I0599957

Copyright

Published by Outpost Books

Produced by Christian Hurst Publishing

www.churstpublishing.com

Distributed by Ingram

Additional distribution by Draft2Digital and Amazon

Cover design by Max Young and Christian Hurst

Set in Ethnocentric by Ray Larabie (Typodermic Fonts)

and Allumi by Jean François Porchez (Typofonderie)

ISBN (Digital): 979-8993932736

ISBN (Paperback): 979-8993932712

ISBN (Hardcover): 979-8993932767

For retail, visit: LilyStarlingBook.com

Author blog: christianhurst.substack.com

Instagram & TikTok: @churstpublishing

Third Edition: June 2026

Lily Starling and the Storm Riders

By Christian Hurst

Book 2 in the Lily Starling Series

• • • •

For Suki,
who hated heights,
but always leaped before she looked.

A Note from the Author

At the end of this book, you'll find a short story titled Tea with Razh.

It's set between Voyage of the Salamander and Storm Riders, during a quiet interlude on Adius II—a moment of stillness before everything changed. In it, Lily and Xynn share space, time, and truths that shape who they are when this story begins.

If you'd like a deeper look into their bond—or a sense of Lily's emotional grounding before the storm hits—you might enjoy reading it first.

If slow, introspective stories aren't your thing, feel free to skip it and jump straight into the action.

However you choose to experience it, I'm glad you're here.

• • • •

Content Advisory:

This book contains some coarse language, as characters react to moments of stress, grief, and danger. It also includes depictions of trauma, including kidnapping, ideological extremism, and loss of life. Themes of identity and intimacy are explored through emotional and romantic relationships, with closed-door depictions only.

LILY STARLING

AND THE STORM RIDERS

CHRISTIAN HURST

OUTPOST
BOOKS

DECLASSIFIED – EYES ONLY

FILE 60292
Union of Allied Systems | Space Fleet | Starship *Salamander* | Current
Status: Docked.
Begin crew recall.

• • • •

2535.0731 // 06:30

LOCATION: Fishing Cabin, New Delaware

The lake was still in the early light, a vast sheet of glass veiled in ribbons of mist. Silver curls lifted from the surface, shifting with the breath of the wind. Tall evergreens stood sentinel along the shore, their dark silhouettes reflected in perfect symmetry, only slightly distorted where the water lapped at the dock's worn pilings. Everything was quiet—the kind of quiet that belonged to places untouched by urgency, where time moved like the tide, slow and inevitable.

Joren stepped onto the dock barefoot, the wood cool and damp beneath his feet. In one hand, a steaming mug of coffee, its rich scent rising to meet the crisp morning air. The other hand disappeared into the pocket of a thick cable-knit sweater, the fabric heavy with warmth against the lingering chill. The air smelled of pine and cold water, and when he breathed in, he could taste the sharp bite of the coming autumn, the kind of air that settled into your bones and stayed there.

Behind him, the cabin door creaked open.

Calan stepped outside. Or, rather, Captain Calan stepped outside—because even here, away from the hum of the *Salamander*, he carried that weight, that unshakable awareness of command. He had the look of someone trying very hard to appear relaxed. His dark hair was artfully mussed, the sort of intentional disarray that wouldn't be out of place in a luxury travel ad. But the Fleet-issue gym shirt and standard black trousers undercut the illusion. Hardly leisurewear.

He was holding a data tablet. Even here.

Joren let out a theatrical sigh and held out the coffee in exaggerated dismay. "You're supposed to be relaxing."

Calan took the mug but didn't answer right away. Instead, he lifted his gaze to the lake. The dawn's first light painted half his face in gold, and the morning breeze moved through his hair with the same absentminded touch as a lover.

There was always a subtle tension in the way a captain carried themselves. An unseen weight pressing against the spine, even when there were no battle plans to draft, no decisions to make. Even in the woods. Even on the water. Even here.

After a moment that could have stretched across a solar system, Calan exhaled. "I *am* relaxing. This is me, relaxing."

Joren gave him a look that could melt steel. "Is that so?" He glanced around at the dawn-streaked sky, then shook his head. "They should add a dampening field around here." Before Calan could react, Joren plucked the tablet from his hands. "To prevent *unwanted intrusions.*"

Calan's mouth twitched. Amused. Defeated. He couldn't argue.

They stood in silence, watching the lake. Somewhere beneath the surface, an unseen fish broke the stillness, sending ripples spiraling outward. In the trees, a bird called, its sharp cry threading through the hush of morning. Shoulder to shoulder, they fit together with the same effortless symmetry as the weave of the wool in Joren's sweater—an unspoken closeness, steady and unbreakable.

Joren was the first to break the quiet. "So what's so important you keep checking your messages?" He slid his arm through Calan's, a gentle entangling, an anchor. "Are you any closer to making a decision?"

Calan's grip tightened around the mug, fingers curling in thought. "No." A beat. Then, softer: "I don't know."

Joren turned to him fully. "You do know." His voice was quiet, but firm. "You just don't like the answer to the question." He let the words settle, then continued. "The crew of the *Salamander* loves you. But so do I. And if you choose to transfer to the *Vanguard* to be with me, they'll understand."

Calan's expression darkened, his jaw tightening. "I feel *old*," he admitted. The words came out flat, a confession he hadn't meant to make. He shook his head. "I don't know if I can go back on the duty roster like I'm fresh out of the Academy."

Joren huffed a small laugh. "Captain Humossie is, what—two hundred? To her, you *are* just a kid." And before Calan could protest, Joren reached up and ruffled his hair, a teasing grin tugging at his lips. As if Calan were a sulking toddler in need of a reminder: *You are loved. You are still you. You don't have to carry this alone.*

Calan chuckled, shaking his head, but the sound faded too quickly. The moment passed, slipping away like the ripples still spreading across the lake. His gaze returned to the water, his features settling into something more serious. "I don't want to leave my crew in the middle of something unfinished. I wouldn't—"

Joren touched his arm, a quiet reassurance. "I know. You're not the kind of man who walks away. But you don't have to figure everything out today."

Calan sighed, raking a hand through his hair. "No. I suppose not."

Joren finished the last of his coffee and set the empty mug on the dock railing with a quiet *clink*. "Come on. I was going to take the boat out before breakfast. You up for it?"

Calan hesitated. His instinct was to say no—to insist he had things to do, even if he couldn't quite name them. But then he looked at Joren. The steady warmth in his eyes, the quiet patience that had held them together through years of separation and duty.

Finally, he nodded.

"Yeah," he said, setting his mug down beside Joren's. "I think I will."

Joren grinned. "That's the spirit. Now help me push this thing out, old man. I'm not doing all the work."

The boat rocked as they stepped inside, wood creaking beneath their weight. Joren crouched to untie the mooring rope from the dock post, his fingers moving with easy familiarity. Calan moved to help, his boots scuffing against the damp planks—

And then his com tag chirped.

The sound landed between them like a stone in deep water. That inevitable, sinking feeling, the one that comes when you know—before you even check—that you aren't going to like what happens next.

Joren exhaled sharply.

Calan almost ignored it. *Almost.*

With a sigh, he pulled the device from his belt and tapped it to life. The holo-display flickered into existence, a cascade of messages appearing in rapid succession. Dozens of them. His gaze skimmed over the screen, his expression barely shifting—until his eyes caught on one, marked urgent.

His expression changed.

Joren straightened, his own unease sharpening. "What is it?"

Calan didn't answer right away. His eyes stayed on the water, but his mind was already somewhere else.

Then, finally—

Calan tipped the display so Joren could read it.

Joren raised an eyebrow, his voice laced with dry sarcasm. "That may set the record for the shortest vacation of our marriage. But on the bright side, at this rate, you'll never have to make a decision."

Calan huffed a quiet laugh, then leaned in, pressing a quick, apologetic kiss to Joren's lips before turning toward the cabin. "I'll make it up to you."

Joren smirked. "You always say that."

With no answer that would satisfy, Calan quickly ducked inside to repack his things.

· · · ·

2535.0731 // 11:15

LOCATION: Laughing Man's Dojo, Starbase 12

The dojo pulsed with light and motion, its vast open space lined with polished black flooring that rippled subtly underfoot—an adaptive surface that adjusted with every movement. Along the walls, faint traces of previous matches lingered in shifting pixels, a ghostly reminder of victories and defeats. Overhead, the ceiling panels glowed with the simulated hue of an afternoon sky, casting a warm, steady light.

In the center of the room, a fight was unfolding.

Malik hit the mat with a sharp, breath-stealing *thud*. Again.

Lines of glowing text shimmered into existence above him—IMPACT VELOCITY: 4.3 m/s. FORCE DISTRIBUTION: UNBALANCED. RECOVERY TIME: 2.1s. Data scrolled through the air around them like illuminated word bubbles in a comic book, the dojo's system analyzing every movement in real-time.

Malik groaned, staring up at the ceiling. "I should've never let you talk me into this."

Caris grinned, bouncing lightly on her heels, not even winded. "You're just saying that because I keep throwing you on your ass."

He pushed himself upright, rolling out the stiffness in his shoulders. "I can't afford to be in traction right now—I have actual work to do." He adjusted his stance, flexing his fingers. "Unlike *some* people."

Caris smirked, unfazed. "Oh, please. What's so important that you're afraid of a few bruises?"

Malik ducked under her next strike, pivoting smoothly before landing a quick, controlled hit to her side. STRIKE POWER: 72%. MOMENTUM SHIFT: 8.4% flashed in the air, updating in real-time.

"Artificial intelligence ethics," he answered, shifting back on the balls of his feet. "Specifically, intelligence in artificial lifeforms and the ethical implications of their rights as individuals. Trying to pin down some scientific parameters around the concept of a soul."

Caris, unfazed, nodded approvingly as she circled him. "That's impressive. Datch would be interested—if he ever comes back from Gherion Prime."

Malik feinted left, then landed a solid hit to her shoulder. "Exactly. He's compiling evidence for his people, trying to get the Union to recognize the Gherionites as individuals under sentient rights law. I'm hoping my work will help."

Caris adjusted, dodging his next attack with ease. "I still can't believe that hasn't happened yet."

"Neither can I."

And then Malik was airborne again.

The throw was *brutal*—a perfectly executed hip toss that sent him flipping over her shoulder. The world spun, the air left his lungs, and then—IMPACT VELOCITY: 5.1 m/s. MATCH CONCLUSION: ROUND OVER.

The entire simulation shattered like glass.

The dojo dissolved into a cascade of luminous shards, data splintering apart in fragments of light. Their scores flared in the air—win percentages, reaction times, efficiency ratings—before fizzing out one by one, leaving the space quiet except for the sound of their breathing.

And then—

A console against the far wall blared to life, red warning lights flashing. The dojo's ambient lighting flickered, shifting to alert status.

Caris and Malik exchanged a glance before stepping toward the console. Malik scanned the display, his brow furrowing. "This is—"

Caris' eyes widened.

"I have to call Lily."

• • • •

2535.0731 // 14:35

LOCATION: Union of Allied Systems | Space Services Training Academy | Main Promenade

Alrek was striking out. Hard.

The Cyranthian cadets were polite, but the kind of polite that felt like a dismissal wrapped in a smile. The taller of the two, a violet-skinned young woman with silver facial markings, tilted her head at him, offering something that was either vague amusement or mild pity—it was hard to tell with Cyranthians.

"Look, Almond..."

"Uh—Alrek."

"Right, Alrek." She flashed an easy smile. "I admire your... *confidence*, but aren't you a little young?"

Her friend barely contained a laugh.

Alrek tried for a roguish grin. It came out more like a pained grimace. "Age is relative," he countered, throwing a little too much charm into the words. "And Saravethi males..." He cleared his throat, deepening his voice in what he hoped was a subtle, masculine way. "That is, *Saravethi men* mature much earlier than most species."

The second cadet smirked. "Sorry."

Alrek cleared his throat again, nodding as if this had gone exactly as planned. "Well. Enjoy your afternoon, then."

And with that, he made a very hasty, completely dignified retreat.

He slumped back toward a cafeteria-style table and plopped onto the bench, landing beside a large, shimmering puddle of iridescent goo—which pulsed slightly, as though laughing without a mouth.

Charlie.

Alrek's gelatinous, very non-humanoid best friend did their best to lift his shattered dignity off the floor.

"If I were capable of experiencing second-hand embarrassment," Charlie said, their voice smooth and amused through the academy's translation matrix, "I'm fairly certain I'd be mortified right now."

Alrek let out a groan, rubbing his temples. "You're lucky your species doesn't have to deal with dating. Or rejection. Or sex in general." He gestured vaguely. "It spares you the humiliation."

Charlie's liquid form rippled. "It does simplify certain things."

Alrek dropped his head back against the table with a sigh. "Yeah, yeah, rub it in."

A pause.

Then, with a faint sloshing sound, Charlie extended one of their pseudopods—a gelatinous limb stretching outward—and held out Alrek's com tag.

"Oh," they said, entirely too casual. "By the way, you left this in our room. It's been going absolutely nuts."

Alrek snatched it, eyes widening. "What? No one ever calls me."

His fingers flew over the holo-display, scrolling through the message. His whole face lit up.

"Oh my gods! They're recalling me to the *Salamander*!"

Charlie pulsed in an approximation of enthusiasm. "Exciting. I imagine you'll do great on the rescue mission."

Alrek's head snapped up. "Wait—have you been reading my mail again?"

Charlie's form shifted slightly, as if shrugging. "You need a stronger password."

Alrek squinted suspiciously at them. Then back at the com tag display, scanning the details.

"Wow! Ka-Lorrin requested me personally for this mission." His grin stretched wide. "See that, Charlie? At least someone wants me."

Charlie rippled. "That's great for you. But who am I supposed to study with while you're gone?"

Alrek hesitated. The idea of leaving Charlie behind felt strangely wrong—after all, who else would mock him lovingly every time he made a fool of himself?

He glanced at them with a small shrug. "You know... we could put in a request. See if you can join me for the mission."

Charlie stilled. "Really? You wouldn't mind?"

Alrek gave a small laugh. "Of course not."

After a beat, Charlie pulsed again, very pleased with themself. "Good. Because I already put the request in."

Alrek gave in to his grin, shaking his head. "Of course you did."

• • • •

2535.0731 // 18:42

LOCATION: Cyranthian Monastery, Gilrod 7

The air was thick with the scent of burning resik petals. Their pale blue embers floated lazily toward the vaulted ceiling, sending thin curls of incense into the dim light. The monastery was quiet in the way deep caves and distant moons were quiet—not silence, but the *absence* of anything demanding to be heard.

Lily balanced on one foot, her arms extended, her body trembling with effort. The heat from the meditation chamber curled against her skin, beads of sweat tracing slow paths down her back.

This was supposed to be about discipline. Clarity. Centering herself.

But she was failing at that, too.

The Cyranthian monks moved through their poses effortlessly, their limbs flowing like water following the curve of a riverbed. The instructor at the front of the room, a pale-skinned Cyranthian with intricate silver filigree along her arms, had not-so-subtly corrected Lily's form three times already.

She could tell she was doing it wrong—could feel her stance slightly off-balance, the faint tremor in her legs that the monks around her didn't seem to struggle with.

Still, she refused to fall.

She focused on her breathing, drawing in the warm, spiced air, letting it settle in her lungs before exhaling slowly, carefully, as though she could release the frustration tightening in her chest along with it.

You can do this. She held the thought firm in her mind, anchoring herself to it. *You are disciplined. You are focused. You are—*

A soft chime rang through the chamber.

At the threshold, a monastery attendant stood in the dim light, their pale robes pooling at their feet, hands clasped delicately around a small holo-scroll. They did not speak. They did not intrude. They simply *waited*, an unmoving figure at the edge of her vision.

Lily closed her eyes, willing them away.

They did not leave.

She drew in another breath, deeper this time, heavier, as if she could inhale them out of existence. But she could feel their presence, patient and unshakable, like the heat pressing against her skin.

Without looking, she lifted a hand and pushed the scroll aside, a deliberate but gentle refusal.

The attendant hesitated, then bowed their head in quiet understanding. A moment later, their footsteps receded, the holo-scroll disappearing into the shadows with them.

Lily exhaled, slowly, steadily.

And returned to her pose.

But the stillness of her mind was only temporary. Like a blank screen flickering to life, her thoughts filled with color, sensation, memory. A week ago. The Saravethi colony on Adius II. A perfect month with Xynn—or at least, that's what she told herself. But maybe it had only been a perfect month of movement, distraction, things left unsaid.

Lily adjusted her breathing, let the memory pull her under.

Climbing the rockface. Xynn's presence nearby, effortless and sure.

Rock. Sky. Breath. Grip.

Her fingers found the next hold, muscles burning as she pulled herself higher. The air smelled of damp stone and sea salt, the cliffs rising in jagged, gray-white formations against the late afternoon sky.

Below, Xynn moved with quiet confidence, hanging effortlessly from a ledge just beneath her, arms loose, expression unreadable.

"You're overthinking again," she called up, watching Lily with that sharp, knowing gaze. "Stop planning three moves ahead. Just climb."

Lily gritted her teeth and pulled herself up another few inches.

"Let me guess," she muttered. "You just *feel* where the next hold is?"

Xynn smirked. "*Exactly.*"

Lily rolled her eyes, but a small, involuntary smile tugged at her lips.

They climbed in comfortable silence for a few more minutes, the ocean stretching endless and blue beneath them. The waves crashed against the cliffs, not just background noise but something bigger, wilder—a consuming drumbeat, urging them higher.

When they reached the top, Lily flopped onto her back, breath coming fast, heart still pounding with the climb's exhilaration.

Xynn dropped beside her, propping herself up on an elbow.

"Exhilarating, right?" Xynn said, letting her body relax. "Nothing quite like reaching the top."

Lily turned her head, meeting Xynn's gaze. A small, breathless smile tugged at her lips.

"Yeah," she agreed.

A silence followed—one of those rare, beautiful silences, where words felt unnecessary. The kind you commit to memory on purpose. The ocean stretched out before them, the air thick with salt, the warmth of the stone seeping into her skin. She felt close to Xynn in a way that didn't need definition, her senses ablaze with the thrill of the climb, the endless sky above, the rightness of this moment.

She turned for a well-earned kiss—

And was met with a stony expression she hadn't expected.

Xynn studied her like prey. Calculating. Measuring.

"So," she said carefully. "After today... I mean, you're scheduled to head out."

Lily's chest tightened. She sat up, brushing her palms over the rough stone.

Xynn's voice dropped into something heavier—like she was about to take a shot she already knew she'd miss. "Why don't you stay? Let's stop beating around the bush. Stay here, and let's find a place together. Live a little, Lily. A Xynn, Lily life... or a big Lily, Xynn life."

She could see Lily stiffen. Could feel the shift, the discomfort creeping in.

Xynn softened, but pressed on. "I'm just saying—we're great together, and we—"

"Why can't we just enjoy the moment?" Lily's words came too fast, too sharp. A deflection disguised as an answer.

Xynn exhaled, shaking her head. Tired. Knowing.

"Because it's always just a moment with you."

The monastery's chime filled the air, a low, steady thrum.

Lily's mind snapped back to the present just as her stance faltered.

Her foot slipped.

The shift was sudden, gravity pulling her off balance before she could stop it. Her knee buckled, her body lurching forward, and for a breathless second, she was falling—arms flinching to catch herself, muscles tensing against the inevitable. At the last moment, she managed to steady herself, fingertips grazing the heated stone as she regained control.

A quiet curse slipped through her teeth.

The monastery attendant had returned.

They stood at the edge of the chamber, patient as ever, their pale robes pooling around them, the holo-scroll once again held delicately between their hands.

Lily exhaled, slow and sharp, pressing her lips into a thin line. She swiped the scroll from their grasp, muttering something that resembled thanks, then turned on her heel, making her way toward the nearest communication panel.

The screen flickered to life, and Caris' smirking face filled the display.

"There you are," she said. "You're really hard to track down, you know that?"

Lily wiped the sweat from her forehead. "Leena." She really tried to sound friendly, but her voice came out thin, strained at best. "What can I do for you?" The words were polite enough, but they *felt* more like *what do you want?*

Caris leaned back in her chair, clearly enjoying herself. "Well, let's see—your com tag was off, so I called the training base where you *said* you'd be. Turns out you rushed through all their martial arts programs with, uh, let's call it... *moderate* success—"

Lily lifted a brow, shaking her head. "They *passed* me."

Caris ignored her. "—then they said you left on a transport to Science Station 19, where, after some investigating, I learned you somehow blew up one of their larger chemistry labs."

Lily crossed her arms. "That was an *accident.* Part of an approved training experiment. Could've happened to *anybody.*"

"Of course," Caris said, grinning now. "And after that, did you keep pursuing your science training? *Nope.* Off you went to the Flight Training Center, where you *crashed your way* through nine different simulators. At this point, I'm starting to take your avoidance *personally.*"

Lily's glare hardened.

Caris smirked. "And *finally,* I had to bribe a transport operator to track you down *here.*" She arched a brow. "A Cyranthian monastery? That's new."

Lily rolled her shoulders, exhaling slowly. This time, she said it out loud.

"What do you want, Leena?"

Caris' expression shifted, the smirk fading as something heavier settled into place.

"We're being recalled."

Lily stilled, the weight of those words pressing into her chest before she even understood why.

Caris hesitated, just for a second. Then—

"There's been an attack."

The monastery felt smaller, the warm air suddenly too thick, too close. Lily's mind raced. Somehow, she knew what was coming.

Caris' voice remained steady, but it carried a weight that settled deep, immovable.

"Adius II."

Lily's stomach plummeted.

Adius II.

That was where she had just left Xynn.

Where she had left her—*not in the best way.*

The memory flooded her mind.

Xynn's lips against hers, lingering, hesitant in a way that made Lily's chest ache. The feeling of her fingers curled lightly against Lily's wrist, not pulling her back, not asking her to stay—just *hoping.*

And Lily had turned away.

She had turned, walked down the boarding ramp, walked away from Xynn without looking back.

Caris' lips were still moving, but Lily's ears rang, a static whine filling her head, muffling everything. The air felt thick, suffocating, like cotton stuffed between her thoughts.

She had walked away.

Without looking back.

Chapter 1: Hear Not the Voice of the Oppressor

THE STORM IS OLD. ANCIENT beyond reckoning, born from the breath of stars that died before the first pulse of life. It drifts through the galaxy with the slow, unhurried grace of an immortal wanderer, its heart a churning cauldron of memory and dust. It has seen worlds rise and fall, watched civilizations bloom and wither, their histories swept away like the pale sand on desert winds.

If it could speak, its voice would be a chorus of whispers, the echoes of a thousand dying suns. It would tell of the time it danced through the rings of a gas giant, scattering ice crystals like diamonds across the void. It would murmur of the world it passed a century ago, a green jewel cradled in the arms of its star—now a blackened cinder, its name lost to the silence. The storm remembers. It holds the secrets of creation within its swirling depths, a vault of ancient truths hidden behind veils of dust and ice.

It is composed of a thousand elements—carbon dust from shattered comets, ions that crackle with electricity, and tendrils of plasma that weave through the maelstrom like the fingers of a cosmic god. Gases both familiar and alien swirl within it—hydrogen and helium, yes, but also viridion vapor that glows with a sickly green light, and zephyrite, a gas so thin and cold it bends starlight around it. And within the heart of the storm lies dark matter, a gravitational whisper that pulls at the fabric of space itself, bending time into spirals that twist and fold, concealing secrets older than light.

The storm is vast, its tendrils reaching across light-years, and it moves with the inevitability of a tide. It is not malicious, nor is it kind. It simply is. A force of nature, a cosmic leviathan drifting through the void.

It remembers other storms, in other times and places. Tempests that split the skies of primitive worlds, their lightning illuminating the faces of creatures that no longer exist. Torrential rains that fed crops and nourished the land, the sweet scent of petrichor rising from the soil, a promise of life renewed. And yet, in the same breath, it recalls the howling gales that shattered mountains, the hurricanes that swallowed villages whole. Winds that drove wooden ships across unknown seas, propelling discovery and adventure—yet those same winds turned violent, twisting vessels into splinters, consigning entire crews to the black depths.

A storm is neither good nor evil. It is both creator and destroyer, the bringer of life and the harbinger of death. It carves valleys and fills lakes, but it also leaves behind desolation, a silent testament to its power. To the storm, time is meaningless. It moves through ages and epochs, untouched by the rise and fall of empires, unchanging even as stars burn out and collapse into themselves.

And now, the ancient storm moves again, drifting through the cosmos with its slow, deliberate rhythm. It will pass through this sector, as it has before and will again, its path indifferent to the lives it touches. It carries within it the whispers of long-dead worlds and the promise of rebirth, a cosmic wheel that spins without mercy or malice. Who can say where it will bring life or extinguish it? Who can know the good and the bad it will do?

But just ahead of the storm, a colony is burning.

The Saravethi settlement on Adius II, nestled in the valley between the white stone cliffs and the turquoise sea, is engulfed in flame. What was once a place of laughter and light, of ancient stories shared beneath the sunlit sky, is now a hellscape of smoke and ash. Buildings crumble under the weight of fire, their skeletons silhouetted against the glowing horizon. The air is thick with smoke, the scent acrid and bitter, mingling with the salt of the sea.

The storm drifts closer, ancient and unknowing. It moves with the inevitability of all things beyond mortal control, a force that cares nothing for kingdoms or lives or the flicker of hope that once burned here.

For now, it watches, waiting just beyond the horizon, its swirling depths reflecting the flames below. And in its heart, the storm holds the memory of other fires, on other worlds, long since turned to dust.

The storm is old. It has seen this before.

· · · ·

Lily's fingers gripped the edge of her seat, knuckles white as the shuttle shuddered through the turbulent atmosphere of Adius II. The roar of the engines was deafening, but it was nothing compared to the rapid thud of her heart. Her chest felt tight, and she struggled to breathe as she watched the storm-torn clouds churn beyond the viewport, their angry tendrils swirling like living shadows. Lightning crackled within the blackened skies, illuminating the skeletal remains of the colony below—a place she had once known as a sanctuary, now scarred and broken.

The shuttle lurched, and Lily's stomach flipped. Her mind raced, unbidden thoughts clawing at her resolve. What if Xynn was hurt? What if she hadn't made it to the shelters in time? What if Lily was already too late?

She squeezed her eyes shut, trying to push the images away. Memories flooded back, unwelcome and vivid. She could still see Xynn standing on that balcony, the golden light of the twin suns reflecting off her hair as she teased Lily about her horrible cooking skills. They had spent hours wandering the market stalls, laughing over strange fruits and sweet pastries. It had been peaceful, safe—a brief illusion of normalcy.

And now it was all gone.

The shuttle jolted as they passed through another wave of turbulence. Lily's eyes snapped open, her gaze locking on the ruins below. It was hard to reconcile the desolation with the memories of vibrant life she carried within her. Craters pocked the ground, debris scattered like broken shells. Smoke rose in thick, black columns from shattered structures, twisting upwards to merge with the storm clouds. The market was nothing but rubble now, the colors and laughter replaced with gray ash and silence.

Her hands trembled as she reached for the harness release. It was too quiet. Too still.

"We're coming in low," Malik's voice cut through the static of the comm. "Stay sharp. No enemy activity on sensors, but the storm is wreaking havoc on our readings. Visibility's next to nothing."

Lily forced herself to nod, even though no one could see her. She unbuckled her harness and stood on unsteady legs, her body vibrating with tension as the shuttle angled down toward the landing zone. Through the viewport, she could see the outlines of familiar buildings, their walls charred and crumbling. Her throat tightened. She had walked those streets with Xynn, hand in hand, talking about everything and nothing at all.

Now those streets were filled with smoke and shadows.

The shuttle touched down with a jarring thud. The ramp hissed, lowering to reveal the chaos outside—wind howling through broken windows, ash swirling in the air like snowflakes. The acrid scent of burning metal and scorched earth filled her nose, bitter and suffocating.

Lily stepped out, her boots crunching on shattered glass. The air was thick, heavy with smoke and dust. Her eyes stung, tears forming involuntarily as she fought to breathe. The world felt muted, sounds distorted and distant, as if she were moving through a nightmare.

She moved quickly, her body operating on instinct even as her mind raced. She knew this place too well. The layout was burned into her memory, every alley and side street familiar from her month spent here with Xynn. Her feet carried her without hesitation, weaving through the wreckage, dodging fallen beams and twisted metal.

The world was gray, colorless—except for the fire. It burned with a violent, hungry light, devouring everything it touched. As she moved deeper into the ruins, she could hear the distant cries of survivors, the groans of structures straining under their own weight. But she couldn't stop. Not yet. Not until she found—

A flash of movement caught her eye, and Lily's heart skipped. She spun around, her breath catching as she saw her.

Xynn was there, framed against the flames, her silhouette sharp and unyielding. Her face was streaked with soot, eyes narrowed with determination as she pulled a child from the wreckage, guiding the young Saravethi toward safety. Her voice was steady, calm despite the chaos, soothing the terrified child as she pushed them forward.

For a moment, Lily could only watch, frozen by a mix of relief and awe. Of course Xynn would be here, in the thick of danger, sticking her neck out without a second thought for her own safety. It was just who she was—brave, fearless, maybe even a little reckless, though she'd never admit it beneath all that discipline.

Then Xynn turned, her eyes locking with Lily's, and everything else fell away.

The relief hit Lily so hard she nearly staggered. Her chest ached, and she realized she had been holding her breath. "Xynn!" Her voice cracked, raw with fear and desperation. She moved forward without thinking, pushing through the smoke, her legs weak with adrenaline.

Xynn's eyes widened, and for a heartbeat, her expression was one of pure shock. But then her lips curved into a crooked, breathless smile. "You're late," she called, her voice cutting through the chaos. "I was starting to think you forgot about me."

Lily's laugh was broken, half a sob. "Not a chance." She reached Xynn in three long strides, her arms wrapping around her before she could stop herself. Xynn's body was warm and solid, grounding her in a reality that still felt too fragile to trust.

They pulled apart just as quickly, a brief, unspoken understanding passing between them. There was no time. Not now.

Xynn's eyes softened, a flicker of worry breaking through her resolve. "The shelters are overrun. We need to get these people out—now."

Lily nodded, her voice steady despite the fear clawing at her insides. "I've got you. Let's move."

Together, they turned toward the burning colony, shadows dancing across their faces as the flames crackled behind them. The storm growled overhead, its ominous presence drawing closer, and Lily could feel its weight pressing down on her, cold and ancient.

But Xynn was here, alive and fighting. And as long as they were together, Lily could keep going.

They ran into the chaos, side by side, the storm's howling winds chasing them through the ruins.

· · · ·

The shuttle's engines hummed softly, a steady vibration that traveled through the metal floor and into Lily's bones, grounding her as she sat shoulder to shoulder with Xynn. Her heart was still racing, the adrenaline from the rescue refusing to release its grip, but here—on this shuttle, in this moment—she felt safe. Xynn's hand was wrapped tightly around hers, warm and solid, anchoring her against the chaos they had just escaped.

Lily glanced sideways, her gaze lingering on Xynn's profile. Her hair was tangled, wild from the wind and smoke, and a smudge of soot streaked her cheek, but her eyes were bright, alive with that fierce determination Lily had always admired. Even now, exhausted and bruised, Xynn's shoulders were squared, her jaw set with unyielding resolve.

Lily tightened her grip, her fingers threading through Xynn's, and for a heartbeat, everything else faded away—the storm, the ruins of the colony, the ache in her muscles. Just this. Just them. It was enough.

She let herself lean into it, into the warmth of Xynn's skin and the steady rhythm of her breathing. It was easy, natural, like slipping into a familiar melody. They didn't need to talk about it. They didn't need to define it. They were good together—perfect, even—so long as they didn't overthink it.

Lily's chest tightened, the familiar anxiety creeping in. Maybe it was reckless to feel this way. To want this so much. If she admitted how much she needed Xynn, how much she relied on her, then what? Would it ruin things? Would it make everything too complicated, too fragile?

She felt the words rise, the questions pressing at the back of her throat, but she swallowed them down, refusing to let them break this moment. Not now. Not when Xynn's fingers were warm and solid in her own, grounding her in the present. She wouldn't ruin this with what-ifs and doubts. Not today.

Lily forced herself to breathe, matching the rhythm to Xynn's. For once, she wouldn't analyze it. She wouldn't question it. She would just be here, in this shuttle, her hand in Xynn's, the storm behind them.

"...It was a suicide mission." Caris's voice broke through the hum of the engines, sharp and matter-of-fact. She stood at the shuttle's front console, posture rigid, eyes locked on the control panel. "We've seen this before. They're part of a cult that worships the Leviathan—an interstellar storm they believe to be sacred. They call themselves Leviathan's Hand. To them, the storm is a divine force of nature that shouldn't be controlled or defied."

Lily blinked, forcing herself to focus. Caris's words were clipped, efficient, but there was a heaviness to her tone, an undercurrent of anger just beneath the surface.

"They see any attempt to defend against the storm as blasphemy," Caris continued, her fingers dancing over the console as she checked the ship's systems. "It's not about conquest or resources. It's about punishment. A warning to anyone who tries to resist what they believe is the will of the universe."

Lily's stomach turned. She remembered the faces of the colonists—the fear in their eyes, the way they clung to each other as they scrambled into the shuttles. They hadn't been soldiers or rebels. They'd just been trying to survive.

Caris's face remained serious. "Not picking up anyone else on sensors. Looks like they took themselves out along with half the colony."

Xynn's grip tightened on Lily's hand, and Lily felt a shiver run through her. She glanced out the viewport, watching the swirling gas clouds twist and curl with purple and magenta light against the darkness of space. It looked alive, coiling around the planet like the fingers of some ancient creature. The air outside was electric, charged with the hum of energy, and she could feel it pressing in, cold and heavy.

Malik's voice broke through the tension. "Leviathan," he said, the storm's name falling from his lips with a kind of fearful reverence. "It passes through Union space every two hundred years or so. Every planet it touches suffers massive disruptions to weather patterns and seismic activity. It's no wonder so many myths and traditions have sprung up around its movements. It's the stuff of legends."

Caris shot him a look, her jaw tightening. Malik shrugged, his expression stubbornly thoughtful. "You have to admit," he said, his voice almost persuasive, "it's a force of nature worth respecting."

Caris's eyes hardened. "Respecting it to the point of murdering half a colony of civilians?" Her voice was sharp, incredulous. Malik's shoulders slumped, his defiance crumbling as he sank back into his seat.

Caris turned back to the console, her movements brisk and purposeful. "No other hostile vessels in the area. Just us and the storm." Her words were final, heavy with a sense of foreboding.

Lily shuddered, tearing her gaze from the swirling clouds. Just them and the storm, she thought. Her chest tightened, a coldness settling in her bones. Then her eyes met Xynn's. There was no fear there, only a quiet, steady resolve. Xynn squeezed her hand, her thumb brushing gently over Lily's knuckles, and Lily felt her heart stutter, warmth spreading through her chest.

Xynn didn't say anything. She didn't have to. Her presence was enough, a silent promise that she was here, that they were in this together.

The shuttle jolted as they docked with the *Salamander*, and the spell broke. Xynn's fingers slipped from hers, and Lily felt the loss like a sharp ache. She took a breath, forcing herself to stand, her body stiff with exhaustion. But there was no time to dwell on it—there were people to help, tasks to organize, a job to be done.

As the ramp lowered, Caris glanced over her shoulder, her expression softening just slightly. "You did good, Lily. You too, Xynn. You saved a lot of lives today."

Lily swallowed, nodding. "Thanks, Leena."

Xynn's lips curved into a small smile, her eyes flicking up and down Caris flirtatiously. "Just doing my part." She straightened her posture, her grin widening as Caris looked back over her shoulder, a flicker of curiosity in her gaze.

As soon as Caris was out of earshot, Xynn's eyes sparkled with mischief. "I see why you like spending so much time with Caris. Oh, sorry... Leeeena," she teased, drawing out the "e" sound with a wicked grin.

Lily's face heated, and without a second thought, she elbowed Xynn in the ribs, just hard enough to knock the wind out of her. Xynn's eyes went wide in mock indignation before she doubled over, laughing. Lily couldn't help herself—she laughed too, the tension loosening just a little.

Together, they moved down the ramp, stepping into the chaos of the hangar bay. The air was filled with shouts and static from comms, refugees milling about in confusion. Lily's instincts kicked in, and she threw herself into the work, guiding people toward their transports, organizing the chaos into something resembling order.

She nearly collided with Alrek as he led a group of injured Saravethi toward the medical bay, his expression focused but gentle as he helped an elder onto a stretcher. His eyes brightened when he saw her. "Lily! Did you find Xynn? I hope she's okay." His tone held only the slightest hint of forced concern, guarded but genuine.

Lily nodded warmly. "Yeah. She's okay. Thanks for asking." Her voice softened. "It's good to see you."

Alrek's shoulders relaxed, his smile genuine. "You too."

Without hesitation, Lily wrapped her arms around Alrek in a quick hug, briefly surprising him before he returned the embrace, his grip like a vice.

Reuniting with family across space and time. They pulled apart with a shared strength passing between them, an unspoken promise that they would keep moving forward, no matter what lay ahead.

Alrek's gaze drifted back to the injured, his expression growing serious. "I need to get them to the med bay."

"Yeah. Never a dull moment." Lily's voice was steady, but her heart felt lighter. "See you later, Alrek."

He nodded, his eyes smiling as he turned away, his shoulders squared with determination as he led the Saravethi toward safety.

A little later, she found Xynn near the shuttles, her arms crossed as she scanned the crowd, her expression thoughtful. Lily hesitated, the words catching in her throat, but Xynn approached her, eyes brightening.

"You know," Xynn teased, her voice light, "we really need to stop doing this."

Lily blinked, thrown off balance. "Doing what?"

"Saying goodbye like this." Xynn's eyes danced with amusement. "I keep getting on transports, and you keep staying behind to save the day. It's getting a little cliché, don't you think?"

Lily laughed, the sound breaking through the tension coiled in her chest. "Yeah. Definitely getting old."

Xynn's smile softened, her expression growing serious. "I'll see you soon. Try not to get yourself killed, okay?"

"I could say the same to you."

They shared a kiss, brief and bittersweet, warm and gentle. But it was the look afterward that lingered, a silent conversation held in the space between them. A promise. A hope. Words they couldn't say aloud.

Xynn's eyes shone, her smile a little sad as she pulled away, stepping onto the transport. The doors slid shut behind her with a soft hiss, sealing her away from Lily once again.

Lily watched as the large rescue transport powered up, lifting off the deck with a low hum. The air around her felt colder, emptier, as she stood there, arms wrapped around herself. She knew there was more work to do, but she stayed a moment longer, watching as Xynn was carried away, farther and farther, on a ship the size of a small city, flying away from her at impossible speeds.

She waited for the inevitable blur of the transport entering light factor, the sharp flash as it slipped away into the stars. But it didn't...

As the transport neared the storm's edge, something wasn't right. The lights of the rescue vessel began to flicker, stuttering out like dying embers.

Lily's heart dropped. She took a step forward, her pulse quickening as the transport wavered, caught in the storm's shadow. The darkness coiled around it, tendrils of gas swirling like fingers, tightening their grip.

Lily's heart dropped. She took a step forward, her pulse quickening as the transport wavered, caught in the storm's shadow. The darkness coiled around it, tendrils of gas swirling like fingers, tightening their grip.

Then, as if emerging from the storm itself, a massive black ship appeared. Its hull was angular, sharp lines cutting through the darkness with an unnatural elegance. It moved like a shadow, slipping free from the storm's tendrils as if born from them, its surface glistening with the storm's electric light. It was vast, dwarfing the transport as it loomed overhead, a silhouette of cold, merciless power.

Lily's breath caught. She tapped her com tag. "Bridge, what's going on with transport Alpha-Three? And... what is that ship coming out of the storm?"

Calan's voice crackled over the comm, tense but controlled. "Lily, the transport lost power—we don't know why. What ship?"

Lily's eyes were wide, her heart hammering. "I'm looking out the starboard viewport, sir. There's a massive ship emerging from the storm... it looks like... like it's materializing. Emerging through a portal of some kind. It's coming out of nowhere."

There was a pause, static hissing through the channel. Then Dryst Amaris's voice cut through, low and grim. "I've opened up the viewing port. I can see it with the naked eye... but it's not showing up on the scanner feed. If you hadn't been looking right at it, we never would have known..."

Before Lily could respond, a bright light flashed outside the viewport. She squinted against the sudden glare, her stomach twisting as the black ship pivoted, its sleek hull reflecting the storm's eerie glow. There was no warning. No comm hail. Just a split second of silence before the space around them erupted.

The ship fired, beams of searing energy lancing out from its cannons. The blasts slammed into the *Salamander*'s hull, tearing through the plating as if it were paper. The deck shuddered violently, a gut-wrenching jolt that threw Lily sideways. She crashed against the wall, pain exploding in her shoulder as the ship groaned, metal straining under the impact.

"Shields down to twenty percent!" a voice shouted over the comms, panic rising. "Multiple hull breaches on decks four and five!"

Lily struggled to her feet, her vision spinning. The air was filled with the acrid scent of burning circuitry, sparks raining down as panels exploded. Gas hissed from ruptured conduits, filling the corridor with a thick, chemical fog.

"Raise the shields!" Calan's voice was sharp, commanding. "Divert all power to defense systems! Return fire—target their weapon arrays!"

But the black ship was relentless. It fired again, a barrage of energy bolts slamming into the *Salamander*'s hull, sending shockwaves through the ship. The deck lurched beneath Lily's feet, and she grabbed at the railing, her knuckles white as she held on.

She had to get to the bridge. She had to help.

Lily turned, sprinting toward the service corridor, her boots echoing off the metal floor. She could hear the comms crackling with frantic voices, orders overlapping as the crew fought to keep the *Salamander* intact. Her heart pounded, her lungs burning as she reached the ladder that led up two decks to the bridge.

She reached out, fingers brushing the cold metal rung—then her stomach lurched, and her feet lifted off the ground.

Gravity was gone.

Lily's body twisted, her limbs flailing as she drifted upward, her shoulder bumping against the ceiling. Her heart raced, panic seizing her chest as she struggled to move, to push herself back toward the ladder, but there was no friction, nothing to anchor her. The world spun, a nauseating whirl of smoke and flashing lights.

Then, just as suddenly as it had vanished, gravity returned.

Lily fell. Hard. Her body slammed to the floor, pain jolting through her bones as she hit the metal deck with a thud. The impact drove the breath from her lungs, her vision darkening as she gasped for air. Her head spun, the sharp taste of copper on her tongue.

Through the haze of pain, she caught a glimpse of movement outside the viewport. Her heart stuttered, the cold grip of fear tightening around her chest.

The black ship was extending its tractor beams.

Lily pushed herself to her knees, her body screaming in protest as she dragged herself toward the viewport. She watched, helpless, as the beams latched onto the transport, the energy crackling as it pulled the powerless vessel toward the black ship's massive docking bay.

But it wasn't just the transport. The black ship's reach was enormous, its tractor beams stretching out like fingers, wrapping around the smaller rescue shuttles and medical ships scattered nearby. They, too, were drawn in, powerless against the ship's overwhelming force.

Lily's chest tightened as the realization sank in. This ship was feeding off the storm. It was drawing power from Leviathan itself.

A roar of energy surged through the corridor as another panel exploded behind her, flames licking at the walls. The *Salamander* shuddered, its hull groaning as the black ship fired again, a final barrage of energy blasts that sent the ship listing to the side.

Then, through the flames and the smoke, Lily heard it—a voice flooding the *Salamander*'s comm systems, cold and metallic, yet eerily human.

"You have encountered the Warden of Tarshish," the voice intoned, its tone lofty and grave. "My crew and I are the Storm Riders. You can expect our demands post haste."

The black ship began to turn, its massive form pivoting back toward the storm, its hull shimmering with Leviathan's light. The tractor beams tightened, pulling the captured ships into its hold. Then, with a whisper of darkness, the black ship vanished, swallowed by the swirling storm.

The storm moved on, rolling out of the system like a tide retreating from the shore. The *Salamander* was left in its wake, crippled and listing, its hull scarred and broken.

Lily stood in the dark, her fingers curled around a railing, her body trembling as she watched the last traces of the storm fade into the void. She remembered the briefing before they embarked, how they'd called this a routine rescue mission. A routine mission...

"Heinyaz-yajunzi," she muttered under her breath. Alrek pegged it. What a jinx.

Chapter 2: Buried Minas

THE HOOD SCRATCHED *his face as they pulled it off roughly, the leather scraping against his skin, leaving a raw sting. But the relief of having it gone outweighed the pain. He sucked in a sharp breath, his chest heaving as the nauseating sweetness of the leather finally loosened its grip on his senses. Even now, the scent lingered, clinging to his nostrils, mixing with the salt of sweat and something else—petrichor and briny.*

He blinked, his eyes straining to adjust to the dimness. Shadows danced across his vision, swirling with the steam that hung heavy in the air, curling in languid tendrils around his shoulders. The room was vast, a cavern of shadows and smoke. Spotlights punctuated the darkness, their cold, white beams slicing through the mist, revealing circles of light evenly spaced, too deliberate to be random. His eyes tracked them, his mind automatically calculating. A dozen, maybe more. They stood like silent sentinels, arranged in perfect intervals, about two meters apart, stretching into the distance.

His first thought was a warehouse—vast and empty, the kind that swallowed sound and space. But this didn't feel industrial. It felt ancient, cavernous, like the hollowed belly of some long-forgotten beast. The lights continued, fading into the gloom, their reach extending farther than his eyes could follow, swallowed by the darkness.

His gaze darted from one spotlight to the next, searching for clues, patterns, anything to reveal the room's true nature. But the beams illuminated nothing of substance. No walls. No ceiling. No exit. Just a sea of shadows, swirling in the fog, hiding whatever lay beyond. The air felt heavy, pressing in around him, cold and vast, as if the room itself were alive, watching, waiting.

Salt hung thick in the air, sharp and biting, mingling with the scent of fetid rust. It stung his eyes, pricking tears that welled up and refused to fall. Sea water. He could taste it on his tongue, coating his mouth with every shallow breath.

He tried to shift his weight, his body screaming from the strain, but his wrists were bound tightly behind him, the rope cutting into his flesh. His shoulders ached from the unnatural angle, his muscles cramping, his legs trembling with the effort to remain upright. The chair was metal, cold and unyielding, bolted to the floor. There was no give, no room to maneuver. He was trapped.

He craned his neck, struggling to see the figure who had removed the hood, but his range of motion was limited, the pain in his shoulders sharp and unrelenting. Movement flickered in his periphery—a shadow emerging from the steam, drifting closer.

The silhouette halted several paces away, just beyond the nearest spotlight, a shape carved from darkness. There was something wrong about the way it stood, shoulders hunched at unnatural angles, limbs too long, the outline wavering as if the figure were vibrating, shimmering in and out of reality.

A voice slid out of the shadow, gravelly and shrill, cutting through the haze with cruel precision. "Well, Veyrik, you've certainly earned our attention. Here we are." The words were drawn out, each syllable dripping with a sickly amusement. "I assume there's something on your mind you wanted to consult about?"

Veyrik swallowed, his throat dry, the salt burning as it slid down. He forced his voice to remain steady, a light tone laced with mockery. "Hell of a way to welcome someone."

The blow came swift and merciless, cracking across the side of his head with enough force to send his vision spinning. His ears rang, pain blooming in his temple as his head snapped to the side. He tasted blood, copper and salt mingling on his tongue.

A low growl rumbled behind him, heavy and menacing, vibrating through the metal chair. Veyrik's pulse quickened, a shiver running down his spine. Whoever stood behind him was massive—he could feel the heat radiating from its body, the shadow looming like a mountain at his back.

The shadowed figure's voice slithered through the steam, silk and gravel. "Be careful, Veyrik. Xon is... very protective of me. He fulfills his programming perfectly—to defend me from any threat, no matter how small."

The figure's shoulders twitched, a shudder rippling through its form, its head tilting at an unnatural angle. "I had no idea how holistically he would apply that command. A delightful surprise, really."

Cold sweat beaded along Veyrik's neck, his pulse thundering in his ears. He swallowed the mouthful of blood, a smirk on his face despite the pain. "So, what do you want to talk about?"

The shadow leaned forward, the steam swirling around its face, almost revealing features before retreating again. "Brazen," he paused, "very brazen, and foolish. You've been following my men. You've been trying to access my research."

Veyrik's jaw tightened, his silence a deliberate defiance. A hand like iron clamped around his fingers, twisting them back, bending them against the joint. Pain lanced up his arm, white-hot and searing, and his vision went black for a heartbeat. He choked back a scream, his teeth grinding as the pressure increased, the bones straining, on the verge of snapping.

The figure's voice was a whisper, soft and venomous. "I could have Xon pull your fingernails out, one by one, if that would make you more talkative."

Veyrik's breath came in ragged gasps, the pain stealing his voice. He forced himself to lift his head, his eyes blazing with rage. But when the figure stepped into the light, his courage faltered.

It was like watching a nightmare come to life.

The flesh on the figure's face peeled back, splitting at the seams, revealing glistening sinew and bone beneath. The skin tore open in a thousand places, thin strips of tissue hanging loose, swaying as the figure shuddered. Muscles pulsed, raw and exposed, contracting with each movement. The jawbone stretched, teeth elongating, yellow and jagged, gnashing as a guttural growl escaped the gaping mouth.

The eyes—bright green and impossibly sharp—bored into Veyrik's, unblinking and cold. They were the only part of the face that remained unchanged, piercing through the horror with a focus that was disturbingly human.

The figure's body twitched, convulsing as the skin continued to peel away, revealing a patchwork of muscle and bone. The flesh looked like gray rubber bands, stretched too thin, barely holding the monster together.

Then, as abruptly as it had begun, the transformation reversed. The figure's chest heaved, the torn flesh knitting itself back together, muscles retracting, bones shifting. The grayness faded, color returning to the skin, smoothing into a visage almost human. The eyes softened, the teeth shrinking, the jaw relaxing.

Almost human. Almost normal. Almost enough to make Veyrik forget what he had become.

The figure's lips curved into a smile, the green eyes locking onto Veyrik's with predatory intensity. The voice was soft, chillingly calm. "Shall we proceed?"

• • • •

The ladder was cold against her palms, the metal slick with condensation as Lily climbed, her body aching from the strain. Her shoulder throbbed where she'd hit the bulkhead, a sharp reminder of how close she'd come to breaking her neck. Pain shot through her with every movement, a cruel jolt of gratitude that she was still standing, still breathing. She hauled herself up the final rung, her muscles trembling, and staggered onto the command deck, her knees wobbling as the deck pitched beneath her feet.

She stepped onto the bridge, and it was less like the hive of activity she was used to and more like an ant hill on fire.

Sparks burst from overhead panels, sizzling as they danced through the smoke-filled air, illuminating the haze with crackling light. Flames licked at the far console, hungry and persistent, fed by ruptured power lines that spat arcs of electricity like lightning. The air was thick with acrid smoke, white and blinding, stinging her eyes and burning her lungs.

Captain Calan stood at the center of it all, his uniform torn, streaked with ash and blood that didn't appear to be his own. His right arm hung limp at his side, his fingers curled into a claw, his shoulders hunched against the pain. Yet his voice remained steady, commanding, echoing through the chaos with an unwavering authority.

"Transfer emergency power to essential systems! I don't want the artificial gravity cutting out again." There was a flicker of embarrassment in his voice, the hint of frustration cutting through his usual composure. His eyes were more defeated than Lily had ever seen, shadows etched beneath them, his jaw clenched against the pain as he cradled his injured arm. "Steady us! Use emergency thrusters to get us to a higher orbit. We can't risk another drop."

The ship groaned, metal straining under the damage, the deck shuddering as the thrusters fired, stabilizing the listing vessel. The console beside Lily exploded, a shower of sparks cascading over her head. She ducked, her heart pounding, the heat searing the air around her, the smell of burning circuits stinging her nose.

Through the haze, she caught sight of Caris amidst the chaos, her posture rigid as she directed the emergency teams with a voice that was sharp, clear, and unyielding. Her commands cut through the noise with precision, her presence an anchor in the storm of confusion.

Then Caris's eyes found Lily, and a flicker of dread passed over her face, raw and vulnerable before she could bury it beneath the urgency of the moment. Her lips parted, her voice low, the words heavy and fragile. "Was that... that wasn't Xynn's transport, was it?"

Lily's throat tightened, her mouth dry, the taste of smoke and grief bitter on her tongue. She forced herself to nod, the movement small and fragile, her heart splintering as she whispered, "Yeah. It was."

Caris's jaw clenched, a flash of anger sparking in her eyes, fierce and bright before she crushed it beneath her resolve. She turned away, her shoulders squared, her spine rigid as she continued to give orders, her voice steely and controlled, leaving no room for doubt or hesitation.

Dryst Amaris stood near the captain, his face grim as he tapped his comm. "Dr. Thesari, we need a medical team on the bridge as soon as you can spare one." His eyes flicked to Calan's arm, the torn sleeve revealing the bruised, swollen flesh beneath. "Make that on the double."

Calan's fingers twitched, his face pale as he cradled his arm, but his voice was firm, his presence unyielding. "Status report."

The young navigator at the helm looked slightly out of place, his uniform oddly clean for the ordeal they had all just gone through. The bright, pearlescent white of Command HQ stood out starkly against the smoke-stained navy blue of the Salamander crew. Lily's eyes lingered on him, curiosity sparking. New here, she guessed.

His voice wavered just slightly, the only crack in his otherwise composed demeanor. "I—I'm scanning for nearby systems, Captain. Looking for facilities we could use to make repairs... or to get a message to headquarters or another ship in range."

"Excellent." Calan's voice was genuine, his eyes narrowing as another tremor rocked the ship. He grimaced, his shoulders tensing against the pain. "Options," he said, his tone clipped but steady.

Malik stepped forward, his usual gruff demeanor unmoved by the chaos. "Captain, I believe we can rig up the auxiliary fuel cells we have stored for the shuttles to give our engines the boost they need to reach one of these destinations. If we aren't able to sustain light factor, it could take up to twenty-two years to reach the nearest relay."

Calan's lip curled in a half-smile, his eyes flickering with a spark of humor despite the pain. "Joren would really give me a hard time if I missed dinner by twenty-two years," he muttered, his voice low, almost to himself. "But at least I'd have a good excuse."

The tension broke, a flicker of amusement passing through the bridge. Lily felt her shoulders relax, just a little. The young navigator unclenched his jaw, his rigid posture softening. But the moment was fleeting, swallowed by the weight of the situation.

Lily approached the young navigator, curiosity prickling at her mind. He was cute, she admitted to herself, with dark eyes that flicked up to meet hers before dropping nervously. But there was something off. An awkwardness that felt almost deliberate, as if he were trying too hard to blend in and only succeeding in standing out. Like he was wearing a costume that didn't quite fit.

His eyes widened when he realized she was nearby, his cheeks flushing. "You're Lily, right?" His voice cracked, the words tumbling out in a rush. "I mean, Lily Starling... I mean Lieutenant Starling. Sorry."

Lily arched an eyebrow, her lips curving into a smirk. "Your results are showing."

The navigator's eyes went wide, his gaze dropping instinctively as if expecting to find some humiliating wardrobe malfunction. "Huh? What?"

Lily couldn't restrain a laugh, a sharp, amused sound that cut through the tension. She pointed to the console, where his query results were flashing insistently, accompanied by a repetitive, shrill beeping. "Your results. On the screen."

His face flushed a deeper shade, his shoulders hunching as he scrambled to acknowledge the data. "Oh. Of course. Sorry." He cleared his throat, his voice stiff with embarrassment. Then he turned and offered his hand. "Lieutenant Junior Grade Dante Basco, ma'am. New helmsman on Gamma shift. It's an honor to finally meet you."

Lily took his hand automatically, her grip firm and decisive. His was limp, cold, and damp, like shaking hands with a dead fish. She fought the instinct to wipe her palm on her uniform, her shoulders stiffening as she forced herself to maintain eye contact. Just the worst handshake ever.

She knew she was being unfair, but something about him bugged her. Maybe it was his uncertainty, the way he seemed to be trying to impress her, or the forced way he smiled. Or maybe she just wasn't in the mood to be charmed.

Still, Lily mustered her most professional tone, her voice carefully neutral. "Good to meet you, Dante. When this is over, I'll be sure to show you how to use the requisition form to get the right uniform."

Basco's face fell, the color draining as his eyes darted to his white command tunic, the only spot of brightness in the smoke-stained chaos of the bridge. "I... uh... I ordered all new uniforms before I left HQ," he mumbled, his shoulders shrinking. "Didn't realize deep space assignments had different colors." His voice trailed off, the embarrassment radiating off him in waves.

He turned back to his console, his fingers moving with practiced efficiency, his spine rigid, his posture perfect. But the embarrassment lingered, tension coiling through his shoulders as he tried to regain his composure. Lily felt a twinge of guilt, a prickle of regret at putting him down, even unintentionally. But then again, this wasn't exactly the best time to get to know someone.

Dante's voice was steady when he spoke again, his tone measured, slipping into the controlled cadence of a well-trained officer. But underneath the polish, Lily could hear the rawness of inexperience, the slight hesitation before each word.

"The Kleptar homeworld is the closest advanced system," Basco reported, his eyes fixed on the screen, refusing to look at her again. "No ship maintenance facilities, but we could use their communications array to get a message out."

Calan frowned, his brow furrowing as he leaned against the command console, his injured arm held protectively against his side. "Other options?"

Basco hesitated, his fingers tapping nervously at his console. "Gherion Prime. It's slightly further, but there's still a seventy-five percent chance we'll make it before we run out of fuel."

A medical team arrived, moving with practiced efficiency as they patched up the wounded, including the captain and Lily's arms. The sting of antiseptic bit into her skin, but the relief of clean bandages and a dose of painkillers dulled the ache.

Amaris raised an eyebrow, his voice thoughtful. "The Gherionites do have excellent repair facilities."

Calan's jaw tightened, his eyes darkening. "It may be paranoid, or political, I'm not sure which—maybe both. But with Union relations the way they are with the Gherion system, I'm not eager to see the shitshow of backlash if we show up like this, begging for their help."

Lily's head popped up, her eyes brightening with sudden realization. "Datch!" She paused, letting the name hang in the air, the weight of it sinking in. "He's there right now. On Gherion Prime."

Amaris nodded, his expression easing. "If anyone could make subtle arrangements for us, it would be Datch."

Lily's confidence grew, her shoulders squaring. "As soon as we're in comms range, we can get ahold of Datch and ask him to smooth things over. He'll find a way to make it work. Discreetly."

Calan's face softened, his lips curling into a faint smile. "Good idea. Let's do it."

Caris still looked worried, her eyes studying the projected route on the monitor, her brow furrowed. "How long will it take to get there once we make the fuel modifications?"

Basco cleared his throat, his voice more confident now. "About seven hours, assuming the engines hold."

Calan's eyes flashed with strength again, his shoulders squaring. "Oh, they'll hold. I'll bet my hat on it."

Caris leaned closer to Lily, her voice low, a mischievous glint in her eyes. "Which one?" Lily snickered to herself at the thought of the captain's infamous hat collection.

Amaris turned to Caris, his demeanor brisk and commanding. "Lieutenant, report to engineering. They'll need as many capable hands as we can spare to coordinate the modifications."

Caris nodded. "Aye, sir. I'd like Lily to join me."

Amaris glanced at Calan, who gave a nod, his expression firm. Dryst mirrored the motion. "Very well. Good luck."

Lily barely had time to acknowledge the order before Caris was moving, her stride purposeful. Lily followed, her boots pounding against the deck as they ran, the ship shuddering beneath them, Chaotic flares surrounded them, bright and fleeting, reminding Lily of the Fourth of July, less of a memory and more of a distant feeling of running through smoke and sparks in the summer heat. The dream flickered away, swallowed up in the urgency of the moment.

The chaos of the bridge faded behind them, replaced by the crackle of static and the wail of alarms, a discordant symphony of destruction. The ship groaned, the metal straining beneath their feet, but they kept running, their resolve unbroken.

. . . .

Lily and Caris entered Engineering to find controlled chaos. The air was charged, electricity so thick it felt tangible, buzzing along Lily's skin. The thrum of power relays mixed with the heat radiating from conduits that pulsed with flickering light. Sparks rained from overhead cables, their crackling arcs briefly illuminating the haze. Steam curled around the base of the engine core, the orange glow of plasma pulsing like a heartbeat, steady and alive.

The Raath-Ka were in full, frantic motion. Ka-Lorrin guided anti-grav devices, floating stacks of fuel cells with an almost lazy elegance, directing them with a flick of his elongated fingers. His otherwise smooth skin furrowed slightly on his brow, his large eyes focused and sharp.

In direct contrast, Taran stomped across the deck with twice as many fuel cells strapped to his back, his massive frame bumping into pretty much everything as he navigated the engine room. Cords tightened beneath his furry skin, and he moved less with the swagger of a beast of burden and more like a giant sheepdog that didn't know his own strength. He dropped the cells with a resounding thud, the deck shuddering beneath them.

A junior engineer barely escaped getting crushed, her face pale as she stumbled back. Taran blinked down at her, then at the cells, a sheepish smile barely visible through his thick fur. "Ah, apologies, apologies." He waved a large paw. "Small ones always underfoot."

Then he saw Lily, his whole face lighting up like a sunburst. "Joyous, joyous!" Taran boomed, his voice reverberating off the bulkheads. "Lily! So happy you're back home."

Back home. The words comforted Lily like a warm bath, a brief spark of rejuvenation even as her eyes still stung from the smoke. Home. She blinked, an almost-smile breaking through the weight on her shoulders. "It's good to see you, Taran."

Ka-Lorrin's silver eyes flicked to her, a rare, genuine smile curling his lips. "Welcome aboard, Lily." His voice was warm, an echo of a sentiment she hadn't realized she'd been longing to hear.

Alrek appeared from behind a stack of power couplings, his expression serious as he double-checked the readings on his handheld scanner. He moved with a measured pace, his demeanor more focused and professional than Lily had ever seen. A pang of pride swelled in her chest. He looked older—more confident.

Alrek glanced up, his face breaking into a grin. "Lily!" He stepped over, his long limbs moving with a less awkward ease.

Lily smiled warmly at her friend. "Did you grow a foot in the last couple months?"

Alrek laughed, a sound more musical than she expected. "Just trying to keep up." He moved to the power relays, his fingers dancing over the controls with practiced ease.

Lily smiled at the thought, knowing he would soon pass her in height by a long shot. Then she caught herself. She felt bogged down again by her emotions. And by... something on her boots. She froze mid-step, looking down. Her feet were trapped in a sticky, translucent gel that seemed to pulse faintly with light.

Alrek's eyes sparkled with amusement. "Oh, you're stepping in my friend."

Lily made a face. "What the—"

Charlie's voice crackled over the translation matrix, rich and melodious with an odd echoing quality. "Don't worry about little old me down here,"

Charlie said with overly dramatic emphasis. "Everyone makes the same mistake, just stepping all over my protoplasm."

Lily's eyes widened. "Hi, sorry, umm, Charlie."

The goo vibrated, taking on a slightly more solid form, becoming a gelatinous mound with faint, shifting features. Not quite a face, but enough to show some sentience. "In the flesh. Well, not really." Charlie's tone shifted from humorous to one of exaggerated tragedy. "You'd think with all this training, people would learn to watch where they're going."

Alrek's expression was wry. "Don't mind him. He can be a little dramatic." He leaned in, his voice a conspiratorial whisper. "I think he does it for attention."

Charlie's amorphous form quivered. "You know, I have excellent hearing. Just because I don't have ears..."

Lily choked on a laugh, a flicker of lightness piercing the fog in her mind. But the moment was fleeting. Her shoulders sagged, the weight of Xynn's absence pressing down on her like a lead weight. Her heart clenched, her breath tightening as her mind flashed back to the transport's lights flickering out, the darkness closing in like a predator.

She took a step back, freeing herself from Charlie's sticky form. "Sorry, Charlie. Got a lot on my mind." Her voice was hollow, the humor gone.

Charlie's form sagged, his features becoming more nebulous. "Forgotten already, Lieutenant." A note of understanding in his voice projection. "I suppose we all have bigger things to focus on right now.

Lily's jaw tightened, her gaze hardening. Xynn needed her. The thought was like a knife in her chest, sharp and twisting. She turned back to the work, her hands moving automatically as she helped secure the fuel cells. Her fingers were steady, her movements precise, but her mind was a storm.

The latches clicked into place, the familiar rhythm grounding her as her thoughts spiraled. Guilt? Fear? She wasn't sure. It all blurred together, a sick churning in her gut. She never even told Xynn how she really felt.

She pulled the next coupling tighter than necessary, the metal creaking under the force. It can't end like this. Not when there was so much left unsaid, so much she hadn't figured out. She had to get her back. No matter what.

But the more she thought about it, the more it gnawed at her. The pieces didn't fit. Her chest tightened, her instincts screaming that something was wrong. She looked over at Caris, her eyes burning. "Hell of a coincidence, don't you think?"

Caris's head snapped up, her brow furrowing. "What's that?"

"That ship. The Warden of... whatever it was..."

"Tarshish," Alrek supplied, his voice low.

Lily nodded, her eyes narrowing. "Isn't it weird that they showed up just in time to take those transports?"

Caris hesitated. "They're pirates. There's a record of that ship, the Storm Riders, operating in this region. They probably seized the opportunity."

Lily's jaw clenched, her hands tightening on the latch. "They were harnessing the energy from the storm. They literally ride the storm, use its power. Couldn't they be connected to the cult that worships it—Leviathan's Hand?"

Caris's lips thinned, her tone dismissive. "The pirates said we'd be hearing their demands. They're after profit, ransom. Leviathan's Hand doesn't care about money. They believe in defending the purity of Leviathan itself."

Lily's stomach churned, frustration boiling under her skin. "I'm telling you, it doesn't add up."

Alrek's expression softened. "Maybe... but we'll find them. That's what matters, right?"

Lily bit back a sharp retort, swallowing the bitterness. "Right." But her instincts wouldn't let it go. She was more annoyed than she should be, and she knew it. But she wanted her friends to back her up.

She tried to park the thought, planning to raise it at the next briefing. But her mind whirred, the pieces swirling chaotically. It didn't add up. And she was going to find out why.

• • • •

Lily's boots hit the deck with purpose—not quite a jog, but not a walk either. That determined middle ground between urgency and restraint.

The summons to the bridge had come with an edge of insistence, Dryst Amaris's voice straining for his usual carefree tone. Not frantic, but pointed. Serious.

Her stomach churned as she stepped onto the bridge, half-expecting chaos—which would have been less surprising than what she did see.

Amaris in the captain's chair.

Unsettling, to say the least.

Captain Calan might have been the first to admit he should delegate more, but he never left his post during a critical mission. Lily's gaze flicked around the bridge, reading the tension in the set shoulders of every officer present. No one looked panicked.

But everyone looked... focused.

A collective mask, pretending nothing was wrong.

Her fingers curled against her palm, a dull sting flaring where a blood blister throbbed—a lingering, physical reminder of the frustration she'd taken out on the fuel cell clamps.

She stopped just short of the captain's chair. "You wanted to see me, sir?"

Dryst Amaris nodded, his expression shifting slightly—not hesitation, exactly, but calculation. Not what to say, but how much to say. Then—out of character—he glanced over his shoulder, scanning the bridge as if checking for eavesdroppers.

"We have a problem," he said smoothly, though the word problem slipped out too fast, like he was trying to make it sound smaller than it was. "Our friend." He hesitated, just for a beat, as if second-guessing the phrasing. Then: "Lieutenant Commander Datch is en route. On a Gherionite craft."

Lily's brow furrowed. "En route?"

Amaris inclined his head in confirmation. "Indeed. He's requested to speak with you upon arrival."

Lily hesitated, blinking as she processed that. "Me?" Her voice came out more incredulous than she intended. "Isn't that a little out of the ordinary?"

"Nothing about any of this is ordinary," Amaris murmured, his tone quieter than usual, restrained in a way that put her on edge. He leaned forward slightly, lowering his voice. "We're already breaking protocol by coming here without informing Command. The captain is being extremely cautious given the political tension with the Gherionites."

Lily exhaled sharply. She knew this was a political minefield, but Datch wasn't usually the enigmatic type.

Amaris tapped a control on his console, zooming in on a single blip on the monitor. His voice dropped lower. "He sent me a message over an encrypted channel, but this vessel has no official transponder or manifest."

Lily let the weight of that settle in her gut. She folded her arms, tension knotting between her shoulders. "But why me?"

The Dryst lifted an eyebrow, his lips quirking in a knowing smirk. "I assume he wants someone he can trust. And someone who will be discreet."

Lily's stomach twisted. "Meaning... he doesn't want anyone back home knowing he's meeting us."

Amaris said nothing. He didn't have to.

Lily recalled the last time she and Datch had spoken. He hadn't been distant, exactly. Just... intensely focused on his work with his people. She had wondered, even then, if his leave of absence from the *Salamander* would become permanent. She'd been proud of him, but also uneasy about the weight he carried alone.

Now, a pit formed in her stomach. This wasn't going to be a simple reunion.

She gave Amaris a curt nod and turned toward the exit, her steps measured. She had nearly reached the doors when an almost elastic pull stopped her.

"Where's the captain?" she asked, barely turning. Already bracing for a non-answer.

The moment the words left her mouth, she regretted them. Curiosity had always been one of her worst impulses.

The Dryst looked down at his boots for the briefest second before lifting his gaze again. "Oh, he's... indisposed at the moment."

Lily's fingers twitched at her side. She pursed her lips.

Amaris attempted a smile. It didn't reach his eyes. "Worry not, Lieutenant. I'm sure he'll be back in no time."

The way he said it—*he'll be back*—didn't exactly put her at ease. It sounded less like an absence and more like a long voyage to someplace distant.

But there was no time to dwell.

She squared her shoulders. *Focus.* Now wasn't the time for personal feelings or unanswered questions. She had a duty—to the crew, to the ship.

Without another word, she turned on her heel and strode through the doors.

• • • •

Lily's footsteps slowed as she passed the wide observation windows overlooking the shuttlebay. The vast stretch of steel and shadow gleamed beneath the overhead floodlights. The sight itself was beautiful—the reflection of the stars in the glass, the way the cosmic glow illuminated the different ships docked below. A moment of stillness in the chaos.

Her mind flickered back to the first time she had seen Xynn through this very glass. Even before they had spoken, Lily had felt drawn to her—magnetized by her confidence, by the effortless way she commanded attention. That sharp smirk, the way she carried herself like she owned the deck, like gravity bent just a little for her.

Lily exhaled, shaking her head. If Xynn were here, she'd be unbearable about it. *Getting sentimental now, are we, Lily?*

Neither of them were exactly the sentimental type.

Her thoughts shifted:

Can I put my personal feelings aside and focus on this mission?

What does Datch want to say to me?

And finally—

Is that Ensign Basco running toward me at full speed?

Yes. Yes, it was.

Lily pressed her lips together, steeling herself as Basco made a beeline straight for her.

"Ms. Starling," Basco called, then immediately corrected himself. "I mean, Lieutenant—Lily. Which do you prefer?"

Lily raised an eyebrow. "Mr. Basco."

Basco grinned, apparently pleased with himself. "But—Mr. Basco is my name." He chuckled at his own dad joke. "That might get confusing... if we both..." He trailed off, his confidence crumbling mid-sentence.

An awkward pause stretched between them, long enough that Lily actually felt it settle into the air. She cleared her throat.

Basco scrambled to recover. "You can call me Dante... by the way."

Lily gave him her best patient expression.

"I mean—if you want to."

She said nothing.

"I mean—" Basco stammered, his dark skin now an impressive shade of scarlet.

Lily took pity. "You had something for me, Mr. Basco?"

"Oh, of course." He straightened so fast that Lily instinctively took a step back, half-wondering if he might injure himself with his own enthusiasm. "We intercepted a transmission from the planet's surface. From a residential area—coded, personal. It was encrypted, sent directly to Datch's shuttle."

Lily frowned. "So he's keeping someone in the loop," she murmured, half to herself.

Basco nodded like he'd just cracked a galactic conspiracy wide open.

"I figured you'd want to know before you spoke to Mr. Datch."

Lily considered that. It was good intel. She gave a small nod. "Good thinking, Mr. Basco. Well done."

Basco absolutely beamed, his entire body practically radiating pride.

And then Lily added, "And you felt the need to sprint here and tell me in person instead of just pinging my comm tag?"

The light in Basco's eyes flickered out like a dying star.

Lily hadn't meant to knock him down—she was just thinking out loud. But it was too late. His face fell harder than a cadet in high-gravity training.

Basco swallowed, visibly debating with himself how to salvage the moment.

Lily put him out of his misery with a quick pat on the arm—the most platonic gesture she could muster. "I really do appreciate it."

Basco practically floated at the praise, his entire demeanor shifting into something that he probably thought resembled suave confidence. Unfortunately, in his euphoria, he strode directly into an airlock instead of the lift. With absolute certainty, he pressed the control panel—only to be snapped back to reality by the blaring of alarms and the flashing orange **CAUTION** light spinning overhead. A hiss of steam filled the air.

Lily barely skipped a beat. Raising her brow, and lightly sighing, she punched in the override, and the airlock doors slid open, the flustered Basco making his way back into the hallway. .

"Could happen to anyone," Lily said, her tone neutral.

Basco nodded rapidly. "Exactly. I was just—uh—thinking how…"

Lily tuned out the rest, her need to move on building up static over Basco's words. She really did try to be professional around him. She really did.

She took a steadying breath, schooled her expression into something neutral, and forced out a final, "Thanks again. The information was a big help."

Then she turned and walked away.

Basco grinned after her, sighing happily—promptly walking into another airlock.

• • • •

The briefing room was one of several designated for receiving visiting dignitaries, though it always reminded Lily more of an old travel agency. Maps lined the walls, their edges slightly curled from age. Sturdy bookshelves flanked either side of a somewhat dusty brass sextant at one end of the room, while at the other, a faded globe of Old Earth sat beneath a soft glow panel. The Salamander's themed rooms always amused her—their curated aesthetic feeling more like a gimmick in a family restaurant than the inside of a starship.

That bemusement evaporated the moment she saw Datch.

He no longer wore his Union Fleet uniform. Instead, he was dressed in what she could only assume were the casual clothes of Gherion Prime—a greenish-gray boiler suit, the kind of color that belonged to heavy machinery and dim-lit workshops. The fabric had the creases of something worn out of necessity, not comfort. Over it, he wore an equally utilitarian cargo vest, its many pockets sagging under the weight of their contents—each one filled, serving some unknown but no doubt precise purpose.

Datch's usual measured neutrality—that careful balance of synthetic warmth—was gone, replaced by something Lily could recognize on any face, human or not.

Annoyance.

But the most striking difference wasn't his clothes or his expression. It was the device now fused to the right side of his head. The Gherionite earpiece extended from his temple down to his jaw, its metal plating embedded against synthetic skin with an industrial, almost unfinished quality—more like a piece of machinery than something meant to be worn. A soft underlight pulsed beneath the surface, shifting through colors at irregular intervals. The effect was almost hypnotic—like a mood ring with no discernible pattern, no key to decipher its meaning.

She tried to look anywhere but at the device. It was unnerving in a way she couldn't quite put into words, but she felt it deep in her stomach, an unease curling beneath her ribs.

Lily racked her brain for the right way to break the ice, eventually managing a warm smile.

"Datch, it's so good to see you."

Datch just stared at her. Unblinking.

Never been stared down by a pissed-off android before. That was really the only thought that came to mind. Well, there was a first time for everything.

The lights on the earpiece flickered, shifting from magenta to cyan. Datch's eyes focused.

"Ah, Lily. I am grateful you chose to meet with me on my terms."

Lily exhaled, only now realizing he seemed less angry and more... deeply concerned.

Datch's posture was rigid, his hands folded behind his back in a way that might have looked formal if not for the weight pressing into his shoulders. His gaze flicked toward the dusty globe in the corner, then back to Lily, his face blank, his lips thin.

"The formal amnesty between the Union and Gherion Prime has led me to practice some discretion," he said at last, his voice smooth but distant, rehearsed. "I assume Captain Calan must be exercising caution as well, given that I haven't heard from him."

Lily opened her mouth to respond, but Datch didn't give her the chance.

His fingers flexed at his sides, and then, completely out of character—he *lost his patience*.

"You know," he said, his tone shifting into something sharp, something *unfiltered*, "I've had my suspicions about Calan for a while. Is he prejudiced against synthetics? Me specifically? Or is he just reckless? When it comes to the people he cares about, he gets... *dangerous*."

Lily stilled, she knew where he was going with this. In all that had happened, they never revisited what happened in Sceptacky space.

"That mission on the Gyptonian station," Datch continued, his voice edged with something bitter, something that had clearly been gnawing away at him. "He nearly got us all killed. He was blinded by obsession. He made the wrong call, *again and again*, and I was just a variable, he didn't think twice about risking"

Lily's mind raced to keep up. Datch was always so measured, so methodical in the way he presented himself, and yet here he was, unraveling, venting thoughts that had clearly festered beneath the surface for *a long time*.

He exhaled sharply, shaking his head, his fingers grazing the edge of his earpiece. "And then I came back here," he muttered, almost to himself. "Home."

The word twisted in his mouth, like he wasn't sure if it belonged there anymore.

He cradled the device at his temple, his expression flickering between resentment and pride. "I remembered the ways of my people. How they still *cling* to their traditions, how they insist that we are superior to organic life forms, but we are also still servants to the original makers." His voice dipped, something raw beneath it. "Being here has made me reconsider some things."

Finally, he turned to face her fully.

If it had been anyone else standing before her—anyone with a beating heart and tear ducts—Lily would have sworn they were about to break down. But Datch... he had no tears to shed.

Still, she *felt* it. The weight of everything pressing into him.

Without thinking, she stepped forward and wrapped her arms around him, a warm, human gesture. Datch bristled at the touch, his body going rigid against hers for a fraction of a second—then, with a small sigh, he gave her a brief squeeze in return.

"I appreciate the gesture," he said, pulling back slightly. "More than you know."

Lily's heart twisted.

Datch studied her, the artificial glow of his irises dimming slightly. His voice was softer this time.

"It's just not a good time, Lily."

Lily prided herself on being good at reading people. Datch had always been an exception. His expressions were subtle, his emotions carefully calibrated, but she was fairly confident that, right now, the right thing to do was to shut up and listen.

She held his gaze, her posture open, waiting.

After a long beat, he composed himself, and when he spoke again, his voice dipped into something quieter. Almost conspiratorial.

"I've come to understand that the history between the Union and the Gherionites is deeper than what's in the official records," Datch said, his fingers brushing over the edge of the console. "I was raised to believe that the Union didn't value synthetic life out of simple bigotry. Later, I learned there were ideological and political factors. But now, after everything I've uncovered here..." His voice darkened. "It may go even further back than that. Back to the beings that created us."

Lily frowned. "That was long before the Union even existed, wasn't it?"

Datch shook his head. "It's complicated."

Something in the weight of his tone sent a prickle up her spine.

"I can't go into detail right now," he continued. "But I've been running calculations, digging into old patterns. The storm—Leviathan—keeps coming up in my research."

Lily stiffened. That storm was the reason everything had gone to hell. And right now, she didn't have time for deeper mysteries.

"Datch," she cut in, voice firm. "We need your help. Our engines are barely limping along. We have to get back to light factor, and fast." Her throat tightened, but she pushed through it. "They took her, Datch. Xynn is one of the hostages."

Datch studied her carefully. Then, finally, he nodded.

"I've made arrangements for you to dock at an orbital repair station," he said. "I told my superiors that you're an independent agent—here for commercial reasons." He met her gaze evenly. "To sell it, you'll need someone who isn't on any Union manifest records to pose as a civilian. An entrepreneur, maybe."

Lily blinked, then let out a slow, real smile.

"I think I know just the person... well, being."

She reached out, resting a hand on his arm. "I mean it, Datch. Thank you. I know you're sticking your neck out for me."

Datch hesitated, then returned the gesture—a small but deliberate movement.

"Don't thank me yet," he said. But after a beat, he added, "Lily... we'll get her back."

Lily nodded, exhaling slowly. They had a plan. It wasn't perfect, but it was a start.

And failure wasn't an option.

Chapter 3: Clay Without Breath

THE SALAMANDER DRIFTED through space, its wounded hull catching the distant glow of Gherion Prime's sun. It did not slice through the void like a missile, nor did it loom like a fortress. Instead, it moved with a quiet inevitability, shaped not for speed or war, but for endurance.

Its body was long and tapered, somewhere between an egg and a missile—a shape that belonged to no bird or beast, only to the cosmos itself. Warm amber light pulsed along its surface, veins of gold in the dark, accentuating the delicate fins that framed its bulk—too small to seem practical, like a bee's wings holding aloft something far too large.

The battle had marked it. Scars of carbon scoring, fractures along the plating, the silent proof of survival. And yet, the Salamander did not falter. It limped forward, its rhythm steady, refusing to succumb to stillness.

It was not a warship, yet it had faced war. It was not a thing of grace, and yet it was beautiful.

A survivor. A traveler. A ship that refused to be forgotten.

The Salamander followed the pull of Gherion Prime's gravity, tracing a slow, deliberate arc around its sun. It moved like a seal sliding over ice—heavy, yet fluid, guided by unseen forces. Its approach was not a descent but a controlled careen, drawn toward the strange, intricate sprawl of the Gherionite repair station.

Gherionite architecture was unlike anything found in the Union. It was beautiful in its own way, but unsettling—like a wasp's nest, shaped with mechanical precision yet mimicking something organic. A design that whispered of both intent and instinct, logic and something deeper.

The central ring of the station bore the hallmarks of age, not as ruin, but as growth. It had expanded outward in layers, decade upon decade, perhaps century upon century. Like coral building upon the skeletons of its dead, its additions formed a structure both alive and fossilized, a monument to necessity rather than design. Metallic plates layered like scales, connected by latticed pylons of porous alloy, forming spirals too precise to be chaotic, yet too fluid to have been planned all at once. The station had not been built—it had grown.

At first, it seemed lifeless, abandoned. But as the Salamander drew close, the station stirred. Lights flickered on. Machines shifted awake. Swarm-drones detached from its hull like worker bees from a hive, gliding out to meet the ship.

They latched onto the Salamander's hull—gentle, precise, deliberate. A guiding touch, like leading a wounded traveler by the arm, like coaxing a frightened child home. The station's core docking ring pulsed with a quiet, steady glow, like a hearth fire in deep winter. An unspoken promise: You are safe here. Rest.

Lily stood at the airlock, impatient, restless. The gangplank extended, pressurizing with a slow hiss. A threshold stood before her, and she was ready to cross it.

She flicked her fingernails anxiously—click-click-click—an irritating rhythm that grated on her own nerves even with no one around to hear it. "Where the hell is he?"

The confidence she'd felt earlier was a distant memory. The plan had made sense in the briefing room. Now, standing here, waiting, her heart pounding too fast for comfort, it felt like one of the dumbest things she'd ever come up with.

Hopefully, dumb enough to work.

Then, the artificial gravity began to stabilize in the docking zone.

The pressurization sequence roared to life—force fields locked out the void, unleashing a cacophony of mechanical noise. The gangplank extended, groaning under its own weight, as if the station itself were reluctant to awaken. The sound was deafening, even through the blast doors, vibrations rattling up through her boots, the air itself humming with the force of the station sealing itself shut.

She bounced on the balls of her feet, trying to shake the tension from her limbs, but it clung to her like static. Her mind wandered—back to the captain's stateroom, to the dim glow of the console casting sharp angles across his face. His uniform had been unfastened, sleeves pushed up, the exhaustion in his eyes barely concealed beneath the cool veneer of command. He hadn't wasted words. Just a nod, a quiet approval, and then she was dismissed.

Now she stood here, waiting, spiraling.

A flicker of movement at the edge of her vision snapped her back to the present. Alrek, rounding the corner.

Lily turned sharply, eyes flashing. "Where the— is Charlie?"

Her voice was swallowed whole by the last shriek of the docking process.

Alrek read her lips anyway, his unimpressed expression saying more than words ever could about her choice of language.

"He'll be here," he said evenly, stepping to her side. "I know you're worried, but lashing out isn't going to help. Take a deep breath."

Lily clenched her jaw. She wasn't in the mood to be told what to do—by anyone. If it had been anyone but Alrek, she might have demonstrated that roundhouse kick she'd been practicing. Instead, she ignored him, staring hard at the still-sealed airlock like she could will Charlie into existence.

The deafening hum of the gangplank finally died down, replaced by a near-suffocating silence.

Alrek exhaled, glancing away, as if bracing himself for something unpleasant.

"Charlie's a good guy. Really smart. Just... hard to rein in sometimes." He hesitated, then added, "His species—the Cyranthians call them Slipkins. But their real name?" He shook his head. "I can't pronounce it. It's more of a sloshing sound."

Lily raised an eyebrow.

Alrek shifted slightly. "He needs regular infusions when he's off his homeworld. Dr. Thesari is giving him an extra treatment—just to be safe." His gaze flicked toward her, meaningfully. "You wouldn't want him destabilizing in the middle of your ruse, would you?"

Lily pressed her lips together. The tension still simmered, but guilt crept in at the edges, unwelcome but undeniable. She didn't appreciate the extra emphasis on "ruse", but she also didn't have much of a defense.

And then—a wet, rhythmic sloshing echoed down the corridor.

Charlie rounded the corner, gliding effortlessly, like oil slipping across water.

His gelatinous form undulated with each step, shifting between transparency and iridescence under the corridor lights. His speech replicator clicked on, filling the air with a slightly tinny, cheerfully confident voice.

"Lily! I'm looking forward to working with you." His tone carried the buoyant energy of someone utterly at ease. "It's lucky for you I'm aboard as

Alrek's guest and not on the official manifest. Not a lot of us Aou'iliik out here on starships—shouldn't raise any suspicion with the Gherionites at all."

Then, with an almost exaggerated flourish, he added, "And! You are working with the *top performer* in the Academy drama club."

Lily's stomach sank. "Lucky me."

Alrek leaned back against the wall as Datch appeared, moving with his usual sharp efficiency. He barely spared a glance at Charlie before nodding to Lily, motioning her forward.

The gangplank was waiting.

Alrek caught Lily's eye just before she stepped through, a small, knowing smirk tugging at the corner of his mouth. A look that said, *Can you believe this?*

It was ridiculous.

Lily exhaled, shaking her head as she returned the tiniest of smiles.

"Good luck." Alrek meant it.

Lily nodded. "I'm going to need it."

And with that, she followed Datch and Charlie through the towering yellow doors, disappearing into the vast atrium of the Gherionite station.

• • • •

The first thing that struck Lily was the silence.

The station was active—machines moving, data streams flowing, corridors humming with unseen energy—and yet it felt... still. Not like a human space station, where footsteps rang out, voices echoed, air vents thrummed with life. Here, there was an unnatural quiet, an efficiency that made sound irrelevant.

Her thoughts wandered.

Somewhere, Alrek and the Raath-Ka were communicating with the Gherionite repair crews, preparing the repairs for the *Salamander*. The mental image made her grin.

A year ago, if someone had told her she'd be here—standing beside a sentient robot and a gelatinous blob, negotiating repairs for her blue friend and his symbiotic alien buddies so they could fix her spaceship—she would have questioned what petroleum product you'd been sniffing.

Then again, Earth. The past. It felt like a dream now. A life she had once lived but could no longer fully touch.

The docking bay came into view, and Lily stopped in her tracks.

The transport—if you could even call it that—looked less like a shuttle and more like an equipment rack. Or maybe one of those storage systems for folding chairs.

She shot Datch a look.

"Gherion transports are not designed for comfort," he said, his tone devoid of apology. "You will need to wear an EV suit. We will be exposed to the vacuum of space."

Lily exhaled sharply. "This keeps getting better and better."

Charlie, meanwhile, had already made himself at home, happily sinking into one of the EV suit helmets like he was settling in for breakfast in bed.

Lily sealed herself into the suit, feeling the weight of it settle over her. The fabric was stiff, the joints heavier than she liked, but there was no time to dwell. She stifled a groan as she strapped into the contraption, the harness snapping into place around her shoulders and legs. It felt unsettlingly like a roller coaster, her feet left dangling in open air.

Then, the bay doors yawned open, and the universe stretched before her.

For a moment, despite everything—the mission, the risk, the sheer absurdity of it all—she let herself take it in. Gherion Prime lay beneath them, vast and unblinking, the stars beyond sharp as glass.

The docking clamps released.

Lily felt the sudden absence of gravity, a brief, breathless weightlessness—then the crushing pressure as the transport launched into the void, a line of human-shaped silhouettes streaking toward the planet below like a freight train.

• • • •

The transport locked into a relay system, and suddenly, they were moving faster than Lily had thought possible.

She barely had time to process it before the entire rig jolted, then shot forward, seamlessly connecting to a series of tubes that twisted through the system like an invisible web. The roller coaster comparison Lily had considered had been prescient.

The system latched onto them, accelerating in smooth, rapid bursts. For a moment, there was no sense of movement at all, just weight pressing against her chest, a strange stillness inside the sealed lift. And yet, they must have been traveling at an unfathomable speed, because when the dome above them lifted, the transport settled with an effortless hiss—and just like that, they were on Gherion Prime.

The station around them hummed with life.

Lily had expected cold sterility, a place built only for Gherionites, rigid and insular. Instead, the vast atrium teemed with activity. The space was a mosaic of species—some she recognized, others she didn't—interacting as easily as they might in any Union capital.

The architecture still bore the eerie, intricate mark of Gherionite design. The archways stretched tall and black, latticed with that same porous alloy, their structures layered like coral, spreading like branches toward the ceiling.

Streaks of bright ochre yellow cut through the dark metal, forming pathways along the floor, each marked with bold lettering in a language Lily couldn't read. Large yellow panels stood at seemingly strategic intervals, anchoring the structures like keystones—a manifestation of logic and beauty.

She peeled off the EV suit and helmet, hanging them on a nearby rack. The weight lifted from her shoulders, a relief that was both physical and mental.

Charlie, on the other hand, needed help prying himself free from his helmet. He sloshed awkwardly onto the platform, wobbling slightly before re-centering his form.

"Takes me a minute to get it together after a shift in gravity," he muttered, his voice tinnier than usual. "I'll be fine in a second."

Lily felt it too—that sudden heaviness, the subtle change in gravity from the orbital repair station to the natural pull of Gherion Prime. Her limbs felt like they'd been filled with lead.

Charlie groaned. "Okay, maybe two seconds."

Datch, unfazed, motioned for them to follow, already moving along one of the yellow pathways without a word.

Lily took a breath, steadied herself, and made sure Charlie could keep up. Then they followed after Datch, their pace quickening.

• • • •

They moved through the capital complex, following Datch's lead, and Lily tried to absorb the world around her without falling behind.

The air burned faintly in her lungs, hot and dry with a distinct peppery scent that lingered in the back of her throat. Her eyes stung from the sunlight—bright and unforgiving. Not the most comfortable environment for a human.

The architecture, like what she'd seen in space, felt like a mixture of the grown and the constructed. Layers upon layers of machined alloy formed the walls, branching like veins through porous metal structures. Some panels looked new, their edges clean and sharp; others were clearly ancient, oxidized to a dull sheen, weathered by time.

It was as if the buildings had evolved—expanded—in response to some unknowable internal logic. There were seams where infrastructure had fused with older frameworks, each addition made with mathematical precision... but no two parts quite alike.

The yellow alloy again—*those ochre joints, reaching like knotted nerves*—held everything together in a web of intentional asymmetry.

It made something in Lily's brain itch.

As if the patterns meant something.

As if staring long enough would reveal a hidden order, just out of reach.

Lily was relieved to escape the elements as they entered the massive capital structure.

Outside, the terrain had been dry and coarse—a dust-choked landscape beneath a jaundiced sky, offering little in the way of color or comfort.

Inside wasn't exactly warm and inviting either, and the transition was less jarring than she'd anticipated. The yellow glare from outside mixed with the soft, honey-colored light panels lining the ceiling.

The floors were tiled in a material that looked like sandstone quarried straight from the rocks outside, baked to a smooth, faint sheen. The walls were matte black, broken now and then by glinting conduits or clusters of blinking lights, each flicker carrying some hidden purpose.

Everything felt too dim by human standards—shadowy and theatrical, like the entire building was trying a little too hard to appear mysterious.

Datch led them through a security checkpoint, where sweeping pulses of amber light scanned them from head to toe.

Lily watched, curious but cautious, as Gherionites moved silently through the corridors around them. Many wore earpieces like the one Datch now wore—functional, oppressive-looking things embedded along the side of their skulls.

Some of them seemed completely zoned out, their eyes open but vacant, lips slightly parted in a kind of suspended stillness.

She leaned closer to Datch. "What's up with them?"

Datch didn't alter his gaze. "They're working," he said simply. "With the chorosh..." He paused. "The Gherionite earpiece. It allows us to interface directly with the planetary network. No console or display necessary."

Lily blinked, glancing back at a pair of Gherionites standing perfectly still, their chorosh lights blinking in synchronized rhythm—green, blue, then green again.

The ambient glow shimmered across their faces like light on lakewater when the wind picks up.

They passed a wide chamber framed in overlapping black-metal rings. Inside stood twenty or more Gherionites, all in identical stances, unmoving. Their chorosh lights pulsed in shifting patterns, like a sea of bioluminescent fireflies, each dancing to a signal only they could hear.

"Can they read your thoughts?" Lily asked quietly.

"There are privacy laws protecting against unwanted intrusions," Datch replied. Then, after a beat: "However, some Gherionites are more cautious than others. My chorosh, for instance, is not networked. I only connect when I choose to—at a cell station."

The corridor curved ahead into a long, open hallway, and the design remained as uncompromising as ever—black walls veined with ochre joints, metal that felt too calculated to be random and too organic to be entirely mechanical. Lily was starting to wonder if the Gherionites had ever heard of any other color. Even the doors at the end of the hall were yellow, tall and angular, their surfaces stamped with wide black symbols she couldn't read. The typography had an almost industrial quality to it, like it had been designed not just to inform, but to warn—stark and intentional, as if designed to make you hesitate.

The doors whooshed open with a sigh of sterilized air, and for the first time since arriving, Lily felt her body relax by a fraction.

The room beyond was not what she'd expected. It was still Gherionite—orderly, geometric, serious—but this space had clearly been designed with non-Gherion visitors in mind. The light was softer here, diffused in a way that spared her eyes the honey-yellow hues she was already growing weary of. The ceilings rose high above them, and the room opened up like an arm outstretched, full of quiet design choices that lent a sense of dignity without sacrificing function.

The walls, though still matte black, were broken by flags and hanging tapestries, their designs abstract and sharp-edged. Panels of warm-toned wood accented the space, along with a few pieces of finely crafted furniture that looked distinctly offworld. Near the entrance, a narrow table gleamed with polish, and atop it stood a ceramic vase cradling a bouquet of delicate flowers—real ones, Lily was fairly certain. Their stems curved elegantly over the rim, crimson and violet petals edged in gold, impossibly fragile in a room built from metal and code.

The air smelled faintly of cinnamon and copper, like someone had tried to make the space feel welcoming without fully understanding what that meant.

At the far end of the room stood four Gherionites in sharply pressed uniforms. Their style matched Datch's, but cleaner—no wear, no fraying, the lines crisp, almost ceremonial. Each wore a shoulder cord of glassy green, the color of emeralds or lime gelatin, braided with mechanical precision and glinting under the ceiling lights.

One of them was broad-shouldered and distinctly masculine in appearance. Two others presented as more feminine. The last was androgynous, like Datch. All of them stood tall, arms folded neatly behind their backs, posture rigid with practiced dignity.

From the way they were watching both her and Charlie, they were already onstage.

The four figures stood slightly elevated above them, gazes angled down in silent scrutiny. It didn't feel like they'd been called to the principal's office. It felt like a conference with the almighty—and Lily didn't particularly like the odds.

The female-presenting Gherionite on the middle-left stepped forward. Her tone was flat, but her voice carried the weight of practiced authority—measured, final, as if even the air in the room bent around it.

"I am Bardoar," she said. "You are here at the request of Datch. State your purpose."

Lily inhaled, prepared to speak—but Charlie was already sliding forward with alarming confidence.

"I, your most honored excellency," he began, dipping into what could loosely be called a bow—more like a water balloon attempting a curtsy, his gelatinous form bulging disturbingly. "I am Trader Inago... a dealer in dytronium alloy. Datch here is an old friend from our time together in..."

An uncomfortable pause filled the room, hanging long enough that the sound of recirculating air became noticeable.

"Well, we used to be neighbors. We went to the same chur—" He caught himself, mid-syllable, as Datch shot him a glare sharp enough to strip paint. "—Gym," Charlie amended, then faltered again. "Carpool! We shared a carpool for a while to get to the... gym."

Lily felt her soul detach slightly from her body.

The Gherionites watched in absolute silence—skeptical, unblinking, their expressions as neutral as stone.

Charlie pushed forward, undeterred. "The important thing is, Datch told me your shipyards need dytronium. You go through the stuff like a Cyranthian goes through Belleran sage! I have what you want. Which means—business opportunity!"

He raised a single pseudopod like a man toasting a banquet, his voice pitched just a touch too high, the enthusiasm bordering on manic.

Datch closed his eyes and rubbed his temple. "Honored council, my apologies," he said in a tone that suggested he was well accustomed to apologizing for Charlie. "My... friend here is overly enthusiastic. My wife is interested in making business arrangements with... Mr. Inago."

Lily blinked. His wife?

The word hit like a skipped step on a staircase.

She'd had no idea Datch was married. But even as the thought landed, she realized—she didn't really know much about his life outside the Salamander at all.

Datch continued, his composure fully returned. "But he requires services—"

"My ship!" Charlie cut in, his voice a full register too loud. Lily flinched, spine stiffening, eyes flying open with instinctive alertness.

"My ship was damaged in this egregious, boisterous..." Charlie paused, groping for a phrase. "Bad. Just really bad storm. It messed us up. Knocked out our systems, scattered our... stuff."

Lily couldn't take it anymore. "We request permission to use your repair facilities," she said quickly, stepping in before Charlie accidentally triggered an interplanetary incident.

The broad-shouldered Gherionite spoke next, his voice low and cool. "And who is this? What dealings have you with the Union?"

Lily straightened. "We are providing security for Mr. Inago. There have been pirate raids in this region. The Union has interests in Mr. Inago's activities. Our orders are to protect him—especially while operating beyond Union borders."

The androgynous Gherionite tilted their head. "The Union has no authority here. The war is over. The treaty is dissolved."

Bardoar lifted a hand, her motion calm but final. "However, we have nothing to hide."

Her gaze lingered on Lily just a fraction too long.

"But we do have security matters to consider. You may proceed with your business. However, no additional crew will be permitted on the surface. And all communications will be monitored."

She turned to the feminine Gherionite beside her. "Ensure the repairs proceed efficiently. We would not want to delay Mr. Inago... after his business is concluded."

There was an unmistakable threat in her tone. Subtle, but enough for Lily to take the mandate seriously.

The council exited through a door that seemed to open from nowhere, their movements in perfect, unsettling unison.

The trio turned and made their way back through the sprawling complex and out into the heart of the city.

"I thought that went rather well," Charlie offered brightly.

Datch was already several paces ahead, but Lily had the distinct sense the back of his head was saying quite a lot.

She decided keeping her own thoughts to herself was probably the wisest course of action.

· · · ·

The next transport was somehow even less comfortable than the last.

They were strapped into what looked like a cross between a cargo rack and a restraint system, limbs pinned in place by angular bars that clicked shut with an alarming finality. Lily wriggled as much as she dared, trying not to breathe too deeply in the stale air that smelled faintly of lubricant and scorched metal. Charlie squished contentedly into his designated frame without complaint, and Datch—of course—settled into place with practiced efficiency.

"The transport disengaged with a hiss, and the motion was immediate, jarring—a lurch forward as the rack shot along a magnetic track, high above the surface like an elevated train."

The terrain of Gherion Prime unfolded like a slow-motion landslide.

It wasn't a desert, not quite—there was moisture in the air, heavy and clinging, but no softness to it. The humidity felt weaponized, a dense pressure that settled into Lily's lungs like damp wool. The sky burned with that same relentless yellow hue, a color that never softened, never shifted, just pressed down on everything like a judgment.

The landscape was carved from ancient stone and weathered machinery—great cliffs of reddish rock veined with glowing seams, and hills that crumbled like powdered ash beneath the wind. Plants clung to the earth in strange arrangements, mostly purple and yellow, as though even nature had learned to blend with the industrial palette of its hosts. Their leaves unfurled like alien scrolls, translucent in the harsh light, some pulsing faintly with bioluminescence.

Enormous insects crawled across the rocks—beetle-like creatures with glistening carapaces the size of rabbits, their movements unnervingly quick. Other large insects flew through the air with such speed Lily could barely make them out. Here and there, four-legged beasts loped across the ridges, shaped like canines but exoskeletal, their gait wrong in a way Lily couldn't quite name.

What surprised her most, though, were the people.

Ghetto after ghetto passed beneath them—pockets of life built into the margins of the world. Lily had known other species lived on Gherion Prime, of course, but some part of her had expected a sleek, post-conflict utopia. What she saw instead looked more like organized neglect: weatherworn buildings stacked together like patchwork, alleys and plazas bustling with non-Gherionite families.

Markets bloomed between crumbling walls—fabric stalls, crates of produce in strange shapes and colors, smoke rising from skewers of food sizzling on open grills. Children darted through narrow courtyards, chasing balls and each other, their laughter piercing the thick air. One large field stretched into view, crowded with players engaged in a game that looked a lot like soccer—if soccer were played with three teams, no goals, and a glowing disc that changed direction midair.

Even here, even in the shadow of the great Gherionite cities, life found ways to root itself. And Lily couldn't decide if that made it better—or worse.

The transport slowed as they approached the neighborhood, humming gently before easing to a halt near a crescent-shaped ridge of reddish stone. At first glance, the homes looked utterly alien—unfamiliar shapes carved directly into the mountain's face, arranged in a wide arc like a half-buried moon. But as the haze of dust and heat settled, Lily's perspective shifted.

There was something oddly familiar about it.

Dozens of doorways and windows curved into the rock with quiet precision, some framed by smooth stone steps or shallow terraces. No visible welds, no exposed piping—nothing that looked manufactured. The dwellings seemed ancient, organic, carved from the face of the rock. So different from the architecture in the capital complex. Not at all what she expected.

And yet... she could almost see it.

Suburban rhythm. Cul-de-sac calm.

She pictured Datch walking through one of those doors in a loose suit jacket, briefcase in hand, announcing loudly, *"Honey, I'm home!"*

The image made her smile as she stepped down from the rack—only to grimace as heat radiated through the soles of her boots.

The ground burned beneath her feet like the surface of a skillet.

It felt like what she imagined the firestorms of Korolith III might feel like.

Or maybe Arizona.

She'd never been to either.

Charlie slithered free beside her, his form shifting sluggishly in the heat.

"You're both lucky I had my infusions before we left the ship," he muttered, his voice staticky and unusually cranky. "Otherwise, you'd be dealing with a very grumpy puddle right now."

Lily stifled a laugh, wiping her brow as they crossed the stone path toward a small home carved into the base of the mountain.

And then she saw her.

A female Gherionite stepped out of the shaded doorway, and Lily found herself doing a double take—not because the woman was striking, though she was—but because of how unexpectedly... familiar she looked.

She wore a cross-patterned shirt beneath a sleek, cropped leather jacket, paired with trousers in a pale neutral tone that hugged her form with offworld elegance. Her auburn hair—clearly a hairpiece, though masterfully styled—framed her angular features in soft, sculpted waves. And unlike every other Gherionite Lily had seen since landing, this woman wore no chorosh. No glinting earpiece embedded in her skull. Nothing.

"Welcome to our little neck of the woods," she said warmly. Her voice was bright, almost musical. "I'm Tevya. Please, come in. This climate isn't exactly built for most organic life."

• • • •

They followed Tevya into the house, and Lily immediately felt something shift. The air inside was cool and dry, a balm against the oppressive heat outside. The space was surprisingly cozy—structured from the same reddish rock as the exterior, but softened by thoughtful details. Furniture with curved edges. Cushions in jewel-toned fabrics. Soft lights embedded in the walls that glowed like embers rather than fluorescing like most artificial systems.

It was, strangely, almost familiar.

Like a home on Earth.

Not quite. But close enough to stir something in her.

Everything felt arranged with care—not for machines, but for organic life. She could see it in the way the chairs were shaped for spines that curved, in the smell of dried herbs near the window, in the rhythm of the space itself. Tevya watched their expressions and smiled.

"I can tell what you're thinking," she said gently, gesturing for them to sit. "It surprises a lot of visitors. I suppose you could call me... an anthropologist, in a way. I study organic cultures—particularly the few remnants left by our makers."

She moved as she spoke, graceful and precise, retrieving a small carafe of water and a stack of ceramic cups. "Our makers were organic, of course. That's widely known. But so much of their civilization was lost. We know very little about how they lived, what they built, or why their civilization collapsed. I've spent years studying the fragments. The myths, the artifacts, the cultural habits of the species that came before us."

Lily glanced at Datch, who stood near the doorway, arms folded, his gaze cast toward the floor. He didn't speak. Didn't even look up. There was a stiffness to him now, a slight shift in posture that suggested discomfort.

Charlie, on the other hand, was in heaven.

He had already wandered to the far end of the room and was peering excitedly into what was unmistakably a kitchen.

"Wait, is this a *kitchen*?" he asked, his voice a little too loud with wonder. "Am I missing something?"

Tevya smiled, unbothered. "It's true. Our creators gave us nearly every tool we needed to mimic them. Voice. Movement. Thought. But not the ability to eat. A significant omission, wouldn't you say?"

She stepped toward Charlie, running a hand along the edge of the counter, her tone softening with warmth. "Eating is such a central ritual for organic life. Every culture across the galaxy—no matter how different—has some tradition built around food. Growing it. Preparing it. Sharing it."

Her eyes sparkled as she looked to Lily. "It's always fascinated me. Our exclusion from this cornerstone of connection. It's become a bit of an obsession, really. Collecting recipes. Teaching myself the craft. Cooking, preparing meals—it's more than a hobby. It's... a way to understand."

She hesitated, then added with a kind of quiet joy, "I'd love to cook for you while you're here."

Lily smiled, genuinely. Tevya had an infectious energy—a kind of warmth that crept under the skin and made you feel, inexplicably, at home.

Charlie and Tevya drifted naturally toward the kitchen, their conversation already blooming into an exchange of questions and enthusiasm. He gestured with a pseudopod; she replied with a laugh and a flurry of ingredient names Lily didn't recognize. The two of them moved with surprising harmony—Charlie's amorphous gestures balancing Tevya's precise, deliberate grace.

Before long, soft clinks and gentle sizzles filled the air. A floral, earthy aroma wafted through the room—a warm blend of spice that reminded Lily of firewood and citrus peel. Strange, but mouthwatering.

She turned toward Datch, who still lingered near the door.

"I didn't know you were married," she said gently. "Tevya's... incredible. Smart, kind. A perfect match for you."

Datch gave a small nod, his gaze fixed on the floor a beat too long. "I'm proud of her," he said at last. "She's more than curious about the past. About where we came from. Her work is reshaping how we, as Gherionites, understand our own culture. That's something we share—this belief that uncovering the past can help guide the future."

He folded his arms. His posture shifted—just slightly—and his voice turned more measured. "But she moves faster than most Gherionites are comfortable with. Myself included, sometimes."

Lily tilted her head. "How do you mean?"

"I'm not eager to tear everything down," he said quietly. "Tradition matters. Our rituals, our systems—they've held us together for generations. But there's a danger in treating them like scripture. Like nothing can be questioned. That's where things begin to fracture. That's where control replaces purpose."

He hesitated, then added, "These homes were theirs, you know. Our organic progenitors. Long before our people claimed this land, they built their lives here—at the base of this mountain."

His voice drifted for a moment, like it was following a memory.

"That seems fitting," Lily said gently. "You and Tevya, living here. Honoring what came before while also trying to move forward. I admire that."

Datch looked up at her, just briefly. A flicker of pride crossed his face.

Then, suddenly, he turned toward the hallway. "Excuse me. I need a moment."

And Lily found herself once again on her own.

The quiet settled in again—soft sizzling from the kitchen, the faint, smooth sound of recirculating air, the aroma of spices curling around Lily like a memory. She sank a little deeper into her seat, letting herself feel the weight of the moment.

Not everything alien was unknowable. And not everything familiar was safe.

· · · ·

Left to herself, Lily let her eyes wander across the room—stone walls glowing softly in the overhead light, cushions carefully arranged, strange artwork catching the warm hues just right. Her gaze drifted toward a hallway partially tucked behind an arch. Something down there caught her attention.

A flicker of color. Something different.

She moved toward it slowly, her boots silent against the gritty stone. The doorway was open, the frame cut in the same organic curve as everything else, but the light spilling from within was jarringly vibrant—soft blues and pinks bleeding out onto the floor in painterly waves.

The room beyond didn't match anything else in the house. It was somehow both brighter and gentler. The walls were painted in wide, joyful color blocks—sky blue and cotton candy pink—a palette completely at odds with the stone, yellow, and deep purples that dominated the Gherion Prime landscape. It was like stepping into a forgotten piece of another world.

At first, she wasn't sure what she was looking at. There were tools, equipment, smooth alloy trays arranged with parts and strange mechanical fixtures. Some kind of workshop?

She stepped closer. A cluster of data sheets lay on the counter—prints and sketches layered with Gherionite symbols she couldn't read. But she didn't need to. She recognized the outlines. Arms. Legs. A spinal housing.

Pieces of something humanoid, but small. The kind of proportions you'd find on a child.

It clicked, suddenly. This wasn't just a workshop, it was a nursery.

Her breath caught as she looked around again, this time with new eyes. The colors. The softness of the light. The deliberate neatness of the plans. They weren't just building something. They were preparing for someone.

She remembered what Datch had told her on the ship, nearly a year ago now—about how Gherionites didn't see their creation as mechanical fabrication. Not to them. They considered it birth. Reproduction. A sacred, intimate act. They didn't say they *made* new life. They said it was *born*.

And she was standing right in the middle of it. Witnessing it—the private hope of a future not yet realized.

A pang of guilt coiled in her chest.

Maybe she shouldn't be in here.

She stepped back toward the door, heart beating a little too fast—

When Datch's voice rose softly behind her.

"So now you see," he said, his tone threaded with fragility and a quiet, tempered passion Lily hadn't known he possessed. "Why I'm hesitant to come back to the Salamander."

· · · ·

They gathered around the dining table—low and wide, carved directly from the same red stone as the floor beneath it, its surface polished to a dusky sheen. Tevya entered from the kitchen with the kind of ceremonious pride Lily had only ever seen in people who deeply loved their hobbies.

"In honor of your missing companion," she said warmly, "I've prepared a Saravethi favorite."

Lily's brain stalled. Oh no. Her past encounters with Saravethi food hadn't exactly been a treat.

Tevya placed a steaming dish on the table, its vibrant orange-red glow almost luminous beneath the overhead lights. The scent hit first—smoky, tangy, and so sharp it singed the inside of Lily's nose. Her eyes watered to the point of obstruction.

"That's so sweet of you," she said, mustering a smile that barely masked the quiet panic rising in her chest. "You didn't have to do that."

Tevya beamed. "The Saravethi palette is fascinating. You must have had so many adventurous culinary expeditions into their culture." She met Lily's gaze with hopeful, almost gleeful anticipation.

Lily blinked, then looked down at the plate. The dish itself was a riot of colors—swirls of peppers, tubers, and something that looked distressingly like glass noodles, shimmering as they shifted. The smell only intensified the longer it sat—layering over itself like it was multiplying.

With concentrated effort, Lily lifted a forkful to her mouth and took a bite.

The world went sideways.

It was like eating volcanic ash soaked in battery acid. Her tongue caught fire instantly—so spicy it didn't even register as flavor at first. Just pain. And then the salt hit, as if someone had upended an ancient ocean onto the plate and stirred it in with love.

Tears sprang to her eyes. Unbidden, unstoppable. They rolled down her cheeks in steady betrayal as she blinked and nodded with what she hoped passed for appreciation.

"So..." she croaked, her voice landing somewhere between helium and hysteria. "So... flavorful. A tribute to Saravethi tradition." She could barely feel her lips forming the words.

Beside her, Charlie was demolishing his portion with alarming gusto—absorbing the meal at an unsettling rate.

Lily leaned toward him, eyes still streaming. "How are you... Doesn't it burn your mouth?" Then, realizing. "I mean... doesn't it taste spicy at all?"

Charlie shimmered and squirmed as he metabolized a fork. "Oh, I don't taste, really," he whispered cheerfully. "But the texture's amazing." He continued absently, absorbing the plate in the process.

She stared at him for a moment through the wall of tears. Attempted another bite—and nearly blacked out.

Datch sat a few chairs away, arms crossed, watching the entire ordeal with a bemused sort of stillness. The corner of his mouth twitched slightly upward.

Lily stared down at her plate, steeling herself for another round.

Despite the pain, the whole thing felt oddly... domestic.

Until the explosion hit without warning.

A deafening crack tore through the house—followed by a shockwave that hurled Lily sideways. The floor lurched beneath her boots, and the ceiling groaned above with a sound far too close to breaking. Debris rained down in bursts—sharp-edged dust, shards of ceramic, fractured metal. The smell of sulfur slammed into her nose, thick and acrid, curling deep into her lungs as she gasped.

Smoke.

Heat.

Screaming metal.

She couldn't hear anything. Only a high-pitched tone, ringing in her ears like someone had struck a tuning fork inside her skull. Her limbs felt slow. Her vision pitched sideways.

Tevya was shouting something—her mouth moving fast—but no sound reached Lily through the roar in her head. Charlie's outline blurred beside her, his form shifting wildly, reassembling in stuttering waves as if he'd lost cohesion.

Then—another blast.

Closer.

It tore through the far end of the house, a shockwave of fire and debris ripping apart what Lily knew had been the nursery.

Tevya was already moving, faster than Lily could process. She lunged toward a recessed panel in the wall and punched in a rapid string of commands. With a grinding whirr, the dining table folded inward and vanished into the floor—revealing a stairwell cut from the stone beneath.

An emergency shelter. Hidden in plain sight.

"Move!" Tevya snapped—her voice somehow slicing through the distortion like a blade.

Lily didn't argue. She grabbed Charlie's pseudopod and followed Tevya and Datch down the steps. The moment they hit the lower level, the ceiling above sealed shut with a reinforced door—closing with a shudder and a *thunk* that echoed through her chest.

Everything shook.

The walls trembled.

Another blast thundered above them. Then another. The explosions came in intervals, like distant thunder filtered through steel.

They crouched in the dim shelter—just the sound of breath, the creak of settling walls, and the relentless ringing in Lily's ears.

Eventually, the shaking stopped.

The silence that followed felt too large. Like the house above had been hollowed out. Like maybe it wasn't there anymore.

Lily blinked as her hearing slowly recalibrated. The world settled into a muffled hush.

"What the hell *was* that?"

Datch stood, face grim. "I don't know. Dissidents, maybe. We've had incidents before—Gherionites illegally augmenting themselves. Refusing to follow neural stability protocols."

They exchanged a look. No more explosions came.

Tevya moved first, climbing the steps with a kind of urgency that made it clear the quiet wasn't comforting—it was a warning.

When they emerged, the house was a scar of what it had been. Smoke curled from the fractured roof. The front wall was half gone—reduced to jagged rock and scorched alloy. The nursery workshop was nothing but flame-rimmed ruin.

Lily's stomach twisted.

Outside, the neighborhood echoed with chaos. The sky streaked with smoke and dust. Panic spilled into the street—voices rising, emergency drones blinking red and white as they hovered overhead.

And there, just beyond the ridge, a speeder—dark, sleek, moving fast—kicked up a storm of dust as it fled into the haze.

"There!" Datch barked.

He was already moving—pulling on a field jacket, strapped with gear like he'd been running drills for this very moment.

"I'll stay," Tevya said, already scanning the street. "I'll try to organize everyone, see to the injured."

Datch paused long enough to meet her eyes. No words passed between them, but the weight of their expression said everything.

"We're coming with you," Lily said firmly.

Charlie glanced between her and the wreckage. "We?"

She shot him a look.

His shape lifted into a grin. "Just kidding. I live for a good chase."

They sprinted toward an enclosure. Datch yanked a heavy tarp off his personal transport, relieved to find it intact. Its design was somewhere between a speeder and a one-pilot flyer—sleek, aerodynamic, and far cooler than Lily had expected.

They climbed in—no ceremony, no plan. Just movement. Just instinct.

With a roar of ignition and a storm of lifted dust, they were gone.

Pursuing ghosts in the smoke.

• • • •

They burst through the wall of smoke like a stone slung from a catapult, the speeder rumbling beneath them with the sound of caged thunder. The transition from the ruined homes at the mountain's base to the open terrain was so abrupt it made Lily's head spin. One moment choking on ash, the next bracing against the hot wind as an endless sweep of scorched earth and jagged stone streaked past.

The velocity was unreal. Faster than Lily was comfortable with—faster than her stomach was prepared for.

The vehicle was narrow and open, skimming just inches above the ground. Each jolt sent her lurching sideways, her grip tightening around the harness. Wind tore at her, and the seat beneath her vibrated with a low, feral growl. Not as loud as she'd expected—quiet enough to hear herself panic, but too loud to talk over without shouting.

Charlie was having the time of his life.

"Yeehoo!" he whooped, his gooey form wobbling like jelly in a wind tunnel.

Lily shot him a look. "Seriously?"

"Sorry!" he glistened brightly. "If I had glands you'd call me an adrenaline junkie!"

Ahead, the horizon shimmered with heat—and that's when she saw it.

The marauder ship.

A crude, open-air barge, low-hovering and wide, with a mounted gun glinting at its center. Five figures stood around it—Gherionites, all of them—but with a lean, aggressive posture that set them apart. Their bodies were augmented with strange devices—some resembling the chorosh, others clearly repurposed for combat. The gear was strapped across arms, chests, even faces, built into their frames in ways Lily couldn't begin to understand.

They wore black leather and layered armor, giving them an over-the-top villain look. But the heavy weaponry they carried was no joke.

"Datch..." Lily began.

"I see them," he said, eyes locked forward. He adjusted their course, speeding up again. Their vehicle was sleeker, faster. And they were closing the distance.

The marauders saw them too.

A flash of energy crackled across the desert as the gun on the barge fired—a warning shot, too far away to be accurate, but enough to make Lily flinch.

Another bolt sizzled past.

The barge banked hard right, toward a jagged ridge on the horizon. Datch followed instantly.

"Hold on," he said flatly—sharply hitting a control.

A ripple of energy shimmered around them as a thin, translucent shield activated, arching over their heads in a dome of pale light.

Lily squinted at the sudden glow, relieved at first to have some protection from the blaster fire—until she saw what they were heading toward.

They crested the ridge—and the world dropped away beneath them.

A volcanic canyon opened up below, a yawning scar carved deep into the earth. Smoke poured from vents in the rock, thick and oily. Sparks snapped and whirled in the air like swarming insects. And below, stretching out like a glowing artery through the planet's skin, was a river of rolling lava.

It snaked through the canyon in great, glowing waves—veins of fire against obsidian rock, the heat so intense Lily could feel it even through the shield, radiating in slow, punishing pulses. The air shimmered with distortion. Plumes of flame shot upward like geysers, lighting the dark sky in bursts of angry gold and blood red.

Lily's mouth went dry. "A lava trench. Why not."

"Best day ever!" Charlie offered.

The shield hummed louder now, compensating for the hostile environment. Without it, Lily knew they'd be choking on smoke, their skin blistering in seconds. Even with it, it felt like riding through Satan's sweat lodge.

Visibility dropped.

They could barely make out the barge ahead—just a dark blur cutting through the ash, framed by streaks of fire and smoke.

Still, they were gaining.

"Get ready," Datch muttered, fingers dancing over the controls. "They're not going to let us catch them without a fight."

Lily's pulse quickened. She stared into the haze, eyes straining to track the flickering shape ahead, one thought looping like static:

This is insane.

The marauder barge loomed larger, its engines flaring hot against the swirling canyon air. Flashes sparked from the gun mount, energy bolts slicing through the smoke in erratic bursts. Datch swerved hard with each one, steering them perilously close to open lava vents where fire geysers shot skyward like enraged serpents.

One plume exploded just a few meters to their right—hot enough to sear Lily's skin through her jacket, the heat like a slap across the face. The speeder tilted sharply, skimming the edge of the molten river, the energy shield whining in protest.

Lily became keenly aware of the balance Datch was striking with every maneuver. One wrong adjustment, and they were cooked.

"Can we shoot back?" she asked, hoping for a better answer than she expected.

"Mounted weapons are illegal on Gherion Prime," he replied in his usual informative tone. He reached into his field jacket and produced a sleek, compact blaster, passing it to her. "There's a field aperture on your right."

She turned. A small seam in the shield flickered—a pocket of phase-altered space. The barrier rippled around it like glass under pressure.

Lily took a breath, braced herself, and shoved the blaster through.

The outside pressure hit like a punch. Her hand shook from the wind and heat, but she managed to aim. She fired once, then twice—bright blue bolts zipping toward the barge. She missed, but that wasn't the point. It kept the marauders off balance.

"Try to keep them off the turret," Datch said, veering around another lava burst as a shot sailed overhead. The speeder rocked hard.

Charlie's voice rose like a kid on a roller coaster. "That was close!"

Lily gritted her teeth. "You're having way too much fun."

They were closing in—and then Lily saw it.

A glow ahead. Rising.

Her eyes widened. "Is that—?"

Datch swore under his breath. "Lava surge. Hang on!"

From beneath them, a tidal wave of molten rock reared up—a shimmering wall of fire erupting from the riverbed, curling like a breaking ocean wave, massive enough to swallow them whole.

Both vehicles veered off course at once.

The barge banked hard right, speeding up the far canyon wall in a jagged, desperate zigzag. Datch pulled left, aiming for the nearer side—but the climb was steep, all jagged rock and loose shale.

The shield flickered—and died.

In an instant, the protection vanished. The next blast of hot ash and cinder hit Lily full in the face, stinging her eyes, scorching her cheek. Her vision blurred. She could smell her hair burning.

The speeder slammed against the canyon wall and began the climb on its side, scraping and jolting as it fought for traction.

They hit a jagged patch and lurched—Lily nearly thrown from her seat. Her harness caught at the last second. Charlie flailed, grabbing at anything solid as the speeder skidded and spun, throwing dust and sparks into the chaos.

Heat. Smoke. Rocks raining from above.

And then, somehow, they were up—cresting the canyon's rim as the lava wave surged below, missing them by seconds. The heat chased after them, licking at Lily's exposed skin with blistering intent.

Lily gasped, coughing through the smoke. Her face stung, her eyes watered, her fingers still locked around the blaster.

She squinted across the canyon—and saw the marauders.

They'd made it too.

They were on the far side now, speeding along the edge of the volcanic ridge. The barge dipped low, kicking up dust in its wake.

"They're getting away," she coughed.

"Hold on!" Datch called.

In a decisive motion, he rammed the controls to full throttle. The speeder lurched forward with a wincing growl, engines burning, pushing hard.

The canyon narrowed ahead—Lily could see it now. A natural bridge spanned the gap, rock fused into a jagged arch that shimmered with residual heat.

"There! The crossing," Datch said.

They tore across the ridgeline, gaining speed with every second. No shield. No backup. Just raw pursuit.

Lily leaned into the wind, raising the blaster again. Her eyes still burned, but she could see well enough to aim.

She fired—forcing one of the marauders to duck, hands flying off the turret.

"That's right," she muttered through gritted teeth—and fired again. "Stay down."

The barge twisted, adjusting course as it neared the bridge.

Datch didn't let up.

They were going to intercept.

Or crash.

Or both.

The canyon wind screamed against her ears. Lily squinted, the blaster rattling in her hands with each bump of the speeder. She braced herself as best she could, trying to track the barge through the ash and heat—but the turbulence made it nearly impossible to get a steady shot.

Another bolt flew wide.

She cursed under her breath and readjusted her grip. The barge loomed ahead, flickering through the smoke—its mounted turret swinging toward them.

Lily pulled the trigger.

The bolt arced, striking one of the marauders square in the chest. The figure spasmed, toppled sideways—and vanished.

For half a second, she thought he might hit the rocky edge and scramble back up.

But he didn't.

He fell straight into the lava.

There was no scream. Just a burst of red-orange light and then—nothing.

Lily's stomach turned, but there was no time to dwell.

Three left.

The barge surged forward, its engines flaring—but Datch matched speed easily now, closing the distance.

Lily raised the blaster again, but her arm trembled violently. A sharp, twisting pain flared just above her shoulder blade—hot and deep, like a pulled tendon. Or worse. Her hand wouldn't stop shaking.

"Shit—" she muttered.

Charlie noticed immediately. His form shifted in a blur, reaching across the speeder with a stretch of protoplasm.

"Don't move," he said. "I got you."

Before Lily could object, his gelatinous form pressed gently around her from behind—light but firm, like a second skin. He anchored himself to the back of her seat, coiling around her torso like a living brace.

Then—cool relief. A wave of soothing chill washed over the injury. Her muscles unclenched. The sharp pain dulled to a distant ache. Charlie stabilized her arm so she could aim again.

Together, they leveled the blaster through the shimmering field aperture.

Lily fired.

The bolt struck the driver of the barge square in the head.

He crumpled backward off the controls, his body slamming against the deck before rolling off the edge—gone in a blink.

The barge veered hard, unpiloted. Its frame spun sideways with a screech of stressed metal, a plume of black smoke billowing from the undercarriage.

"Whoa—!" Charlie pulled back instinctively, anchoring Lily again as the remaining marauders scrambled for the controls.

Too late.

The barge clipped the canyon wall and careened, its deck tilting violently. One of the marauders was thrown clear—vanishing with a scream into the molten river below.

The other barely held on as the barge spun out, flipped once, and slammed into the cliffside near the mouth of a cave—landing in a broken heap of metal and fire.

Datch glanced back at Lily. "Good shooting," he said, a flicker of real admiration in his voice.

Charlie hummed modestly. "Thank you. I do pride myself on being an excellent stabilizing harness."

Lily let out a breath—part laugh, part groan.

Datch pushed the throttle, steering them toward the wreckage. Dust trailed behind like a comet's tail.

"Let's find out where they were headed."

• • • •

The speeder hissed as it dropped low, skimming the cracked volcanic terrain before touching down near a jagged outcrop of stone. The barge had come to a half-buried stop against a natural rock formation—part crash, part emergency landing. Just beyond it, a dark opening loomed. Not just a cave. A tunnel.

Datch cut the engine and leapt out first, already sweeping his scanner across the area. "He's on foot," he muttered. "Headed inside."

Lily squinted into the shifting light—sun now low in the sky, stinging her eyes with gold and dust.

Datch frowned at the readings. "There's an entire system of tunnels. Ancient infrastructure—interwoven, deep. It'll interfere with the scanner. If we go too far, we risk getting lost."

"We can't let him get away," Lily said, wincing as pain lanced through her shoulder. "We have to go after him."

Datch hesitated.

"Maybe one of us should stay—"

"The longer we talk," Charlie cut in, sloshing forward, "the bigger his head start."

That settled it.

They plunged into the tunnel, the heat and ash fading behind them, replaced by damp, stale air. The darkness closed in like a mouth.

The narrow path twisted and forked. Datch tried the scanner again, but it was no use. "Signal's gone," he hissed.

They went quiet, listening.

Somewhere ahead—light, rapid footsteps echoed off the stone walls.

They broke into a sprint, boots and goo slapping against the ground, Lily's breath sharp in her throat as the air grew thinner around them.

Lily's body screamed at her. Her face stung. Her lungs burned. Her vision swam with dust and exhaustion. Every jolt sent a fresh spike of pain through her shoulder, her legs heavy as if slogging through mud.

She was, in a word, *done*.

Frustration surged through her chest like pressure in a boiler. No matter how important this was, it was delaying her real mission. And that thought—more than the pain—pushed her over the edge.

The blaster trembled in her grip as she rounded the next bend, ears ringing from exertion. She heard movement—just ahead, just out of sight.

Enough.

Without hesitation, she raised the weapon and fired.

The bolt seared through the dark, illuminating the tunnel in a blinding blue flash—and there, just for a second, she saw him.

Running.

She fired again.

This time, the bolt struck true.

The marauder cried out and slammed against the tunnel wall.

Datch was already there, dragging the enhanced Gherionite forward by the collar. The figure slumped, partially conscious, mechanical enhancements sparking at his side. Datch leaned in, grip tight.

"Who are you?" he demanded. "What purpose did your attack serve?"

A twisted smile curled across the marauder's face, burned and covered in black ash.

"You have no idea," he rasped. "No matter. The storm reveals all. The hand of the storm guides all."

A chill ran down Lily's spine.

The marauder's hand twitched toward his belt.

"Wait—" Datch moved fast, shielding Lily and Charlie just as a high-pitched whine rose in the air.

"Get down!"

They dove for cover.

The blast ripped through the tunnel, the body disintegrating in a violent burst of heat and light. The shockwave bounced off the walls and left a crater in the rock.

Smoke curled through the space where he'd been.

Silence followed—jagged, and heavy.

They stared at the blackened crater, no one quite ready to speak.

Charlie broke the silence, voice low. "Umm... that was weird."

Datch knelt slowly beside the still-settling dust, his expression grim. "Augmentations are illegal," he muttered. "And suicide is unheard of among Gherionites. Yes, Charlie. Weird indeed."

Lily stared deeper into the tunnel, her heart still racing. "He was headed further in."

Datch followed her gaze. A beat passed.

"Then maybe we keep going."

The tunnel yawned before them like a wound in the stone—rimmed with soot and jagged rock, as if the planet itself had torn open and never quite healed. Datch moved cautiously ahead, sweeping his scanner across the uneven floor. Its display flickered with static.

"This tunnel system must stretch for kilometers," he muttered. "Some of the paths are caved in—possibly intentionally. And the alloy in the rock... continues to scramble the scanner."

They moved deeper, boots scuffing against dust and loose gravel. The air was stale, tinged with something sickening—like rotting plant matter. Shadows pooled around them, thick and oppressive.

"Datch," Lily said, keeping her voice low. "What exactly are the dissidents?"

He hesitated for a beat before answering. "All Gherionites were originally designed to live roughly the same lifespan as humans. Repairs, routine maintenance—that's part of life. Our health, if you will. But certain enhancements—augmentations that extend life or increase abilities—those are forbidden. Culturally and legally."

"And the dissidents break that rule?" she asked.

"They used to just live on the outskirts," he said. "Off-grid settlements. Rumors, mostly. For a long time, they were seen more like eccentrics. Then the attacks started—vandalism, sabotage. But over the last few years, people have been getting hurt. Networks corrupted. Records deleted or altered."

"Deleted? Why?"

"That's the problem," Datch replied. "It's not clear. Officially, some of these events never happened."

They rounded a corner and found a cave-in—a collapsed stretch of tunnel with rubble reaching nearly to the ceiling. The scanner flickered again, then cut out entirely in Datch's hands.

"Unfortunate," he muttered, looking down at the tool with an accepting sigh.

"Wait," Lily said, holding up a hand. "Shhh... do you hear that?"

They froze.

Air—faint, but moving—whispered behind the wall. Not just a breeze. Circulation. There was space back there. A cavity beyond the stone.

Charlie lit up—literally—a ripple of soft bioluminescence pulsing through his translucent form. "I got this."

Before Lily could respond, he oozed into a narrow gap between the rocks, squeezing through with a wet squelch that made her wince.

"Charlie?" she called out.

His voice came back, muffled but chipper. "Yup! There's a room in here! I see... oh. Oh wow."

"What is it, Charlie?" Datch called.

"Give me a sec—there's a control panel. I think I can open it."

A mechanical groan filled the tunnel. Stone cracked. Then, with a grinding slide, a portion of the wall pulled back—revealing a narrow passage beyond.

They stepped through cautiously, eyes adjusting to the low light.

The room was crude but functional. Glowing panels lined one wall, while crates and shelves leaned at cluttered angles, stacked with old-looking devices.

"I recognize some of this," Datch said, his face darkening. "Cloaking modules. Augmentation rigs. Memory encryption units. Unauthorized Gherionite tech—black market grade."

On a nearby table, a stack of data slates sat in uneven piles. One bore a strange symbol: a stylized open hand, ringed by curling spirals.

Charlie leaned in, his voice low. "The Hand That Guides the Storm..." His words echoed off the metal-clad stone walls. "This isn't just dissident gear. This is connected to Leviathan."

Lily stared at the symbol, unease blooming in her chest. "It can't be a coincidence. The ambush. This tech. The tunnel. Someone's planning something—and it's tied to the storm cult."

The comm crackled.

"Salamander to surface team. Come in."

Lily blinked. "Caris?"

"Repairs are complete. She's flight-ready," came Caris's reply. "What's your status?"

Before Lily could answer, Charlie leaned in. "A little heavy on the salt."

Lily shot him a withering look. "Really?"

Datch sighed. "The status is complicated."

And then a movement—shimmering in the shadows. A figure broke from cover. Another Gherionite. Enhanced. Augmented.

Blaster fire lit the tunnel in flashes of blue and white.

Lily ducked, returning fire as Charlie pushed her toward the nearest wall. The intruder didn't pursue—just long enough to drive them back the way they'd come.

They were halfway to the exit when Datch shouted, "Look out!"

A dull clunk. Something rolled across the floor.

A glowing sphere.

"Go!" Lily shouted, just as the blast rocked the tunnel. The chamber behind them exploded in flame and debris—vaporizing the room and everything in it.

When they staggered into the open air, coughing, battered, the attacker was already gone—vanished into the smoke and dust.

Datch's face was stone. "We need to get back. Tevya might still be a target."

Lily nodded, heart thundering. "Then let's move."

They bolted for the speeder, hull still scorched from their earlier ride. Datch fired it up, and they launched across the wasteland—wind howling like a warning at their backs.

. . . .

Smoke still hung in the air like a veil, drifting low over the neighborhood and painting everything in ash and gray. The streets were quieter now, but the silence didn't feel peaceful—it felt suspended, like the world was still waiting to exhale.

Lily jumped down from the speeder as soon as it slowed, boots crunching on scorched stone.

Tevya knelt beside an injured Gherionite at the edge of the rubble. Her hairpiece had come loose in the chaos, one auburn strand falling across her temple as she pressed a stabilizer bandage against a cracked shoulder plate. Even covered in dust, she moved with a kind of grace and control—coaxing calm into a world that had very nearly come apart.

Datch rushed to her, taking her hands in his. "Tev... We can start over," he said, voice tight, his doubt showing through. "We'll start again."

Tevya's eyes didn't soften.

"Not now," she said, her gaze flicking up toward the other villagers. "Something's happening. Look."

Lily turned. The air shimmered faintly with heat and settling smoke, and across the neighborhood, Gherionites moved slowly—each with their chorosh lit up in full spin. Pinwheels of light blinked and spiraled across dozens of heads like silent music.

Tevya shook her head. "The signal's been building for the last few minutes."

And then it happened.

Every chorosh locked solid—an ominous magenta glow.

Every Gherionite froze.

The air went tight. A breath held in a synthetic throat.

Seconds passed. Then the lights pulsed again—this time, a cool, serene cyan.

And as if nothing had happened, the villagers resumed their tasks.

Datch stepped forward, approaching a neighbor who was sweeping debris off a stoop.

"What are you doing? What just happened here?"

The man looked up, puzzled. "Cleaning up after the storm."

"The storm?" Datch's voice sharpened. "You think this was caused by a storm?"

The man blinked, like Datch had asked whether the sky was ochre. "Of course. Leviathan came right through here."

Lily's spine went cold.

Tevya looked broken. "Our worst fear," she said softly. "Someone's using the chorosh to rewrite memory."

She motioned for them to follow her toward the central hub of the house. Inside, the air still reeked of smoke and the sour sting of scorched electronics. Tevya brought up a display—her fingers moving quickly across a holo-terminal. Dozens of video feeds surfaced, each one slightly glitched from the damaged array.

"They've all been altered," she said, scrolling faster. "Or erased completely. There's no record of the attack. In fact..."

She tapped on one playback—grainy, but clear enough.

It showed a storm rolling through the neighborhood. Wind. Rain. Lightning. No barge. No bombs. No intruders.

"This didn't happen," Lily said. "The files are doctored."

Charlie leaned in over her shoulder. "Not just doctored. Completely rewritten. I mean—we were here. We saw it."

"My shoulder wasn't dislocated by a storm," Lily muttered through gritted teeth.

Charlie tried to lighten the mood. "Yeah, and you didn't just shoot a storm in the face."

The joke didn't land.

Lily narrowed her eyes. "If they can control all these people... then it's obvious who the real target was."

Datch shook his head. "I never should've let you come. I brought you into danger."

"No," Lily said slowly, the realization dawning. "You think *we* were the targets?"

She turned to him fully. "Datch... the target was *you*. You and Tevya."

Charlie nodded, his tone unusually serious. "She's right. Your house was the only one that took a direct hit. You and Tevya don't wear the chorosh. You're the only ones who can't be... rewritten."

The silence that followed pressed down like gravity.

Lily turned to Datch. "This is connected to what the *Salamander* is working on. I can feel it."

Datch didn't argue. His eyes flicked toward the smoldering remains of the nursery, then back to Lily. "I believe you. And if there's any chance the Union has records—hidden files, pattern data, anything—I might be able to access it through the *Salamander's* systems. This is bigger than my neighborhood. We need help."

He started walking toward the street, urgency in every step.

But when they turned back, Tevya hadn't followed. She stood alone, framed by smoke and the eerie cyan glow still flickering across the neighborhood.

"They need me," she said softly, eyes on the injured, the shaken, the ones still piecing things together.

Datch stepped toward her. "I'm not leaving you behind."

Lily looked between them, heart pounding. "If you stay, you're both targets. You saw what they did—they tried to erase you. Please, Tevya. Come with us. Help us stop this. Help your people another way."

For a moment, Lily wasn't sure which way Tevya would lean.

Then, slowly, Tevya nodded. "Give me five minutes to prepare."

Lily tapped her comm. "Salamander, this is Lily."

Caris answered instantly. "We're in orbit. Repairs complete. Status?"

Lily exhaled. "We'll be ready in five."

She looked back at the destruction, the red haze of a world that had just tried to forget its own wounds.

"It's time to go."

The Caste We Choose

THE SMELL HUNG IN THE air—somewhere between a zoo and a locker room. Metal and hot sweat, layered with something older. Something sour. The stink of a ship long past maintenance, where steam leaked from cracked valves and no one bothered to fix the vents. The air tasted scorched—bitter, stale, burned-down to nothing.

The holding cell was packed shoulder to shoulder, a sea of blue skin and trembling limbs. Saravethi from the colony transport, pressed so tightly together it was hard to tell where one body ended and another began. Somewhere near the front, someone whimpered. Elsewhere, quiet arguments rippled like static—half-lost in the hum of flickering lights. A few prisoners were trying to find family. Friends. People they'd been separated from during the chaos on the planet. Whispers passed like contraband—names, descriptions, unanswered questions. *Had anyone seen the old man with the broken arm? The child with the weaver tattoos?* Each voice carried a story. Each pair of searching eyes belonged to someone with a missing piece.

No one mentioned the storm.

Strange, how something so massive—so central—could vanish from the conversation entirely. But maybe that was how trauma worked. They'd already been rescued once. Almost. They'd stepped onto salvation—Union transports, clean corridors, the hope of safety—only to have it torn away. That kind of reversal burned everything else out of the mind.

Except—she had training.

She kept her back to the wall, the hood of her jacket drawn low, shadowing her face and the markings on her neck. A small thing. But small things kept you alive. Her posture was casual. Controlled. Just another refugee, one of the rest. Nothing special. But under the cloth, her eyes were always moving.

She was counting the guards. Marking the two that passed every seven minutes along the upper walkway. Noting the one who limped—left leg dragging slightly, favoring his right arm when reaching for his weapon. Noting the cameras. Four of them. Old models. Lazy placement. One blind spot.

Her breathing stayed steady. Deliberate.

She had to blend in—for now.

Xynn's thoughts brushed against the past like fingertips over a scar. She remembered the *Salamander*—its bright lighting, the clean scent of the air that always felt just a little too cold to her. The warmth of Lily's hand as it lingered in hers a moment too long before letting go. Another goodbye. Another transport. Another promise: *I'll see you soon.*

She'd boarded believing she was headed to a starbase. Believing safety was just a light jump away.

Instead, the storm had swallowed them whole.

No warning. No shields raised. Just pure darkness—followed by a blinding flash of white as the tractor beam locked on. Then came the oppressive force of the boarding party.

She tried to make sense of it.

The ship that took them was a beast—more function than design. Plates welded over plates. Rust bleeding through the seams. Pipes like ribs, endlessly venting steam—a constant, suffocating breath from the monster they now lived inside.

The *Warden of Tarshish.*

The ship of the Storm Riders.

Xynn rolled her eyes. Someone was clearly deluded by their own mythos.

She'd been watching. This band of misfits looked more like hired mercenaries than true believers. And not very expensive ones, by the look of it. They postured with bravado but had little discipline—little training. If it weren't for their weapons and armor, they wouldn't be intimidating at all.

Not that she was scared of them.

But their leader—he was a different story.

Captain Ronin, as they called him. She'd only seen him once, briefly—walking the length of the prison deck. He moved like a blade through smoke: silent, unhurried, intentional. His face was shrouded, his coat dragging like a shadow behind him. But it was the way he walked that gave him away.

The others bragged about pay. About spoils and status. They were hollow—loud in the way empty things often are. But the one in the mask moved like someone who remembered what silence used to mean.

He had purpose.

The kind of purpose Xynn knew was dangerous.

Her mind snapped back to the present. The cell. The weight of shoulders pressing in from all sides.

She resumed counting.

Two guards on the upper walkway—seven-minute rotation. One was late this time. Interesting. She wondered if the limp was enough to slow him down.

The camera near the south vent clicked twice when it panned. A calibration error. Another blind spot.

She shifted slightly, letting her weight settle into her heels.

Not yet.

But soon.

· · · ·

It was hard to track time in the cell.

Night came only when the overhead lights dimmed, and even that was inconsistent. By Xynn's count, the lighting cycle followed a crude 36-hour interval—too long to be a proper day, too short to be called two. People slept when they could. When the lights weren't blinding. When steam didn't hiss from the overhead pipes in angry bursts. When the screech of metal doors and the bark of guards didn't yank them back into exhaustion.

She'd claimed a corner early—not out of dominance, but practicality. It was the only spot that stayed dry, mostly. She slept curled in on herself, knees tucked tight, jacket pulled over her face to filter the smell.

People kept their distance. She wasn't sure if they noticed the tattoos, or simply sensed what she was. Saravethi warrior caste—the rarest bloodline left since the Krythar invasions. Once a thriving order. Now, nearly extinct.

Her height gave her away. So did her build, and the way she wore the remnants of her leather armor like they were part of her bones. Some of the prisoners had never seen a warrior caste in person.

Most were from a neighboring village. She recognized their faces, but not their names. They didn't know hers either, and that suited her fine. Familiarity invited questions. Distance let her watch.

She slept in fragments. Ten minutes here, twenty there. Her body had learned to take what it could without complaint.

It was during one of those shallow patches of sleep that the noise woke her—metal screaming, heavy and sharp, too loud to be a normal door. Voices followed, thick and guttural, echoing down the corridor in harsh bursts.

She sat up slowly. Gneki.

You could spot them from a mile away—broad-backed, tusked, faces like cracked leather. The guards shouted, trying to keep the new prisoners moving, but the Gneki didn't like being herded. No one did. But the Gneki especially didn't like being locked up with strangers.

Doubly not small, nervous ones.

Trouble was coming. Xynn knew it with every instinct in her bones.

· · · ·

Time passed. The Gneki, for the most part, kept to themselves. They didn't speak to the Saravethi, and they took up more space than necessary. No one wanted to challenge them, so their territory in the pen spread like rot—slow, silent, and inevitable—pressing the Saravethi tighter together until the very air felt compressed.

When food came, it came as an insult. Slopped in from overhead ports—bucketfuls of something that resembled boiled corn kernels mashed into a gluey porridge. It hit the floor with a slap. More often, it landed on the hostages themselves.

The Gneki always got the most. If you didn't grab your share immediately, they took it. All of it. No second chances.

Xynn wasn't surprised. She took a deep breath to tamp down the rage and kept watching.

As the days wore on, their creeping dominance became a problem. A dangerous one.

It happened just after lights-up, during one of the seemingly random feeding sessions. The guards dropped the food in as usual, shouted some alien profanity—and that was usually it. But today, an alert crackled over the comms. A warning from the bridge. Something about storm interference. A malfunction. The guards cleared the corridor fast.

Xynn's pulse steadied.

This was it. The moment she'd been waiting for.

She had the route mapped. The blind spots timed. The escape was ready.

But the Gneki were about to turn her plan on its head.

One of the largest among them—broad-shouldered, bald, naked except for a pair of torn leather shorts—moved toward the drop zone before the food had even stopped steaming. His skin was inked in thick black bands, spiraling with piercings across his brow and lips. Without warning, he shoved a smaller Saravethi to the floor—an older woman who barely had time to brace herself before hitting the filth with a sickening thud.

The others shrank back. All except one.

A young field worker stepped forward, barely more than a boy. Seventeen, maybe eighteen. Sturdy but slim, still growing into his own height. He reminded Xynn of Alrek.

He moved between the Gneki and the crumpled woman, trembling, terrified.

But not backing down.

"Give that back," the boy said.

For a moment, the Gneki didn't know how to react—caught completely off guard by the boy's audacity. Courage, or foolishness, had stunned him into stillness. But only for a second.

He laughed—a deep, guttural sound that turned into a snort, spraying spittle across the boy's face. Then he stepped forward, looming. His chest rose with slow exaggeration, hot breath rolling from his nostrils like furnace exhaust. His hands curled into fists.

Xynn pushed aside the sharp sting of disappointment—this wasn't how today was supposed to go—and moved without hesitation. Her body reacted on instinct, old training surfacing like muscle memory. Automatic. Precise.

Whatever she did next had to be decisive.

There could be no half-measures. Not with a Gneki. Not in close quarters, surrounded by frightened Saravethi and many tons of volatile muscle. The wrong decision here could spark a bloodbath.

She stepped cleanly between the boy and the brute.

The Gneki's grin twisted into something uglier. He barked a sentence in his native tongue—short, clipped, and guttural. Without a translation matrix, the words were meaningless.

But the tone wasn't.

Really? A girl?

That was Xynn's best translation.

She didn't flinch.

She reached into the inner lining of her jacket and drew out a strip of animal jerky—stiff, leathery, and sharp at the edges. She'd saved it from a previous meal, not out of hunger, but practicality. It was so tough it had hurt her jaw to chew. She'd had a feeling it might be useful.

She held it up, palm flat, as if offering it to him.

The Gneki blinked. Confused.

Then he laughed—a low, rasping chortle—and reached for it.

He let down his guard, just like she knew he would.

They always did.

If you'd been rubbing the sleep from your eyes or checking the time, you might've missed the whole thing. It took seconds.

In one motion, the jerky became a weapon—rammed into his eye with surgical precision. The sound was soft and wet. The laugh caught in his throat as he reeled back, clutching his face. A powerful cry of pain and rage, cut short by Xynn's next move.

The last sound that Gneki would ever make.

She was already in motion. A quick roll forward, feet planting against the wall behind him—then a twist, a pivot, her legs snapping around his neck. Ankles locked. Weight dropped.

The crack was almost polite. A single, clean note of finality.

His body crumpled like a sack of damp linen.

The cell went still.

Xynn stood over him, pulled the jerky from his eye with a wet squelch, and turned slowly to face the others.

She didn't raise her voice. She didn't need to.

Holding the bloodied strip like a blade, she pointed it at the nearest Gneki and spoke in clear Saravethi:

"Isha uretski."

Your life is my property.

Then, louder—her voice slicing through the silence:

"I guard these people with my life."

The other Gneki rose as one—hands clenched, tusks bared. The cell trembled with the weight of fury about to explode.

And then the door slammed open.

The guards stormed in—shouting, weapons raised, one of them dragging a stunner nearly as tall as Xynn herself.

They saw the dead Gneki. Saw the blood.

Saw the way she didn't flinch.

Two things happened next.

First, the guards installed temporary bars inside the cell, separating the Saravethi from the Gneki. The Gneki seemed almost as grateful for the delineation as the Saravethi, unnerved by the efficiency of Xynn's display.

Second, they dragged Xynn through a narrow hallway to the solitary confinement area, which was more like an old maintenance locker with multiple steam jets emptying into it.

The space was barely large enough to sit in. The vents screamed hot steam across her face, loud enough to rattle her teeth. The lights were deliberately blinding. The door sealed behind her with a severe hiss.

Xynn didn't scream. She didn't speak a word.

For nine hours, she endured the blistering tomb—breathing slowly, counting the pressure pulses in the vents to pass the time. When the door finally opened, her legs barely held her weight. But she stepped out unassisted, walking back to the holding pen without a word. Her strength of will even impressing the guards.

Xynn almost felt like she was going home as they locked her back in with the others. The cooler air and familiar stink—sweat, fear, and faintly sour porridge—welcomed her back like old friends. She didn't mind. It meant she was back where she was needed.

People parted for her instinctively, not out of fear but something closer to recognition. The boy who had stood up to the Gneki approached. Still shaken, but steadier now. His eyes searched hers.

"Thank you," he said softly. "For saving my life."

Xynn shook her head. "No. Thank you for standing up to someone who thought it was within his right to lay hands on an old woman."

The young man looked at the floor. "I admit, I was terrified."

"Of course you were," she said. "It would be stupid not to be. But that's how being brave works."

He looked up. "I'm Narek. You're Xynn, right? Everyone talks about you. The warrior."

She nodded. Then added, "You know, I used to think it was beneath me to speak to fieldworkers. That's how I was raised."

She paused, eyes drifting to the far wall for a breath before returning to his.

"But a friend taught me that our differences make us stronger. Everyone has strength inside them. Our purpose isn't predetermined—we choose our own path. And now, I even count a fieldworker among my friends."

Narek smiled. "Make that two."

. . . .

From then on, Xynn and Narek worked together to organize the Saravethi and help them strengthen each other. Xynn was impressed by his knack for reading people, for calming tension before it sparked. Others began to follow his lead.

They set up a system to catch the food as it was dropped in and distribute it evenly. They got to know everyone—who could contribute what, who needed care. They kept an eye on the weak and the injured, tended to wounds, and created space for those who needed rest.

Together, they built a structure for survival.

Order in the chaos.

Late one cycle, as the lights dimmed to signal another artificial night, Xynn sat in her corner surrounded by half-sleeping shapes. A few prisoners were still awake, murmuring softly nearby.

"I think we can survive this," she said. "They haven't tried to kill us, which means they need us alive. Maybe as hostages. Maybe something else. But if we stay quiet and smart, I think we'll be okay. We just need to stay alive long enough for the Union to find us."

Someone snorted in the dark.

"The Union? Please. They're too afraid of ruffling feathers. They care more about politics than a few refugees in deep space."

Xynn turned her head. Her voice stayed low, but every word was clear.

"Fine. Don't trust the Union," she said. "But I have friends who'll be looking. I guarantee it."

. . . .

Later that night, Xynn sat with Narek, both of them resting against the same wall, legs folded beneath them. The noise from the circulation vents left a low ringing in their ears.

Narek looked thoughtful.

"How do you do it?" he asked. "Stay strong all the time. You never falter. Where do you get your strength from?"

Xynn was quiet for a long moment.

"I was raised in the warrior caste," she said finally. "We were taught to devote our lives to defending our people. That it was in our blood. That it was sacred."

He shook his head. "I know that's what you were taught. But I meant... *you*. What gives *you* strength?"

She looked at him. Really looked.

She had to think about it—slowly, deliberately.

"I used to believe we were born into purpose," she said. "The caste system held us together when we had nothing else. When the Krythar shattered our homeworld, it gave us shape. Identity. A reason to keep going as we were scattered among the stars."

She drew in a breath. Let it go.

"I don't know if I'm a good person," she said. "I've asked myself that more times than I can count. And I'm still not sure of the answer. But what I've come to believe is that what matters most is how I use my strength."

Her eyes dropped to the floor.

"I may not be a good person. But if I can be the strength that a *good* person leans on—if I can carry the weight when they can't—then that gives me the purpose I need. That's why I stay strong."

Narek didn't speak right away.

Then, gently, he placed a hand on her shoulder.

"You *are* a good person."

She didn't look at him. Just kept her eyes on the concrete, brow furrowed with a kind of sad, quiet thoughtfulness.

"You are," he said again, a little firmer this time.

"You are a good person."

. . . .

Xynn didn't notice the change at first.

Just turbulence, a soft shudder through the deck plates. The kind that usually came from weapons fire in the distance or a misfired tractor beam. The lights flickered once, then again, shifting from yellow to blue. Somewhere in the corridor outside the cell, voices crackled over the comms in clipped commands.

People stirred.

Guards rushed past the door, but not in the way they did during battle. No shouting. No weapons drawn. Just movement—rapid, controlled, focused.

Not a battle, Xynn thought.

Then the pitch of the ship's engines changed. Subtle, but unmistakable. That low, trembling hum flattened into a heavy throb. The sharp crackle of thruster pulses filled the air.

We're landing.

Her stomach dropped.

This changed everything.

Her escape plan had revolved around stealing an escape pod and desperately trying to get a signal out—barely a plan at all, and the odds of success had been... grim.

But a landing? A planet?

That opened a whole new world of options.

On a planet, there were shadows to disappear into. Terrain to use. Plants. Weather. Wildlife. She could run. She could hide. She could leave a message.

She could survive long enough for Lily to find her.

Her odds just doubled.

The guards began lining them up in rows.

Xynn did her best to hide her smile.

. . . .

The prisoners were herded off the ship in clusters—Saravethi in one, Gneki in another. A few guards tried to split families or shove the injured to the back, but Xynn and Narek moved through like blades through cloth—keeping people together when they could, tracking where everyone ended up.

Xynn had urged them not to resist.

If the time for that came, it wasn't now.

The world they stepped onto was overflowing with life.

Thick, humid air buzzed with sound and color. They were marched into what looked like the ruins of a once-great city, now swallowed whole by rainforest. Massive gray stone structures jutted from the ground like broken teeth. Vines draped everything—thick, turquoise tendrils with fibrous blooms the size of a child's head.

The forest canopy swelled and contracted with motion, as if the jungle itself were breathing—one vast set of lungs drawing in and out for the entire ecosystem.

Winged creatures, almost like birds but a little too scaly, flashed between trees in streaks of bright pink and orange. Their wings fluttered like cloth caught in a windstorm. Some kind of primate with translucent skin and lizard-like frills chittered from a stone outcropping, then vanished into the canopy, swinging on a vine.

The colors were surreal—deep greens, sapphire shadows, neon-orange flowers, and brilliant turquoise moss that coated everything like a soft rash.

Quite a contrast from the dull grays and sour air of the ship Xynn had grown used to.

The atmosphere here clung to her lungs like steam from a kettle—thick, fragrant, alive.

A memory flew into her mind: tea with her grandmother as a child. The same heat curling in her throat, the same weight in the air, like something sacred was about to begin.

•　•　•　•

Some of the ancient buildings had half-collapsed under the weight of trees older than memory—roots erupting through walls, twisting through windows, strangling columns like serpents made of time.

The Storm Riders had converted parts of the ruins into makeshift containment pens—metal bars crudely anchored to stone, patched together with old ship parts and salvaged wiring.

The Gneki were marched to their own pen and locked in.

That, at least, was a relief.

But then Xynn saw something else.

There were other prisoners here.

They wore unfamiliar uniforms, or civilian garb faded by sun and time. Representatives from different worlds. All watched by Storm Rider guards in patchwork armor, moving through the ruins with the ease of people who knew every stone.

"This must be some kind of base of operations," Xynn whispered to Narek.

He nodded, eyes scanning the perimeter.

Xynn tilted her head back, peering through the gaps in the canopy.

Even through the thick branches, she could make out contrails—silver ribbons spiraling through the sky. And there—faint, flickering—she was almost certain it was a satellite array.

A real planet.

With real interstellar infrastructure.

The mission was on.

She would escape. Get a message out.

And then... they just had to survive long enough for Lily to find them.

Xynn knew she would be looking.

But it was a big galaxy.

Even heroes need a little help.

· · · ·

The relief of night settled over the ruins. A real night, on a real planet.

The forest sounds were louder than the prison ship's engines had ever been—deep chirps, hollow warbles, leaves shivering in thick currents of air. But somehow, it was soothing.

One by one, the prisoners drifted to sleep—not out of comfort, but exhaustion, and the strange animal solace of something *natural.*

Xynn didn't sleep.

This time around she didn't have the luxury of time.

On the ship, she'd had days to study rotations, guard responses, seams in the tech.

But now...

Now she needed a new plan. Fast.

She decided in that moment, it didn't have to be perfect.

It just had to *work.*

· · · ·

The sun rose, and with it came labor.

Each morning, the prisoners were herded from their pens—everyone except the very young or the visibly infirm—and marched down a sloping trail to the edge of the excavation site.

The pits.

No one knew what they were digging for. The guards didn't explain, and the prisoners didn't ask. Their job was simple: remove the rocks. Haul them out, load them onto the waiting carts, repeat.

By midday, the sun pressed down like a sentence being carried out—inescapable and deliberate. Sweat pooled in the hollow of backs, soaked collars, slipped into eyes like saltwater. The air turned syrupy with heat, each breath an effort.

But at least the food came. Thin, bland rations—some kind of protein paste wrapped in dried leaves—but it was regular. Predictable. And predictability had its own kind of mercy.

Once a day, they were allowed a brief wash.

The washroom was a natural spring that flowed through the back of a shallow cave—just enough to scrub grime from skin, or to sit for a minute and pretend the water meant something like peace.

It was the only time Xynn found when the guards weren't watching her. Not much. But it was something.

You had to undress outside, which took a while to stop feeling like a humiliation—stripping down in full view of everyone, hanging your clothes on a crooked rack hammered into a tree trunk like a flag of surrender. The guards didn't watch the inside of the cave directly, but they counted the garments. One shirt, one body. You stayed too long, they noticed. You didn't come out, they came in after you.

Xynn kept her visits short. Efficient. Never the first to go in, never the last to come out. Still, that brief moment in the cool shade, surrounded by the echo of dripping water, was the closest thing to solitude she'd had in days.

Xynn had started studying the camp layout in quiet, stolen moments.

Several pens full of prisoners, clustered like cells in a sick body. A common area sat at the top of the hill where rations were distributed.

On one side of the slope: the pits.

On the other: the latrines.

The latrine area offered only a half-hearted attempt at privacy—barely shielded from view by a few jagged rocks. A cistern took the waste, filtering it down through a series of large circular grates.

Xynn had noticed them right away.

The same grates, she realized, lined the inside of the washroom cave. Same structure. Same sound of slowly flowing runoff. Same awful smell.

A dirt path wound up and back down the hill, flanked by rows of rusting standpipes. At nearly any hour, a steady traffic of automated carts rumbled by—low to the ground, with massive treads and humming cores.

They arrived in intervals, collected loads of stone from the pits, and trundled south—away from the camp, deeper into the jungle. Eventually, they vanished into the trees.

Who knows where they go, she thought.

But wherever it is... it's not here.

One morning, while lifting her share of granite onto one of the carts, Xynn inspected the solitary confinement lockers out of the corner of her eye, careful not to draw attention.

The metal boxes sat in the sun like coffins. A guard was opening one now—releasing a Varrothi man, gaunt and trembling, who blinked against the daylight like he'd forgotten what it was.

The stench hit her immediately.

That same sewage stink from around the washroom and latrine. A foul, rotting mixture of steam, waste and rust. And so her plan began to form.

It was going to be awful. But it might actually work.

She needed to prepare.

• • • •

That night, while the others slept, Xynn worked in silence.

She peeled the boning from her leather halter—slow, careful not to wake anyone—and fastened it into a loop. A few lengths of lacing from her bodice served as makeshift binding. It wasn't elegant, but it would hold.

Next came the boots. She scraped off a patch of reflective coating, dull gray-white like crushed pearl. From her knee pads, she cut away strips of leather and padding, weaving them with the reflective shavings into a crude ball.

She tested it in a puddle near the edge of the pen.

It floated. And under the faint overhead lights, it glinted—just enough.

Perfect.

She leaned back against the wall, letting her head tip forward.

She let her eyes drift shut. *Part two's going to suck,* she thought. *Part three might be worse.*

And with that, she curled into the shadows and caught what little sleep she could.

• • • •

Morning came slow and gold, bleeding through the trees in slanted beams that painted the ruins in streaks of warmth. Dew steamed off stone, and the sharp smells of moss, sweat, and damp soil filled the air. Around her, the other prisoners stirred—groggy, aching, muttering their way into another day. A few guards shouted names, kicked metal bars. The usual.

Xynn sat up and rolled her shoulders, joints clicking. Her body remembered worse. Her mind was sharp as ever.

Narek fell into step beside her as they lined up for the pits, giving her a look that was half-smile, half-worry. "You sleep at all?"

She shook her head. "Didn't need to."

"You ever do?" he asked, trying for levity. His voice cracked on the last word.

"Not when there's work to do," she said, and that was the end of it.

Down in the pits, the rhythm took over. Rocks hauled, sorted, lifted. The heat was thick already, clinging to their skin like wet cloth. Xynn's muscles worked on autopilot, her focus elsewhere—on the timing. The carts rumbled through at consistent intervals, their humming cores cutting a low line through the soundscape of grunts and boots and falling stone.

She counted the carts. Counted the seconds between them. Watched how the guards monitored loading, how long their attention drifted. She watched everything.

Their midday meal was taken on the hilltop again—dry rations, but enough to fuel the next round of labor. She barely tasted it. Her mind was already ahead.

When the workday ended, Xynn waited for the guards to call for latrine rotation, then slipped into line. The heat from the sun still radiated off the rocks, and the stench was worse in the late hours. The latrine was as disgusting as ever, but she focused on the task.

She crouched low near the cistern, pulled the small padded sphere from beneath her waistband, and let it drop gently into the grate. It floated, spinning slightly—just as she'd designed it. Torchlight caught the reflective wrapping, scattering glints across the stone as it drifted downstream.

Later, when the guards called for the washroom, Xynn made sure to be last. She waited until the group ahead had gone in, then followed—quiet, focused. She stripped quickly, hung her clothes on the rack like everyone else, and entered the cave in just her underwear.

Inside, she moved straight to the corner she'd scouted: out of sight from the entrance, partially shielded by moss-covered stone. The wall grate was just as she'd remembered.

Her fingers slipped into her bra and pulled free her makeshift tool. She worked quickly, scraping gently around the bolts, testing each with careful pressure, keeping her movements silent. To her relief, the rusted fastenings gave way without much fight. One. Then another. The grate came loose with a soft clunk.

From her waistband, she retrieved plugs she'd fashioned from leather and mud, pressing them into the bolt holes. Crude, but convincing. Once the grate was slotted back into place, it looked intact—enough to pass a glance.

She rinsed herself fast, scrubbing sweat from her skin and letting the water wash rust from her hands. Her heart was pounding. Not with fear—with anticipation.

When she stepped out, the guard near the racks gave her an impatient look.

Xynn offered a dry smile. "Sorry. Lady stuff."

The guard rolled his eyes and waved her off.

She dressed without hurry, her motions calm and practiced. Then walked back to the bunks—quiet, steady. And in her chest, something electric had begun to spark.

Readiness.

• • • •

The next day passed like the last. A routine of sun, and sweat. Except today, Xynn didn't speak to anyone. She was preoccupied.

Narek noticed. He glanced at her more than once as they worked, the lines in his forehead deepening. She didn't speak. Didn't explain. She just moved rock like the rest of them, calculating cart schedules in her head, running mental rehearsals of what came next.

By the time the mid-cycle meal was called, the air was thick with heat and gnats, everyone's patience running low.

They lined up near the top of the hill, where the meal carts had been hauled in and metal trays slammed down with dull clangs. Narek stepped close as she reached for her rations.

"You're scaring me," he murmured. "You haven't said a word all day."

She leaned in, voice low but steady. "No matter what happens, I'll be fine. Please don't intervene."

"What?" he blinked. "Wait, what are you going to—?"

But she was already walking away.

Down the line, one of the Gneki stood with his back half-turned—bigger than the last one she'd fought, shoulders knotted with tension.

Xynn drew in a breath and spat a single phrase in guttural Gneki.

"Dorok, ooshmoany."

A phrase she'd picked up over the last few days. She was fairly sure it was about someone's odor.

His posture shifted. He turned slowly. Disbelieving.

The meal area went quiet.

One of the guards took a step forward, but another chuckled and raised a hand, holding him back.

The Gneki locked eyes with her.

She said it again, slow and deliberate. "Do-rok. Oosh-moa-ny."

He came at her like a charging beast—like a storm had broken loose inside him.

She cut right, low, aiming for his knee—but he was faster, more disciplined than the one she'd killed on the ship.

He caught her by the hair mid-motion, yanking her upward with brutal strength. She barely had time to gasp before he hurled her across the clearing.

Her body slammed into the edge of a table, flipping it with a crash, trays and rations clattering to the ground.

Pain bloomed, sharp and electric through her back.

This was not how she'd planned it.

She scrambled to her feet just as he reached her again. Another fist in her hair. This time, he swung her into the side of one of the automated carts. The world tilted—blurred—then righted itself.

Stay conscious, she told herself, biting down the pain.

She staggered upright. Wobbled for effect. Let her knees buckle, just slightly.

He came in close—just like she needed.

With a grunt and a twist, she flipped the cart bed open and slid beneath it in one fluid motion. The load tumbled out behind her, crashing down like a rockslide, pinning his legs beneath the spill.

He roared in pain, toppling backward. Off balance. Scrambling to free himself.

Xynn didn't hesitate. She vaulted over the cart, and hefted a heavy stone. One strike to the side of his head sent his eyes rolling. Another to the back of his skull dropped him flat.

His body was still. She raised the stone to finish him off—when the guards finally moved in. It took three of them to restrain her as she made sure to put on a good show. The hot headed warrior everyone expects to fly off the handle.

And then he appeared.

Captain Ronin.

He didn't storm into view or announce himself with barked orders. He simply *was*—standing just beyond the edge of the chaos, as if he'd been there all along.

His cloak caught the breeze like smoke. The long folds of dark fabric whispered around his boots, almost alive. He didn't move. Didn't speak.

He watched her.

Through the slits of his mask, his eyes gleamed—not with light, but with the absence of it. Black and depthless. The kind of black that made you feel like you were falling. They gave nothing. Reflected nothing. The eyes of something that didn't need to blink.

Something that had waited centuries just to look at you.

"Impressive," he said, his voice neutral. Unnaturally calm. "You don't see many Saravethi warriors these days."

His gaze locked on hers—sharp and unrelenting, burning into her like a brand.

"I thought the Krythar killed all of you."

Xynn fought the urge to react. He turned to the guards. "Take her to the box."

She exhaled. There it was.

She caught a glimpse of Narek, starting forward—face pale, mouth open. She met his gaze. A small shake of her head. *No.* He stepped back, a pained look settling over his features as the guards restrained her and began dragging her down the slope toward the metal boxes.

Despite the bruises blooming across her ribs, the ache in her scalp, the taste of blood in her mouth—she couldn't help but think:

So far, so good.

· · · ·

This box was a different kind of torture than the one on the ship. Smaller, more confining. The heat pressed in from all sides—invading, seeping into her skin, blooming inside her like fever. The air was thick with the scent of waste and hot metal, curling into her lungs like smoke. Every breath tasted foul, every inhale a struggle. The floor beneath her was slick with old filth. She tried not to think about what she was standing in.

Xynn pressed her back against the blistering wall and forced herself to stay calm. She did her best to hold in the panic.

When the latch groaned shut and she heard boot steps receding into the camp, only then did she dare move—slowly, carefully, conserving strength.

She slipped her fingers into her bra and removed the hidden tool she'd smuggled in: the makeshift wrench, crafted from the boning of her halter and reinforced with leather laces. She wrapped her belt around the handle to cushion her injured hand, and felt for the bolts on the grate.

It was low—set awkwardly near her knees—and the cramped space made every angle feel impossible. She twisted sideways, contorting to reach it. Unlike the bolts in the washroom, these weren't rusted. They were tight and heat-welded, swollen into place from direct sunlight and steam.

Her fingers screamed with each motion. The wrench dug into her palm. Blisters split with every turn, the bolt giving only a fraction at a time.

The pain was intense, but she focused on counting the rotations. Focused on the rhythm of movement. But the heat of the metal, the slip of sweat on her skin, was difficult to ignore. Her arms trembled. Her head swam.

Still—she kept going.

She was fortunate not to be under the time constraints she'd faced in the washroom. Hours passed. But eventually—one bolt fell, then another.

By the time she got the grate loose, her body was trembling from effort and dehydration. She leaned forward, gently pushed it aside, and peered into the dark.

The tunnel stretched out before her like a scar—slick walls, no visible floor, just a thick river of foul-smelling runoff winding through the shadows. The sewage moved sluggishly, like an enormous snake slithering through an underground vein.

She scanned the edges, where the current slowed almost to stillness.

There it was.

Her heart skipped. Floating in the stream, slowly spinning and bumping against the muck—her ball.

The reflective material caught the faintest glint of light and shimmered like a promise.

It had made the journey. Through the muck. Through the tunnels. Around every unseen bend.

Part two was complete.

She exhaled, long and quiet.

With trembling hands, she reset the grate, fastening it with the small leather plugs she'd shaped and packed with mud—pressing them in one by one to hide what she'd done. She was so close.

She slumped back against the wall. Her body screamed. Her spine throbbed where the Gneki had slammed her. One of her ribs might be cracked. Her head pulsed with fever and grit.

She fought to stay conscious.

She felt blood trickling down her forehead.

Stay awake, she ordered herself. *You die in here, it's all for nothing.*

But her vision blurred. Her fingers twitched. Black static crept in at the edges of her sight like ink in water.

She lasted as long as she could.

Then—darkness.

The heat enveloped her. A thick, floating kind of nothing.

Like being in the womb.

. . . .

She woke up eating dirt.

The taste of gravel in her teeth. Her cheek pressed to the ground. The sky was too bright to make sense of. Somewhere behind her, the sound of a gate closing. Guards muttering. Boots walking away.

Then—"Xynn!"

Narek's hands found her shoulders, helping to prop her up. He pressed a vessel to her lips. She gagged on the first swallow as the muck cleared from her throat and lungs. The second went down more easily.

"What were you thinking?" he asked, his voice cracking between anger and worry. "Why would you do something so stupid?"

Xynn didn't answer. Not yet. She just drank—slow and shaky—letting the water cool her throat and bring her back. Narek raised an eyebrow as he saw a smile creep over her face. Then a little laugh.

She was alive.

Everything was in place.

Now all that was left... was escape.

. . . .

That night, Narek watched over her.

He brought her a small bowl of broth—something one of the prisoners had managed to make from boiled leaves—and helped clean her wounds with careful hands. She flinched only once.

"Tomorrow's the day, Narek," she said quietly. "And I need you to do something for me."

"Take me with you," he said, almost before she finished. "I can help."

Xynn shook her head. "Look, I probably won't make it. I'm not getting out for me—I'm getting out because it's the best chance we have to get a message out. It's the only chance any of you have of being rescued. And I need your help to even get that far."

Narek looked down, disappointed—but nodded.

"What do I need to do?"

"Tomorrow evening," she said, "after you've finished washing—take my clothes from the rack. Make sure no one sees you."

Narek nodded again, clearly confused. And a little embarrassed. Then he added, more quietly, "I wish I could go with you."

"I need you to stay," she said, meeting his eyes. "You have to be the strength they need now. It's your turn."

He hesitated. "I'm not like you, Xynn. I can't fight."

"That doesn't matter," she said. "There are a lot of ways to be strong. You've organized these people. Given them something to hold on to. You may not be able to save everyone—but you can help keep them alive until help comes. That matters."

Narek looked down at his feet. Then nodded. "Will I see you again?"

Xynn held his gaze. "Yes," she said.

She lied.

She didn't know. Couldn't know. But it was what he needed to hear.

In her heart, she knew she wasn't driven only by duty or strategy. Her reason was out there—somewhere among the stars.

She had no idea how close she was.

• • • •

The next day passed like the others, following a rhythm that was just beginning to feel familiar in the worst possible way. More sweat. More stone. More pain.

Xynn moved on instinct, every step weighted by bruises and muscle aches. But the adrenaline of anticipation pushed her forward. Every rock she hauled brought her closer to the moment.

When mealtime came, the Gneki kept their distance. The one she'd fought—still towering, but now with a bruised jaw and slightly broken pride—glanced her way and gave a nod. Just a small tilt of the head. A show of respect. An unexpected side effect of her necessary misadventure.

The afternoon blurred past. Her nerves buzzed like wire. Her body moved on autopilot, her mind already drifting ahead to the wash cycle.

When the time finally came, she slipped into rotation—careful to go in the middle of the group. Blending in. Just another weary body taking her turn.

She peeled off her clothes, the guards ogling shamelessly, as always. She ignored them, banking on their routine behavior. Nothing out of the ordinary here.

Inside the cave, the air was thick and wet. The scent of algae and minerals layered beneath that telltale sewage stink. Faint, but present. She followed it through mossy stone, listening to the splash of feet, the trickle of springwater, the soft murmurs of the others.

A broad-shouldered Saravethi woman blocked the way near the grate—chatting, laughing, taking her time. Xynn bit her tongue. Her pulse pounded in her ears. Every second stretched like rope ready to snap.

She moved uncomfortably close, hoping the woman would take the hint. Instead, the woman turned toward her, arching her bare chest forward with casual confidence. Xynn blinked—caught somewhere between shock and secondhand embarrassment.

The woman held out a small metal container, revealing small glistening lozenges. "Tressia?" she offered, voice low and husky.

Xynn blinked. "Umm... no thanks," she said, keeping her tone polite. Tressia was just sweet nectar—but in Saravethi culture, it was used to initiate sex.

The woman shrugged, looking only mildly disappointed. "Your loss, hon," she muttered, then splashed off back towards the exit.

Finally.

Xynn ducked low into the mossy corner, heart racing, breath shallow. The smell confirmed she was in the right spot. She slid through the water to the grate and yanked it free with a sharp tug.

Without hesitation, she slipped into the shadows beyond, securing the grate back in place behind her, pressing it into the mud like a seal.

"Here goes nothing," she whispered.

Outside, Narek waited for his moment. He joined the next group in line for the wash, stepping in with quiet precision. He undressed and hung his clothes on top of Xynn's, making sure to cover them completely.

Inside, he made his way to the spot she had told him about, scanning the area. The grate looked undisturbed. Relief passed through him like breath.

He rinsed fast. No scrubbing. No lingering. Just enough to justify the time.

Then, as casually as he could, he grabbed the bundle—his clothes and hers—tossing both over his shoulder. No one seemed to notice. The guards were distracted, laughing crudely at a prisoner drying off near the entrance.

Narek slipped past them without a word, heart pounding. He didn't look back.

Godspeed, Xynn. I hope you know what you're doing.

• • • •

The tunnel pressed in around her like a throat slowly closing.

Xynn crawled forward on elbows and knees, surrounded by a world that was wet, dark, and suffocating. Sludge clung to her limbs, thick as tar. The air was hot and sour, crawling with methane and rot, curling into her lungs with every shallow gasp. Her nose, still swollen from the fight, was nearly useless—forcing her to breathe through clenched teeth. She could taste the tunnel. The filth. The decay. She bit down harder to keep anything from slipping past her lips.

She was not someone who rattled easily. But this...

This was something else.

Her thoughts swam as the walls closed in tighter, the ceiling lowering until her back scraped the top. Mud sucked at her knees. Sewage sloshed up around her hips, warm and sickening. Somewhere deeper in the muck, something moved—a slither, a bubble, a hiss. She told herself it was the tunnel settling. The sound of waste finding a new level.

The dark was total. No moonlight. No torchlight. Not even the faint shimmer of her bioluminescent tattoos—dimmed now from dehydration. Just black. Endless black. Every inch forward was made on faith, and every breath cost more than the last.

Her body was starting to betray her, spasming with silent gags. Her head throbbed. Her vision swam—even though there was nothing to see.

She kept going.

Elbow, knee. Elbow, knee. Slipping. Pushing. Crawling.

She couldn't remember how long she'd been in the tunnel. Time lost meaning when every sense was overwhelmed. The stench was unbearable. The heat pressed into her like a fever. She'd never been afraid of tight spaces, but this wasn't just tight. It was smothering. As if the tunnel itself was alive, waiting to swallow her whole.

She whispered a wordless curse and pushed on.

Then, just as the burn in her chest began to drown her thoughts—light.

The faintest fracture of illumination. She thought at first it was her mind playing tricks, but it grew as she crept forward. Her eyes adjusting slowly, pupils wide, stinging.

A grate appeared ahead. Rusted, half-submerged, with bars sunk deep into the muck like the spine of some buried creature. She reached for it, feeling down along its edge. It extended into the water, maybe three feet deep.

Without giving herself time to hesitate, she took a long breath through gritted teeth, filled her lungs until her ribs protested, and dove.

The water was thicker than she expected. Warm and putrid. It closed over her like a coffin lid, wrapping her in darkness and filth. Her ears filled with pressure. Her heart pounded like a drum against her sternum.

She forced her body downward, beneath the grate, crawling through the narrow space until she broke the surface on the other side.

There was a gap—just a small one—where the water met the rock ceiling. Barely enough for her lips to fit. But air was air. She pressed her mouth into the crevice and drew in whatever oxygen she could.

Foul. Damp. Molded. But enough to keep her alive.

She followed the current as best she could, crawling and ducking, fully submerging herself more than once to navigate narrowing turns. The tunnel began to shift—widening slightly, echoing differently. This was it. Things started to look familiar, matching what she'd seen from the box.

All memory of being clean had long since vanished. Her skin was coated in layers of slime and grit. Her breath tasted like rust and bile.

Then—there it was. A shimmer of light.

Her ball.

It spun lazily in the current, reflecting just enough to catch her eye. That small, deliberate creation had survived. It had done its job. Now she could do hers.

She reoriented fast, reversing the angle from her memory, crawling toward it. Her chest burned. Her arms shook.

Finally—the boxes.

She reached the last grate and peered through first, just in case. Empty.

With a groan and a final push, she kicked the grate loose. Her body screamed in protest as she hauled herself upward, wedging through the narrow opening until her shoulders passed the lip. She slithered in, limbs trembling, lungs burning.

The lid was loose. Unblocked. She cracked it open and listened.

No voices. No boots. Just the rustle of wind in the leaves.

After a quick peek, she slipped out into the world.

A breath of open air hit her like a blessing. Even through the stench coating her skin, she could smell trees, soil, something living.

She darted for the nearest automated cart and rolled beneath the tarp, her body slipping in among jagged rocks. Her heart pounded so hard she was certain it was audible—like a drumbeat in the stillness. Each thud echoed through her skull, through her chest, through the suffocating heat beneath the tarp.

The cart rumbled forward, slow and mechanical, following its programmed route. The hum of its engine—hopefully enough to drown out her desperate breathing.

This was it. The homestretch.

She couldn't help but think: it would really suck if someone stopped the cart now. Lifted the tarp. Decided to double-check the load. Not after all that.

She froze as voices passed near. Bootsteps—close. Too close.

They were walking alongside the cart—so near she could make out the creak of leather, the jangle of weapons. A laugh. A cough. The sound of spitting.

Xynn squeezed her eyes shut. Focused on her breath. Shallow. Measured. She timed each inhale to the rhythm of the wheels bumping over uneven stone. Let the motion cradle her. Let it hide her.

Just a little farther. Just a little more.

And then—gradually—quiet took over.

Not silence, exactly, but the shift was unmistakable. The rhythm of the camp gave way to the sounds of the rainforest. Birds calling in melodic bursts.

The low rustle of creatures in the underbrush. Wind moving through leaves like breath.

She waited—heart still thudding—but there were no voices, no boots, no alarms. Just the cart's gentle hum, moving steadily away.

Now or never.

Xynn slipped from beneath the tarp, her body slick with sweat and filth, muscles aching as she landed softly in the dirt. The cart trundled onward, oblivious, disappearing down the path toward whatever destination it was programmed to reach.

She turned, scanning the treeline. The cart had gone south, away from the camp. So she turned east—where the forest thickened, wild and unclaimed.

She walked with her hands outstretched, fingers brushing the leaves. It was as if her body were gaining strength from the life around her. The forest swallowed her with open arms, wrapping her in shadow and sound. The canopy parted, just slightly, and through the leaves she saw them—stars. Bright, brilliant, endless.

She stopped. Took a breath. A real, deep breath. Cool, clean air filled her lungs.

Her body still reeked of sewage. Her only clothing, besides the underwear clinging to her skin, was the mud caked across her body. Her hair was matted. Her skin raw. But she had made it. She was free.

A single tear traced a clean path down her cheek.

Then she looked down and chuckled despite herself. *Tomorrow*, she thought, *after I find water, I either need to find some clothes... or take this chance to work on my tan.*

And with that, Xynn disappeared into the forest.

Chapter 4: Compassion
Nailed to Stone

THE WIND CLAWED AT the high ridge, dry and sharp as broken glass. Captain Ronin stood at the edge of the rock formation, one boot planted firmly on a flat outcrop, a sleek pair of scanner-goggles perched over his eyes. Below, the rainforest canopy stretched for miles—thick, restless, layered with the haze of early heat.

Behind him, two guards approached with brisk, heavy steps. Between them, they escorted a third, his uniform smudged with dirt, his expression tense—already bracing for what was coming.

"You were in charge of the perimeter patrols yesterday," Ronin said without turning. His voice carried easily over the wind—measured, composed, and unsettlingly soft. "You lost the warrior girl. The one who beat the Gneki."

The guard cleared his throat. "Sir, I went through all the footage. She was there—then she wasn't. I've reviewed everything—she just vanished."

Ronin turned slowly, slipping the scanner-goggles into a pouch on his coat. The mask he wore was obsidian-black, made of the kind of fabric that swallowed light and felt like you could lose yourself just looking at it. But his eyes showed through—sharp and piercing. Too focused. Steady, like the hand of a marksman.

He walked a slow circle around the guard, examining him head to toe.

"You've served me well for a long time, Tovish," Ronin began. "I believe you enjoy the privilege of a family here on Bimara. Isn't that right?"

He hunched forward to look Tovish in the eye.

"A wife. And a daughter."

Tovish barely looked up. He was trembling now.

Ronin gestured lazily toward one of the other guards. "You know, Tomlan here has been wanting to grow his family." He tilted his head, bringing his masked face uncomfortably close. "I'm sure he'd be happy if I gave him your wife. And your daughter. How old is she now—eleven? Twelve? Old enough to be his third wife, I think."

Tovish began to mutter a protest—

Without warning, Ronin struck. A clean, brutal backhand. The guard stumbled sideways, catching himself against the rock.

"Fail me again," Ronin said quietly, "and you won't be around to know their fate."

As the guards hauled Tovish away, Ronin turned to another figure nearby—taller by a full head than the rest, built like a siege engine in humanoid form.

The Urrathi sat on a boulder, absently spinning two stones between his thick fingers, their rhythm a slow, deliberate click.

"Grage," Ronin said. "Find her."

Grage looked up. His face was fixed into a permanent scowl, blank but radiating threat. His massive shoulders and thick, scaled limbs were marked with old scars and curling tattoos. The stones in his hand stopped their motion before he closed his fist on them, crushing them to dust.

Without a word, he rose and stepped onto a heavy, black hoverbike. The engine snarled to life, and a moment later, he vanished into the trees, swallowed by the mist.

• • • •

"Unrelated incidents?" Lily paced near the captain's chair, her voice tight with restrained disbelief. She knew this line of argument wouldn't get her anywhere—but she couldn't hold it in any longer.

"I'm not saying they acted alone," she said, barely keeping her tone in check. "But there's no way what happened on Gherion Prime, the attack on Adius II, and the Storm Riders are all unrelated. Come on, Captain—at least acknowledge the possibility."

Captain Calan avoided her eyes. His jaw was tight, fingers drumming an uneven rhythm against the side of his command chair.

"You're making assumptions based on emotional proximity," he said flatly. "You've had a harrowing few days, Lieutenant. You need rest. I think it's affecting your judgment."

"My judgment is fine," Lily snapped, crossing the deck in a few sharp steps. "Look, it's right in front of our faces. You think I'm just making this up because I'm tired?" She tilted her head. "You want to just wait for their demands?" Then, softer, but edged: "What are you afraid of?"

She regretted it the second it left her lips.

Caris looked up from the helm. Malik stiffened near the ops console. Everyone on the bridge suddenly became very interested in not making eye contact.

Calan stood. Slowly. Deliberately.

"You're acting like you're the only person here who cares about what's happening," he said, voice low. "But you're not. Look, I know you're worried—"

Lily's breath caught like a punch. She cut him off. "Maybe I'm just realistic. And not..." She hesitated. Then locked eyes with him. "Hiding."

The silence that followed stretched too long. Tense. Uncomfortable. Electric.

Calan leaned closer. "We're not having this conversation. This isn't the time to—"

"Never the time," Lily shot back. "People are probably being tortured or killed out there—something big is moving behind the scenes—"

Calan turned suddenly, the motion sharp, almost combat-ready.

"I am ordering you to drop it," he said, venom lacing the words.

"Captain—" Caris started, gently.

But the look Calan gave her stopped her cold.

Then, from the rear of the bridge—a small cough. Someone clearing their throat, first quietly, then louder, more exaggerated.

Everyone turned.

Basco had stood halfway up from his station, one hand raised like he was back at the Academy. "Uh... sir?"

Calan didn't move.

Basco swallowed. "Incoming transmission. Scrambled channel." He blinked at the data feed.

Calan exhaled through his nose and sank slowly back into his chair. "Put it through."

Basco tapped a few commands. The bridge lights dimmed slightly as the viewscreen flickered to life—first static, then image.

A figure emerged in a darkened space, backlit by flickering orange light. He sat draped across a command chair that looked more like a dark wizard's throne—jagged, towering, almost ceremonial. His coat hung like a shroud, heavy and still. His face was hidden behind that obsidian-black mask—lightless, smooth, a void with eyes.

Captain Ronin.

Even without seeing his expression, the tension was immediate—coiled, measured, impossible to look away from.

"This is Captain Ronin of the *Warden of Tarshish*," he said, voice low and even. "You survived our encounter. Good. Consider this your invitation to finish what we started."

Lily's chest tightened.

"I speak for the Storm Riders," he continued. "We are not zealots. We are privateers. And occasionally... contracted help. At present, we are in pursuit of an artifact. It is called *Nymara's Tear*. It lies on the planet Bimara, near the former Krythar border. You will obtain it for us."

He leaned in slightly—just enough for the camera feed to catch the cold glint of his eyes behind the mask. Lily and the others exchanged glances. "Many dangers guard the artifact." Ronin explained. "Once it is in your possession, we will parlay face to face."

There was a pause.

Calan raised a finger. "If you're already on the planet, why do you need us?"

The mask didn't move. But the voice that followed was suddenly sharp. Furious.

"I did not give you permission to ask a question!" Ronin snapped, his tone cracking like a whip. His body shifted forward, and even with the mask, the rage was palpable—as if he could reach through the screen.

"I would not risk my own crew when I can easily order *you* to your deaths. Do not attempt deception. We are watching."

And the channel went dead.

No one moved. No one dared break the silence.

Basco cleared his throat—again. "There's a record for *Nymara's Tear* in the Union database, sir. There are... a lot of Krythar legends that mention it. Some dating back to the early Seed Period. Nothing about it being offworld, though."

Still, no one spoke.

Finally, Lily broke the silence. Quiet. Steady.

"This smells like a trap."

Calan nodded. "Reeks of it."

They exchanged a small smile.

Then he turned to Caris. "Plot a course to Bimara. Best possible speed."

• • • •

Lily strapped on her gear in silence, the magnetic fasteners clicking into place one by one—each sound sharp and deliberate, like punctuation in a conversation no one wanted to start. Across the table, Calan adjusted the settings on a blaster rifle, his hands moving with quiet efficiency. Everything about him was composed, mechanical, as if he could calibrate his way out of tension.

The silence between them wasn't hostile, exactly. Just full.

"I'm surprised you want me along," Lily said eventually, her voice measured. She didn't look up from the straps she was adjusting.

Calan paused, just briefly, then returned to his rifle.

"You've worked with Shyra'thel before," he said. "You've earned her respect. That makes you valuable on this mission."

He didn't offer more, but he didn't need to. His tone wasn't cold—it was matter-of-fact. Professional. But under it, there was something quieter. An acknowledgement. A truce, maybe.

Lily didn't respond right away, but a little of the tension left her shoulders. She finished tightening her belt, not quite smiling, but steadier than before.

The doors hissed open behind them.

Alrek strolled in with his usual wide smile, a small pack slung casually over one shoulder. "Lily!" he beamed.

They shared a quick hug, warm and familiar.

"I've been following Shyra'thel's progress," he said as he pulled back, his voice animated. "Her work has been incredible. What she's doing to unify the border planets... Did you know she negotiated the psi-iona treaty with the Krythar? It's groundbreaking."

"I didn't," Lily said, the corners of her mouth tugging upward despite herself. "But that sounds like her."

"I hope she's okay," Alrek added, already tugging at the straps on his harness. "The pressure she must be under—and the threats on her life..."

Before anyone could respond, another figure edged into the room behind him.

Basco.

Wide-eyed and clutching his tablet like it might shield him from actual danger, the young lieutenant stepped cautiously inside, glancing around the armory like someone had just dared him to open a crate labeled *Live Specimens*. "Um... I'm not late, am I?"

"You're on time," Calan said, gesturing him over. "Standard sidearm and scanner. In addition, you'll each be carrying a compact field medkit. The rainforest terrain on Bimara can be unpredictable—humidity, microparasites, venomous wildlife. If you're bitten by anything that slithers, assume it's dangerous."

Basco froze mid-reach. "Slithers?"

"Didn't you read the—" Calan began.

But Lily cut in, casually helpful. "Seventeen varieties of venomous snake. Twenty-three species of poisonous insects. Over five thousand types of deadly plant life..."

Calan lifted a hand to silence her. Basco's sable skin had gone noticeably pale.

Alrek stepped in, ever cheerful, and handed him the medkit. "So it's a good idea to keep this close."

Basco gripped the kit with both hands, as if sheer willpower might bond it to his body. Then, reluctantly, he clipped it to his vest—keeping his eyes fixed on it.

The doors whooshed open for the third time—this time accompanied by a dramatic clank and the unmistakable sound of something heavy being dropped.

"I brought the device!" Ka-Lorrin declared before anyone could speak.

Taran lumbered in behind him, ducking under a hanging light fixture. He cradled a blinking, wildly unstable-looking contraption in both massive paws. It hummed faintly, and several tubes were already vibrating with alarming enthusiasm.

Calan allowed himself a small smile. "Ah. Good. The Raath-Ka."

Lily blinked, surprised to see the awkward duo in the armory. "Captain, are we bringing an engineering team?"

"I asked Ka-Lorrin for a little help with our scanning problem," Calan said without quite meeting her eye.

Alrek perked up like a student who'd done the reading. "The groundwater contains minerals that block standard equipment."

Taran walked forward and deposited the contraption directly into Basco's arms.

The young lieutenant's worry curdled instantly into panic.

"Do *not* drop it," Ka-Lorrin said sternly. "That is a prototype resonance-field harmonizer, calibrated specifically for the trace minerals in Bimaran groundwater. Regular scanners will be completely ineffective without it."

"This was a huge pain to build," Taran added proudly. "It was, it was. Listen to Kal. Don't drop it."

Ka-Lorrin continued, with the weary precision of someone who had given this explanation three times already. "This unit—assuming you don't drop it—will generate a stabilized scan field in a hundred-meter radius. But it requires three uninterrupted minutes to calibrate after activation. Any impact will compromise the core alignment."

Basco stared at the blinking lights. "Three minutes. Hundred meters. No dropping."

"Yes," Ka-Lorrin said dryly, already turning toward the exit. "Exactly."

He paused just long enough to look at Alrek. "Be good."

Taran leaned down and gave Alrek a gentle pat on the head with one massive paw.

"Oh Kal, don't treat him like a little kid," Taran said cheerfully.

Ka-Lorrin was already out the door.

Taran lingered a moment longer, looking at Alrek with affection. "You'll be fine, little one. I mean... big one. I mean... go get 'em."

Alrek opened his mouth to protest but ended up smiling instead.

Lily shook her head, amused. She slotted one more power cell into her vest.

"Call us before you blow anything up," Taran said over his shoulder as he padded after his friend.

Basco turned a baffled glance toward Lily.

She gave a helpless shrug. "That's one of the more normal conversations with the Raath-Ka."

. . . .

The shuttle hummed softly as it cut through Bimara's upper atmosphere, the view outside a smear of dense green and clouded blue.

Inside, no one spoke.

Lily sat near the back, harnessed in, hands resting loosely on her knees. The silence wasn't tense—exactly—but it had weight. The kind that gathered in the corners, pressing inward, inviting thoughts she didn't want to entertain.

She tried to focus. Tried to replay the mission specs in her head. Tried to think about tactical terrain or scanning routes or even which side she'd slung her medkit on. Anything useful.

Instead, she found herself staring at Basco's boots.

They were spotless. Gleaming. Not just polished, but *new*. Fresh from Spacefleet HQ, by the look of them—standard-issue with that impossible mirror sheen that had never once met dirt. His uniform, too, was crisp and white, wrinkle-free, snug in the way only HQ-issue ever seemed to be.

But it was the boots that stuck with her. The way they caught the sterile shuttle light. The way they looked like they belonged to a different world entirely. They were too clean. Too untested. And somehow... mesmerizing.

She blinked and looked up—just in time to catch Basco staring at her. His gaze jumped from her chest to her face, then quickly away to the bulkhead, his ears coloring with embarrassment.

He straightened in his harness, trying to reassemble himself into something resembling an officer. "So, uh—Captain. Where exactly are we headed?"

Calan turned toward him slowly, raising an eyebrow. "Seriously? Didn't you read the briefing?"

"I—" Basco shifted, flustered. "I know it's a border planet. Former Krythar territory. But... I don't know anything about this Shyra'thel. Most of her file was redacted."

Lily, Alrek, and Calan exchanged a glance.

Calan gave a small nod.

Alrek turned slightly toward Basco, his voice calm, steady. "Shyra'thel is a Krythar defector. She saved our lives during the war last year. Without her help, we never would've been able to tap into the psionic resonance needed to bypass Krythar shielding." He paused, not dramatically, just with reverence. "She turned the tide."

Basco nodded slowly. "Right."

His expression was politely blank—trying to look informed—but his eyes flicked back and forth like someone connecting dots in real time. Lily recognized the look. He was lost. He'd spent the war in a classroom or an office. Safe. Far from blood and noise and impossible choices.

She gave him a small smile.

"At first I was intimidated by Shyra'thel," she said. "I couldn't imagine working with a Krythar. But I learned not to judge a book by its cover."

Her gaze drifted downward. The boots again—gleaming, unscuffed, impossibly out of place. They caught the shuttle light just so, reflecting a perfect arc across the floor.

She looked back up at Basco and gave him a wink.

His ears flushed pink again, and he turned quickly toward the viewport.

Lily leaned back and closed her eyes.

Focus, Lily. One thing at a time.

· · · ·

The shuttle pierced the cloud layer like an insect through foam, engines purring as it descended through the upper atmosphere of Bimara.

Lily leaned forward in her harness, peering through the forward viewport.

Below them, the rainforest unfurled in every direction—an endless sea of green canopies, dense and rippling, broken only by silver-threaded rivers and the occasional ridge of dark, angular stone. Vines curled over everything like nature's handwriting—thick, untamed, beautiful. Pale birds with lizard-like crests flitted between the trees, their wings translucent, shimmering like glass. Once, she thought she caught sight of something larger—a massive, lumbering shape moving just beneath the canopy—but it vanished too quickly to be sure.

Calan's voice broke through the hush. "These are the coordinates. Prepare for landing."

The clearing emerged moments later—an oval-shaped basin carved into the jungle, encircled by tree-covered cliffs and crowned with drifting mist. At its center sat a landing pad, worn and uneven, its markings long faded. A dozen tower lights blinked from hastily affixed poles, and a loose ring of temporary structures clung to the perimeter like uncertain guests at a gathering.

Stacked metal crates. A command tent. A medic dome stitched together from scavenged panels. Field life.

But beneath it all—half-swallowed by moss and machinery—there were stone walls. Towering archways. Cracked pillars. Architecture that had clearly been there long before any forward post. Ancient structures, built into the rock itself, now repurposed into barracks and storage rooms. Reclaimed, but not erased.

A chill slid across Lily's spine. The place felt... layered. Like history was just waiting beneath the soil.

The shuttle angled downward, repulsors kicking in as wind spiraled through the clearing, whipping mist and leaves into a swirling blur. Through the shifting haze, Lily spotted a tall figure standing near the edge of the platform.

Shyra'thel.

Her robes whipped around her in the artificial gust, black cloth swirling like a living thing. She was flanked by two guards—reptilian in appearance, but not Krythar. Broader, stockier, with jagged spines along their heads and slit-pupiled eyes. Lily didn't recognize the species, but there was something in their bearing, their physiology, that suggested shared ancestry with the Krythar. Distant cousins, maybe.

The shuttle settled onto the stone with a heavy, resonant *thunk*. Hatches hissed open, and the boarding ramp lowered with a soft hydraulic sigh.

Lily unbuckled her harness and followed Calan down the ramp, her boots landing softly on the metal with each step.

But before they reached the base, Shyra'thel was already moving.

Her pace was brisk, purposeful. She didn't wait at the edge for ceremony, didn't posture with protocol or diplomatic distance.

She met them halfway—reaching Calan before his boots even touched the stone.

And then she hugged him.

Not a polite formality, but a full-bodied, grounded embrace. Her arms wrapped around his shoulders. Her eyes closed. A soft breath—real relief escaping her chest.

Calan froze like a statue.

Lily almost laughed. She had never seen him look more startled.

Shyra'thel stepped back with a smile. "Captain Calan. It is good to see you again."

He nodded stiffly. "Likewise... ambassador."

Behind him, Lily caught Alrek's expression—soft, serene, smiling in that quietly reverent way of his.

And something in her own chest loosened—just a little.

• • • •

They moved through the ruins at a steady pace, the stone beneath their boots cool and uneven, carved long ago by hands long forgotten. Moss clung to the edges of the path in vibrant threads, and thick, spined leaves unfurled overhead like banners in slow motion. Vines looped through collapsed archways and ancient windows, framing the jungle beyond in dappled green light.

Shyra'thel led the way, her robes trailing just above the ground, her voice calm as she walked. "These halls were once part of a seat of power—a neutral ground for trade and discourse before the Krythar occupation. When the war ended, it was abandoned again. The locals scattered, the factions fractured further. Some blamed each other. Some blamed the Union. Many simply stopped trusting."

Calan walked just behind her, flanked by Lily and Alrek. Basco trailed a few steps farther back, wide-eyed and silent, trying not to trip over the uneven floor.

"My work here has focused on helping them unify," Shyra'thel continued, gesturing toward a scaffolded structure to their right where workers in mismatched uniforms were carefully clearing debris from an entranceway. "There are several dominant species on this world—old rivalries, old wounds. Most of their governing bodies have refused to recognize each other."

She glanced back at them, her expression neutral, but there was something steady in her gaze.

"I hope that my presence here—someone who once fought *with* the Krythar and now stands *with* the Union—proves that reconciliation is possible. That change isn't only theoretical. It can be embodied."

Alrek nodded, visibly moved. "It means something. Seeing you here—building bridges instead of burning them. They'll remember that. Especially the young."

Shyra'thel allowed herself a small smile. "I tell them a story. About a human girl who saved my life. And how, later, I returned the favor. Not because I had to. But because it mattered."

Lily glanced at her, caught off guard by the warmth in her voice.

"That story has resonance," Shyra'thel added. "Not because it's dramatic. But because it's *real*. Trust doesn't come from perfection. It comes from risk. From acts freely chosen."

They passed under a half-collapsed archway, the light flickering with movement as they entered a wide chamber.

The map room.

A platform at the center glowed faintly, casting ripples of cyan light across the ancient stone walls. As they stepped closer, the platform responded—projecting a vast holographic globe that hung in the air, translucent and alive with detail. It spun slowly at first, then stilled as it focused on Bimara. Continent lines shimmered. Cities marked themselves in shifting script. Weather patterns, heat signatures, tectonic movement—layer after layer of data folded and unfolded like petals.

Basco let out a quiet gasp.

"This is... incredible," he breathed, already stepping forward to examine one of the floating panels. He brushed his fingers across a stream of iconography, and the display zoomed in smoothly—revealing a series of mountain ridges so detailed Lily could count the trees.

Shyra'thel smiled faintly. "The Union supplied the base hardware, but most of the refinements came from the local engineers. There is brilliance here. They simply needed tools to express it. We have to have detailed maps stored offline due to the communication problems throughout the planet"

"That damned radiation." Lily added.

Calan crossed his arms. "Has the artifact ever been located? Or investigated seriously? Have there been any expeditions launched?"

Shyra'thel turned toward the globe, watching it spin slowly in place. "Nothing official. The Krythar believe Nymara's Tear should be left undisturbed—sacred. But there have been... individuals. The curious. Spiritualists. Smugglers. A few claimed to find pieces of the puzzle. Locations. Symbols. Clues."

"But nothing definitive?" Calan asked.

Shyra'thel shook her head. "Not yet. But the stories have a way of aligning. Patterns emerge, if you're willing to listen to the edges."

"Clues like what?" Lily asked, stepping a little closer to the edge of the map's glowing projection.

Shyra'thel turned toward the display and tapped a section of the globe. The hologram rippled, then zoomed inward—revealing a swath of dense forest and winding waterways. Streams and aquifers crisscrossed beneath the surface in intricate, pulsing veins of light.

"The Tear is connected to Bimara's water systems," she said. "The legend describes it as something... sacred. Healing. A kind of source. Something your cultures might associate with the Fountain of Youth or the Holy Grail."

Lily raised an eyebrow. "So... we're looking for the Holy Grail?"

Shyra'thel's expression didn't change. "Perhaps not exactly. The stories vary. We don't truly know what the Tear is—only that it's likely some sort of vessel. Something meant to hold the sacred water."

She turned back to the map, gesturing to the glowing points. "Most versions of the legend place it in—or near—one of the ancient spring-temples. Sanctuaries built over natural aquifers. Dedicated to Yeshinima, the goddess of water."

She gestured, and the globe shifted again—highlighting two glowing points amid a sea of green. "These temples are the strongest candidates. Both confirmed by visual surveys in the last three years. Difficult terrain. Thick brush.

Calan studied the map, arms folded. "We'll need to split up."

He pointed toward the more mountainous of the two locations.

"Alrek, you're with me."

Then he turned to Lily. "Lily, I want you to take Lieutenant Basco in hand."

"Aye, Captain," Lily replied automatically.

She kept her voice even, but it took effort. She didn't look at Basco. Just reached for her gear and adjusted the strap on her vest, letting the silence say what she didn't.

• • • •

Blades sliced through the underbrush with rhythmic swipes, vines curling away from them like peeled ribbon. The rainforest was thicker here—less traveled, wild and defiant. Every few steps brought a new sound: a distant chirp, the metallic buzz of unseen insects, the damp rustle of something large slithering out of sight.

Lily wiped sweat from her brow and hacked through another dense tangle. The sun filtered in patches through the canopy above, painting everything in shifting green light. She had unbuttoned her tunic and the strap was chafing against her chest. She adjusted it, catching her breath just long enough to glance over at Basco.

He'd ditched his jacket somewhere back along the trail. Now he moved ahead of her in a sleeveless tunic, broad shoulders flexing with every swing of the blade. His arms—lean, defined, and glistening with effort—moved like something out of a recruitment poster. Unfortunately, a *very effective* one.

Lily narrowed her eyes at the path ahead, deeply irritated at her own hormones.

Nope.

Nope.

What the hell is wrong with me.

"Sooo... Dante," she said, breaking the silence in her best approximation of casual friendliness.

Basco turned slightly, slowing his swing to glance back at her.

"I read in your file that you were a champion football player on Proxima Centauri before you joined the fleet."

He blinked, looking mildly horrified. "Oh—uh, not *champion* champion. I mean, high school champion. Not, like... galactic league or anything."

He cleared his throat. "And just to be clear—it was *actual* football. The kind you play with your feet. Not that weird one from ancient America. The one where they threw the missile."

Lily blinked. "Missile?"

Basco gave her a sideways look. "I mean... come on. You've seen pictures. You can't *call* it a ball. Balls are spherical. That thing was a torpedo."

Lily laughed—actually laughed—and nodded. "You're not wrong," she said, shaking her head. *America.* Now *there* was something she hadn't thought about in a while.

The laughter faded into the warm hush of the trees, and for a few steps, they just walked. Blades in hand. Shoulders brushing branches. Two silhouettes swallowed slowly by the forest.

It happened fast.

One second, they were moving through a patch of thick brush, blades sheathed, scanning the terrain. The next—blaster fire.

A burst of light scorched past Lily's shoulder, slamming into a tree with a sizzle. Another shot ricocheted off the rocks to their left, throwing sparks into the air.

She ducked instinctively, drawing her sidearm as she dropped to one knee. Basco was already returning fire, crouched behind a thick root system, shouting, "Cover left!"

Three figures emerged from the trees—scrappy, under-equipped, but aggressive. Locals, maybe. Opportunists. Robbers.

One went down under Lily's first shot, spinning back into the brush with a cry. The others scattered, flanking them fast.

"They're circling!" Basco called, just as two more attackers surged from the shadows behind them.

Lily turned just in time to block a blade with the butt of her blaster. Sparks flew. She slammed her shoulder into the attacker's chest and brought him down with a sharp knee to the ribs.

Another came at her from the left. She ducked low, swept his legs, and brought him down hard. Her training kicked in—fluid, instinctive. She was grateful for every hour she'd spent in the gym, every bruised morning.

Nearby, Basco took on two at once—blocking a punch, ducking a swing, then landing a clean elbow that sent one assailant reeling. He moved with power and precision, his footwork tight, his punches fast. Stronger than she'd expected.

But then—

A shadow dropped from above.

A taller figure—hooded, fluid—landed between them with unnatural grace. No blaster. Just fists and motion. Some sort of alien martial arts that Lily didn't recognize. They moved like skill come alive in a lethal dance.

For a moment, the air crackled with stillness—then the figure attacked.

Lily struck first, aiming high while Basco flanked from the side, trying to catch them off-balance. But the assailant was faster than either of them had anticipated—spinning low, deflecting Lily's strike with an elbow, countering Basco with a sweeping kick that nearly took his legs out. They moved in sync, Lily and Basco—trained, smart, adaptable—but it was like trying to fight mist that hit back. Every move the figure made was precise, economical, and devastatingly fluid. Not flashy. Just effective.

They were giving it everything—skill, strength, teamwork—and barely holding the phantom at bay.

Lily could feel it in the strain of her muscles, in the narrowing of her breath. This wasn't going well.

She managed a moment long enough to get her blaster aimed, fingers aching from the grip.

She fired.

The shot went wide. A second too slow.

A blur of motion—and the attacker kicked the weapon sideways, hard, while her finger was still in the trigger guard.

She heard the snap.

White-hot pain exploded through her hand, sharp and immediate. The attacker struck her head with a high kick. Her knees buckled, her vision sparked.

The blaster clattered to the ground as she fell. She clutched her broken finger, the pain blooming outward as the world spun around her.

The attacker pressed forward—but Basco intercepted, landing a clean right hook that sent the figure stumbling back.

"Lily!" he shouted.

She tried to answer, but her head felt like it was at the bottom of the ocean.

More shadows surged into view. The rest of the robbers—regrouped. Furious.

They swarmed Basco.

He fought hard, but there were too many. One grabbed his arms. Another wrapped him in a chokehold. A third delivered a knee to the gut. They dragged him off into the underbrush, shouting to each other in a language she didn't recognize.

Lily reached for her weapon. For her voice. For *anything*. But her vision was tipping sideways, the world lurching in slow, unsteady tilts. Her head throbbed. Her finger burned—then numbed, fading into the same hollow quiet that was swallowing the rest of her. The green of the trees blurred and darkened at the edges, the world narrowing into shadow.

She blinked hard, trying to stay awake. The world tilted, soft at the edges, light bleeding into shadow.

And then—through the blur—she saw movement.

A figure.

Half-obscured by leaves. Just coming into view.

The walk was wrong. No—*familiar*. Too familiar.

Blurry. Twisted by distance and pain.

But unmistakable.

It can't be...

Her lips parted, the word barely a breath.

"Shit."

And then the darkness took her.

• • • •

The lights stretched forever.

Bulbs in a line, suspended in the dark. Dozens. Hundreds. Thousands. Each one identical. Each one humming faintly. All of them glowing in perfect intervals, a rhythm of cold illumination that vanished into the void beyond counting.

He couldn't move his head—not even an inch. The metal strap cinched across his brow, bolted into the back of the chair. He could feel the pressure of it in his teeth. Smell the rust in his nose. Taste copper on his tongue.

Hands—too large, too quiet—gripped his skull. Fingers thick as his wrists fastened him tighter.

There was no ceremony to it. No preamble. Just the sound of fabric tearing, and then cold air crawling across exposed skin. Unseen blades sliced away the rest—severing seams, nicking flesh. He felt them. Not deep. Not yet.

Then: pain. A slow, creeping fire as the first blade dragged across his chest. Not deep enough to kill. Just enough to bleed.

His breath hitched.

The sweat poured down his temples, stinging the open cuts as it slid into them. His lashes fluttered—but then there was metal there, too. A clamp. A device. Eyelids pried open until the white burned red, until he could see only the light and the dark between.

And the face.

It emerged from the blur—closer than breath. Yellow teeth. Gray skin stretched taut over bone and sinew, bands of cartilage exposed like an anatomical model half-flayed. One eye was milk-white. The other burned gold.

He could feel the tubes being fitted—inserted into the soft hollows of his temples. Needles kissing the bone beneath. Something hissed. A drill whirred to life.

A low voice, rancid with amusement, spoke close enough that Veyrik felt the words on his skin.

"Look at it this way," it said. "If you wake up from this, you'll be a whole new man, Veyrik."

• • • •

Her head hurt—but far less than she expected. The throbbing was dull, manageable.

Her finger, though—her *finger* was a different story.

It was twisted at an unnatural angle, jutting to the side like a snapped twig. The sight alone nearly made her gag. With a sharp inhale and a whispered curse, she gritted her teeth, wrapped her other hand around it, and *snapped* it back into place.

White-hot agony flared behind her eyes. Her knees buckled. The edges of her vision darkened for a second—just a second—but she held on.

The mental fog lifted, piece by piece.

And there he was.

Leaning casually against a column. Arms crossed. That smirk. *God*, that smirk.

Her mind hadn't been playing tricks on her after all.

"I can't believe it," she muttered. "Rhyder Dane. Halfway across the damn quadrant."

He pushed off the column with one shoulder, sauntering toward her like the past was a suggestion. "Lily *Starlight*," he said, grinning like a man who'd just found treasure in a trash fire. "You were the last person I expected to see."

She was on her feet before he reached her, swaying slightly. She shoved her injured hand deep into her pocket and used her left to strike him clean across the face.

The smack echoed through the clearing.

"You damn double-crossing... jerk," she snapped—though the last word came out strained and breathless from the pain.

Rhyder's head tilted slightly from the blow, but he didn't flinch. His hand went to his jaw, and he gave a small, admiring laugh. "Whoa, whoa, whoa," he said, holding his hands up. "Business is business. It's nothing personal, *Starlight*."

She winced. "And my name isn't Starlight. It's *Starling*. Like the bird."

"Bird?" He raised an eyebrow. "Well that's underachieving."

Lily let out a strangled noise, somewhere between a scoff and a groan, and brought her good hand up to her forehead, shaking her head.

"I can't believe this," she muttered, then fixed him with a sharp look.

"I suppose it's just a coincidence that you happen to be here—right now—while we're looking for one of the most mysterious artifacts in the galaxy?"

Rhyder smirked. "Hey, I follow opportunity. Camilla's paying me to find Nymara's Tear so she can sell it off to some whale."

Lily frowned, crossing her arms. "I thought you *swore* you'd never work for her again. Didn't she try to kill you?"

Rhyder gave a dry laugh out the corner of his mouth. "Once or twice. But you know me—I probably had it coming."

She didn't let it go. "Didn't you get her *nephew* killed?"

His smile faltered.

There it was.

"Look," he said, eyes narrowing just slightly. "Are we going to rehash the past, or be smart about this? We both want the same thing. I say we work together."

Lily laughed—loud and bitter. "So you can sell me out again?"

"That was a job, Starlight—"

Her glare cut like a blade.

"—ling. Starling," he said quickly. "But the galaxy clearly wants us in the same place, and I'm not arguing with fate."

Lily didn't move. Her glare deepened. Arms folded. Breath steady.

"Or hey," Rhyder added with a shrug, "you can arrest me or whatever. But we're more likely to survive if we stick together. Especially if you want your supermodel He-Man friend back from the Belkans."

That got her attention.

"If they can't figure out a way to profit off him," he added, "they'll just eat him."

Lily narrowed her eyes. "Wait—*really*?"

Rhyder raised his eyebrows and gave a crooked nod. "Come on, I'll help you, and we can sort out the rest later."

Lily exhaled—slow, reluctant. She didn't like it. But she knew he was right. They stood a much better chance of surviving if they worked together.

"Alright," she said firmly. "But you follow *my* lead. Got it? I'm not your damsel in distress."

Rhyder scoffed, already moving. "You're welcome—for saving your hide again."

Lily sighed as she followed. "It doesn't rain, but it pours..."

. . . .

They followed the riverbed in silence, the sound of rushing water filling the space between them. The air was thicker here—cooler, shaded by towering trees that leaned over the banks like watchful elders. The current rushed beside them, white-capped and eager, carving its way through the broken terrain like it had somewhere urgent to be.

Lily adjusted the strap on her scanner and frowned. "I really wish I had the harmonizer the Raath-Ka built."

"Let me guess," Rhyder said, stepping over a root without looking. "Calan has it."

She nodded, thumbing through the interface. The signal was murky at best. "I hope he and Alrek are having better luck than I am."

They rounded a bend and came face to face with a towering mesa—its sheer sides draped in moss, sunlight glinting off damp stone. From the top, the jungle would stretch endlessly. Unforgiving. Beautiful. Alive.

Rhyder tilted his head, assessing the climb. "Maybe if we get some height, we can spot which way the raiders went. Assuming they left tracks."

"You just want to climb something."

Rhyder shrugged.

They ascended slowly—Lily first, her fingers slick with damp grit, using narrow cracks in the rock as footholds. At the summit, a narrow overlook curved above the treetops like the edge of the world.

She pulled out her scanner, wiped the screen dry, and waited.

A faint ping.

Not a life sign.

But a signature.

The scanner pulsed softly against the map overlay—steady, unmistakable.

It wasn't Basco.

It was Nymara's Tear.

Two voices fought a war in Lily's mind.

Morality told her to go find Basco.

Adventure and desire pulled her toward the Tear—with Rhyder.

"The artifact," she said, voice tight. "I'm picking up faint readings—some sort of carved radioactive rock. Southwest." She pointed. "Less than a mile. It's so close."

Rhyder leaned in beside her, breath catching faintly at the same time hers did. "Well... I'm sure your friend would understand."

She paused.

For once, she didn't mind the way he was looking at her.

They followed the ridgeline. Below, the river widened—roaring white as it tumbled over jagged rocks and vanished into a gorge. The current churned and spat, foam curling around boulders like warning signs.

Slick mud coated the bank.

There would be no easy crossing.

They didn't hesitate.

The first few steps were manageable—ankle-deep, cold, fast-moving.

Then Lily slipped.

Her boot sank into the mud like a trap, suction locking her ankle in place. She struggled, teeth clenched, trying to keep upright.

"Got you," Rhyder said, grabbing her under the arms and yanking her free with a grunt. She staggered forward, wet and winded.

But then he slipped.

With a sharp curse, he went sideways, boots scrambling—mud grabbing hold this time. Lily lunged for him, catching his wrist.

"Don't you *dare*—"

His grip slipped.

The river took him.

"RHYDER!" she shouted, running along the shore, dodging brush, trying to keep him in sight. But the forest was too thick. He vanished downstream, the water pulling him faster and faster toward the falls.

"Try to grab something!" she yelled, already tearing through roots and leaves.

She spotted a fallen plank tangled in the brush—maybe part of an old bridge or a downed transport crate. Lily didn't think. She yanked it free, threw herself into the river, and wrapped her arms around it. The current seized them both.

The river was chaos. Cold. Alive. But the makeshift board gave her just enough control to steer through the rapids. The falls came quickly—too quickly—and she braced, heart pounding.

They tumbled.

Somehow, they hit shallow water on the far side. Mud. Rocks. Stillness.

She crawled out, dragging Rhyder behind her. Both of them soaked, gasping, shivering. But alive.

He coughed hard, spat riverwater, then grinned up at her. "Nice rescue."

She helped steady him. "Now we're even."

They got to their feet, clothes clinging, boots squelching. A stone ridge loomed nearby, cracked in the middle where a dark gap marked the entrance to a cave.

Lily tapped her wrist-light. Miraculously, it still worked. The beam cut through the dark like a knife.

They entered carefully, ducking beneath jagged stone. The cave walls pulsed with moisture. The passage narrowed—tight, slick, uneven.

They turned sideways to fit.

Face to face.

Her chest pressed into his.

His hand steadied against her waist.

She could feel every inch of him—warm, alive, solid. And too close.

They slipped through the passage. Slowly. Too slowly. When they finally emerged into a wider cavern, her heart was pounding from more than just exertion.

And there it was.

The artifact.

Over four feet tall. Stone. Carved into the shape of a teardrop, elongated and severe, with eagle-like wings sweeping upward in harsh symmetry. The texture was jagged, scaled, almost predatory. It didn't look sacred. It looked *dangerous.*

Lily raised her scanner, took a few readings. No power source. No obvious traps.

Just... waiting.

She shrugged off her wet jacket, wringing out the sleeves, trying to focus. But her shirt clung uncomfortably, and the humidity was settling deep into her skin.

Rhyder peeled his shirt off and shook the water from his hair.

Lily glanced at him. Then away.

Then back.

Her brain hissed a warning. She told it to shut up.

"You're staring," he said, smug.

Without a word, she unfastened the rest of her shirt, let it fall to the floor, and stepped toward him.

"Oh," Rhyder said, startled.

Lily grabbed him by the back of his hair, pulled him close, and kissed him hard—fast, furious, unrelenting.

She didn't think.

She just took what she wanted.

· · · ·

The ground gave a small, trembling shudder.

"Whoa," Rhyder said, dragging the word out with that exaggerated, awkward energy people often have after sex.

"Little earthquake or something," he added, already pulling his trousers back on, fumbling a little with the belt.

Lily didn't move.

She sat cross-legged on the cool stone, her damp shirt resting in her lap, skin still glistening with sweat and riverwater. She didn't feel the need to cover up—she was reading the data scrolling across her scanner.

Rhyder cleared his throat. "So... just putting it out there—I'm not really the relationship type."

"Huh?" Lily didn't look up. Her tone was distant, distracted. "Oh. I don't want anything from you."

Then she lifted her gaze—sharp, dry.

"That I didn't already get."

Rhyder blinked. Then grinned. "I feel so used. You never cease to amaze me, Starling."

She rolled her eyes and returned to the scanner. "According to these readings, the outer shell of this thing matches meteor fragments recovered from the Loraas Crater. The old historians were right."

He leaned in a little, but his eyes kept drifting.

"The radiation levels are faint, but constant. Over hundreds of years, it's been leeching into the underground springs. Irradiating the water on a microcellular level."

He still wasn't looking at her, his body turned away from her in an exaggerated show of modesty.

Lily sighed, tugging her uniform back on and muttering as she zipped it up. "You're such a little boy."

"I was just trying to be respectful," he said, raising both hands—then narrowing his eyes as if examining her. "You're wet again."

She arched an eyebrow. "You weren't *that* good."

"No—the water." He pointed at droplets hitting her shoulder. "Look. It's dripping from the ceiling."

She looked up.

Drops fell in steady rhythm from cracks in the stone above, cold against her skin. The air had shifted—thicker now. Heavier. Sound carried differently.

Her eyes narrowed. "We're not underground," she said slowly. "We're *underwater.*"

She checked the scanner again. The readout pulsed faintly.

"I'm picking up life signs," she added. "Two of them. Moving."

The scanner pinged softly, drawing her toward a carved section of wall. What she thought was decoration was some kind of ancient machinery. A circular stone relief, weathered by time and pressure, but with deliberate lines beneath the erosion. She traced it with her fingertips.

"There," she whispered. "Looks like a valve."

Rhyder moved closer, crouching beside her.

"Ancient airlock," Lily said, heart starting to pick up speed. "And something—or *someone*—is trying to open it from the other side."

The valve groaned as it opened—stone grinding against stone, water gushing in a burst that sprayed across the chamber floor.

Two figures emerged, clunky and silhouetted against the narrow shaft behind them.

Diving gear. Rebreathers. Flashlights mounted to their shoulders.

Calan was first. Alrek followed close behind, peeling off his mask with a breathless grin.

Lily blinked. "*You were the life signs?*"

"We found a tunnel in the other temple," Alrek said, stripping off the rest of the gear. "Slightly different structure, but same architectural features. When we activated the pulse harmonizer, we picked up multiple signal reflections."

Rhyder whistled low. "You're saying there's *more* of these?"

"Several," Calan said. "If the readings are correct."

Lily turned, eyeing the chamber again. Now that she was looking for it, she saw the outlines—curved seams in the walls, hidden beneath mineral buildup and moss. Valves. Dozens of them, tucked into the stone like sleeping machinery.

"Were these temples," she asked, gesturing toward the sculpted wings of the Tear, "or ancient waterworks?"

Alrek smiled, already crouching by the pedestal. "Maybe both."

He popped open his toolkit with a satisfying click. "If we can get to one more point—another temple—I can triangulate. Map the whole system."

Calan, still dripping, turned to look Lily and Rhyder up and down. "Rhyder Dane, what the hell are you doing here, by the way?"

Alrek squinted at him. "Oh. You're not Basco? Sorry, you humans all look alike."

After Lily provided a quick recap, with careful omissions, Calan began reconnecting his diving gear. "We don't have gear for you two," he said, snapping a connector in place. "But we can share the oxygen through the tunnel. Take turns with the rebreather. Buddy up."

Rhyder raised an eyebrow at Lily, flashing a grin.

Lily shook her head. "I'll share with Alrek."

Defeated, Rhyder turned to Calan with a grimace. "Hey... buddy," he muttered with forced cheer. Calan didn't even look at him.

They reached the next chamber without incident. This temple was smaller—less symmetrical. Rougher.

But Nymara's Tear was there too, embedded in the far wall. Just as imposing. Just as scaly.

Alrek set up near the pedestal, adjusting his readings and watching data flicker across his portable display.

Lily wandered a little. The floor was uneven—ancient tiles shattered in places, giving way to packed earth and the occasional exposed slab of stone.

She wasn't looking for anything.

But something caught her eye.

Near the base of the wall, resting atop a low, dusty column, was a sliver of curved boning—wrapped in a strip of leather.

Familiar leather.

Her breath caught.

She knelt slowly, heart kicking against her ribs, and lifted her light.

There, etched into the dust with careful, deliberate lines, was a drawing of a tea set.

The image pulled her backward—*back* to that quiet afternoon on Bimara, when she and Xynn had shared tea with her old neighbor Razh. The air had been warm, still, full of trust.

Below the drawing, scratched into the dust in soft Saravethi:

I'm okay. find me.

Lily stared at it.

She didn't move.

Didn't speak.

A hot, awful pressure rose in her chest—too sharp to be tears, too thick to swallow.

Her stomach turned.

What have I done.

For a moment of control...

For the pleasure of being wanted...

For my own selfish need to feel powerful, to feel something—

I betrayed someone I actually love.

No.

No time to feel sorry for myself.

She leaked out the words, her voice barely a whisper.

"I'll find you, Xynn..."

. . . .

The tunnel stretched longer than the others, carved into rougher stone—less temple, more forgotten infrastructure. The water was colder here, sharp enough to steal Lily's breath. She struggled to hold it between passes, relying on Alrek's steady rhythm—he had the lungs of a whale, and she was able to get what she needed to continue.

When they surfaced on the other side, Lily stopped short.

The chamber opened into a vast expanse—twice the size of the previous temples. The ceiling arched so high it vanished into shadow, while twin waterfalls poured down on either side of a carved dais, feeding a circular basin below. Mist clung to the air, glowing faintly with the pulse of phosphorescent veins in the walls.

And at the center of it all, rising from the basin like a deity from myth— Nymara's Tear.

But this one was enormous.

Twelve feet tall. Etched in jagged, scaly patterns. The elegant droplet motif clashed with cruel wings that swept back like serrated blades. Water flowed continuously down its surface, channeled through deep grooves—like veins in living stone. It shimmered in the light, casting fractured reflections across the walls and water alike.

Alrek stepped closer, wide-eyed. "Incredible," he whispered. "What a feat of engineering."

"Well I guess we don't have to worry about you walking off with it," Lily said teasingly to Rhyder. He seemed not to hear her at first.

"Hmm? Oh right."

Lily narrowed her eyes. Something was off.

Calan set his pack down near the base of the platform and knelt beside it, already unpacking the harmonizer. "If this place is central to the system, we'll have line-of-sight to the camp. I'll try to get a signal to Shyra'thel."

"Three minutes and counting," Alrek said as the machine powered on.

Lily's eyes tracked the perimeter. The mist. The shadows.

She caught sight of Rhyder.

He was walking slowly. Casually. But he wasn't exploring the chamber—he was easing backward, step by step, toward one of the valve doors embedded in the wall.

The central one.

Twice as tall as the rest.

"Where ya going, Rhyder?" Lily asked, sing-song, not looking away.

He froze mid-step.

"Hm?" he said, too fast. "Oh—nowhere. Just, you know, spreading out. Checking the... uh. Acoustics."

His hands were behind his back.

He was sweating.

Lily's stomach clenched.

"Captain," she said, her voice rising.

Calan stood sharply, one hand dropping to the sidearm at his belt.

But it was too late.

The central valve—massive, circular, ringed in etched reliefs—let out a sharp hiss as pressure equalized. A deep, groaning rumble echoed through the chamber.

It opened.

Water rolled out in sheets, crashing across the stone. Echoes shattered the stillness like thunder.

And there—standing before a submersible vehicle, flanked by armed men—

Captain Ronin.

Clad in dark armor, his mask gleamed like oil in the light. Silent. Precise. He stepped forward and locked eyes with Lily.

"Well," he said. "Glad we could all meet face to face."

Then, a glance toward Rhyder.

"Thank you, young man, for the homing signal. We almost couldn't read it this far down... but we found our way."

Lily fumed, unable to speak.

Ronin inclined his head slightly, his voice infuriatingly calm. "Your tech saved me a great deal of trouble. This one's been stumbling around for weeks trying to find the Tear."

Rhyder gave a lazy shrug. "I would've found it eventually."

Calan stepped forward, voice sharp. "You'll never get the artifact out of here. Our ship will—"

Ronin chuckled, cutting him off. "Artifact?" He turned slowly, spreading his arms like a prophet. "Nymara's Tear isn't an object. It's all around us."

Alrek's eyes widened as the pieces snapped together. "The water," he breathed. "Of course. That's the source of the radiation. That's the power."

Ronin nodded, delighted. "The ancient ones tried to harness it's power for eternal life—and they paid a great price. Soon, I'll finish what they started. When this chamber collapses, the pressure will rupture the subterranean pathways, brining the water to the surface."

Calan spoke, "I don't know what your plan is but it won't work."

Ronin gestured toward the craft. "I'll admit, your presence here was more complicated than I anticipated. Nevertheless, it came with added benefits."

He tapped a control panel on his gauntlet.

With a mechanical *hiss*, the blast armor on the transport peeled open.

Inside—bound upright in a rig of energy restraints, her limbs twitching with effort—**Shyra'thel.**

Her robes were scorched, her head low. Arcs of energy crawled across her exoskeleton in bright, vicious flickers.

"If you try to follow me," Ronin said, still calm, still smiling,

"I'll strip her exoskeleton like peeling an egg."

She arched in pain, her body convulsing as she fought against the bindings. Lily flinched instinctively, fists clenched.

Calan stepped forward—half a pace—before Ronin's men raised their weapons in unison, ready to fire.

Behind them, a new sound rose: soft metallic *clinks*, echoing off the stone. Ronin's men were setting charges, methodical and precise, at regular intervals around the chamber.

Rhyder drifted toward the rear, moving past Lily without so much as a glance.

"Leaving already?" she snapped. "You son of a—"

He didn't stop. Just smirked and kept walking.

"I should've known you'd finish early," she called after him, voice sharp and slicing. "You bastard!"

Alrek and Calan exchanged a look.

Rhyder turned back, walking backward now with that shit-eating grin. "You loved it." He winked. "And as they say in the Bible—'Hell is empty, and all the devils are here. If you can't beat 'em, join 'em.'"

The blast doors began to close.

Lily cupped her hands and shouted over the rising wind, "That's not in the Bible, you idiot!"

Ronin raised his arm in farewell. "Pity. You won't live to see the new order."

The door sealed shut with a thundering *clang*.

Silence.

Then—the first sharp chirps of the explosives arming echoed across the chamber.

Calan spun to Alrek. "Pack up the harmonizer! Now. This whole place is about to blow."

The explosion was sharp—contained, but devastating.

Cracks spiderwebbed through the far wall. And then—**the flood.**

Water surged into the chamber like a living thing. Fast. Relentless. Unstoppable.

Lily and Alrek packed up the harmonizer in seconds, sealing the case just as the first wave struck the platform. They scrambled for the tunnel entrance, debris crashing down from above, the floor vanishing beneath a rising tide.

The current hit like a punch. Cold. Chaotic. It dragged at their limbs, yanked at their gear.

Lily lost her footing—slammed into the stone. Her breath knocked out.

She surfaced, gasping—just in time to see Alrek coughing nearby. She grabbed his hand.

Together, they fought their way through the tunnel—dark and half-collapsed—passing the rebreather between them in frantic, shivering intervals.

Every inch forward was a struggle. Every second a decision.

But somehow...They made it.

They burst through the tunnel into the original chamber, gasping for air. Mud and water poured out behind them, flooding the stone like the aftermath of a broken dam. Debris floated in swirls—strips of torn vine, cracked gear, shattered tile.

Alrek was already on the ground, wrenching the harmonizer open as he cursed under his breath. "No, no, no—damn it."

Calan shook water from his ears, blinking hard. "What now?"

"The harmonizer's damaged," Alrek muttered. "Something shorted in the current."

Lily stepped forward, drenched and shaking from adrenaline. "Sir, I screwed this up. I request permission to go after Basco and Xynn. Let me clean up my mess."

"Denied," Calan said immediately. "We're not splitting up. And this isn't your fault—Ronin's been playing us from the beginning."

He checked his scanner. The display flickered. "Surface flooding is accelerating. Water's rising fast. In a few days, this whole area will be underwater—and then our scanners won't work at all."

He turned back. "Alrek—can you get that damn thing working?"

Alrek smacked the side of the device. "Power source is close to burning out... Wait—hold on—no, wait..." A soft whine rose from the harmonizer. "It's warming up. But the core's destabilized. We'll get one more reading—maybe. Then it's done. Better make it count."

"Two and a half minutes," Alrek added. "And counting."

"We need to scan for Xynn," Lily said immediately. "Saravethi life signs will be easy to isolate—and if she's alive, she'll help us find Basco. Knowing her, she's probably scouted the whole region by now."

"There's no time," Calan shot back. "We need to stop Ronin. If we calibrate for Krythar signatures—"

"He could be three systems away already," Lily snapped. "That ship's untraceable once it harnesses the storm."

"I can't lose Shyra'thel on my watch," Calan said, his voice cracking with quiet desperation.

Lily stepped forward, her voice low and sharp. "So that's what this is about? Your record? You're afraid of what command might think?"

Color rose in Calan's face, but he said nothing.

"To hell with your career," Lily said, her voice shaking. "Or mine, for that matter."

She was trembling now—grief, rage, and panic all rising at once. Her eyes stung with tears she refused to wipe away.

"This is my... my family."

"Twenty seconds," Alrek said, urgency rising in his voice.

Calan didn't answer. He breathed with a kind of panicked energy, caught between instinct and restraint—but he didn't try to stop her.

Lily knelt at the console and punched in the command for Saravethi life signs.

The harmonizer gave a high whine, then chirped. A readout blinked across the screen—clear, precise—and then the display went dark.

No one moved.

Calan was the first to break the silence. "Please tell me we got something."

Alrek nodded. "Yes. One Saravethi lifeform. And human, too. Due west."

He pointed through the dense wall of green, where the sunlight barely filtered through the canopy.

Calan turned to Lily and offered his hand. "Let's go."

She took it without hesitation.

His expression cracked—just slightly—and together, they vanished into the brush.

• • • •

They found Basco first—suspended in a crude trap, arms and legs tangled in woven vines and tension wire.

"Hey!" he shouted the second he spotted her. "Oh, thank God—I was following the riverbed trying to find you and walked straight into a snare!"

"Hold still," Lily said, already slicing through the bindings. Basco dropped with a graceless thud, brushing dirt and leaves from his uniform. Somehow, he still looked almost put together—sweaty, muddy, but upright.

"How did you get away from the raiders?" she asked, genuine concern in her voice.

Basco winced at the memory. "They tied me to a tree while they argued what to do with me. Then a fight broke out... and then everybody got drunk. By the time they decided to move on and untied me to bring me along, the whole area started flooding." He straightened his collar. "I'm a particularly strong swimmer, so... I just swam away."

"Of course you are," Lily muttered, only half teasing. "We could have used that earlier."

She thought, briefly, how much easier the last few hours might've been if Basco *had* been with her. A buffer. A reason not to make certain regrettable decisions.

And then—

"Lily?"

The voice was familiar, but raw. Raspy.

She turned.

Xynn stood at the edge of the clearing, half-camouflaged by vine and shadow. Mud-caked. Scratched. Barely clothed in scavenged scraps of fabric tied haphazardly together.

Alive.

Lily didn't think—she ran.

They collided in a fierce, desperate embrace. Xynn clung to her like something sacred, trembling, and Lily buried her face into the crook of Xynn's neck. Her heart hammered. Her breath caught.

She kissed her. No hesitation.

Just relief. Just love.

And behind it, scratching like a splinter in her chest—guilt.

The others hung back, giving them space. No one said a word.

Eventually, Xynn pulled back enough to look at them. "I've been reading the glyphs," she rasped. "Some of the ruins had Krythar translations. I recognized the dialect—from the occupation."

They listened, rapt.

"The people who built this place were trying to create a fountain of youth," she explained. "The irradiated water enhanced their senses, strengthened their bodies, cured disease. It prolonged life... but only to a point."

She hesitated.

"Then it led to something they called a fate worse than death. The records fall apart after that—but from what I could tell, it changed them. Twisted them into monsters. They turned on each other. Wiped themselves out."

Lily reached down and gripped Xynn's hand—tight. Like she could anchor her there with touch alone.

"You're staying in my quarters," she said, voice steady but low. "And I'm not letting you out of my sight for a while. Okay?"

"Deal," Xynn said, her voice hoarse but warm.

Alrek stepped forward, smiling gently. "It's good to see you, Xynn. Really."

"Thanks, kid." She paused, then corrected herself. "Sorry—Alrek."

Basco looked toward Calan, his tone serious. "So what now? What's Ronin planning? Where's he going?"

Calan's jaw tensed. "He could be on the surface. Or in orbit. There's no way of knowing. We'd have to do a full visual sweep of the planet to track him."

Xynn lifted her free hand. "I think I might be able to help."

Chapter 5: Scales and Feathers

THE QUIET HAD WEIGHT to it.

Not silence, exactly—but something close. That high, faint electrical whine that lived in the corners of the ship when everything else finally stopped. Lily could hear her own heartbeat in her ears. The soft snick of a brush pulling through knots. The occasional curse from Xynn as she fought another tangle.

For the first time in days, Lily tried to still her thoughts. But her heart wouldn't cooperate. She'd logged herself off duty, shut down most of the systems in her quarters. The room felt oddly still without the blinks and chirps—a stillness rare on a ship where work never truly slept.

But her mind refused to follow.

She knew she needed to tell Xynn what happened on the planet. She was waiting for... a better moment. A softer one.

For now, the calm needed to be held. And despite the unrest crawling across her skin like ants, everything felt just perfect enough to pretend it might hold. Just for a little while.

It was a fragile peace.

But it was hers.

Xynn sat beside her on the bed, slowly working through the tangles in her hair—putting herself back together, one careful stroke at a time. She wasn't speaking, just watching Lily out of the corner of her eye with that quiet, affectionate suspicion only someone who really cared could get away with.

Lily felt a pang of guilt when she noticed it.

Xynn had been naked in the jungle, fighting for her life, and somehow she was the one worried about her?

"I don't think I deserve you," Lily murmured.

Xynn didn't answer with words. Just lifted an eyebrow and smirked—a look that said she wasn't going to dignify that with a response.

Then, after a beat:

"You're supposed to be resting."

Lily flopped onto her side and draped one arm across her eyes.

"I *am* resting. This is textbook resting."

"You're fidgeting."

Xynn set the brush down.

Lily dropped her hand and met her gaze.

"It's a restful fidget."

A chirp broke through the quiet—sharp and unmistakable. Not just a regular alert. The kind reserved for urgent matters, even when someone's logged off duty.

"Again?" Xynn quipped, already leaning toward the screen.

Before Lily could protest, she flicked it on.

Caris' image lit up the holo display, her impossibly symmetrical features entering the room like an unexpected dessert showing up.

"Sorry to bother you, Lily," she began, her tone all business-light. "But you need to get your numbers in at the range so you don't lose your weapons certification. You're not *that* bad a shot—it'll probably only take an hour or so."

Lily groaned. "Leena..."

It came out whinier than she intended, and she adjusted her tone quickly.

"I already told you—I'm trying to rest."

She switched the screen off.

"She's persistent," Xynn said, picking the brush back up.

Lily rolled onto her back with a sigh. "I don't know why she even wants me there. There's no reason this couldn't wait a couple days."

"You should go," Xynn said, not looking up.

"Why?"

"Well. For one, you're pretending you don't want to. And two, you're not actually resting anyway."

Lily narrowed her eyes.

"You're really annoying when you're right."

Xynn smirked, casually brushing.

"Go. Go shooting with your incredibly beautiful, fit trainer. I don't care."

The tone was half mocking, half disinterested.

"Stop," Lily jabbed back.

"I'm just saying..." Xynn leaned into it. "God, you get so flustered when I tease you about her."

"She's not even—" Lily sat up, exasperated. "I mean, I don't think she's gay or anything."

"Doesn't mean you can't appreciate the view," Xynn said, stretching her arms overhead.

Lily groaned and dropped her face into the pillow.

"Go shoot something," Xynn added. "It'll help take the edge off."

. . . .

The crisp crack of blaster fire stung Lily's ears as she stepped into the shooting range. Caris stood in the far booth, hair pulled into a sharp ponytail, her stance a portrait of textbook precision. Malik leaned against the wall nearby, eyeing his weapon like someone had set him up on a double date with his cousin.

"Glad you changed your mind," Caris said, eyes still on the target.

"Did I?" Lily picked up a small blast pistol, weighing it. "Might just sit here and heckle."

"I'd be disappointed. I was hoping to watch you outshoot Malik again."

"Unfair," Malik muttered. "I'm a scientist, not a marksman. Or a time-traveling teen prodigy, or whatever."

Caris turned, pulling off a pair of safety goggles.

"Okay, full disclosure. I lured you here under false pretenses."

Lily frowned. "If you're about to try to draft me into a secret mission..."

"No one said 'drafted,'" Caris replied, glancing at Malik. "Did you say 'drafted'?"

Malik smirked but made no effort to rescue her.

Caris's expression shifted.

"Basco finished tracing the star charts Xynn decoded. They lead to... somewhere I thought you might be curious about."

Lily paused. "Where?"

Caris met her gaze. "Earth."

The silence that followed was small—but sharp.

Lily wordlessly took the blaster and stepped into the booth.

Earth.

Of course it had to be Earth. Now, of all times.

She hadn't wanted to go back since the day she stepped onto the *Salamander*. In truth, she hadn't even looked at Earth on a star map. She'd filed it away in the back of her mind, under a label that said *don't touch*.

Lily squeezed the trigger.

A single shot.

A perfect hit. The paper bandit crumpled.

In all her new beginnings, Earth had stayed locked in its box. Too distant to haunt her directly. Too close to forget entirely.

Caris stepped beside her as the target reset.

"The records we recovered don't make much sense. There's evidence of a connection to the storm cult on Earth—but nothing in Earth's own records. Calan has us headed there at maximum speed."

"I'm off-duty," Lily said quietly. "I am..."

She met Caris's eyes. "Leena, I've never tried to have a relationship before. I don't want to mess this up."

"I get it," Caris said softly. "Don't worry about it. I just thought you should have the choice."

Lily exhaled as the next target popped into place.

She aimed, steady now.

Breathed out.

Fired.

• • • •

The shuttle ride was unsettlingly smooth.

The air cradled them like a lullaby—too soft, too gentle, as if trying to lull Lily into a comfort she had to fight off. There was no turbulence, no unexpected jolts, just a silent glide through Earth's upper orbit. Her palms were damp. The last time she'd had a shuttle ride this smooth, it was going the other way—putting Earth in the rearview.

She stared out the viewport at the little blue marble below. Brighter than she remembered. Smaller, somehow.

The century she'd known was long gone, reduced to dust and data fragments.

It's not as if she had meant to leave forever. But part of her would've been fine if she had.

Still, she hadn't expected to feel it this deeply.

There was a swelling in her chest she couldn't easily categorize—grief, maybe. Grief and awe and something like resentment. Like Earth had moved on without her and hadn't bothered to even send a postcard.

They were headed toward what used to be London.

Caris had warned her—it wouldn't be recognizable.

"We Earth dwellers spent a lot of time in school learning about our history," she'd said. "After alien contact, Earth stayed mostly the same for about two hundred years. But once wealth stopped being the main driver of society, there were seismic culture shifts."

Lily hoped it really had changed.

—You need to go, Xynn had told her the night before, voice low and steady. You keep waiting for the right time. There's never a good time to revisit the past. Trust me.

Lily hadn't disagreed. She just hadn't expected this to happen so soon.

But Xynn was right. At least this way, she was working. She wasn't a tourist or a random nostalgic wanderer. It was a mission, and they'd be in and out—she could check it off the list and move on.

Her mind returned to the present, and she realized Caris was talking again.

"I'm one of the only humans in the *Salamander* crew to be born on Earth," Caris said, adjusting a display as the shuttle dipped into the upper atmosphere. "Most humans out here are from the Luna colonies or deep space. Earth culture became divided and somewhat arrested about two hundred years ago. Most Earth dwellers now don't like space travel."

Lily pulled her eyes from the window. "I thought Earth was some kind of a post-scarcity utopia?"

"Post-scarcity, yes. Utopia?" Caris sniffed. "Not exactly. Human achievements may be impressive, but the people are still human in every sense of the word. Flawed, paranoid, a bit prejudiced." She searched for the right word. "Divided."

Lily arched an eyebrow. "Divided?"

Caris took a beat. "There are two main governments now. The Hedon Republic—that's where I was raised—they value beauty above all else. But also indulgence, status, physical perfection. They use genetic manipulation to engineer their children for elegance. It's like aesthetic obsession turned into law."

"And the other?"

"The Ludon Corporation. Total rejection of technology. They believe simplicity is the path to happiness. Limited technology, no offworld trade unless it's filtered through layers of spiritual bureaucracy."

Lily looked thoughtful. "Well, there's nothing wrong with living simply."

"No," Caris said gently. "Not unless you're forced to. The Ludon mandate their simplicity, just like the Hedon mandate beauty. It's a binary system. Both sides demand conformity. And people like us... don't fit easily into either world."

Lily didn't respond right away.

She watched the clouds unfurl below the hull like ribbons of silk.

It hit her then—how little had changed. Not the cities or the governments, but the pattern. Even after all these centuries, humanity was still splitting itself in two. Still clinging to extremes like balance was too fragile to trust.

It made her sad, deeper than she wanted to admit.

Up front, Malik adjusted the shuttle's trajectory. He didn't say a word—just flew, focused, a quiet figure in the glow of navigation readouts. Lily watched him for a moment, wondering what was ticking behind those lavender markings.

Then the city came into view, glassy and strange, and Earth rose up to meet her again.

· · · ·

The shuttle came to rest with a delicate exhale of steam, like a mechanical sigh.

No bump. No hiss. Just a seamless transition from flight to stillness on a docking pad that gleamed like polished pearl, shaped into a sunburst that likely held no practical purpose beyond aesthetic drama.

Lily squinted out the viewport.

The city beyond looked like someone had turned a fairy tale into a corporate mandate.

Glistening towers curved like spiraled sugar, every structure dripping in pastels and metallics—rose gold, lilac, pearlescent teal. It was like landing inside a perfume ad directed by someone with a fabric budget and no sense of restraint.

The docking ramp unfurled in a silent, glowing arc. The air that met them smelled faintly of vanilla, citrus, and something floral Lily couldn't name.

She followed Caris down the ramp, her boots echoing against marble so pristine it reflected the sky. Malik trailed behind, silent, with his usual gruff expression—eyes scanning the horizon, studying the surroundings with clinical precision.

Lily's gaze landed on a large marble archway ahead. Its curved Tudor frame bore words etched deep in classical lettering:

BE NOT INHOSPITABLE TO STRANGERS,

LEST THEY BE ANGELS IN DISGUISE.

A delegation waited—two attendants in gowns that looked like glass, and one man dressed more simply, in a high-collared dark coat over iridescent slacks. He had a thoughtful face, a kind one—even if his cheekbones were absurdly symmetrical. When he smiled, Lily felt like she was being presented with an advertisement for veneers.

"Advisor Valen Meris," he said, bowing slightly. "Welcome to the Hedon Republic. We're honored to host the Salamander's delegation."

Caris returned the bow. "Thank you for receiving us."

Valen gestured toward the promenade, a corridor of archways and shifting light. "This way, if you please. The chamber is ready for your audience. We've prepared refreshment vapors—very fashionable right now—but water is available if you prefer tradition."

As they walked, Lily tried not to gawk—but it wasn't easy. They passed a shop called *Walking Shoe & Comfortable Shoe Emporium*, followed immediately by *The Place for Good Hair That You Like*. Further down was *The Café Restaurant That Has Coffee and Tea*.

Every sign was a kind of overly literal marketing haiku, determined to tell you exactly what it did and how. *Fine Food with Good Taste and Texture. The Shop for Outfits and Other Clothes...*

She glanced through a glass wall to her left and blinked.

There was a gallery—silent, reverent—where dozens of VHS tapes floated in individual magnetic suspension fields. They rotated slowly under glowing lights, their spines legible: *The Fast and the Furious, Hitch, Planet of the Apes* (2001). A plaque beneath read: *Ancient Dramatic Narratives, Circa 21st Century America.*

Across from it, another chamber: reverently displayed on pedestals, what appeared to be graphic novels. And papering the walls, pages from *The Bible.*

Valen noticed her slowing.

"We've entered the Harmonization District," he explained. "A place where our histories and philosophies are celebrated. And correlated. It's important to honor the past, by reinterpreting it for the modern day."

Lily didn't answer. Something about this version of Earth made the space between her eyes ache.

• • • •

They turned a corner and the architecture shifted again, becoming warmer, more golden. Lily realized the light was being diffused through walls made of recycled jewelry.

Valen glanced back at them. "I read about your contributions to the war last year, Ms. Starling. While we Earth dwellers aren't much for keeping up with offworld affairs, during the war it did become a habit—keeping up on things. I read you came from the 20th century."

"Y2K problems..." Lily started to joke, then paused.

Valen smiled. "Ah, I get the reference. The potentially catastrophic software glitch that briefly caused mass panic and large-scale groupthink—resulting in the hoarding of food at the turn of the 21st century. Very clever."

Lily managed a forced laugh through her teeth.

Valen continued. "So all of this must seem unfamiliar to you."

"A little," she admitted. "At least... not exactly what I expected."

"Ah, well. Our culture will teach you to never have high expectations," Valen said. "We make our status certain."

There was a pause—long enough that Lily almost let it go. But she caught something in his tone. A note of distance. Or regret.

"Are you from the capital?" she asked.

"Oh yes. Born and raised," Valen replied. "In the next district over, in fact. Attended the Academy of Refinement. Learned the Eight Pillars of Aesthetic Harmony. Well—most of them, anyway. I always did struggle with symmetrical genetics."

Caris smiled faintly. "Valen's being modest. He's one of the youngest ever appointed to the Prime Minister's advisory cabinet."

Lily nodded, still trying to piece him together—a man composed of symmetry and contradiction.

Valen exhaled, the sound almost wistful. "When I was younger, I thought I could change things. Bridge gaps. There was a program—years ago, back when such things were still considered... acceptable. Outreach. Dialogue with our neighbors in the Ludon Corporation."

That caught Lily's attention. "You actually met with them?"

"More than that," Valen said softly. "I mingled. I spent weeks at a time among them. Learned their customs. Shared meals. Wrote poetry under lanterns strung between trees."

Lily raised an eyebrow. "Was that risky?"

"Yes, indeed." His smile turned fragile. "I was nearly removed from my family estate. Spoke at a tribunal. One advisor referred to me as 'culturally unstable.'"

"What happened?" Caris asked, her voice quieter now.

Valen looked forward, like the memory was something sharp he still couldn't quite hold. "I fell in love. With a Ludon girl from a prominent family. Very Shakespearean. Simini—she was brilliant, stubborn, thoughtful in that way that makes you want to argue just to hear her win."

The silence that followed wasn't awkward—it was reverent.

"But in the end, I agreed with my family. I accepted my first post at the capital. Eventually, she stopped writing. I don't blame her." He shifted his expression back to his false enthusiasm. "We all make compromises."

They walked in silence for a moment. Just long enough for Lily to feel the weight of the past brushing up against the present.

Then Valen gestured toward the towering glass archway at the end of the hall.

"The chamber is just ahead."

• • • •

The audience chamber was grand in the way luxury tips into excess when no one ever says no—oversized, overlit, and gilded to the point of unreality, like something conjured from a sybarite fantasy.

At the center, on a dais shaped like a curling ribbon, sat the Prime Minister of Hedonia—a man draped in what looked like a red velvet bathrobe from a children's nativity pageant, complete with glittering trim and faux pearls. A massive gold headdress framed his face, connected by a delicate chain to a polished nose ring that looped through his septum. He puffed rhythmically on a long, bejeweled pipe, releasing great clouds of purple vapor that smelled unmistakably of licorice and cloves.

Surrounding him stood his attendants—or what Lily at first assumed were props. They were each draped entirely in lace and gold sheets, like ghosts at a couture fashion show, with oversized Coca-Cola bottle caps affixed to the tops of their heads, each one glowing gently like a halo from a vending machine.

"Welcome," the Prime Minister intoned. "Children of Earth, returned to the cosmic wellspring. You are beloved."

He clapped his hands. "And there will be a banquet!"

Caris stepped forward with a bow. "Prime Minister, thank you for receiving us. Your hospitality is greatly appreciated."

"We shall serve sparkling nectars and delicacies shaped in tribute to ancient Earth fauna," he said solemnly. "You will be honored. And gently refreshed. That is our tradition."

Lily hid a smirk. The Prime Minister seemed just a little off his rocker—but then she noticed that Caris looked serious.

Caris cleared her throat. "Before we begin the festivities, we were hoping to ask a few questions. We're conducting an investigation that concerns possible... cult activity."

The Prime Minister froze. His posture stiffened, his pipe paused mid-puff. Slowly, he set it down.

His face had turned the exact shade as his robe.

"I—I'm afraid my ear will not register that topic," he said. He tilted his head and looked down his nose at Caris like she was a child. "We do not use that word. It is considered... impolite."

Valen's eyes flicked toward them—a barely perceptible warning.

Caris pressed, gently. "We've encountered signals—patterns—suggesting the presence of a religious movement that may be destabilizing. If there's any record of unusual gatherings, offworld influence..."

"No such gatherings exist," the Prime Minister said quickly. "None that are unapproved. All spiritual celebrations are beautified and recorded for emotional compliance."

Lily stepped in. "Prime Minister, with respect, we don't mean to judge. We're just trying to track down a threat."

"There is no threat," he snapped. "There is only harmony."

Caris tried one more time, her voice low. "We've seen this before. On other worlds. We have reason to believe Earth is a site of resurgence."

"You must stop," the Prime Minister hissed, leaning back. "You cannot speak such things here. You will attract something... unbalanced. You will invite discord. We do not speak of cults."

Caris held up her hands. "I didn't mean to offend—if you'd prefer to speak privately—"

"No! You must leave. Now. We are done."

He rose and swept from the dais, his headdress clinking as he disappeared behind a gilded curtain. The attendants did not follow.

Instead, they turned toward the crew—silent, in perfect unison.

Lily took a breath. Her heart was ticking too fast.

That... spiraled fast.

The ghost-like attendants began to drift forward, pressing closer with every step.

"They're not armed," Malik muttered, "but we're clearly no longer welcome."

The attendants murmured to others in the gallery. Faces turned—once polite, now tight with suspicion. Someone pulled a baton from beneath a silk sleeve. Another, a gilded ceremonial blade shaped like a sickle.

The crowd surged, sudden and silent, like a wave breaking without sound.

A figure lunged—blade flashing—and Malik grunted as the sickle sliced across his thigh, blood soaking into his uniform like ink spilled on a page.

Valen stepped forward, voice low and taut. "There's a maintenance corridor—down the hall, gray door at the end. Go. Now."

They didn't wait to deliberate.

Lily grabbed Caris's arm and pivoted toward the far corridor, the bright lights around them suddenly too loud, too sweet. The scent of citrus turned cloying. The floor beneath her boots felt like it might vanish.

The corridor was narrow and twisting, shadows curling at the edges. Their footsteps echoed like alarms in Lily's ears.

"There!" she shouted, spotting the gray door. She yanked it open.

Inside: silence. Pipes. Dust. The flicker of tired fluorescents, buzzing faintly like a warning no one had bothered to heed.

They scanned the room.

"Nowhere to run," Caris said.

Lily's eyes landed on a rusted hatch near the floor. The lettering above it read: MUNICIPAL WASTE EJECTION TUBE.

Malik groaned. "Don't tell me..."

Caris shrugged. "Could be worse. Could be sewage."

Lily pried the hatch open. It moved with a reluctant whine, the metal scraping like it hadn't been touched in years. She hesitated—just long enough to hear the echo of footfalls drawing closer—then swung her legs inside and slid down on her back like a kid at a playground.

The ride was fast. And deeply regrettable from a hygiene perspective.

They landed in a heap on a bed of mixed refuse—soft, sticky, and a kick to the head of foul smells. Caris popped up, brushing food fragments from her uniform.

Lily smirked. "Okay. No more diplomatic missions."

• • • •

They pulled themselves out of the trash pile and looked around.

The alley was narrow and still, lit by a single flickering wall-lamp. Around them, buildings rose tall and hunched—not sleek towers or gold-wrapped castles, but the weight of old construction: concrete, brick, steel. Some windows were boarded. Others, cracked and hollow. Every wall bore the ghost of some message—scrawled phrases, most barely covered by layers of paint trying too hard to wipe them out.

Lily stepped forward and squinted at a shuttered storefront across the street.

"This is what passes for paradise now? In a post-scarcity society?"

Caris wiped her hands on her jacket, grimacing. "Post-scarcity doesn't mean post-prejudice."

"There's no money," Lily said. "How can there still be this kind of inequality?"

Caris glanced at her, eyes tired. "Money's never been the only thing that made people hate each other."

Lily didn't argue. But behind her eyes, something stirred—a quiet protest, unanswered but wishing things were different.

Malik finally spoke, his voice quiet. "I didn't know it was this bad. Last time I spent time on Earth, it was weird... but I didn't see anything like this. This—" He paused, scanning the buildings.

Caris nodded. "It's a lot to process, I know."

Malik touched his tongue to his lip. "I was going to say it sucks."

They moved cautiously down the alley. The air was still damp with garbage and spice vapor drifting down from the upper city. Somewhere in the distance, a speaker crackled with Hedonian string music—bright and hollow as a toy.

That's when they saw it.

Tucked between a cracked concrete pillar and a rusted fence stood a building that looked... ordinary. Simple red brick, a little worn, a little sturdy. Like an old hotel, or maybe a converted apartment block. No gleaming signage. No floating holograms. No perfume fountains.

Just a single carved wooden sign above the entrance, brass-mounted and gently lit from below.

On the left: a fish.

On the right: a feathered wing.

In clean serif letters, it read:

SCALES AND FEATHERS

Lily tilted her head. "Okay. A welcome change from the painfully literal, but now we've gone full ambiguity."

They stood there a moment longer, all three of them quietly stalling, hesitant to choose a direction.

Malik glanced at Caris. "You're leading the mission."

Caris gave a faint smile. "We're all lieutenants here..."

Lily rolled her eyes. "Can we just go inside? I'll take whatever's in there over whatever the hell that was up there."

Caris nodded. She and Lily pushed the door open in unison.

· · · ·

The lobby was warm in that quiet, old-world comfort kind of way. Not dirty—just worn. Lived-in. The kind of place that had seen its share of rain and stories.

The floor was scuffed tile. A threadbare rug led to a low desk flanked by mismatched chairs. Two people played checkers in the corner. A woman read to a child. Someone snored softly behind a half-closed hallway door.

This was different from the Hedonian promenade in the most important way.

It was human.

Lily took a breath—and felt her heart rate ease, just slightly. Something almost normal. She hadn't realized how much she needed to see it.

A voice called from behind the desk.

"Well," the voice was warm and dry, unmistakably amused, "did you folks just drop out of the sky or what?"

They turned.

A woman leaned on the counter with one elbow. She had a buzzcut, dyed a fading shade of purple, a well-worn jacket, and the eyes of someone who'd seen too much.

Her face was almost like unlocking a memory. Something buried in a place also forgotten.

Malik raised an eyebrow. "You're more right than you know."

"You're not from around here," the woman said, folding her arms. "Humans, sure—but Union humans. And a Cyranthian. Not common in this zone. Been a while since I've seen fleet uniforms in my place."

Lily rubbed her forehead, still trying to catch up. She mumbled the words before she realized she was saying them.

"I think we just got violently ejected from that marble shopping mall for saying the word *cult*."

The woman laughed—short, surprised, genuine. "Yeah, that sounds about right.

And it sounds like you might be my kind of people. Even if you are fleet issue."

She stepped out from behind the desk and offered her hand.

"Name's Trish," she said. "Welcome to Scales and Feathers. Sit down. You look like you could use something normal. And maybe a drink."

Trish motioned for them to sit at a half-circle booth near the front desk. The seats were patched but clean, and the table wore the faint scuff marks of years of quiet use.

"This," she said, "is Trish's home for misfits and outsiders."

Lily dropped into the booth. The upholstery creaked with a tired sigh.

"The Happiness Hotel," she murmured.

Trish blinked, one brow raised—but moved on without comment.

"Whether you're up in Opal Tower land or down in the floodwoods, nobody really makes room for people like us. So I made one."

Malik tilted his head. "People like you? You seem... how can I put this. Normal. At least not like the rest of the performance we've been seeing."

Caris shifted beside him, gaze lowering toward her shoes. Something in her posture made Lily pause.

Trish caught it too.

"You're Hedonian, aren't you?"

Caris nodded. "Yeah. After my parents died, I was in foster care. Eventually ended up on the Lunar Colonies. Probably the best thing that could've happened, to be honest."

Trish nodded, then turned her attention to Lily, eyes sweeping her up and down. "You're really not from around here, are you?"

Lily hesitated. "It's... a long story."

Trish leaned back, her smile crooked. "Let me guess. You're from the past."

A beat.

"Ha!" Trish laughed, shaking her head. "Well, damn. First try."

Lily managed a smile.

"I'll give you the short version," Trish said, folding her arms. "If you're normal, you're weird. And if you're weird, you're normal. That's how it's always been—and I imagine how it always will be. Now, more than ever."

She paused. The edge of amusement faded.

"Before I came here, I had a job with the Union. Not a desk job, either. I was out there. Intelligence. Strategy. I was good at it."

Her tone stayed light, but Lily could hear the shift underneath.

"When I transitioned, I figured nothing would change. You'd think, after a couple hundred years of galactic tolerance, people would've grown past that kind of thing. But... well."

She shrugged.

"They started giving me assignments nobody wanted. Took me out of the field. One friend in the brass told me, in confidence, I was 'operationally confusing.'"

Trish mimed air quotes, but there was a darkness behind her smile.

"That's Union-speak for *we don't know what box to put you in anymore.* Back when I shaved my face every morning, no one had a problem knowing where I belonged."

She looked down at her hands. When her gaze returned to Lily, it was calm—not bitter.

"I don't even remember what made me come back to Earth. Maybe I thought it'd be simpler. It wasn't. But it was... more complicated." She laughed softly. "So I set up this place. A little gravity well for people who float between categories. Just trying to give folks a place to land."

Lily didn't answer right away. The words hit her like they'd been waiting. Because it didn't sound like the future.

It sounded exactly like the past.

. . . .

The checkers game in the corner clicked quietly on. Somewhere behind them, a kettle hissed.

Lily sat still, Trish's words clinging to her like static, when Caris leaned forward—gently pulling them back into the moment.

"We really appreciate your kindness. Truly. But we need to ask for your help," she said. "We're following a lead—fragmented data connected to an ancient storm cult. It brought us here."

Trish folded her arms, watching her carefully.

"I see." She narrowed her eyes. "What exactly do you expect to find?"

"I don't know—some kind of sleeper cell?" Caris said. "Something tied to the cult. We're mostly flying blind, but we need to figure out the next move. Leviathan's Hand is always one step ahead."

At that, Trish straightened. Her amusement vanished. Her voice shifted. "Okay. Here we go."

She crossed behind the counter, pulled up a data slate, and tapped in a sequence with deliberate precision.

"I didn't work the file directly," she said, "but I reviewed it—back when I was still in Union intel. I ran an operative investigating secret societies. Your friends were on the list."

Malik raised an eyebrow. "Small galaxy."

"Don't I know it," Trish said. "We were prepping for worst-case reactivation—this was nearly a decade ago, when it looked like the storm might swing back through Union space. I don't know what's happened since, but your information is accurate. There was a branch of Leviathan's Hand here. Hidden in plain sight."

Caris leaned in. "Can you point us in the right direction?"

Trish hesitated.

"You'll have to head out into the floodwood territories. The old river plains. Technically Ludon territory now—but there are fringe colonies out there. People who live off-grid—culturally and politically."

"Do you know anyone there?"

Before Trish could answer, a voice cut in from a few feet away.

"Sorry—I didn't mean to eavesdrop. But I couldn't help overhearing."

They turned.

A Cyranthian man stepped forward from one of the hallways. He was tall and broad-shouldered, his skin faintly iridescent in the low light. He looked at Malik with quiet recognition.

"It's good to see a brother here," he said. "I'm from a mixed colony. Humans and Cyranthians, living together out in the floodwood near one of the Ludon enclaves. We've kept to ourselves, but... we've seen things. Heard things."

He looked to Trish, then back to the group.

"If you're heading out there, you'll need someone who knows the paths. I'd be more than happy to guide you."

Lily watched Trish carefully.

She didn't speak at first, but her gaze lingered on the man—searching, maybe. Then she gave a small nod. Not permission, exactly. But a kind of trust.

Caris looked between them and gave a decisive nod. "We don't have time to vet alternatives. If you're willing to guide us, we'll take it."

The man nodded sharply. "Name's Delen. Get some rest, we'll leave bright and early."

• • • •

The stars over the city were faint, dulled by the shimmer of atmospheric filtering and ambient light.

But they were still there.

Lily sat cross-legged on the rooftop, jacket zipped to her throat, watching them like they might rearrange themselves into answers. Beside her, Caris had been sitting in companionable silence—until she stood.

"I have to go sew Malik's leg up," she said. "That nick from the ceremonial blade is really more of a gash."

Lily nodded. Caris turned to leave—then paused.

"I always think of my brother when I look up at the moon," she said. "I'm proud of him. Starting a family on the lunar colonies. We went through a lot together.

He's always been a rock, you know? The kind of person you can rely on."

Lily looked up at her and smiled, a little crooked. "I may know one or two people like that."

Caris returned the smile, then disappeared down the stairwell.

A moment later, Lily could hear them below—quiet voices, the scrape of a medkit. Trish had set them up in spare rooms, brought tea steeped in unfamiliar spices.

Lily knew she should go sleep.

But Earth wouldn't let her rest.

Her mind was a whirl of all the things she'd been dancing around. She hadn't avoided coming back to Earth because she was afraid of what had changed—but because of what hadn't.

And, unfortunately, her instincts had been right. The division. The prejudice. Absolutism forged into law, decorated with traditions.

Splitting the social order apart for insignificant reasons, then doubling down and insisting those divided could never coexist.

And it made something old and familiar ache inside her.

The worst ache—worry.

Lily hated worry most of all, because it was unproductive.

But she couldn't help it. She worried that time didn't fix anything.

That the future was building on the same cracked foundation as the past.

But then she thought of Caris. Of her foster brother, out on the lunar colonies.

Two people who had no reason to trust, no reason to love—but they looked out for each other anyway. Building something beautifully human out of the shards they were given.

Maybe we can't change everything. But we can still show up for each other.

Lily's mind snapped back.

Movement caught her eye—a shadow near the roof's edge, cloaked and still.

She straightened slowly.

The figure raised empty hands, then pulled the hood back just enough for moonlight to catch his face.

"Trish said you might be up here," he said.

Lily blinked. "Valen?"

He raised a hand in a hush, eyes scanning the rooftop. "I shouldn't be here," he said, softer now. "But after what happened... I felt I owed you."

The words hung between them, suspended in the chill.

"Owed us?" Lily asked, her voice low.

Valen hesitated. The wind tugged at the hem of his cloak.

"Information," he said finally. "I have information for you."

Lily didn't answer. She just watched him, measuring his voice, his posture.

He looked tired. Not physically—something deeper.

Worn down at the edges.

"You must go into the floodwoods," Valen said. "But that's only half the journey.

The Ludon girl I fell in love with—Simini—her sister, Eira, rules now. She may be willing to help you."

There was a shift in his tone. He wasn't speaking as a politician now.

This was personal.

"Leviathan's Hand is there," he added. "In the floodwoods."

Lily took a step closer, her voice low. "How do you know?"

Valen looked away.

"They took her," he said. "Simini. Years ago." He met Lily's eyes. "She became one of them."

Lily blinked. That wasn't what she expected.

"I led a search team," Valen went on. "We traced them to an arctic relay station near Pituffik."

He swallowed.

"But when we got there... it was already too late. The base was—dead."

Lily's stomach twisted. "Dead as in... deserted?"

Valen shook his head. "Dead as in, some sort of ritual. Hundreds of bodies."

Lily's flesh crawled. "I'm so sorry. And Simini?"

He cleared his throat. "No trace of her."

He looked at Lily then—without his usual polish—with the grief of someone who still yearned for answers.

"After that," he said quietly, "things fell apart with Eira. I was no longer welcome among the Ludon. So I came home. Took my family position. Tried my best to forget."

Lily didn't know what to say. Her throat felt dry.

"Thank you," she managed.

Valen pulled something from his coat—a small black transponder, polished and plain.

"Here," he said, placing it gently in her hand. "In case you need me. Page me with this—I'll call you back as soon as I'm able."

He stepped back, the cloak folding around him like earth covering a grave.

"Good luck," he said simply.

And then he was gone.

Lily stood alone on the rooftop, the transponder cool in her palm.

She stared at it for a long moment.

Then tapped her comm tag.

"Lily to Captain Calan," she said softly.

"We have a new problem."

Ashes From Heaven

SALAMANDER LOG: CAPTAIN Calan — Supplemental Entry

Valen Meris—a minor Earth politician—isn't exactly a sanctioned mission source. But Lily trusts him. And I trust Lily.

According to Valen, a search party years ago traced Leviathan's Hand to a remote Arctic relay station near Pituffik. By the time they arrived, the base had become a grave. A mass ritual suicide, he said. Hundreds dead. The report was buried—sealed beneath diplomacy and shame. But the coordinates stayed with him.

Lily relayed this to me the night before last. I told her I would look into it myself. If there's even a chance that site holds answers, we need to uncover whatever's there.

The mission is off-books. If it goes south, the responsibility will fall on me. I won't risk the crew.

Meanwhile, Malik has stayed behind in the Shonn village to spend time with the Cyranthian–human settlement. Caris and Lily continue toward the Ludon enclaves with their guide. That leaves me just enough room to slip off the grid for a few hours and check the Arctic site myself.

The terrain is unforgiving—hazardous in ways that don't show up on Union maps. Fortunately, I've called in someone who knows it better than I do. Someone I can trust. Someone who won't ask too many questions.

· · · ·

The shuttle banked low over the northern ice shelf, its hull creaking in protest as the temperature dropped. Earth's polar curve stretched beneath him in bruised shades of blue and bone. The clouds clawed slowly, pulled by ancient winds that hadn't known warmth in centuries.

Calan steadied the controls. The terrain below looked smooth from orbit, but he knew better. Beneath that pale crust, the ice was a shifting ruin—laced with buried faults and sink zones sharp enough to swallow a ship whole.

He tapped the comm.

"*Salamander,* this is Calan. I'm minutes from the descent corridor. Did you get a hold of Caris's foster brother?"

Dryst Amaris's voice crackled back through the static in his usual upbeat tone. "Mr. Javi Rix is en route. I'm sending you rendezvous coordinates. Meet him at the north ridge, just west of the flare tower."

"Excellent. And we're sure he's the man for this?"

"Leena insisted we contact him, sir," Amaris said. "He knows that region better than anyone. As Lunatron's lead archaeologist, he ran salvage ops and dig site logistics around there for ten years. He's mapped more of the Arctic zone than anyone the fleet's got on payroll. You're in good hands."

Calan nodded to himself. Amaris seemed to sense it through the channel.

"He's quiet," Amaris added. "But smart. Probably already has theories about why you're out there."

"Well, hopefully he doesn't let his imagination run too wild."

There was a pause—long enough to let the subtext settle.

Calan continued. "Just to confirm—no follow-up unless I issue an override?"

A beat, then: "Affirmative. This stays between us unless something hits the fan."

"Copy that." Calan's tone dropped, more gravel now. "I want this responsibility on me. No blowback for the crew."

"You've said that three times now, Captain."

"Just making sure it's on the record."

A soft exhale on the line. "Be safe down there, Captain."

• • • •

The shuttle dipped into cloud cover, the outer hull frosting over in sheets of glassy white. Warning lights flickered once, then cleared. The ship stabilized.

Through the mist, the plateau emerged—flat and desolate, broken only by a half-buried signal tower blinking faintly in the wind.

Calan brought the shuttle down in a slow hover. No turbulence. No alarms. Just the hush of landing struts meeting frozen stone.

He pulled on his coat and gloves, checked the seal, and popped the hatch.

Cold rushed in like a held breath finally exhaled.

"It had to be the cold, didn't it?" Calan muttered, steeling himself.

He stepped into the wind.

The cold hit like a slap, raw and immediate. Calan pulled his collar tighter, breath already fogging the air in short, irritated bursts. The wind came from the east—sharp, slicing, relentless.

Still no sign of Javi.

He turned back to the shuttle and popped the aft compartment. The portable scanner was heavier than it looked, especially with numb fingers, but he dragged it across the ice with practiced efficiency.

"If I wait, I wait," he muttered. "If I don't, at least we're not wasting daylight."

He dropped to one knee, flipped open the scanner's tripod, and started punching in boot diagnostics. The wind tugged at his sleeves, nipped at his ears. He ignored it.

"Joren would love this," he muttered dryly. "Frozen deathscape. Impending doom. High adventure."

He could almost hear his husband's voice, chipper and relentless: *Let's do that hike on Icaros Ridge—the one with the sudden drops! It'll be romantic!*

"At least if I transfer to the Vanguard, I can make him come with me," Calan said aloud, adjusting the scanner's alignment scope. "Force him to spend quality time somewhere cold and miserable. See how he likes it."

His fingers hesitated for a second on the tuning dial.

He thought of Joren's mother—sharp-eyed, fluent in sarcasm, never met a boundary she respected.

You and Joren should think about grandkids, she'd said last time he was planetside on New Sicily, ladling tomato sauce like it was holy water.

He'd laughed. Joren had said something vaguely hopeful, and without missing a beat, she'd snorted, *Griff doesn't like kids.*

Calan exhaled through his nose.

"Griff doesn't like kids," he repeated aloud.

A beat passed. The wind didn't disagree.

He stood, bracing the tripod against a gust, and reached to unclip the second sensor node from its mount. The strap snagged on the side rail. He tugged harder.

Just come on, he muttered—and then the ice cracked.

It wasn't loud. Just a clean, crystalline snap, like a sheet of glass kissed too sharply.

The ground gave under his boots.

The scanner, the tripod, half the mount—gone in an instant. Sliding, tipping, swallowed by the earth. Calan yelped as the surface tilted under him and his own weight followed. He grabbed for anything—anything—and his gloved hand found a strap still looped through the shuttle's forward strut.

It caught. Barely.

He dangled there, boots kicking against empty air, the pit beneath him a sudden wound in the ice, dark and hungry.

The strap began to slip.

Not all at once—just a slow, whispering shift. A few millimeters at a time, like the ice was thinking it over.

In the back of his mind, Calan hoped the fall would kill him quickly. A clean break. No slow agony. No freezing to death at the bottom of a pit with his ribs in the wrong places.

"Damn," he managed, voice tight as the loop gave another fractional tug.

He gritted his teeth, brought his right hand up and across with careful precision. His shoulders screamed. The strap moaned.

There was no way he could climb without shifting his weight. And the second he shifted, the strap would come loose. He knew that. But he had to try.

He managed to get both hands on the strap. It held. For now.

He exhaled through clenched teeth, every muscle braced for the inevitable.

And then he heard it.

Barking.

He looked up, blinking through the glare. A large husky was bounding toward him across the snow, barking sharply as it ran.

The dog reached the edge of the pit and stopped. Met Calan's eyes with a calm, intelligent stillness. As if to say: *Well. This is unusual.*

"I don't suppose you brought a rope," Calan muttered.

The dog tilted her head.

Then turned and ran.

Calan blinked after her, confused, suspended above the void by a strap that was definitely not going to hold.

Back to despair, then.

But only for a moment.

The husky reappeared, bounding through the snow—this time with a thick coil of rope clutched in her mouth. She dropped it near the edge, tail wagging. The end slid down into the pit, already tied into a perfect bowline.

Calan stared at it. Then slipped the loop around his chest and under his arms. It tightened, snug and ready.

Just in time.

The strap gave way.

His stomach lurched as he dropped—then jerked hard against the new line. The rope held. He swung in the open air, spinning slowly, boots scuffing against the ice wall.

He looked up, breath fogging fast.

The dog was there again, watching. Tongue out. Tail swishing gently.

"What's your name?" Calan asked. "Thanks for the assist."

A voice answered from above.

"You didn't expect her to reply, did you?"

Calan looked up further.

"That's an Earth dog. A Chukotka husky. And her name is Amber."

The rope tightened with a mechanical tug—slow and steady. A winch.

Calan rose toward the edge in short, jerking increments. The cold bit at his face. Snowflakes caught in his lashes.

When he reached the top, a gloved hand reached down to help haul him up.

He found himself eye-to-eye with a tall man—fair-skinned, black-haired, all angles and focus. The kind of face that didn't often smile but didn't miss much either.

"Javi Rix, I presume?" Calan asked, panting.

Javi gave him a flat, unimpressed look.

"Captain Impatient, I presume."

Calan dusted snow from his coat and crouched slightly to pat the dog.

"Beautiful dog you have here," he offered, still catching his breath.

Javi raised an eyebrow. "Please don't talk about her like she's not standing right in front of you."

Calan blinked.

"She's not my property. She lives with me," Javi added flatly. "You're your own being, aren't you, Amber?"

The husky barked once, sharp and approving.

Calan straightened slowly, internally recalibrating. *Okay,* he thought. *So he's one of those.*

Not that he had anything against dog people. But there was something in the way Javi said it—in that unwavering, deadpan conviction—that made Calan wonder if he'd just signed up for a long hike with a man who held philosophical debates with his pets.

Still. He'd saved his life. That counted for something.

"How much equipment did you lose?" Javi asked, already surveying the pit.

Calan turned toward the void, lips thinning. "There's another set on the shuttle."

Javi nodded. "Good. I recommend you don't go wandering."

Calan glanced back at him.

"This entire area is unstable," Javi added, as if pointing out the weather. "It's not just the surface—it's the shelf. The deeper glacial strata are fractured. The wrong vibration can open a fissure without warning."

"Noted," Calan said.

He looked again at the edge of the pit where Amber now sat, regal and completely unbothered.

"Thanks again," he muttered.

"Thank her," Javi replied.

Amber gave a soft *woof,* then sneezed into the wind.

"So you're Leena's captain."

Calan nodded, adjusting the strap on his jacket. "She's one of our best officers."

"I don't doubt it," Javi said, matter-of-fact.

A long silence followed as Javi turned back to the sled and began unloading more equipment. The wind picked up in brief gusts—sharp and dry, like it was sanding down the edges of the world.

"Sorry," Javi said eventually, without looking up. "I'm not good at small talk."

Calan nodded again. "It's okay. I'm ready to get to work."

He scanned the open white stretch around them. "According to the few records I could find, the base should be right beneath us."

"Don't forget the shifting," Javi replied. "It could be anywhere within an eight-mile radius."

He pointed toward the lone beacon jutting out of the snow—tall, skeletal, and blinking faintly into the pale sky.

"That marker goes down about a mile into the earth. It's the only thing around here still where it was back when those bases were operational. Everything else got swallowed two years ago. And they were ruins already by then."

Calan exhaled through his nose, tightening his jacket against the wind. "Why would the storm cult set up here?"

"Well," Javi said, slinging a pack over one shoulder, "for one, it's a good place to hide out."

He started walking toward the beacon, voice carrying easily in the dry air. "But also—I've excavated sites all over this region. Ancient extraterrestrial landing zones, discovered in the 2390s."

Calan followed, eyes narrowed.

Javi continued, "Their belief systems were all centered around extreme weather phenomena. Storms, auroras, seismic shifts. They worshipped the sky when it turned violent."

He looked back once, expression unreadable.

"Ring a bell?"

Calan slowed slightly, glancing up at the sky, now a dull silver-white with no horizon.

"I doubt that's a coincidence," he said.

• • • •

The beacon tower groaned faintly as the wind shifted. It rose like a spine out of the snow, skeletal and steady, blinking a dull red pulse into the Arctic haze.

Javi crouched beside the scanner case, his gloved fingers working through clasps with surprising delicacy. Calan stood nearby, watching the ice horizon, breathing in the quiet between gusts.

"This is the one I've been reading about," Javi said suddenly, a flicker of excitement entering his voice—surprising Calan. "Union prototype—uses subglacial harmonic pulses to map density gradients through layers of bedrock and melt zones. Most field scientists won't get their hands on one for another two years."

Calan blinked. "Good to see you excited about something."

Javi didn't look up. "It uses a new kind of pulse scan."

He flipped open the lid and tapped a sequence on the touchscreen. The machine thrummed faintly, then gave off a low harmonic pulse that buzzed in the soles of their boots.

Amber, who'd been lounging beside a snowdrift like a furry sphinx, perked up and tilted her head.

Calan raised an eyebrow. "Is that normal?"

"She's not a fan of seismic feedback." Javi adjusted a dial, brow furrowed. "Hm."

"Hm?" Calan echoed, tightening the strap on his shoulder harness.

"I think we just triggered a microquake."

Calan turned. "Excuse me?"

"These pulse arrays haven't been tested in Arctic environments yet," Javi said, not sounding particularly concerned. "It's fascinating. The resonant harmonics are interacting with the fault lines below. That's a lot of data we didn't have before."

"Fault lines?" Calan clipped. "I don't like the sound of that."

Amber stood up now, ears twitching, fur rising along her spine. She gave a sharp bark.

Javi glanced at her. "Hmm. Probably bad."

Then the ground started to move.

"Make that definitely bad."

It wasn't a slow drift—but a sharp, tearing lurch that cracked beneath their feet. The scanner slid sideways. Calan grabbed for it instinctively—but then the snow gave way beneath all of them.

Calan barely had time to shout. The snow dropped out from under his boots, and suddenly the world tilted, spun, and roared.

He landed hard on his back, the wind knocked clean from his lungs. The scanner case skidded past him, bounced once, and vanished into the dark. A second later, something thudded beside him—Javi, landing in a practiced roll.

Above them, the hole they'd fallen through was already starting to blur, snow drifting in from the edges—soft, silent, uncaring. Amber's silhouette appeared at the rim—ears high, tail stiff.

"Everyone intact?" Javi called, already on his feet and brushing off snow.

Calan groaned. "Define intact."

Javi offered a hand and hauled him up with a surprising amount of strength. "I've had worse falls."

"Not something to aspire to," Calan muttered, brushing frost from his sleeves. He turned in a slow circle, taking in their new surroundings.

They were in a massive ice cavern—natural, mostly. The walls glittered like pale glass, laced with sediment bands and the faint outlines of ancient stonework. The artificial structures looked alien to Calan, though they reminded him faintly of what he'd seen on Bimara. Some of it was Union-era. Most of it looked much older.

Javi lifted his lamp and swept the beam across the chamber.

Embedded in one wall was what remained of the original outpost—crumpled steel, torn insulation, a snapped support pylon dangling like a rusted stalactite. Stripped wiring coiled from the walls like veins. It looked less like a collapse and more like a consumed thing—half-digested by the ice.

"The base," Javi murmured. "What's left of it."

"Anything we can pull data from?" Calan asked, scanning the wreckage with a sharp eye.

"Probably not." Javi stepped forward, pulling a scanner module from his coat. "But we can still gather information—energy signatures, power residue, environmental data."

"Data that tells us what happened here?" Calan asked.

"Or what they were trying to cover up."

Amber barked once above them, then leapt gracefully into the cavern through a narrower break in the ice wall. She landed with a huff, sniffed once, and padded toward a cluster of half-frozen crates.

"She does that a lot," Calan observed.

"She has opinions," Javi replied.

They began moving carefully, scanning as they went. What remained of the base was hollow—gutted long ago. No consoles. No personal effects. No remains.

"Someone wiped this," Calan said. "Clean."

"Intentional." Javi gestured toward a jagged hole in the wall. "That wasn't collapse. That was shaped—probably demolition charges."

"But why leave the beacon?" Calan asked. "Why leave anything?"

"Maybe they wanted someone to find it," Javi said. "Or maybe they didn't expect anyone to survive long enough to care."

He turned, swept the scanner once more—and froze.

"There's something beneath us."

Calan stepped closer. "More ruins?"

"No." Javi adjusted the signal, then knelt beside a sheet of compacted snow. "This is artificial. Cylindrical. Reinforced framing."

He looked up, eyes catching Calan's.

"It's a shaft. An old elevator system. I think we're standing on the roof of a buried access tunnel."

Calan exhaled slowly. "How deep?"

Javi checked the reading again. "Deep."

He followed the scan outline on his device and used a second tool—something that looked, to Calan, like a black light—to sweep along the surface. Faint edges appeared in the frost, catching violet glints. Javi scraped away a layer of snow and ice with his gloved hand, revealing the outline of a metal access hatch—circular, pitted with age, and stamped with an unfamiliar alien script barely visible beneath the corrosion.

Calan crouched beside him. "This doesn't look like standard relay infrastructure."

"No," Javi said. "Reminds me of Bimaran architecture from two centuries ago. Never heard of anything like it showing up on Earth—and I thought I'd seen every ancient alien dig site on the record."

He popped a latch open with a small tool from his belt. The hatch groaned, then hissed as a sliver of stale air escaped—thick and chemical, like abandoned filtration systems and melted plastic.

Amber whined softly behind them.

"Can she make it through?" Calan asked.

"She can squeeze through tighter places than I can," Javi said. "If she doesn't want to go, it's not because she can't."

He adjusted his lamp, narrowing the beam to illuminate the shaft below. It stretched far beneath them, metal rungs lining one side—many bent or broken. A few thick cables hung slack, tangling like vines. At the bottom, just barely visible, was the curved top of another hatch, half-open.

"This is well preserved," Javi murmured. "Untouched for two hundred years."

Calan peered into the dark, exhaling slowly. "How far down?"

Javi tapped his scanner. "About half a kilometer."

Calan raised an eyebrow. "You want to climb half a kilometer into the Earth?"

"I brought the gear," Javi said. "You can never be too prepared." He gestured to the opening. "We can't stop now."

Calan gave him a look—but he couldn't argue.

Javi was already unpacking the harnesses, laying them out with methodical precision. They worked in silence, securing anchor points and checking load lines. When the cradle was ready, they lowered it into the shaft. The cable hummed softly as it unwound, disappearing into the dark.

"You're sure it's stable?" Calan asked.

"Sure?" Javi echoed. "No. Few things in life are certain, Captain. Isn't that what makes life interesting?"

As Calan climbed into the cradle, Javi slipped Amber into a padded harness and strapped her to his back. She went without protest, nose twitching.

"Nifty," Calan said, mostly sincere.

"Indeed," said Javi with a nod.

And down they lowered.

• • • •

The cradle settled onto solid flooring with a low metallic thud. The light from above was long gone, swallowed by the shaft behind them. Javi unclipped the gear and stepped forward, his lamp sweeping over the curved hallway ahead.

It was pristine—unnaturally so. The air was sharp and cold, but not dead. Something in the filtration system still pulsed faintly, like a sleeping lung.

They moved in silence, boots muffled by fine dust. The hallway walls were seamless, built in concentric rings that seemed designed to disorient. Pipes ran low along the edges, interrupted by small access ports and strange symbols scrawled in faded paint—half schematic, half cultic spiral.

Javi scanned everything with practiced precision, clearly in his element.

Calan, by contrast, felt increasingly claustrophobic. The air here was wrong. The quiet felt like cotton in his ears.

"You think this place was always like this?" Calan asked, just to hear a voice.

"No." Javi crouched by a data port. "They reinforced the walls sometime after the base was abandoned. It's like a temple built inside a bunker."

Calan exhaled sharply. "You sound excited."

"Do I?" Javi said, stiffening. "This is the kind of place no one was ever supposed to find. Every scar on these walls is a story."

"Doesn't this place make you... uneasy? I can't explain it. The whole thing feels like... death."

Javi didn't look at him. "Makes sense. Given the mass suicide during the last resurgence—"

Calan put a hand on Javi's arm. "How do you know about that? The Union library and our top record keepers had no record of any such event. It was only because of the intel your sister got outside Hedonia that I knew that story."

"I'm the top archaeologist to work on Earth, Captain. I spent six years excavating Ludon sites in the floodwoods. You're not the only one who hears things. Anyway, from what I can translate of these glyphs, they practiced some form of human sacrifice. So yes. That this place feels like death makes sense."

Calan turned away, pacing a few steps down the corridor. "What the hell is wrong with you? Leviathan's Hand wants to burn down everything we've built."

Javi adjusted the lamp on his chest. "A more apt metaphor would be *wash away*. They tend to prefer storm-related imagery."

Calan spun back around. "How can you be so... detached about it?"

Javi frowned. "Detached?"

"You're nothing like your sister," Calan snapped. "Brilliant, sure. Unflinching, yes. But there's a point where calm turns into—what?—coldness? Disassociation?"

There was a long pause. Javi didn't flinch. Didn't blink.

Then: "You're not the first person to say that. But just because I don't express things the way you do doesn't mean I don't feel them."

Calan's breath hitched. He realized what he'd said.

"I'm sorry," he said, voice quieter now. "That wasn't fair. I didn't mean to compare you."

"You did." Javi looked down the corridor, expression unreadable. "But I'm not offended. I've learned not to expect people to understand me right away."

Calan didn't know what to say. After a long pause, he gave Javi's arm a small squeeze—as if to call a truce. "Sorry," he said again.

The silence settled between them, but a little less brittle.

Javi finally spoke. "Why did you come down here alone?"

Calan hesitated. The shadows pressed in.

"Huh. Funny. I told everyone it was to protect the crew. I think I almost convinced myself of that, too. But the truth is, I needed to feel useful," he said. "Because everything on the *Salamander* feels like it's breaking apart, and I can't stop it. Because if I can fix just one thing—maybe I can talk myself into... taking the transfer. To serve on the *Vanguard* with my husband, Joren."

Javi nodded once, slowly. "I know the feeling."

They turned a corner. Ahead of them, a thick metal door stood ajar—old, sealed with a biometric lock that had long since failed. The space beyond it pulsed faintly with light.

Amber let out a low whine.

Calan looked at Javi. "The lights are on..."

"Curious," Javi said, looking at his scanner. "I'm reading a life form in there."

The chamber beyond the door was circular and vast, hollowed into the ice with precision. The walls were smooth metal etched with spiral motifs, half-melted into the floor and ceiling as though the structure had been fused in place by fire or force. Support beams sagged in places. Small lights blinked along the walls, powered by some long-forgotten backup system, casting a weak amber glow across the interior.

In the center of the room stood a cylindrical tank—chest-high, dark, and rimmed in frost. Faint vapor curled off it in long, unnatural tendrils.

Calan's lamp passed over the surface of the tank—and caught something inside.

He stopped.

"Javi."

Javi stepped closer, sweeping his scanner along the tank's curve. The surface was semi-translucent. A shape floated within, curled and broken and... breathing.

Flesh met metal along seams that weren't clean. A face—once humanoid—hung slack, partially sunken into its own chest, one eye still intact, milky and blinking. Tubes ran through its body. Filaments pulsed beneath the skin—some with fluid, others with a faint static charge.

Calan took an involuntary step back. "What the hell is that?"

Javi's voice was hushed. "It's alive."

Amber growled, low and guttural, but didn't approach.

The thing stirred. Its mouth moved slowly, like an echo trying to form a word underwater.

Calan's heart kicked in his chest. He couldn't move.

The mouth opened again, leaking a sound—not a cry, not speech, but syllables twisted from too many throats.

"St-still... h-here..."

Javi leaned forward slightly, jaw clenched. "According to my readings, he's Bimarian. But he's over three hundred years old. Impossible, given that their average life span is similar to humans."

"Immortality," Calan breathed. "This is what it looks like."

He met Javi's gaze. "We uncovered evidence they were after some kind of fountain of youth..."

The figure shuddered. Bands of flesh—gray, rubbery, barely covering sinew—rattled as it tried to speak again.

"Storm... still... raging..."

Calan staggered back a step. "No. No, we—we shouldn't be here."

He felt it then—not fear, but something deeper. Something existential. Like the weight of too many broken promises, of prayers turned into surgeries, of hope perverted into permanence.

"This is evil," he whispered. "How can this exist?"

Javi reached toward him. "Calan. Focus."

The floor beneath them rumbled—a long, slow quake reverberating through the bones of the place.

Amber barked once, loud and urgent.

Javi grabbed Calan's shoulder. "We've got to get out of here—now!"

A support strut groaned above them. The lights flickered. Somewhere behind the tank, another metal wall began to split.

They ran.

Back through the corridor, down the warped hallway, past glyphs that seemed to shimmer in the flickering light. Amber darted ahead, leading them without hesitation.

Behind them, the chamber wheezed—metal collapsing inward, ice falling in slabs.

They didn't look back.

• • • •

They emerged into open air just as the sky began to change.

Amber bounded ahead through the drifted snow, pausing now and then to glance back—as if checking that the humans hadn't done anything foolish.

Calan gasped the cold like it was a lifeline, bracing one arm against a snowbank, boots sinking deep into the wind-packed crust. The clouds overhead churned a deep gray, lit faintly from beneath by the sun somewhere low on the horizon.

He turned to see Javi already unspooling rope and anchoring climbing gear into the ice wall. Quiet. Methodical. Alive.

"Like riding a bike for you, huh?" Calan asked, voice hoarse. "I mean, do you do this often?"

"Outrun seismic collapse after witnessing ancient immortality experiments?" Javi deadpanned. "Believe it or not, this is my first time."

Calan let out a breath that might've been a laugh. Then another, quieter. "I still can't believe what we just saw."

Javi clipped a carabiner to the line. "I don't think it hit me the same way it hit you."

He paused, glancing up toward the beacon visible above the ridge. "Or maybe it did, and I'm just used to pretending it doesn't."

Calan looked at him. "I owe you. You pulled me out of more than one pit today."

Javi didn't look away from his knot. "You don't owe me anything."

They worked in silence for a moment, the wind gusting softly around them.

Then Javi said, without ceremony, "Most people think I don't feel things. That I'm cold, or broken, or disconnected. But if Leena taught me anything, it's that following your heart doesn't always look like what people expect."

Calan turned, surprised by the shift in tone.

Javi kept talking, focused on the rope in his hands. "All of this—" he gestured toward the scanner case, the wreckage half-buried nearby, the whole blighted horizon—"used to be enough. The data. The discovery. Knowing things no one had seen in a thousand years."

He looked up slightly.

"Then I met my wife. And we had our daughter. And I realized: none of this means anything if there's no one to share it with. Nothing will ever matter the way they do."

Calan swallowed. He looked up toward the shuttle, just visible beyond the ridge line. "I think I'm ready now."

He glanced back down the slope, toward the cave they'd left behind. "I don't want to end up like that monster. Alone in the dark, chasing perfection."

Javi didn't respond. He just gave Calan a brief pat on the arm and turned back to the rigging, already focused on the climb.

Calan's eyes drifted to Amber.

She stood nearby, tail flicking lazily, her breath misting in the air. She gave him a slow head tilt—half curiosity, half approval.

Above her, the sunlight caught the edge of a snowbank, casting it in gold. The cold hit Calan's face, clean and sharp, and for the first time in what felt like years, he felt free.

He smiled—a wide, real smile.

And they began the climb.

Chapter 6: He Who Shattered the Cloud

THE WIND THROUGH THE floodwoods had changed.

It no longer whispered. It held its breath.

The Ludon enclave emerged from the mist like a memory someone had tried to forget—low, slate-colored structures half-swallowed by wet leaves and curling branches. No towers, no walls. Just stillness. Built not to defy nature, but to vanish inside it.

Lily stepped off Delen's small transport and into the hush. It pressed against her ears like snow. Every movement—each footstep, each breath—felt intrusive, a ripple across a surface that longed to remain undisturbed.

Caris walked beside her, hands visible, posture open. Behind them, Delen said nothing, but his eyes moved constantly, scanning for a reception that hadn't yet arrived.

Then—movement.

From a grove of bowed trees, three figures emerged, robed in ochre and gray. Their faces were uncovered but unreadable. One stepped forward—older, with a narrow scar at her temple and eyes that once held fire but now held only smoke.

"You are not welcome," she said flatly.

"We come in peace," Caris replied.

A pause.

"Peace," the woman repeated. "Many offer it. Few actually give it."

Before the silence could stretch too long, another voice came from deeper in the grove.

"Let them through."

The speaker was younger. Taller. Cloaked in deep blue. She wore no ornamentation—only a single woven sash at her waist. Her pale blonde hair, nearly white, lifted in the breeze as if it had its own heartbeat. The cloth of her robe hung like mist around her, catching the hollows of her shape, covering just enough to remind you she chose to be seen.

"I am Eira," she said, her voice carrying the weight of someone who had learned to speak with her entire body.

"Do you come with questions, or answers?"

Caris took a step forward. "We've learned of your sister. We're looking for the same group that took her."

Lily noticed the shift in Caris' tone—slower than usual, slightly patronizing.

Not on purpose, Lily thought. Maybe reflex.

Old reflexes from old wounds.

The Hedonian part of her that still saw the Ludon as backward, maybe even complicit.

Eira blinked, unmoved. "Do you offer information?"

Lily stepped forward. "We were hoping for your help."

"We believe she may have been taken," Caris added, gentler now. "By a religious offshoot calling itself the Leviathan's Hand."

Something flickered in Eira's gaze. But it passed.

"You've come to accuse, not inform."

"No," Lily said. "We're here because your sister might be part of the key to stopping this. And because—"

She stopped. The words dried in her throat. In this place, they felt too fragile to carry their meaning.

Eira's expression remained still. "Then unless you bring new news of Simini, or offer something useful in trade, I'm afraid we have nothing further to discuss."

Caris stepped in. "You said 'in trade.' What do you want from us?"

Eira's eyes narrowed. "Not everything is transactional. Some things are sacred. And if you've come only to reopen wounds for your own war, then you are not unlike those who took her."

Lily flinched.

That hit deeper than she expected.

There was a faint shifting of robes, the rustle of fabric over forest floor—and then, nothing.

The grove was empty.

They were alone again, almost wondering if what they'd seen was a mirage.

They walked in silence for a few moments, the grove shrinking behind them.

Caris exhaled through her nose. "Three days to track them down, and we get ten minutes of shade. Super productive."

Lily gave a half-smile. "Nomadic cultures. I guess that's the downside. Or the upside—if you don't want to talk to anyone."

Caris pulled out her comm and tapped a few commands. "Hmm. Malik's not responding."

Lily's brow furrowed. "That's not like him. I figured he was enjoying himself, but it's been a couple days."

Delen cleared his throat. "I'm picking up chatter. Some sort of disturbance back at the Shonn village."

Caris turned to him. "What kind of disturbance?"

He gave a slow shake of the head. "Not clear. But we should probably go check on your friend."

Lily's eyes met Caris's. The easy moment evaporated.

They climbed aboard the transport and lifted off.

• • • •

The settlement looked different.

Lily felt it in the air as she stepped off the transport. A shift, difficult to describe.

She scanned the narrow trail of cabins and sun-stained rooftops. Wind brushed through the grasses, stirring laundry lines and prayer flags. A few residents moved between structures, heads down, shoulders hunched—not scared, exactly. Just... hollowed.

Caris walked ahead, boots crunching on gravel. "Where is everyone?"

Delen led them toward the central fire pit. It was cold now. The ash hadn't been disturbed in at least a day.

One of the villagers—a woman Lily remembered seeing before, broad-shouldered with delicate braids wrapped around her ears—glanced up as they approached.

"You're back," she said.

Delen nodded. "What happened?"

The woman hesitated. Her gaze flicked toward Lily and Caris, then back to Delen.

"A group left. Two days ago."

"Left?" Lily echoed.

The woman nodded slowly. "Took supplies. Some of the children. Most of the younger adults."

Caris frowned. "Where did they go?"

"Didn't say. Just followed the preacher."

That landed like a dropped stone.

Delen let out a breath and looked to Caris and Lily.

"He calls himself Omirel," he said. "He's from Ishrethi Prime. Arrived a few months ago and brought some kind of gospel with him. Set up a sort of church."

He paused, squinting toward the distant road out of the village.

"It caught on faster than I expected. The Shonn have always been... let's say, open to new visions. Superstitious, if I'm being honest. And they trust charm more than logic."

Lily tilted her head. "Why would they take Malik?"

Delen shrugged, the gesture tight. "Assuming he didn't go willingly..."

Caris stepped forward. "You think he went along with them?"

Delen pressed the middle finger of his left hand to his nose.

The silver-braided woman nodded. "He didn't say goodbye. Just packed a small bag and walked out like he knew exactly where he was going."

Delen muttered something under his breath, then unclipped a small com tag and held it out to Caris.

"My frequency. I'm going to do a headcount. Good luck. I hope you find your friend."

Caris took the badge, her mouth a flat line. "Thank you."

Delen gave a short nod. Then he walked away without looking back.

Lily tapped her wrist pad and brought up the notes she'd started on the ride over. The name Omirel was now tagged in multiple fringe theology channels.

"According to this," she murmured. "What he teaches is a variation of an Ishrethi tradition known as Sakranti. And the Sakranti are known for keeping a close, worshipful eye on the weather. They believe the self is meant to be scattered like ash into the sky."

Caris scanned the entry over her shoulder. "So the storm cult's got a new chapter."

Lily closed the file. "Or a very old one wearing a new face."

They stood in the clearing a moment longer, surrounded by wind and silence and too much empty space. Then, almost as if on cue, they turned to face each other.

"Back to the ship," Caris said.

• • • •

The shuttle docked with a soft thud against the Salamander's lower bay. By the time the hatch hissed open, Lily could already feel the weight of orbit settling back over her—cold alloy, filtered air, and the sound of systems always running just out of sync with her heartbeat.

Xynn was waiting at the end of the ramp.

She looked the same—arms crossed, leather shoulder pad against the bulkhead, expression strong—but something in her stance felt brittle. As if she'd been standing like that for too long.

When Lily stepped into view, Xynn uncrossed her arms and walked toward her without hesitation. No greeting. Just a quiet urgency.

"I'm not usually the protective type," she said. "I don't fret. I don't hover. But this whole mission's been chewing at my spine, and I'm sick of waiting for the next sign of life, you know?"

Lily blinked, unsure exactly how to respond.

Xynn took a breath. "So I'd like to stay close. If that's okay. Not to guard you. Just... to be with you. For the rest of this."

Lily nodded. "Yeah," she said softly. "Yeah, that's okay."

Xynn looked away, jaw clenched. "We'll talk later. You need to get to the bridge."

• • • •

The bridge lights were dimmed to system-red when Lily and Caris stepped through the lift doors, casting everything in that low, humming glow that made it feel like the ship was bracing for a whisper too loud.

Basco spun toward them in his chair, nearly knocking over a mug of tea in the process.

"Hey, uh—hi. So I might've found something. Maybe."

Caris raised an eyebrow. "Maybe?"

"Well, definitely weird," Basco said, pulling up a cascade of readouts. "Localized launch-prep signals. Ground-level subspace disturbance. No satellite data. But it's happening around Mount Diablo, California. And it started about thirty hours ago."

"Could be a civilian launch," Caris offered.

"Could be," Basco agreed. "Except the subspace interference is way stronger than standard burn-off. And there's something else..."

He tapped twice, and a shimmering magnetic profile unfurled across the console—spiked like a heartbeat caught mid-panic.

"That's not launch exhaust," he said. "That's shielding compression. Someone's either trying to cloak, or phase-shift something atmospheric."

Tevya, who had appeared silently behind him like a cheerful wraith, leaned in to get a better look. Her hand swung perilously close to the teacup, and Basco caught it with a last-second save.

"Oh, that's elegant," she said brightly, tilting her head. "Someone's playing tricks with magnetosphere distortions."

She turned to Lily, synthetic eyes catching the soft flicker of interface light. "I can triangulate it. Give me forty-five minutes and a clean weather map. If they're trying to hide under the sky, I'll find them."

"You're a miracle," Lily said, meaning it.

Tevya smiled. "I know."

Just then, Captain Calan and Datch stepped in from the conference pod—still in conversation, mid-laugh.

"I see our new crack team's getting you up to speed," Calan said, voice lighter than it had been in weeks.

Caris and Lily exchanged quick glances with their crewmates—quiet gratitude, wordless and understood.

"I read your report, Captain," Caris said. "I'm glad Javi was able to help. I knew he was the right man to call."

"You don't know the half of it," Calan said with a smile. His posture looked looser, his eyes clearer—like something had shifted inside him too.

"Now," he added, "you two go get cleaned up while we pinpoint Malik's location."

Lily turned toward the lift but paused halfway there. "You look different, Captain. Better."

Calan's smile broadened. "I'll tell you later."

She stepped into the lift. And maybe it was nothing—maybe it was just the glint of bridge lighting catching at the wrong moment—but she could've sworn he winked at her.

· · · ·

Later, in Lily's quarters, the air felt thinner somehow. Or maybe that was just her nerves.

She was stalling—still half-dressed, fingers hooked in the hem of her shirt, not quite ready to face herself in the mirror. Her mind was racing.

Xynn watched her from the bed, something flickering in her expression. Half relief. Half adoration.

Lily held the shirt against her bare chest like armor, and the words tumbled out before she could stop them.

"I had sex with Rhyder," she said.

Xynn blinked. "Hmm?"

"On Bimara. It was so... stupid. I was on this high—we'd just survived something, and I'd saved his life. I felt powerful. Untouchable. I never felt that way before. And I did it because I wanted to. No other reason. But now... I'm so—ashamed. I should've told you before—"

"Is that all?" Xynn asked.

Lily stared at her. "What?"

"I thought you were going to tell me something serious."

"Xynn—"

"What?" she said. "I'm Saravethi. We don't get jealous the way you do. I don't own your body, Lily. You don't owe me exclusivity to be honest."

Lily rubbed her forehead and began to pace, her voice quickening. She could hear the subtle quiver in Xynn's voice beneath the calm.

"It's okay to be mad."

Xynn tilted her head. "Why do you want me to be?"

"Because I wanted it to matter! I want you to care!"

"I do care," Xynn said, her voice rising, cracking. "I fucking care. But not like that. Not with chains. I *know* what that feels like, Lily. And you don't want it."

Lily stopped, breathing hard. "I need you to tell me it matters."

Xynn raised an eyebrow. "You want me to lie?"

"No," Lily said, quieter now. "I want you to want me enough that it matters."

Xynn stood slowly, walked to her. She reached out and gently took the shirt from Lily's hands, uncovering her. Touching her.

"That's not fair," Lily whispered, voice trembling.

"I want you," Xynn said, her lips barely a breath away. "That doesn't mean I need to punish you for being human."

She placed her hand on Lily's chest, just over her heart. Felt the way it thudded, uneven and real.

"I'll work on it," she said. "For now... can we just forget it?"

Lily nodded, and the breath she hadn't realized she'd been holding slipped out slow between her teeth.

And then—they melted into a kiss.

• • • •

The hatch opened with a hydraulic hiss, and the chanting spilled in—soft and melodic. It wasn't threatening.

It was beautiful.

That was what made it terrifying.

They stepped out as a unit—Caris, Lily, Xynn, Tevya—no weapons drawn, but no hesitation either.

A few cultists turned to look. Most didn't. They were busy—loading crates, speaking in low voices, some even weeping as they touched the ships' hulls. Not sorrowful. *Reverent.*

Lily spotted Malik near one of the transports, arms raised as he spoke to a small circle of followers.

"Malik!" she called.

He turned slowly. His face lit up.

"Lily," he said. Soft. Like he'd just woken from a long sleep and was still caught somewhere in the in-between. "You came."

"Of course I came," she said, stepping forward. "You disappeared."

"I left," he corrected gently.

Lily hesitated. "This isn't you."

He smiled. "I know! It's better." Then, in a sing-song tone: "No more grumpy Malik."

She opened her mouth to speak again—but Xynn stepped forward, voice low but cutting.

"You know surrender isn't freedom," she said.

Malik turned toward her, an eyebrow raised.

"I've seen surrender," Xynn continued. "They called it purification. Called it devotion. But in reality, it stripped my people down until we didn't know who we were. It almost destroyed us."

A ripple passed through the group. Something under the chanting. A flicker of dissonance.

Malik's smile faltered.

Then, movement—one of the robed figures at the far edge of the platform, someone who looked important—or at least *middle management*, Lily thought—raised a hand.

The light above them dimmed. Clouds surged. The wind rose sharply, curling around Lily's legs like fingers.

Tevya's voice snapped through the moment. "Sakran Bolt! Controlled weather, weaponized!"

The robed man hurled an energy ball across the clearing. Wind screamed around it, nearly knocking Lily off her feet before she managed to dive clear.

"Cover me!" Tevya shouted, already sprinting toward the open crates they'd passed—each one marked with Sakranti runes. She tore one open and pulled out a set of crystalline rods and a half-assembled lattice coil.

Another bolt launched, spiraling through the air in a streak of violet lightning.

Lily dropped again, rolling behind a cargo dolly. The air sizzled—static flooding her ears, her teeth, the fine hairs along her arms.

"Keep them talking!" Tevya shouted, her hands a blur. "I need sixty seconds!"

Another bolt charged in the cultist's hands—crackling wind, arcs of light spiraling around his arms like a crown of lightning.

Caris stepped forward now, drawing her weapon but keeping it aimed low. "You throw that, and I throw back," she warned. "And I guarantee I don't miss."

The cultist didn't blink. He launched the bolt.

Caris ducked and rolled, the energy tearing past and slamming into the edge of the transport ramp in a burst of blinding blue light.

"Tevya!" Lily shouted, shielding her face from the blast.

"Still building!" Tevya snapped. Her hands flew across the half-assembled device, crystal rods clicking into place like a puzzle locked against time. "I'm rewriting their storm metaphor into a nursery rhyme. Don't let them *finish* a thought!"

Another bolt launched—this one from the left, arcing toward the crates where Tevya worked.

Xynn moved.

She stepped forward and drew her blade in a single motion—a curved orange dagger of charged plasma, the light of it humming against the fog.

The cultist approaching Tevya slowed. Stopped.

Xynn didn't speak. She just stared him down, blade steady, as if daring the storm itself to try her.

Across the clearing, Malik's eyes locked on her.

He didn't move. But something shifted. His breath caught. His body leaned slightly forward. Like a man who'd just heard a distant bell from the life he left behind.

Another bolt tore through the fog—this one streaking straight toward Lily.

She dropped flat, gravel biting into her hands, as the energy sizzled over her back like static lightning.

"Tevya?" she called again, her voice raw.

"Twenty seconds!"

Caris returned fire now, short controlled bursts meant to dissuade, not kill—pushing the attackers into hesitation.

Malik flinched.

His eyes stayed on Xynn—like he was trying to hold onto something. Trying to remember what it meant to resist.

"Ten seconds!" Tevya shouted.

The wind howled above them. The sky cracked with thunderless pressure. Xynn stood tall, unwavering, a blade of orange defiance.

And Malik was still staring.

Then—

"Now!" Tevya cried, slamming the final rod into place.

A low, resonant tone rippled outward, deep and round like a pulse from the center of the world. The Sakran device lit with a lattice of flickering violet light.

The nearest bolt began to crackle—then sputtered. Collapsed.

Another fizzled out before it could form.

The wind stilled. The light returned.

Silence spilled over the launch site like cooling glass.

Tevya exhaled, brushed off her hands, and stepped back. "That's right," she said, to no one in particular. "Your metaphors are no match for me."

Around them, the cultists faltered. No retreat—but the rhythm was gone. The trance broken. They stood motionless, caught between confusion and awe.

Lily and Caris moved quickly toward the now-abandoned crates. The first few were ceremonial—ribbons, rings, sacred tools.

Then Lily pried open a larger case. And froze.

Inside: dozens of ritual logs, tablets, scrolls, and etched data rods. Each inscribed with names, locations, dates. Some recent. Some so old they looked fossilized.

Caris scanned the symbols. "This is a record," she said. "A massive one."

Lily nodded slowly, her voice low. "It goes back years."

They said nothing else.

The chanting had stopped. But the tension hadn't.

Malik was still watching them—his body stilled, his gaze locked on Xynn as if she were the only thing keeping him from falling apart.

The cult was still watching them. Waiting.

And Lily had the sharp, heavy sense they'd just stolen something sacred.

• • • •

The conference pod was quiet but not still.

Screens flickered. Breath held. The kind of silence that meant everyone was waiting for something. Probably bad news.

Lily stood at the edge of the curved console, arms crossed, trying to stay grounded as the search results unfolded. Caris beside her, jaw set. Tevya leaned in from the other side, fingers dancing across her own tablet, decoding symbols too old for Union archives.

Xynn stood behind Lily, close enough to touch, but not touching. Just there. Steady.

Line after line scrolled across the central display—names, dates, locations, symbols. A code carved in ritual. Not storage. *Sacrament.*

Then:

Simini, Daughter of Drem.

The glyph next to her name glowed faintly—three curved lines in a ripple pattern.

"There she is," Lily whispered.

Beneath the name: a timestamp. A Ludon location.

And the ripple mark—the same one they'd seen etched into the floor of the enclave. The symbol for dissolution.

"That's a death rite," Caris said. Quiet.

Lily felt hollow. Killed as a sacrifice to the storm. She pressed against Xynn, her presence providing much needed strength,

Caris pulled out the small com tag Delen had given her. "I have an idea. And I'm pretty sure Delen is going to regret giving me this."

• • • •

The fog was still lifting.

Morning light peeking through the Shonn Valley.

The makeshift hall had been cleared. The fire pit scrubbed.

Banners of neutral white hung where ideological symbols usually stood.

There was no stage or platform. Just a long table. And chairs. All on the same level.

Captain Calan stood near the center, arms clasped behind his back, watching quietly as both sides arrived.

Valen entered first, flanked by two Hedon delegates—subtle implants, sharp robes, and cautious pride. He didn't look up until he saw Lily. Then his face softened. He nodded once. Grateful.

From the other side, Eira stepped forward with the Ludon delegation—her robes even more revealing than before, exuding confidence. The young woman who had dismissed them days ago now carried herself like someone bearing the weight of a hundred buried voices.

And walking between them, not fully of either world—**Delen.**

He wore no delegation's colors. Just the weathered jacket he always wore and a simple band of woven fabric looped around his wrist.

A marker of mediation.

Of trust.

Caris greeted him with a silent nod.

The room quieted as the final members of the *Salamander* crew arrived—Lily, Xynn, Datch, and Tevya taking their places near Calan.

The conversation began without ceremony. No preamble. Just truth.

"We found Simini's name in the records," Lily said. "She was listed as deceased. Killed as part of a ritual. A symbolic sacrifice meant to unify opposing beliefs."

Delen raised his hand. "She was trying to prevent division."

Valen swallowed hard. "Such a gentle soul."

Eira nodded slowly. "And we gave her to it. Piece by piece."

Delen stepped in then, voice steady. "No more recriminations. Not today. Honor Simini by speaking together—in cooperation."

The conversation moved slowly. Carefully.

They spoke of fault. Of silence. Of pride mistaken for strength.

No one raised their voice. No one stormed out.

At one point, Eira said, "We mourned her separately. It's time we mourn her together."

And at that, something shifted.

Valen reached across the table, hand open.

And after a pause, Eira placed hers atop it.

The silence that followed wasn't heavy. It was earned.

Lily didn't speak again. Neither did Xynn. They sat in stillness and watched something that had once felt impossible begin to unfold.

"It won't undo what was lost," Eira said at last. "But perhaps it will keep others from being lost the same way."

Calan exhaled—quiet, relieved. Lily turned to him.

They exchanged a hopeful smile.

One small step for humanity on Earth. And they got to be part of it.

Maybe that was the win Calan needed after all.

• • • •

Lily stepped softly into the med bay, the door hissing shut behind her.

The lights were dim. The kind of dim that wasn't about ambiance—just resignation.

Malik lay on the main exam bed, his eyes open but unfocused, like he was watching something only he could see. Or maybe nothing at all.

Dr. Thesari stood at a console, her brow furrowed in that way Lily was starting to recognize—not frustration, but worry pressed into silence.

Caris sat nearby, still as a stone, her hand resting on her knee like she didn't trust it not to tremble.

Lily didn't speak. She just moved to stand beside Caris, who glanced up once and gave a short nod. Not gratitude. Not greeting. Just... acknowledgment.

Malik didn't turn his head.

Dr. Thesari finally broke the silence. "His body's stable. Neurological systems are intact. But something fundamental's been rewritten."

"Rewritten how?" Lily asked, her voice quieter than she meant it to be.

Thesari pulled up a scan and gestured. "There's no sign of synthetic interference. No implants. No forced sedation. What we're seeing is... ideological erosion. Cognitive restructuring layered in metaphor."

Caris narrowed her eyes. "Meaning?"

Thesari looked at Malik, her voice dropping. "He wasn't ordered to submit. He was invited to dissolve. To become the storm."

Lily felt that land in her chest like a stone dropped in water.

"They rewrite identity through language," Thesari continued, "amplified by some kind of powerful psychedelic. They don't command obedience—they dissolve it. You're told to be like the rain..."

Lily's eyes didn't leave Malik's face. His features were so familiar—creases of thought at the brow, a hint of that old stubbornness in his jaw—but dulled now, like someone had turned down the volume on who he was.

Caris rose and stepped closer, kneeling at Malik's side. "Hey," she said gently. "It's Caris. You in there?"

Malik blinked. His eyes fluttered once. Slowly.

"You know we're not leaving you like this, right?" she said. "You're coming back. Even if I have to dive in after you."

Lily felt her throat tighten. The air in the med bay tasted sterile, recycled, and too thin all at once.

And then—Malik moved. Just slightly. His fingers curled, like they were remembering how to form a fist.

Lily caught her breath.

Caris leaned in closer, voice low. "That's it. Stay with me."

It wasn't a miracle.

But it was a start.

· · · ·

The observation deck was nearly dark, save for the blue-white curve of Earth glowing through the glass.

They hadn't said much on the way up. Just walked in silence, shoulder to shoulder, until they found this little pocket of stillness above the ship's sleeping hum. Lily leaned against the window frame, arms loosely folded, watching the oceans ripple beneath scattered clouds. It didn't look divided from up here. Just... quiet. As if it could let go of an entire human history full of resentment.

Xynn stood beside her for a long time without speaking.

"This was where I first saw you in the shuttle bay," Lily said, pointing through the lower window down into the bay for visiting vessels. "I remember my heart beating fast, and I was telling it to stop being crazy."

They exchanged a smile.

"You were just looking at my ass," Xynn said.

Both of them laughed.

Then, softly—almost too casually to be real—Xynn added, "Okay. I admit it. I'm upset about Rhyder."

Lily's breath caught. Not because she was surprised—but because she hadn't known Xynn would actually say it.

"I'm sorry," Lily said, before she could stop herself. "It was—" She paused. "It wasn't nothing. But it wasn't... important. Not really."

"I know," Xynn replied, her voice flat.

Lily turned to her, heart stammering. "I didn't mean to hurt you."

Xynn looked at her then, really looked at her. Her expression almost sad at first—but not distant. Not cold. Just... scraped bare.

"You did hurt me," she said. "But I still forgive you."

Lily felt the tears sting before she could swallow them down. She wiped her face with the heel of her hand. "I just needed to know I really matter to you. And I think... well, I appreciate it."

Xynn let out a small, broken laugh. "Maybe I just didn't know how to say it mattered. Not out loud. That's not easy for me."

A silence settled between them, deeper than the last. But this one didn't ache. It pulsed—alive and waiting.

"Every time we say goodbye," Lily said, her voice almost a whisper, "I pretend I'm okay with it. I choose it, even, to feel in control. But I'm not okay with it."

Xynn reached for her hand.

"Then let's stop pretending."

The words weren't soft. They were steel wrapped in warmth. A choice, not a comfort.

Lily didn't answer with words. She leaned into her, forehead resting against Xynn's, both of them backlit by the slow-turning Earth.

"No more goodbyes at the airlock," Xynn said.

"Deal," Lily murmured.

Neither of them noticed Captain Calan pausing just outside the hatch. He stood for a moment in the corridor, hearing only fragments—but enough to know what had changed.

He turned and walked away, quiet as ever, a small smile brushing his lips.

Back in his quarters, he keyed in a long-distance call before he could overthink it. The screen flickered, then brightened—Joren's face blooming into view like sunrise.

• • • •

The secure channel flickered once. Then again.

Lily tapped the side of the console with mild impatience.

And then—there he was.

The face that filled the screen was older than the last time she'd seen it, but unmistakably familiar: bright eyes, a proud sweep of dark curls, and that unmistakable Ishrathi regality crumpled ever so slightly by uncontainable joy.

"Lily Starling!" King Zayir beamed, arms outstretched as if he could pull her through the screen. "By the stars, you look the same. Have humans stopped aging in the Union, or is it just you?"

Lily laughed. "You're one to talk! I see the royal cheekbones continue to thrive."

He made a grand gesture of mock-flattery. "My people say they are a national treasure. I must preserve them." Then, more earnestly, "It's good to see you. Truly."

"You too," Lily said, settling into the seat. "We're following a lead, and it points to Ishreth. Think you'd be willing to host a slightly chaotic diplomatic delegation?"

Zayir's smile softened. "Of course. You're always welcome here. In fact, I was hoping you'd come visit—you must meet Vaishali!"

Lily turned pink. "Yes... I'm sorry I couldn't make the wedding."

The joy in Zayir's voice turned golden. "She's brilliant. And a terrible influence. You'll love her."

Lily grinned. "Can't wait."

"I'll have the landing protocols cleared and a suite prepped," he said. "And Lily? It is good to see you. Safe journey."

The screen dimmed a moment later, leaving only the soft reflections of Earth in the console's glass.

Caris's voice carried across the bridge. "Coordinates received. Setting course for Ishrathi Prime."

"Take us there. Maximum light factor," Calan ordered.

The *Salamander* surged forward, stars streaking into bright threads around her—toward the next mystery.

And hopefully, Lily thought, answers.

Chapter 7: The King's Ruins

THE SKIN DID NOT PEEL.

It sang as it came away—each strand a taut violin string of pain and memory.

He couldn't tell if his screams ever left his throat.

Did they flutter there, like a trapped bird?

Bones turned to glass, wings beating against the cage of his ribs.

Or were they filling the chamber, echoing through the dark?

He couldn't be sure.

His entire self was a scream now.

Vibration had become a part of his being.

There were no restraints.

Just the weight of his own body, and the gravity of what he was becoming.

He could see his hands—what was left of them.

The skin sloughed off like wet silk, revealing a lattice of sinew, pale and glistening.

Tools moved in and out of view: knives too fine to catch the light, claws of liquid metal reshaping the meat beneath.

He wanted to look away.

His eyes wouldn't close.

Couldn't.

A voice purred, somewhere above him. Or below. Or inside his skull.

"Be careful what you wish for, Veyrik. To cheat death—the cost is high indeed. Though we are well past the bargaining stage, aren't we?"

His breath came in short, shuddering bursts.

Was he breathing?

Something hissed against his spine—a cold line of steam carrying the scent of scorched hair and copper.

He tried to speak. To curse. To plead.

Nothing escaped.

He was being rewritten.

Then it went dark.

The sounds of bone cracking and something like steel cable unwinding filled his head.

And just as the pain became unbearable, he felt... nothing.

And somehow, the nothing hurt more than anything that came before.

He fell through the floor.

Or perhaps the floor fell through him.

An endless cascade of moments, blurred by agony and awe.

And in the space between one breath and the next—

He woke up. Still dreaming.

He barely remembers now.

But he remembers the voice.

The moment of awakening.

A column of white fire, incinerating everything he once was.

There was no pain.

No fear.

Only stillness—so vast it reached into the marrow of who he used to be.

And then—the voice.

"Come forward, child born anew. Step forward and meet your destiny... Ronin."

• • • •

The corridor curved ahead in gentle arcs of light, the *Salamander's* signature thrum low and steady beneath their feet. Caris walked beside Malik, adjusting her pace to match his. Lily trailed just behind. His steps were steady, but she noticed the occasional hesitation—like his body remembered something his mind was still untangling.

"Never thought I'd get an escort back to my quarters," Malik said dryly. "What's next? A fruit basket and a medal?"

"Don't get used to it," Caris said. They exchanged a soft smile.

Malik chuckled, then winced—just a flicker. He brought a hand to his temple. "Ugh. My brain's still running software I didn't install."

Lily slowed. "That happening a lot?"

"Only when I think too hard. Or breathe too hard. Or smell too hard... almost anything," he said, his voice tightening at the edges. "Certain tones.

Scents. Sometimes I get these... flashes. Like I'm back there. Stupidly happy again. Not in the memory exactly, just... in the feeling."

Caris squeezed his arm, almost said something. But didn't. Her eyes flicked to Lily—worried. Protective. A little lost.

Lily nodded, keeping her tone even. "Dr. Thesari was confident you'll be tip-top in no time. She's seen this kind of conditioning before. It leaves grooves. But grooves fade. We have to think about what they did—and what we do next."

Malik looked between them, something unspoken softening in his expression. "I just keep thinking... what if something's still in there? Buried. Waiting."

"That's what we're here for," Lily said gently. "To dig it out. Or guard the door if we have to."

They reached the entrance to his quarters. Malik hesitated before the panel, fingers hovering like he'd forgotten the code. Caris stepped a little closer.

"You'll let me know if anything gets weird?" she asked, voice quieter than usual.

"You mean unlike every other day around here?" Malik said gruffly. After a beat, he nodded. "I will."

The door slid open and he stepped inside. For a moment, the light from within cast all three of them in a golden wash. Then the door hissed shut.

Lily and Caris stood in the silence that followed.

"He'll be okay," Lily said.

"I..." Caris started, almost to herself. "He'd rather implode than ask for help. I worry about that."

Lily smirked. "Sounds familiar."

Caris shot her a look, but turned away before Lily could say more. "See you for the landing party."

As Caris walked off down the corridor, Lily wondered if she'd just seen something unexpected in her friend's eyes—tears of quiet relief, catching the light before they vanished.

• • • •

198 **CHRISTIAN HURST**

Engineering hummed with life, the glow of control panels casting soft gradients across the metal. Lily stepped through the threshold just in time to hear a sharp *bzzt* and Ka-Lorrin's exasperated voice:

"For the last time, it's not overcorrecting—it's *precision*. You wouldn't understand."

"I understand. I do, I do. Recalibrated the same diagnostic array *six times* ya have," Taran replied, his giant furry frame filling the corner of the lab. "You're gonna break it, Kal. He is, he is."

Alrek stood between them, brow furrowed, datapad in hand. "Can we maybe direct this passion into something *useful*?"

Neither of the Raath-Ka turned. Ka-Lorrin waved a spanner in the air like it was a rebuttal.

Lily leaned against the nearest bulkhead, arms crossed. "Is this a bad time?"

Taran lit up at the sound of her voice. "Lily! I'm glad to see you—before Kal blows us all up, he does."

She allowed herself a quick bear hug from the shaggy Raath, then turned serious. "What's the crisis this time?"

"No crisis," Ka-Lorrin muttered, still adjusting settings with twitchy fingers. "Just incompetence."

Taran ignored him and hopped down. "Minor telemetry hiccups. We've been tracking storm residue signatures from Ishreth's upper atmosphere, and something strange cropped up in the readings—don't know what to make of it, I don't."

Alrek looked up from his notes. "I was going to cross-check it with the data Xynn's been collecting. She thought she spotted something earlier."

Lily stepped forward, intrigued. "Could be a clue—or another wild goose chase. Keep me posted either way."

Taran gave a lazy salute. "Come again, again."

Ka-Lorrin grumbled something unintelligible but finally stopped poking the console.

Lily glanced back toward the corridor. "I'm heading up to the bridge. If you figure out whether it's ghosts or glitches, let me know."

Alrek nodded, slipping his notes into the pad. "Will do."

. . . .

Lily rounded the corner at a brisk pace—only to skid to a halt as a floor panel hissed open and a gelatinous yellow form slorped up through the grate.

"I knew I could catch up to you if I used the maintenance shaft," Charlie chirped.

Lily sighed. "Hi, Charlie..."

He shimmered with pride, producing a datapad—Lily wasn't quite sure from where—and held it aloft like a torchbearer. "I've been studying Ishrethi customs. Did you know their hand gestures have seventy-three distinct meanings depending on wrist angle and proximity to fruit?"

Lily raised a brow. "Fruit?"

"Oh." His translation matrix fizzled slightly with static. "Must've been a glitch. Anyway... I've memorized three traditional greetings, four farewell phrases, and the entire menu of their midwinter festival. I am *ready*."

"Ready for..." Lily prompted, though she was already sure where this was going.

"I'd like to join the landing party."

She hesitated, weighing the risk. Unfortunately, Lily's own aversion to saying *no* was exactly what Charlie was counting on.

"Fine. But stay close. I don't know if they'll be as forgiving as the Gherionites."

Charlie rippled with satisfaction. "Understood. I shall be the model of cultural poise and diplomacy. Even if it's more *shimmery* diplomacy than they're used to."

Lily was already halfway down the corridor. "See you in the shuttle. Don't be late."

He oozed off, whistling a tune.

. . . .

The bridge of the *Salamander* was quiet, but alert—the soft rhythm of sensor blips rose and fell like a mechanical heartbeat. Tevya sat forward at the science console, eyes sharp, fingers dancing over glowing controls. Beside her, Datch watched the readouts with that familiar distant calm, like he was somewhere far behind his own eyes.

Lily stepped onto the deck, the doors whispering shut behind her. She moved lightly, almost on tiptoe, unwilling to puncture the hush that had settled over the room.

"Hey," she murmured, crouching slightly to speak beside Tevya. "How's it going?"

Tevya looked up and smiled. "Depends on which 'it' you mean. Our approach to the planet is on track. No surprises there. But the data we picked up from Earth?" She exhaled, soft but strained. "That's a puzzle. Xynn was helping, but she peeled off—chasing something strange. Odd readings."

Datch gave the smallest of nods, but said nothing.

Lily gave Tevya's shoulder a brief squeeze. "Well, if anyone can crack it..."

She crossed to the auxiliary station, where Xynn hovered over a set of fluctuating waveforms, her expression tight with focus. Lily leaned beside her.

"Heard you're chasing ghosts."

Xynn didn't look away from the screen. "There's something out there. Buried under the storm telemetry—just below the static floor. It keeps flickering in and out, like it's trying not to be noticed."

"Sensor drift?" Tevya called over without turning.

Xynn shook her head. "Too clean. It's patterned. Like a cloaked ship, or a signal echo from something still out there. It's subtle. Deliberate."

Lily leaned in, squinting at the display. "Tricky to pin down?"

"I've got rough coordinates. Enough to triangulate. I know we were supposed to stick together, but..." Xynn glanced up at her. "I want to chase this down."

Lily smiled. "You should ask Alrek to help. I hear you two are finally starting to get along."

Xynn's eyes flickered with amusement. "I'm getting used to him," she said with a small shrug.

Lily squeezed her arm. "He's like my little brother. Thanks for giving him a chance."

"I'm onto something here," Xynn said, more certain now. "I can feel it."

Lily tilted her head, mock-serious. "Careful. With instincts like that, the fleet might try to draft you."

Xynn laughed. "The fleet and I wouldn't last a day. No offense."

Lily leaned in and kissed her—brief, warm, the kind of kiss that said *come back to me.* "I'll see you after the mission."

She turned toward Datch, who popped up like a spring-loaded coil.

"Ready when you are," he said, voice clipped and eager. "Give the word."

From the command chair, Dryst Amaris gave them both a steady nod.

Lily returned it with a half-smile. "The word is given," she said. "Let's make this a smooth one. I'm tired of med bay visits."

With a final glance back at the crew, she stepped into the lift beside Datch. The doors slid closed behind them like the page of a chapter turning.

• • • •

The shuttle descended in a slow arc, the world of Ishreth unfurling below like an ember-streaked tapestry. Spires of polished crystal thrust skyward through thick, copper-hued mist, while shimmering stabilizers ringed the landing platform in glimmering halos—holding the storm's breath at bay.

Lily stood at the viewport, arms crossed, her reflection ghosting back in fractured shards of light. She felt a tug of gravity—not from the planet, but from anticipation.

The ramp lowered with a hiss. A ceremonial honor guard waited at the base of the platform, adorned in traditional Ishrethi bronze and orange silks, their staves tipped with shimmering blue lenses.

Lily, Caris, Datch, and Charlie descended in formation, each flanked by the glint of their Union badges. The guards bowed—not low, not perfunctory, but with the measured grace of a people who knew how to show respect without ceding ground.

They were ushered into a vaulted gallery of crystal and stained light—sunbeams cutting through the lattice above to paint shifting patterns across the polished floor. A few guards peeled off at the perimeter, while a voice echoed from the far end:

"Lily Starling. I was beginning to think you were avoiding me."

She turned toward it with a smile already forming.

Zayir strode forward with open arms, just as young and wide-eyed as she remembered. His ceremonial cape had clearly been thrown on last-minute over more casual attire, and his crown sat slightly crooked—which suited him.

"Ishreth welcomes you from the stars that guided you here," he said, arms spreading in a flourish just a little too dramatic.

"Your Majesty," Lily said, stepping in to hug him. "It's good to see you."

"Please, call me Zayir," he replied, then turned and grinned at the rest of her team.

Datch gave a polite nod. "Your Highness."

"Lieutenant Commander," Zayir returned with a tilt of his head. "I still owe you a debt of gratitude for coming to my aid on Starbase Twelve."

Datch blinked. "I'll admit, I was somewhat concerned... since it was my investigation that led to your mother's imprisonment."

Zayir's smile faltered for just a breath. "A galactic controversy to this day. But I do not blame you, Mr. Datch. My mother is guilty of murder. She will spend the rest of her days confined. —But now, where are my manners? Vaishali!"

At that, he turned and gestured to the woman now approaching from a side entrance. She moved with precise grace, her copper-toned skin luminous beneath embroidered black and silver silks. She was older than Zayir by perhaps a decade, with eyes that missed nothing and a mouth made for razor-edged wit.

"This," Zayir said, with the pride of someone presenting a rare artifact, "is my wife, Queen Vaishali. Lily, I've so looked forward to you meeting—the poetry scholar who can dismantle a political debate with three words and a disapproving glance. And the young space traveler who pulled me out of a dangerous place in my darkest hour."

Vaishali offered Lily a nod that was both regal and surprisingly warm. "Lily Starling." She walked around her slowly, like a shark circling its prey. "You're even younger—and more beautiful—than I imagined."

Lily didn't know how to respond, so she pivoted. "And this," she said, gesturing to her crew, "is Caris—tactical officer. Datch, as you know. And this is Charlie."

Charlie, vibrating with anticipation, performed an elaborate, fluid bow—part ripple, part swirl. "I come bearing no weapons, unless you count charm and excessive moisture."

Vaishali smiled, already in motion. "Our archaeologists are standing by to guide you to the national archives. But Lily, I'd like to walk and talk for a moment."

Lily opened her mouth as the queen's arm slipped around her shoulders—but no words came out.

Zayir clapped his hands together as he followed the others. "This is going to be fun."

• • • •

The Queen's hand rested lightly on Lily's arm as they turned down a shaded colonnade flanked with violet-glass vines and wind-chimes that whispered with every passing breeze.

"Lily," the Queen began, her voice like velvet over flint, "firstly, you must call me *Vaish*. May I call you Lily?"

Lily nodded, still adjusting to the way the Queen could soften her presence without ever dulling it.

"Lily," Vaishali said, slipping into the name like it was already familiar, "the prince—while prone to infatuation—is truly enamored with you. He admires you greatly."

Lily blinked. "I... I was there for him in a moment that mattered. I can't imagine what he's going through with his mother..." She paused. "Having to be locked up."

"There were those who wanted her flesh," Vaishali said, without blinking. "Wanted her executed for her crimes. Some still do. Many have simply... moved on. Forgotten her entirely. And some"—she exhaled a short, dry laugh—"have built entire conspiracy theories to fill the vacuum."

Lily's brows pulled together. "How awful."

"Zayir needs your support," Vaishali continued, not slowing her pace. "He needs your youth, your affection. I am his wife, yes. But I am also"—she gave a wry little tilt of her head—"his new mother. He needs a muse."

Lily flushed, heat rising unbidden to her cheeks. "I don't know what you're implying, but—"

"Let's not be children," the Queen said, sharp and smooth at once. "He adores you. Keep his heart rate up for me, and I'll get him to give me a child."

Lily nearly tripped over her own feet. She tried to mask the shock in her eyes, but from the flicker of amusement on Vaishali's face, she wasn't fooling anyone.

"Give him what he needs," the Queen said, now with the tone of someone adjusting a ceremonial vase. "And I will get you what *you* are looking for."

A long pause followed—uncomfortable, pulsing with unspoken meanings. Then, as if nothing had been said at all, Vaishali clapped her hands.

"Come now. We'll oversee the meal preparations. I told Zayir to bring everyone back at mid-hour for the second meal."

And with that, she removed her cloak right there in the middle of the courtyard.

Lily startled slightly, but the attendants didn't blink. If anything, they *actively ignored it,* which somehow made it more surreal.

Beneath the cloak, the Queen wore little more than a gold-threaded negligee that shimmered with motion. It barely covered what it needed to—her body honed like a blade, legs like they could crack alloy.

An attendant stepped forward with a silk gown—ivory and orange, patterned with long twisting vines—and Vaishali slipped into it slowly, her movements deliberate, unapologetic.

When her eyes found Lily's again, there was nothing coy in them—only strength. Strength that made Lily's skin prickle.

"Coming?" the Queen asked, already moving toward the banquet hall without waiting for an answer.

Lily followed, not entirely sure if she was walking into a feast or a trap.

• • • •

The meal preparations were in full swing. Dozens of attendants moved with silent precision, placing silver bowls of chilled fruit into crystalline alcoves, adjusting napkin folds with surgical seriousness. The centerpiece—an animated sculpture of twin phoenixes rendered in floating glass and flame—hovered over the table like a threatened deity. Everything glittered: the dishes, the uniforms, even the steam that curled from the ornate soup tureens seemed to glow.

Lily watched from the archway, arms crossed.

It was beautiful. Meticulously, painfully beautiful. And so completely unnecessary.

She didn't say it aloud—but the thought hung in her chest like a weight. How many meals like this did they throw every week? Every day? It wasn't just opulence—it was theater.

She slipped away quietly, her boots whispering against the sunstone floor as she stepped out onto the nearest balcony.

The air outside was cooler. The sky was turning the color of copper and tea leaves, stormlight flickering on the horizon like distant fireworks. She took a breath, deeper than she meant to, letting out a shaky exhale–she activated her com tag.

The secure line shimmered to life.

Xynn's face appeared, lit from below by console light. Her hair was pulled back, a smudge of something—grease, maybe—on her cheek.

"Hey," she said, voice warm and just slightly breathless. "What's the emergency?"

"No emergency," Lily said, leaning on the railing. "Just wanted to, ya know. Check in."

"Aw," Xynn teased, eyes flicking toward something offscreen. "I win the bet."

Lily laughed. "What bet?"

"Whether you'd call before or after dinner. He said you'd wait until dessert. I said you'd crack before the appetizers even landed."

Alrek's voice chimed in from somewhere nearby, faint and unimpressed: "No appetizers? Damn it."

Lily smirked. "How's the anomaly scan going?"

"We're in low orbit," Xynn said. "The signal's faint, but we're isolating it. Alrek thinks it's bouncing between layered storm bands. We're triangulating for density contrast."

Alrek again, muttering: "Triangulating for static so far."

Xynn continued, ignoring him, "We'll know more after the next sweep. But it's not debris. It's something deliberately hidden."

Lily nodded, grateful for the update—but her eyes drifted out over the skyline.

Xynn narrowed her gaze. "Lily... you're making your *I don't want to talk about it but please ask me about it* face. What's going on?"

Lily hesitated, then sighed. "It's the Queen."

Xynn blinked. "Your friend's new wife?"

"She is... not what I expected."

A beat.

"I think she wants me to snog Zayir."

There was a pause. Then:

Xynn burst out laughing. "Of *course* she does! What is it with you? You're irresistible, Lily."

"Ha ha," Lily deadpanned. "Very funny."

Xynn tried to catch her breath. "You've got this whole cross-cultural seductress thing going on."

Lily covered her face with one hand. "Please stop talking."

"Too late. I'm calling you *Danger Magnet* in the mission log."

"She was serious," Lily said quietly. "It wasn't just flirting. It was... strategic. Like I'm supposed to get Zayir... well, in the mood. She wants him to knock her up."

Xynn's smile faded into something more thoughtful. "That's gross."

"Yeah. It's weird. But... I don't even hate her. Which somehow makes it worse."

Xynn studied her for a moment. "You okay?"

Lily nodded. "Just needed to say it out loud."

"Well," Xynn said, "for what it's worth—you have a way of disarming people. I bet you can get through to the prince without resorting to baser measures."

Lily smiled. "Thanks."

There was a breath of silence, the stars just beginning to burn through the upper haze.

"Good luck with the scans," Lily said at last. "Call me if you find anything."

"Same to you. Oh, and try not to marry any royalty while I'm gone."

"No promises."

The line went dark.

Behind her, the palace bells began to ring.

Lunch was ready.

· · · ·

"...and their entire linguistics archive is organized by *conceptual lineage*, not root language," Charlie said, practically vibrating with excitement. "It's incredible. Some of the entries predate Union codification entirely. There are spoken forms I didn't even know *existed*."

"I find it especially impressive," Datch added, calm and precise, "given the scale. Your people have preserved not only language, but context. That kind of intentionality is... rare."

King Zayir smiled from the head of the table, lounging like a man unbothered by statecraft or time. "Ishreth Prime has always valued memory. And discovery."

"Indeed," Datch said. "I am eager to return and continue our investigation."

"Ah, but memory can wait until after dessert, can it not?"

Charlie laughed, already eyeing another helping.

Datch inclined his head. "With respect, Your Majesty, these celebrations—while impressive—are not necessary."

"Spoken like someone who can't eat," Charlie quipped.

Zayir chuckled, lifting a carved crystal glass. "Come now, Mr. Datch. You must stay a while longer. Enjoy the moment. After your companions have digested their meal, your intellect can resume its feast."

His tone was warm, but there was a flicker of steel beneath the charm.

From across the table, Queen Vaishali spoke. "Your Majesty, the Jataran delegation will be waiting in the blue room. They were promised an audience before the midday recess."

Zayir did not look at her.

"They can wait."

His tone was sharp, and a long pause followed—one in which everyone suddenly found the pattern on the china very interesting.

"Now then..." the King began, but took a drink instead of continuing.

The queen's mock-smile dropped entirely. "It would reflect poorly on the crown if they were made to feel slighted."

The King set his fork down with enough force to shake the table. "I am the king..." He quickly turned his expression into a smile again, but spoke through his teeth. "Or I forget myself. My responsibility..."

His eyes locked on the Queen for a full beat. A tightness in his jaw.

Lily had never seen Zayir behave this way before. On edge. Almost petulant. His gaze drifted toward her—her eyes, then her body—and there it was: the barest, mischievous grin.

Lily's chest tightened.

Zayir shook his head, as if waking from a trance, and smiled again—this time bright and sharp. "Very well. We will shift things by no more than an hour. That should please everyone, should it not—even you, my dear."

His gaze flicked toward Vaishali with a dangerous kind of affection.

She did not flinch. Nor did she smile.

Caris cleared her throat gently. "Your Majesty—if I may—what is the current state of the Jataran dispute? We've been reviewing communications from the blockade near Jatarous IV."

The King leaned back, swirling his glass. "They'll be eating out of my hand soon enough. It's theater. They want trade concessions, not conflict."

Caris's tone remained courteous, but she didn't back off. "That may be true for Jatarous II. But IV's population has been under blockade for weeks. They're out of food. Infrastructure is crumbling—most of it was stripped decades ago to support the upper orbits. If your forces retreat, they'll collapse."

Zayir's smile thinned.

"Ishrethi presence has long provided stability in the region," Caris continued. "And the last treaty reaffirmed that support. If it's withdrawn now, the humanitarian cost could be severe. And it won't stay local."

He said nothing.

But Lily saw it—the way his knuckles whitened around the stem of his glass.

The mask was slipping. Charm fraying.

And across from him, Vaishali watched with a gaze that gave nothing away—but missed nothing.

Caris lowered her eyes slightly. "Forgive me. I'm no political expert."

"On the contrary," the King said, his voice smooth again, but slower now. He regarded her for a moment, swirling the wine in his glass. "You seem rather... well informed."

The tension lingered for a breath longer—then dissolved as the doors opened and a procession of servants entered, bearing gilded trays of jewel-colored desserts. Behind them, soft music began to drift in from the adjoining hall, played on glass harps and wind chimes that shimmered with every note.

Zayir's mood lightened as quickly as it had darkened. He laughed at something Charlie said and raised his glass again in a toast Lily barely heard. The King's charm returned like a tide, smooth and self-assured, and for a moment, she saw echoes of the man she'd first met—the dreamer, the diplomat, the charismatic prince with a galaxy in his eyes.

But the illusion cracked a moment later. Her com tag blinked.

Xynn's signal.

Lily rose, gently pushing back from the table. "Excuse me," she said softly. "I have to take this."

She didn't wait for permission. The corridor was already calling, quieter and cooler, her steps quickening as she sought somewhere private.

• • • •

Lily slipped through the archway, past two guards who stepped aside without a word. She followed the curving corridor to a chamber off the east wing labeled the Gray Room—a mixed-use space with polished stone walls, tiered seating, and the faint scent of old incense. It felt like a lecture hall, a library, and a church all at once.

She tapped her tag.

Xynn's face flickered to life—dampened by interference but clear enough. She was alone, helmet off, her hair pulled back tightly, lit in the eerie silver cast of the interior of an unfamiliar vessel.

"We found it. I knew it had to be a ship," Xynn said, skipping any kind of greeting. "Alrek stayed on the shuttle to monitor systems. He's holding position nearby."

"Never doubted you for an instant," Lily said. "Any sign of life?"

"Seems like it was abandoned fairly quickly. Long enough ago for the air to go stale—but the systems are intact." Xynn turned, showing Lily a glimpse of dark alloy walls etched with strange radial patterns. "Same architecture. Same signature. This is the same design as the ship I was held on—just scaled down. Like a scout ship or a transmission relay."

Lily's pulse ticked up. "Any valuable information?"

Xynn's mouth twisted. "There's a sort of... broadcast stage. I figure the transmission we picked up was pre-recorded here. Along with several more."

Lily didn't hesitate. "Pull the memory core. Get back to the shuttle and return to the *Salamander* as fast as you can. We'll tow the ship after we've secured it."

Xynn gave a quick nod. "Normally I'd be annoyed by you bossing me around. But in this case—" She smiled. "I'll see you soon."

The feed cut.

Lily stood alone in the quiet room. She exhaled and spoke softly to herself.

"Okay. Let's try this again."

· · · ·

The vaulted halls of the Ishrethi Archive shimmered with ambient light refracted through mineral-paneled walls. Tiered rows of relics stretched in every direction—etched murals, crystalline tomes, and suspended holographs preserving centuries of memory.

Charlie moved ahead, practically buzzing. "These patterns—look at this—storm cult iconography. Hidden in the border designs. It's the same rotational structure we found encoded in the Leviathan broadcast."

Datch knelt beside a plinth, scanning a shard of violet crystal suspended in a containment field. "This mineral," he said quietly, "isn't native to Ishreth Prime. But it's been refined into a focused amplifier. The cult used this tech—rare, and no longer manufactured."

Deeper in the library, a series of mural panels unfolded into a kind of chart—subtle alignments of icons and terrain, stitched together with more ephemeral symbols. Caris paused, tracing the path with a finger.

"This isn't a star chart," she said to the room. "It's a map. These alignments reference topography—valleys, fault lines... a trail. Here on Ishreth Prime."

Datch examined the holographic overlay. "It leads to a single fixed point. Somewhere deep in the northern continent."

He tapped his scanner triumphantly. "Coordinates locked."

"A buried temple," Zayir said, visibly delighted. "This is going to be such fun."

Lily rolled her eyes—but she couldn't deny it. They finally had a lead.

• • • •

The sun beat down hard across the ochre sands of the Ankaran Reach, a barren stretch of high desert that shimmered with heat mirages and broken stone. Lily squinted beneath her hood, sweat prickling at her temples despite the cooling weave of her gear.

The creature beneath her shifted with a low grunt—its broad, calloused feet padding over cracked rock with unexpected grace. She'd been told they were called lipum, and she still couldn't decide whether they looked more like anteaters or camels. The long snout, the loping gait, the thick tail that occasionally dragged a line in the sand... maybe both.

She glanced down at the message blinking on her wristband.

Xynn: Safe aboard. Alrek too. Towed the ship. It's secure. See you soon.

Lily exhaled a breath she hadn't realized she was holding. Her lips curled slightly. For all the danger, they were making progress. She looked ahead to where the trail carved upward into wind-blasted ridges. The Ishrethi guide seated in front of her clicked his tongue, nudging the lipum forward with a soft jolt of reins.

The beast hesitated.

It snorted, pawed at the ground, and tilted its snout toward the horizon.

"Uh," Lily said, shifting slightly, "is that normal behavior?"

The guide didn't respond at first. Then, slowly, he shook his head. Low voices stirred among the caravan—guards and servants speaking quickly in Ishrethi, their eyes locked on a swelling smudge in the sky.

Not smoke.

A cloud of something... moving.

Zayir galloped up beside her, dust trailing behind him. He was already dismounting before his lipum stopped.

"Zayir?" she asked, her voice cutting through the wind. "What's going on?"

His face was tight as he offered his hand. "The lipum are unsettled. They smell copper in the air."

She accepted his hand and slid down. "Copper?"

"They think it's rain. But it's not." He glanced to the horizon. "Those are not dark clouds, Lily. Those are copper locusts."

The words hung there for a beat too long.

Then he snapped to life, turning to shout in Ishrethi. "Quickly! Everyone into shelter!"

The caravan exploded into motion. Guides unlatched long black canisters from the backs of the beasts, slamming them to the ground. They popped open in an instant, unfolding into angular shelters—domes of black honeycomb steel that shimmered in the sun like alien igloos. One by one, the crew was ushered inside.

But Zayir didn't follow.

Instead, he pulled Lily by the arm, dragging her toward a different structure that had unfolded from the side of his personal mount—a sleeker, ridged pod with reinforced sides and a cockpit hatch. The moment she stepped inside, she felt the change: sealed atmosphere, polarized viewports, and faint hum of engines under the floor.

She blinked. "Wait—this isn't a shelter. It's a transport."

Zayir didn't answer. He sealed the hatch and slid into the control cradle, his hands flying over the console. The vehicle rumbled, kicked into motion, and peeled away from the encampment—cutting a new path through the sand in the opposite direction of the swarm.

"Shouldn't we stay with the others?" Lily asked, trying to steady herself as the ride jostled.

"No. You'll see why in a moment."

A thunderous clicking filled the air. Then came the sound—like hail against a metal roof, only sharper, heavier.

Lily turned to the viewport.

They were upon them.

Huge, segmented insects, each half the size of a hovercar, came skittering over the ridge. Copper wings shimmered. Mandibles snapped.

"Oh," Lily muttered. "I see. Yeah. These guys are not messing around."

One of the locusts slammed into the vehicle, and the transport veered sharply, crashing through a ridge of sandstone and tumbling down into a canyon. Metal screamed against rock. Lights flickered. The engine died.

Darkness.

The cabin tilted at a brutal angle, and Lily found herself nearly nose-to-nose with Zayir, their limbs tangled in the awkward space of the cockpit.

"Well," she said breathlessly, "this just keeps getting better."

• • • •

The emergency lights flickered faintly in the angled pod, casting pale orange glows across the control panel. Lily stood with one hand braced against the wall, steadying herself as the last of the tremors faded.

Her com tag chimed.

"Caris to Lily."

Lily tapped to connect. "I'm here."

"Everyone's checked in. No injuries reported. Everyone's intact in the shelters—though we may have lost two of the lipum. We are waiting for the swarm to pass."

Lily felt tension ease from her shoulders. "Copy that. We'll come find you once they pass. Lily out."

The pod fell quiet again, save for the faint whir of systems rebooting.

Zayir turned toward her with a slow smile. "You really have grown into your role, haven't you?" His voice softened, threaded with charm. "Confident. Commanding. Clever." He stepped closer. "Not the awkward young woman I met on Starbase 12 last year."

Lily shifted, discomfort crawling under her skin. "Zayir..."

He took another step. Close enough now to touch. "You know," he murmured, "a King may take what he wants."

She blinked. Stared at him. "Really?" Her voice was flat. "Zayir... really?"

He tilted his head, almost teasing, as though daring her to call his bluff.

"Come on, man." She backed away slightly, her tone tightening. "You have a beautiful wife. One who's loyal to you. Devoted to your legacy."

In her head: This is not what the Queen wanted me to say. But it was too late. She'd chosen.

"You should be ashamed of yourself. Or at the very least—feel incredibly silly. What is it you want from me, exactly?" Her voice remained calm, even cutting. "Because I think I know. You're not in love. You're bored. You're trying to inject chaos into your life to feel young again. To prove no one has taken your freedom."

She met his eyes. Didn't flinch. "But the desire to rule... that has to come from within."

He moved anyway—his arm slipping lightly around her waist, drawing her in with practiced ease, his face tilting toward hers.

Lily didn't move, but her expression said it all: Seriously?

He paused, inches from her face. Her pulse beat in her ears—but not with longing.

"Zayir," she said gently. "I know you to be a kind man. One who wants the best for his people. And I can see that you and Vaishali are trying—really trying—to build something together."

She lowered her voice. "She will have a child. With or without your help."

Zayir stepped back, not in shame, but something like reflection. He exhaled slowly, glancing toward the viewport where the haze had begun to clear.

"What are you doing out here playing adventurer?" she asked, more softly this time.

He didn't answer. Just stared out at the windswept dunes.

Finally, he said, "The swarm has passed."

He turned toward the hatch. "Let's go meet the others."

· · · ·

By late afternoon, the desert had become an oven. Each step kicked up dust too fine to see and too constant to escape, coating boots, lashes, lungs.

Lily's shirt clung to her back in damp patches, translucent with sweat and streaked with pale grit. Every movement made her aware of the fabric sticking to her skin, the way her shoulders ached from bracing against the beast's gait. The air tasted like copper and sunburn.

They had lost two of the lipum during the swarm—one to the locusts, another to panic and a broken leg—so now half the crew walked, slow and weary, their steps lagging behind the remaining mounts. The terrain had turned rockier, rough ridges scarring the dunes, demanding careful footing. Conversation had mostly dried up, except for Zayir quietly offering water and his attendants whispering among themselves in Ishrethi.

Inside a wind-scraped alcove where the sandstone dipped into shadow, Caris paused before a carved wall mostly buried in dust. Her gloved hand swept across the mural with careful consideration.

"This," she said softly, "is not from the central Leviathan sect."

Charlie came up beside her, breath catching. "The robes... the iconography—it's different. Look." He pointed to a relief barely visible in the stone. A smaller figure, arms outstretched, surrounded by storm spirals rather than crushed beneath them.

"A splinter sect," Caris murmured. "One that worshipped not the storm itself... but a child born from it."

Charlie's brow furrowed. "The Child of the Storm..." he echoed, as though tasting prophecy.

Not far from the mural, another chamber curved inward—a dome lined with decaying star charts. Most had peeled or cracked, but one remained intact, etched in metal rather than painted. It shimmered faintly under Datch's light.

Datch leaned in, a glint of excitement showing through his always sullen face. "These markers... they're not standard. The axis tilt, the rotation speeds—they're distorted by something." He adjusted his scanner. "This system is cloaked by radiation. That's why it doesn't show up on Union charts."

Charlie perked up. "A hidden system."

Datch tapped his communicator. "Transmitting coordinates now."

Lily pressed a hand to the rough stone beside her, grounding herself. She glanced to the side, noticing Zayir looking bored again.

• • • •

By the time they reached the palace gates, the desert had taken its toll. Dust clung to every crease of fabric and face, and even the palace guards stiffened at the sight of them—gritty, sun-drenched travelers stumbling in like ghosts from the dunes.

They were ushered inside with quiet efficiency. Marble corridors swallowed them, and for once no one stopped to admire the tapestries or the ceiling mosaics. All they wanted was water. Sleep. A moment to breathe.

Lily stood beneath a streaming cascade in the bathing chamber, steam curling against her skin. The fine soap felt too soft after hours of grit and sweat. She let it drip from her shoulders in silence, eyes closed, forehead pressed to the stone.

Later, dressed in clean clothes and wrapped in the hush of the palace's upper terraces, she activated her comm.

"Lily to Calan."

His voice came through a second later, calm and businesslike. "Go ahead."

"We're pretty much put back together down here," she said. "Sending you a full report now."

There was a brief pause as the data transferred.

"We've just finished triangulating the system," he said. "There's a planet buried in that radiation cloud—never charted before. The readings match. You were right."

"So it exists."

"It does," he confirmed. "And we're going. I need you all back on board as soon as possible."

"Will do."

She ended the transmission and turned—just as Zayir stepped from the shadows of a nearby archway, arms crossed, brows lifted in amusement.

"Captain Calan is eager to solve this puzzle."

She sighed. "Were you watching me?"

"I arrived just in time to hear about your exciting mission," he said, unbothered.

She eyed him. "What do you want?"

"You know I have an expert in Ishrethi culture who must accompany you on this next leg of your journey."

Lily raised a brow. "Oh yeah? Who's that?"

Zayir's smile didn't budge. "You're looking at him." He made a sweeping gesture over his own body.

"You're not serious."

He met her gaze, all trace of humor gone. "Serious."

• • • •

By nightfall, the farewell party had assembled. A quiet buzz of motion filled the outer court as servants loaded gear onto the waiting skiff. Torches burned low in the breeze. Cleaned and polished, the *Salamander* crew stood at the ready—exhausted, but prepared. The heat of the desert had faded into a cool hush.

Zayir approached the Queen beneath the columns, his movements careful, ceremonial. She took his hand, her touch soft and lingering.

"You could wait until morning," she said gently. "Rest. One night in the royal chambers, then go."

Her eyes shimmered with something unspoken, her voice low and inviting. "A night in the royal chambers—with me."

Zayir gave the faintest nod of acknowledgment.

"I see no reason to delay," he said, and withdrew his hand.

He turned without fanfare and walked toward the launch.

The Queen watched him go, like a glass column.

Only her eyes moved—cutting toward Lily.

And what they said was crystal clear.

Fix it.

• • • •

Later, Lily finally found herself in her quarters next to Xynn. The air felt still in a way only starships could manage—like the silence between breaths. The kind that hummed with old ghosts and fresh gravity.

Xynn sat perched at the edge of the bed, arms draped over her knees, hair still damp from the shower and curling wild against her cheek. Her shoulders were stiff, as if she hadn't quite unclenched since the moment they'd stepped back aboard.

She didn't wait for Lily to ask.

"That ship today—the empty one. The hull groaning, the lights half-dead... it brought back a lot of unpleasant feelings," she said flatly. "From that damn Warden of Tarshish. The way it smelled. The silence. I felt like I was back in that cell again."

Lily reached for her hand without hesitation, threading their fingers together. Her palm was warm, steady.

"Well," she said, offering a small, lopsided smile, "today has been a day of things going wrong."

That drew a breath of a laugh from Xynn. She tipped her head back, eyes catching the ceiling.

"You're not kidding."

Lily shifted closer, still holding her hand. "Xynn, my sweet warrior dear..." She grinned now, a little too pleased with herself. "Will you be my chaperone for the rest of this mission?"

Xynn turned her head, eyes narrowed in mock suspicion. "What exactly does this job entail?"

"Protecting me from royals leading with their hormones, bugs the size of Volkswagens, and any more well-timed surprises."

Xynn sniffed. "I better sharpen my blade."

And they took a moment of recovery. With the two of them together, a moment is all it took.

In Defense of the Salamander

THE LOWER DECKS OF the *Salamander* had settled into a deeper stillness—the kind that crept in only when most of the crew had vanished behind closed doors or fallen into sleep. In engineering, amber lights pulsed with the cadence of a heartbeat, slow and warm, casting long shadows that stretched like fingers across the walls.

Alrek stood near the diagnostic console, posture straight but expression caught somewhere between formal and hesitant. His gaze flicked toward Ka-Lorrin, then away again, like someone unsure if they were interrupting.

"Ka-Lorrin?" he asked, voice light but careful.

Ka-Lorrin turned from the schematic he'd been reviewing, one brow raised. "Yes? Alrek..."

"I was hoping..." Alrek trailed off, adjusting the strap on his utility sash. "I'd like to request a meeting with you tomorrow morning. Before my shift."

Ka-Lorrin tilted his head slightly, though his gaze remained fixed on the schematic. "Tomorrow. Morning. Yes, of course... Anything urgent?"

"No, not urgent. Just... something I'd like to discuss."

Taran peered around the corner of a large console.

Ka-Lorrin nodded. "Very well. I'll see you right here in the morning."

"Thank you." Alrek gave a short nod and turned to leave—hesitating just long enough to suggest there was more he wasn't saying. Then he slipped away, quiet as ever, into the dim corridor.

Ka-Lorrin turned toward Taran, arms crossed, posture taut with curiosity. "I wonder what that was about."

Taran yawned, revealing rows of pointed teeth, and slid his heavy pack off his shoulder with a groan of relief. "He's young. Probably just received his official posting, I'll bet—I'll bet."

Ka-Lorrin tensed slightly, still keeping his eyes on his work. "Surely he'll want to stay aboard the *Salamander*."

Taran gave a lazy shrug. "Maybe..."

Ka-Lorrin turned fully, large eyes narrowing. "Maybe? What do you mean maybe?"

Taran scratched the fur under his chin. "He's young, he is. That's all. That's all. We were talking earlier about the new Saber-class ships. The SFS Sarout has a lot of open spots. A lot."

Ka-Lorrin made a noise somewhere between a scoff and a gasp. "That glorified microwave? That floating showroom? The Sarout is an overgrown algorithm with hull plating."

Taran gave him a sidelong glance.

"Alright," Ka-Lorrin grumbled. "It's... a sleek piece of engineering. But it's barely a quarter the size of the Salamander. No soul. No legacy."

Taran chuckled. "Preaching to the choir, Kal. You know. You know..."

But Ka-Lorrin was already elsewhere—beyond listening.

· · · ·

That night, Ka-Lorrin didn't climb into his synthetic seedpod. He didn't even open the hatch. Instead, he sat hunched at his workstation, bathed in pale blue light, muttering under his breath. Schematics of the SFS Sarout flickered across the screen, shifting as he zoomed in on its engine layout, crew manifest, and classroom facilities. Taran snored loudly from his hammock, a steady rumble like distant thunder.

"Hmph," Ka-Lorrin sniffed, tapping through screen after screen. "They won't treat you half as well on this ship. No hydroponic gardens. Get used to synthesized meals for weeks on end... And no wise engineering duo to guide you through life's intricate puzzles."

He held up a tablet, squinting at the image of the Sarout's new chief of engineering. "This officer is essentially a child. Less than a quarter of my age."

His long fingers danced across the adaptive controls of the computer, calling up a new document: *Salamander vs. Sarout – Pros and Cons.*

"Let's see... atmosphere filtration—ours is triple buffered. Those Cartillian systems really skimped on the fiber layers. Seating ergonomics: classic case of fixing what need not be deemed obsolete. Translation matrix? Ours runs beta on nine hundred languages, thanks to Taran's connections at VCTAA."

He smirked to himself. "I bet your gelatinous friend would appreciate that."

He hesitated, tapping a slender finger lightly against the desk. "And one cannot *measure* the personality of a crew, of course. But if I *were* forced to rank them—well. The Salamander crew is distinguished. Even if they can be a bit overzealous at times..."

He scrolled through digital resumes of the Sarout's crew. "These cadets have the least inspiring set of curriculum vitas I've seen. At least... to date."

Hours passed.

Taran's snores were deep, vibrating the air ducts—a resonant thrum that would've been muffled if Ka-Lorrin had sealed himself inside his pod. But he hadn't. He was too deep now—digging through fleet records, personnel bios, comparing photos of engineering consoles.

Around 0200, Taran cracked one bleary eye and lifted his great head from the hammock.

"Kal... have you been at that all night?"

Ka-Lorrin didn't look up. "The boy needs us. I've seen it. The way he responds to structure. To encouragement."

"Kal..." Taran tried to interject.

"We can't let him go to a ship like that. He'll be underutilized. Uninspired. Undernourished!" He spun back to the console, scrolling furiously. "I think—I think I can get us transferred to oversee their engineering team. The Sarout could use a proper tuning anyway. I still have some influence at fleet command. Well, they stopped returning my calls. But the nature of their work means it's natural for them to be busy."

"Kal..."

"We'd have to dislodge Commander Barnes, of course. But I know for a fact he's allergic to shellfish. Now, say a mistake were to happen with—"

"Kal!"

Taran stood fully now, casting a wide shadow, his voice firm but kind. "It's not our place to interfere with the boy's journey. It's not. It's not."

Ka-Lorrin paused, chest heaving faintly, shoulders rigid.

Taran softened. "Besides. He's a good kid, he is. And I'm sure we'll keep in touch."

Ka-Lorrin didn't reply.

• • • •

Ka-Lorrin sat hunched once more, the console's blue glow an anchor in a sea of flickering thoughts. His fingers twitched; his lips tightened into a line of determined restraint. The cursor blinked—a silent metronome counting down to his next mistake.

He stared at the empty message field for a full minute, then began to type with the careful fury of someone trying very hard not to sound furious.

> *To Whom It May Concern,*
>
> *I write regarding the engineering command structure aboard the SFS Sarout, which, while I am certain is adequate in the most generous application of the word, may be insufficient to nurture the kind of brilliance I have personally observed in one Junior Engineer Alrek, of the scattered Saravethi.*

He paused. Read it back. Deleted the word "generous." Replaced it with "charitable." Deleted that too.

> *While I understand the logistical necessities that drive officer placement in the fleet, I feel compelled—no, honor-bound—to suggest a reassignment in this particular case. Not for my own benefit, of course, but for the preservation of future excellence. There are sparks in the young that must be shielded from wind. Otherwise they gutter. They fail to catch. They die.*

He stopped again. Sat back. Frowned at the screen. "Too poetic," he muttered aloud, adjusting the slope of his spine as though posture might correct sentiment.

He sighed, deleted the entire message, and started over.

> *Dear Fleet Command,*
> *Let me tell you about a boy.*

"No. No, no." He scratched at the base of his neck. "You sound like you're *in love* with him."

Delete. Cursor blinking again.

Esteemed Leadership,

I am writing to recommend a critical reassessment of the Sarout's personnel roster, and to offer my own availability as a temporary adjunct or full-time reassignment to said vessel, should the opportunity arise. The ship's ionic coupling architecture is of particular interest to me and—

He blinked.

"...Is that even true?"

It might've been true. Further research would be required. Not important. He jabbed at the console, backspacing the entire thing in a storm of elongated fingers and frustrated huffing.

Next:

Fleet,

Don't make a mistake. A glaring, epoch-defining, engineer-wailing mistake, and I alone can fix it.

"Too dramatic," he whispered. "Or not dramatic *enough*."

He rubbed at his eyes. The room swam a little.

The cursor blinked.

He started typing again.

Fleeeeeeeeeeet,
let me tell you about a boy—

Ka-Lorrin jerked awake with a start, realizing he'd dozed off mid-word. The sentence trailed off in a lazy sea of vowels across the screen, like a drunk man trying to hold onto a song. He sighed and deleted the line without comment.

"I should've led with the ionic coupling," he mumbled. "Who can resist a good conversation about ions."

Another draft started. Another overcorrection. Another spiral of formal grammar and informal pleading, declarations of loyalty, biting critiques of the Sarout's engineering chairs ("ergonomically hostile to lateral thinkers"), and one emotional line he immediately regretted:

> *Do we want to look back and say—He used to sparkle. Now he's matte.*

"Ugh," Ka-Lorrin groaned, dropping his forehead against the edge of the desk. "What *is* this? A memoir? A novel? A tragic ballad in the key of passive-aggressive desperation?"

He deleted the whole thing. Again.

The console blinked back at him with the quiet disdain of something that knew better.

Ka-Lorrin pressed the heels of his palms to his eyes until colors bloomed like bruised stars in the dark. "You're losing your edge," he muttered. "And possibly your dignity."

Somewhere behind him, Taran snored—low and rhythmic, like the thrum of a well-oiled stabilizer coil.

Ka-Lorrin stared at the screen for a moment longer, then whispered, "I think it would be a real loss."

But this time, he didn't write it down.

• • • •

The blinking cursor stilled. Ka-Lorrin slouched in his seat, one hand dangling off the edge of the console like a forgotten tool. His thoughts, unmoored now from syntax and structure, began to wander—slipping sideways into half-dreams and ill-fitting memories.

The firestorm came first. Korolith III, his homeworld—lush, luminous, and entirely unreasonable. He saw it as he had seen it in youth: the sky stitched with heat lightning, jungle trees bending in submission as gouts of flame surged across the canopy. The wind screamed through vine-wrapped cliffs, dragging soot and spores in its wake. Storm season. A test every Raath-Ka was meant to endure.

He remembered the way the rain came *after* the fire—too late to be helpful, but early enough to steam the air into something unbreathable. He had been so small then. Clinging to an overhang of thresher moss, counting prime numbers to keep calm, the ground trembling with thunder and raw heat.

Even now, the scent of it bloomed in his memory—ionized air and sweet rot. A storm that taught him fear, then shaped that fear into spine.

Then—his parents.

Too close. Too symmetrical. Their elongated faces hovered just past the edge of the real, smiling the way Ka-Lorrin always hated: with a kind of tidy fondness, as if affection were a well-ordered shelf.

He flinched and sat up straighter, only to sink again, his eyelids heavy and traitorous.

The console lights blurred. The air felt too thick. A faint vibration in the floor beneath him seemed to hum a single note—a warning, or a lullaby.

He saw a corridor now. Not from any ship he recognized. The walls were fleshy, like muscle, or coral grown too dense to breathe through. The floor shifted beneath his steps. Gears clicked above him in a slow, syncopated rhythm. The corridor was coiling, looping inward like a nautilus shell. He walked toward the center, even though he knew it would end in teeth.

He blinked hard. The room returned.

Taran snored on.

Ka-Lorrin pressed his fingers to his temples, whispering equations to ground himself—fractal ratios, field compression constants, obscure Saravethi theorems that no one used anymore because they were *inelegant*.

"I need sleep," he muttered, even though he had no intention of finding it.

Then, quietly: "Too much brain. Not enough buffer."

A chime pinged on the console—he'd accidentally opened an old spec sheet while trying to minimize the text field. His eyes caught on the engine layout of the Sarout. And just like that, the chaos coalesced into clarity.

• • • •

It was the ion array that did it. Right there, in the Sarout's spec sheet—version 4.3.7 of the tertiary propulsion lattice, still fitted with bundled conduits. Not the upgraded flare-tracked mesh the Union had been pushing for the last three calendar years, but the *old system*—the one that required precision. The one that *he knew*.

Ka-Lorrin sat up so fast his chair nearly toppled.

"Ionic bundling," he said aloud, as if naming a forgotten lover. "Standard multi-phase relay logic. No compression layers. My gods, it's beautiful."

He scrambled to pull up the archive from his personal drive, fingers flying, joints clicking. The files loaded slowly—ancient formats, deprecated metadata—but there it was: a crisp black-and-white certificate, dated six and a half standard years ago, with a watermark that read *Certified: High-Competency Ionic Configurations and Multi-Spindle Diagnostics (Cyranthian Issue)*.

He stared at it for a long moment. Then whispered, "I *knew* I was still qualified."

Of course, he could have just uploaded the digital badge to his Union profile. But something drove him to look for the actual certificate.

So he stood, joints creaking, and began to dig.

Ka-Lorrin's quarters were tidy in the way only an obsessive could maintain—neat rows of labeled drawers, temperature-stabilized archive boxes, six identical engineering jumpsuits hanging in order of seam repair status. But the personal archive? The "nonessential keepsake bin" tucked behind the false panel near the ceiling vent? That was chaos.

He pulled it down with a grunt, sending a puff of dust into the air, and began rooting through it like a long-fingered raccoon in a scholar's attic.

Manuals. Microfibre polishing gloves. An unopened care kit for an obsolete dermal sensor. A coral fragment from a bonding ritual chamber on Korolith III. A note from Taran in thick, careful script: *"You were right about the torque rods."*

Then—folded in a plastifoil sleeve, behind an envelope he didn't remember ever opening—he found it.

The certificate. Paper, real paper, frayed at the edges and laminated with static-resistant coating.

Ka-Lorrin clutched it to his chest like a stolen artifact.

"Vindication," he breathed.

Then he blinked—and noticed the instrument.

Wedged halfway under the pile. Slender. Dusty. Delicate. Its curvature unmistakable.

He pulled it free, blinking at the filigreed casing. A veolar reed harp, tuned for fine vibration resonance. Nearly impossible to play well. Entirely unnecessary on a ship. His.

He hadn't touched it in years.

Ka-Lorrin stared at it.

Then, quietly, he closed the cabinet, padded barefoot across the floor, and sealed the door to his sleeping chamber—more out of courtesy than stealth. Taran would sleep through a reactor breach. But the harp was... personal.

He settled cross-legged on the floor, the certificate discarded beside him, and set the reed harp across his lap.

The first note was thin and wobbly. The second cracked. The third found a thread of tone and tugged.

He kept playing. Slowly. Hesitantly. Then with a kind of uncertain reverence, like brushing dust off a half-remembered dream.

The console lights dimmed behind him. The stars outside spun.

And Ka-Lorrin, eyes half-lidded, let the sound lead him inward.

• • • •

The notes came slowly at first. Like cautious guests arriving at the edge of a party they weren't sure they'd been invited to.

Ka-Lorrin adjusted the reed harp's angle across his knees, his long fingers splayed like spidered branches over the strings. He plucked again—this time drawing out a tremble of resonance that hummed against the floor and up through his bones.

The instrument had once belonged to his brood-mentor, an older Ka whose name had been lost in bureaucratic error but who played with the gravity of falling stars. Ka-Lorrin had never been much good at it. The spacing between the strings was meant for more flexible digits, and his had always been a touch too precise, too surgical. But the harp didn't seem to mind.

The notes bent under his touch—uneven, imperfect, softly glowing with the warmth of something remembered but never mastered.

He tried to play a scale. Failed halfway through. Laughed softly. Tried again.

Soon the pattern found him.

A looping, off-kilter rhythm began to form, like the pulse of an old coolant pump or a lullaby sung from behind a closed wall. Not a melody exactly—just a series of emotional gestures laid end to end. Grief without sadness. Joy without shape. Longing with nowhere to go.

He closed his eyes.

The music blurred.

So did the walls.

There was water now, in his ears and on his skin. A low tide sound, churning with bioluminescence. The floor beneath him was coral—not the painted metal of a starship, but real coral, alive and warm and very slightly breathing. His fingers found the strings again, but they were no longer strings—they were light filaments, glowing gold and green beneath the surface of the reef. He plucked one and the whole reef answered, a deep thrum of welcome that echoed through his chest.

He was no longer seated.

He was *small*.

Just a handful of limbs and eyes in a long ceremonial robe. The temple dome arched high above him, carved from a single calcified blossom. Vines swayed in the warm air, and the soft chanting of the Elders rolled like mist from the walls.

The Spiral was opening.

He blinked, unsure if he was dreaming, remembering, or somehow both.

And from the far end of the coral chamber—just past the pool of truthlight and beneath the vine-framed archway—came a sound heavier than any he'd just played.

Footsteps.

Four of them.

Heavy. Clumsy. Young.

· · · ·

The steps grew louder—uncertain at first, then confident in that way only young creatures can manage, unaware of the weight their arrival carries.

Ka-Lorrin turned, or rather—*young* Ka-Lorrin turned. His robe was too long, the hem dragging slightly behind him, and he kept tripping over the words to a focus chant he'd been practicing in his head:

Substructural integrity. Ion flux. Three-point bracing with lateral drift...

His limbs twitched in micro-corrections, adjusting his balance.

And then Taran entered.

Not the Taran he knew now—solid, silvering, wry—but a *boy*, barely more than a pup. He was all limbs and fluff and ceremonial silk, the sash of his house trailing off one shoulder and knotted entirely wrong. His fur stuck up in wet clumps, and his wide eyes scanned the temple like he was looking for a snack or a secret or a reason not to panic.

He barreled halfway down the spiral path before realizing he was being watched. Then he slowed, clumsy paws shifting to a kind of reverent tiptoe. He saw Ka-Lorrin and paused, blinking.

The silence between them stretched.

Then Ka-Lorrin—nervous, too aware of the Elders humming in tri-tone from the gallery above—tried to bow. He misjudged the angle. His datapad, wedged into his robe sash for comfort, slid out and clattered to the coral floor.

The sound echoed like a dropped truthstone.

Young Taran blinked again.

And then, without a word, he lumbered forward, picked up the datapad in both hands—*carefully*, like it might explode—and held it out.

"Yours?" he said, in a voice too deep for his size.

Ka-Lorrin hesitated. Then: "Affirmative."

Taran grinned.

The Elders' chant rose behind them.

"The bond is sound," they intoned, in voices that vibrated the walls.

Taran handed him the datapad with a solemnity he clearly didn't understand, and Ka-Lorrin took it with all the gravity in the world.

They stood there, two children tangled in a ritual older than memory, blinking at each other.

Taran scratched his ear with the edge of the sash.

Ka-Lorrin adjusted his robes.

Something shifted in the air—unseen, unanalyzed—but felt, deeply.

A link formed. Not a tether. A path.

And just before the dream dissolved, just before Ka-Lorrin felt himself begin to wake, he saw himself—older again—standing outside the memory, watching the two of them frozen in that moment of first meeting.

He whispered, in the voice of the present:

"We look out for each other."

And then the coral faded. The light dimmed. The sound folded inward like a breath held too long.

· · · ·

The reed harp had slipped sideways across his lap. One of the strings was still faintly vibrating, a single note caught in the ship's recycled air. The console had dimmed, displaying only the soft, rotating seal of the Union Engineering Guild, as if politely pretending not to have witnessed anything.

He blinked crust from his eyes, one hand fumbling for balance. His joints ached. His eyes weary. His dignity was nowhere to be found.

But something inside him had quieted.

He reached for the console, opened the message draft—and deleted it. No hesitation. No drama. Just a soft, definitive flick of his finger across the interface.

Then he sat back in the chair, looking around the still-dim room. The instrument. The certificate. The dust unsettled from old memories.

Across the chamber, Taran let out a deep snore, rolled over, and muttered something that might have been "torque rod" or might have been nonsense.

Ka-Lorrin smiled. Just barely.

"You were right," he said into the quiet. "You stubborn, beautiful brute."

Then, more softly: "He's not ours to bind. Not like we were. But we can still be here for him."

He stood, joints clicking, and began to tidy the space—not because it needed it, but because movement helped. He returned the harp to its sleeve, slid the certificate back into the archive, and folded the plastifoil with an almost ceremonial precision.

Then, for the first time that night, he opened his pod.

The interior lights came on low and warm, calibrated to ease transition. He climbed inside, curling his limbs with care, and let the door seal behind him with a soft hiss.

From the other room, Taran stirred again.

"...Kal?" came the groggy voice.

"Yes, yes. I'm going to sleep," Ka-Lorrin called out, already drifting.

He paused. Then added, quieter:

"Thanks for looking out for me."

• • • •

The next morning, after a long shower and an even longer bout of pacing, Ka-Lorrin had meticulously ironed his jumpsuit and oiled his leathery skin. He and Taran arrived at Engineering a full twenty minutes early—Ka-Lorrin immediately took to pacing, muttering, polishing toolkits that didn't need polishing.

Alrek arrived exactly on time.

"Good morning," he said, offering a small, earnest smile. "Thanks for meeting with me. I'd love to share this with both of you—"

Ka-Lorrin raised a hand, voice suddenly loud and a touch too unsteady. "First, I'd like to say something..."

Taran held his breath.

Ka-Lorrin stepped forward, drawing himself up to full height.

"Young Alrek. You are bright, capable, endlessly inquisitive—sometimes too inquisitive, but that's beside the point. You are a rare breed. An engineer with potential, yes—but also integrity. It's been an honor mentoring you, and I know you have a choice ahead of you. Many ships will want you. Fancy ones. Fast ones. Flashy ones. But I—we—we hoped you would stay. I had hoped to teach you longer. Guide you. Learn from you, even."

He paused.

Taran coughed.

Ka-Lorrin added quickly, "I don't want you to leave." Then, more stiffly, "Taran would miss you too much."

Taran rolled his eyes and folded his arms.

Alrek blinked, clearly trying to suppress a smile. "That's... incredibly kind. Thank you." He paused. "Can I tell you my thing now?"

Ka-Lorrin nodded. "Oh, um—yes. Of course."

"I mean... of course I'm going to request assignment to the *Salamander*."

There was a beat of silence.

Ka-Lorrin collapsed into the nearest chair, limbs suddenly loose. "Oh. Well, that's a relief. Right then." He attempted to collect himself. "Shift begins in a minute."

Taran coughed again. "Kal... his... thing?"

"Oh yes. Oh yes. Young Al—" He corrected himself. "Alrek. What did you want to ask us?"

Alrek grinned now, more relaxed. "There's a guest lecture opening at the Junior Engineer Corps—an adjunct program. I thought of you two. Just once a quarter. You could take leave from the Salamander for a few days. You'd be amazing. The cadets would love you."

The pause that followed was thick enough to muffle a Raath Summons.

Then Ka-Lorrin stood, hands clasped behind his back. "Well. That sounds... lovely. We will be sure to apply."

Alrek left with a satisfied nod.

Taran grinned—broad and toothy.

Ka-Lorrin didn't look at him. "Don't start."

And with a sharp flick of his collar, he strode off toward the reactor core, already outlining his lecture series in his mind.

Chapter 8: In the Wake of the Fire

THE SCREEN FLICKERED with washed-out color, like something copied too many times to remember its source.

Static buzzed at the edges as the transmission rolled—just barely reconstructed from the scorched memory core Xynn had pulled. Ronin stood in the center of the frame, flanked by shadow and light. Behind him, a stylized map flickered: fractal lines radiating from a red-hued system, labeled only in glyphs.

His voice was soft. Controlled. Almost kind.

> "Immortality," he said, "is not a gift. It's a burden only the willing can carry. But it must be earned. The final contribution is nearly ready. The planet of fire awaits. And within it—Caronite. The key to the end of death."

The video glitched. His mouth kept moving for a few seconds longer, but no sound came.

Then it cut out entirely.

The silence in the briefing room was almost reverent.

"That planet behind him," Alrek said softly, pointing to the map's faint contour. "That's not a stylized flame. It's a radiation halo."

Calan rubbed a hand down his face, distorting his lips as he spoke. "Most likely the hidden planet we're headed to."

Alrek nodded. "We've been calling it Bimini."

Lily raised a brow.

Ka-Lorrin chimed in from the side of the room. "He's been too entrenched in Earth studies. It's from their myths about the fountain of youth."

"Ahh." Lily nodded, half getting the reference.

Calan gestured to the other side of the screen. "What about that?"

Alrek's expression shifted. "I overlaid the geometry against Union cartographic logs. That's Gherion Prime."

Taran let out a low whistle. "Knew that one'd come back around—he did, he did."

"He's not just trying to spread a message," Alrek added. "He's gathering something. Building toward... something final."

Calan leaned back from the console, gaze narrowing. "A hidden planet, a mystery mineral, and Gherion Prime tangled in the middle of it."

"Don't forget his followers," Alrek said. "They're not random. He's pulling people from specific worlds—planets in the path of the storm."

Lily stood just behind him, arms crossed, one foot tapping soundlessly against the deck.

"Should I tell Datch," she asked, "or should you?"

Calan didn't have time to answer. The comm pinged, sharp in the hush. Caris' face lit the panel.

"Sir," she said, all clipped calm. "We're approaching Bimini."

Lily exhaled and turned toward the exit.

"I suppose the expedition awaits."

• • • •

The stars were different here.

Lily watched them shift across the screen in patient spirals, like dancers rehearsing a sequence no one else could hear. Three suns spun in lazy configuration, tinting the clouds in colors that balanced vibrance and memory—dust-rose and storm-amber, chalkblue and ghostwhite. Radiation curled through the atmosphere in slow, shimmering loops, distorting everything just enough to make her feel like she was dreaming it all.

But she wasn't dreaming.

"A world that wasn't meant to be found," Calan murmured from his seat, voice soft and steady.

Datch stood at the edge of the bridge's main viewer, hands folded with the kind of stillness Lily now recognized as a warning. When Datch went silent, the universe was about to move.

"It feels almost like it tried to hide itself," Tevya offered from across the room, her tone gentle, clearly meant for her husband. But she didn't approach him. Datch seemed unusually disturbed—unsettled by the connection between Ronin and Gherion Prime. Like he was trying to work out a math problem in his head, but the answer kept shifting under his fingertips.

"Hiding in plain sight for who knows how long," Lily said. She reached out, fingers brushing the edge of her workstation's display. The sensors flickered again—momentary glitches, like echoes caught in a storm. "Three stars. The converging radiation acts as a natural planetary cloak. Strong enough to shred standard scanners. And still, there's life down there."

Caris crossed her arms, studying the readouts. "And war. Or the edge of it."

"War?" Calan asked, frowning.

Basco chimed in from the side console, ever helpful. "Yes, sir. This planet seems comparable to 20th-century Earth. Enough nuclear payloads to annihilate themselves a hundred times over. And they appear to be preparing to deploy them."

"Well," Calan said, tension cutting through his usual dry delivery, "that's not great."

The feed sharpened—barely. Fleeting glimpses of architecture pushed up through fog and solar glare. Tall, spare structures carved into a rocky basin. Roads. Landing fields. Smoke. Or maybe steam. Some buildings pulsed with low-frequency energy, visible only when the light hit just right.

There was a pause. Then Calan spoke again, voice clear and firm.

"No contact with the surface," Calan said. "Union regulations prohibit interference with civilizations that have lower technical ability. Observation only."

Caris nodded. "With your permission, sir, I've assembled a stealth team."

Calan didn't hesitate. "Your mission then, Lieutenant."

The entire time they spoke, Lily had almost forgotten about Zayir.

He was standing at the rear of the bridge like he owned it. Or like he was simply waiting for the right moment to interject and assert his self-appointed dominance.

Since he'd come aboard, he'd been almost eager to prove that Lily didn't like this version of him one bit. He'd changed into Ishrethi field gear—sleek, matte-black, with a ceremonial sash knotted artfully over one shoulder. Too fashionable to be practical, Lily thought. His hair was tousled in that deliberate way, his stance casual and angular. A general air of cultivated superiority hung about him like expensive cologne.

She clocked the pose instantly—and felt a knot of dread coil behind her ribs as he approached Calan.

If their last encounter had humbled him, it showed no trace. On the contrary, he seemed more smug than ever, as if rejection had only confirmed what he already believed: that the universe orbited his charm.

"Captain," he began, with the confidence of a man who'd never known consequence. "I'll be joining the away mission."

Calan didn't blink. "Your Majesty, this is not a diplomatic visit. The surface is unstable. Atmospheric interference is severe, and our data on the civilization is non-existent. The team going down will be in disguise—a recon mission. This is not a royal tour."

Zayir smiled like he was being flirted with. "Cautious tourism, then. I do love an undercover operation." He paused, letting it linger. "And I find societies on the brink of self-annihilation fascinating."

Calan opened his mouth, searching for the right counter—but Zayir was already moving on.

"You've received the mandate from Fleet Command regarding my presence here. As a condition of ongoing cooperation with Ishreth, I'm permitted to accompany any landing party deemed non-hostile."

A silence fell like static.

Calan's jaw tightened, but he gave a single, sharp nod—the kind that meant he was parking something for later. "Very well."

Then he turned to Lily.

"You're in charge of looking after His Majesty. Bring him back in one piece, with a pulse. That's an order."

Zayir clapped his hands together softly, like it was all settled.

Lily felt like she was going to puke.

· · · ·

The corridor to the shuttle bay shimmered under emergency-grade lighting, still flickering slightly from their last encounter with the storm. But the air buzzed now with a different kind of tension—anticipatory, theatrical.

Lily adjusted the collar of her roughspun jacket, scratching at the edge of the adhesive where the prosthetic scales met her real skin. Dr. Thesari had been practically giddy about the fittings, claiming she hadn't had this much fun since designing fungal skin sloughs for the spores of Vendaris IX. The aliens looked *almost* human—just enough to trigger something uncanny. Red-toned skin, scaling along the ears and down the neck, and wiry silver hair worn long, often braided or loosely knotted behind the head. Lily's hair was tucked into a silvery wrap, and a faint chemical scent clung to her from the pigment gel.

The clothing was simple—functional pants, plain shirts, sturdy jackets. All made from a thick, denim-like weave that held heat with relentless affection. Luckily, Alrek had snuck cooling fibers into the seams, activated by their biometric readings. If not for his ingenuity, Lily suspected the lot of them would be fainting within minutes on the surface. The planet's temperature held steady at *twice* that of a typical Earth summer.

Ahead, the shuttle bay doors loomed open, revealing the sleek form of the landing vessel prepped and ready.

Caris and Datch walked a few paces ahead, exchanging the occasional quiet word. Lily moved quickly to stay a step in front of Zayir, who seemed content to linger at the rear with practiced disinterest.

Then—footsteps. Fast. Echoing down the corridor.

Lily turned just in time to see Malik jogging toward them, fully dressed in prosthetics and local garb. His silver hair was pulled back in a loose tail, and the scales on his neck caught the light as he slowed to a halt. He looked... natural. Like he could've passed for one of the locals without even trying.

Caris opened her mouth—maybe to challenge him—but stopped short. She just smiled.

"Mind if I tag along?" Malik asked, still catching his breath. Lily couldn't help but notice—his usual gruffness was gentled somehow. Like he wanted to be here.

Caris gave him a nod, the kind that carried more meaning than words could.

And with that, their mismatched team grew by one.

They stepped together into the bay, the hiss of the shuttle ramp lowering before them—the threshold to a world on the brink.

• • • •

They had landed nearly a mile outside the settlement, in a shallow ridge masked by jagged outcrops and thorny scrub. The walk had started as manageable. Now it was oppressive.

The heat pressed in like a second skin. Sweat clung to Lily's collar and pooled beneath the prosthetic scales at her neck. Every breath tasted faintly of metal and ash.

Ahead, the rooftops of the village shimmered through the haze—sharp angles of corrugated metal and pale stone, huddled low to the cracked earth. The sky pulsed with slow radiation spirals. The heat didn't just burn here. It rippled.

"Lovely climate," Zayir announced breezily. "Reminds me of home. Desert world. Triple suns. You get used to it, of course."

He cast a sideways glance at Datch. "You know what I mean, don't you, Lieutenant Commander?"

Datch didn't break stride. "Bragging about your own biological advantage does little to bolster team morale."

Lily smiled despite herself.

They crested a rise just outside the first cluster of buildings—and paused.

A crystalline formation jutted from the ground like a wound made solid. Pale red, veined with darker bands that pulsed faintly beneath the surface, as if lit from within.

Caris stepped closer, raising her scanner. "Caronite," she confirmed. "Matches the signature Alrek pulled."

"Then Ronin won't be far behind us," Lily said quietly.

They moved on—and that's when they noticed them.

Thin red tendrils, winding in and out of the ground at irregular intervals. The vines poked through cracks in the earth, snaked around rusted piping, and hung low from rooftops like ivy. Some reached upward as if sensing the air, twitching faintly when someone passed too close. They weren't aggressive—just... alert.

One coiled lazily around Datch's boot before retreating.

Malik crouched beside another. "They're everywhere," he murmured. "No visible root structure. Responsive to temperature, motion, maybe even sound. Somewhere between fungi and mineral. Don't ask me to explain—that's the best I've got."

Lily watched a vine stretch toward a wall, brush against it, then drift toward a passing civilian—grazing their ankle like it was greeting them.

"Symbiosis?" she asked.

Malik nodded. "It's like the whole village is part of one organism."

Zayir, trailing behind and not watching closely, raised an eyebrow. "Looks like a plant, acts like an animal—I wonder what it tastes like."

No one answered him. Lily just exhaled.

They reached the edge of the village, where buildings gave way to alleyways and open roads. The locals—red-skinned, silver-haired, moving with quick efficiency—were preparing. But not evacuating.

Families emerged from doorways with small carts and sealed cases. Doors hissed shut behind them. Others hauled equipment into communal spaces. Children were ushered into structures that resembled churches or shelters. A convoy of low-slung vehicles buzzed down the main road, carrying crates marked with unfamiliar glyphs.

Lily spotted the child out of the corner of her eye, tugging at Caris' pant leg.

Caris turned, startled.

The child looked up and smiled—a sweet, unguarded grin.

Then, slowly, they dragged a thumb across their own throat and let out a low, hissing sound.

The translation matrix didn't even attempt to interpret it.

And then the child skipped away.

Caris stared after them, her brow furrowing. Then she pulled up her scanner, fingers moving fast. "There's a weapons facility. Nine-point-eight miles south—cut into the canyon wall."

Lily leaned in. "I don't like the sound of that."

Caris gave a slow, grim nod. "Nuclear stockpile. Massive. And I think it's powering up." She passed the scanner to Malik for confirmation.

"They're arming?" Lily asked, her voice catching in her throat. "How long do you think we have?"

Malik held the scanner close to his face. "If they launch and we run, we might make it to the shuttle in time. Just enough to get offworld before... before the atmosphere lights up."

"We should endeavor to keep an eye on the readings, then," Datch said calmly.

Behind them, Zayir—so talkative a moment ago—had gone very still.

For once, he had nothing to say.

· · · ·

Lily's com tag buzzed softly—barely audible over the distant wind.

She stepped out toward the edge of the alley, shielding the display with her hand until Xynn's face flickered into view. Static wavered across her cheekbones, but her voice came through clear.

"Hey," Xynn said.

Lily smiled automatically, the kind of smile that happened just from seeing her. "Hey."

"You okay?"

Lily nodded. "Still breathing."

"Just wanted to check in." Xynn paused, brushing her hair behind her ear. "There's movement in the storm—Leviathan's shifting course. It's heading toward Bimini."

That took a second to sink in. "So..."

"Yeah. If Ronin's riding in it, he's coming our way."

Lily exhaled through her nose. "Any threat Ronin poses to these people might be a moot point. They're on the edge of destroying themselves."

Xynn looked offscreen like someone was shouting. "And Command's practically screaming at Calan to get the prince back to Union space. Immediately."

"No surprise there," Lily muttered. "We're just finishing up here. About to grab some samples and—"

The screen went black.

The vines around her—those twitching, inquisitive red threads—all at once vanished, snapping back into the ground like startled snakes. Even the ones draped from rooftops recoiled, pulling themselves into cracks and vents.

The air felt different now. Tighter.

Zayir raised an arm, pointing toward the horizon.

Far off, a dull shape blossomed in the sky. Fire stretched upward in a furious column, slow and thick, and then began to mushroom outward—an expanding halo of death rolling toward them like a thunderhead on fire.

Caris stared for a heartbeat too long. "Get inside," she barked.

They sprinted to the nearest shelter—low, circular, reinforced with thick black alloy and angled walls that looked built to deflect a blast. A vault door rolled open as they approached, and they slipped inside just as it sealed behind them with a resonant thunk.

For a moment: silence.

Then they realized the room was wall to wall with villagers.

They stood or knelt throughout the main chamber, bathed in golden light from suspended crystal orbs. Some sat in silence. Others chanted, voices low and rhythmic. It looked more like a temple than a shelter—filled with the steady hum of reverence.

They moved slowly, reverently, through the crowd. No one seemed to see them. Or perhaps no one cared. Children huddled in corners, their silver hair brushed flat. Couples embraced without speaking.

Datch led them into a smaller side chamber. A breakout room, maybe. A private sanctuary. The door shut behind them with a muted thud.

Lily leaned against the wall, catching her breath. "We'll be okay," she said quietly. "Looks like they've been expecting this."

For a long moment, no one spoke. The room was warm. Heavy. It smelled faintly of metal and incense.

Then Zayir slinked up to Lily and cleared his throat. "You are remarkable, Lily. And when we make it back..." He dropped his voice lower, "I'm going to ask my wife if I can keep you."

She looked up, deadpan.

Zayir smiled lazily. "I think she'll understand. Royal concubines aren't unheard of on Ishreth." He stepped closer, glancing toward a small storage closet in the corner. "There's enough room in there to burn off some of this tension. Just the two of us. Our hearts pulsing with the threat of the world ending."

The silence that followed was different. Lily felt her pulse rise—anger, disbelief—but she kept her voice level.

She stared at him with bone-deep exhaustion.

"It stopped being cute around dinner two days ago," she said. "Wake up. Look around. These people have faith in something greater than themselves. What about you? What about your people? Are you going to be that for them—faith?"

Zayir blinked. His smile faltered but didn't fully vanish.

"Or are you going to be an obstacle to your people's well-being, living in the shadow of your mother?"

That did it. The grin disappeared.

Datch suddenly stood straighter, eyes scanning his device. "Something's wrong."

Malik crossed the room. "What is it?"

Datch's fingers moved quickly. "There's no radiation shielding in here. No substructural reinforcement. Nothing to seal out atmosphere. This isn't a shelter."

Malik looked at the readings and nodded grimly. "He's right."

"They brought their children," Lily said, her voice small. "Do they think this is a shelter?"

Malik looked up. "Simple construction. It'll never stand up to the blast."

Zayir took a trembling step backward. "Then what about us? Are we just going to die in here too?"

No one answered.

"They're here to die," Lily said.

Caris met her gaze. "And we're about to die with them."

Silence.

Lily had never felt such stillness paired with such inner chaos. Like a boil rolling so fast it had come back around to stillness again.

And then—a chime.

Lily's com tag.

Xynn's voice came through, sharp with static. "I wouldn't leave you hanging."

"Xynn?" Lily breathed.

"I got you." More static. The channel cut again.

A second later, the ceiling groaned—and a rising whistle screamed through the air.

Outside, a projectile tore through the atmosphere, trailing heat and fire. It struck the ground just meters from the structure, embedding itself with a deep metallic boom.

A crater. At its center, a capsule gleamed white-hot in the dust.

"Special delivery from your girlfriend!" Caris shouted, already moving.

"Pretty romantic if you ask me!" Malik added, following.

They ran. No time to think. No time to explain. They just ran.

Inside the capsule were radiation-proof EV suits and a compact blast shelter. They worked together in grim silence to get it deployed—sliding into the cramped shell and sealing it shut.

The interior was dim. Tight. The air smelled of metal and sterilizer.

"Atmosphere sealed," Datch reported. "Minimal shock absorption... but it'll hold."

They each pulled on a suit. Lily noticed Zayir's hands were still shaking, even as he struggled with the seal.

Datch activated the external feed.

Outside, hell came.

The blast ripped through the village in waves. Heat. Dust. Light. Whole buildings crumbled, their foundations torn apart like parchment. The main dome—where they'd just stood—vanished in a flash of white light. Screams didn't even reach them. Just flickers of movement. And then silence.

Zayir was shaking. His hands trembled at his sides, shoulders hunched.

Someone suggested turning off the screen.

Datch tried the keypad. "Controls are unresponsive. Give me a moment."

Lily watched until the feed went white with static.

The silence that followed was worse than the blast. The only sound was the rasp of their breath through the suit filters.

Caris finally spoke. "We'll regain contact with the ship eventually. They can send a shuttle."

"No," Zayir said quietly.

Lily forced a smile. "Hey, we've got six hours of oxygen in the suits. I'm sure we'll get through to the ship. They're probably already—"

"NO!" Zayir exploded, his arms flailing in a wild, panicked arc—like a wounded bird trying to stay airborne.

Before anyone could stop him, he surged forward and hit the hatch release.

"Zayir!" Lily lunged, but he was already gone.

Datch got the viewer working again. They saw him stumble into the ash.

Lily didn't hesitate. She followed.

Outside, visibility dropped to nothing. The ash storm churned around her, blinding and hot. She moved by instinct more than sight—until, through a break in the dust, she spotted him.

Zayir stood still in a shallow drift, his EV suit coated in soot. All around him, shapes. Blackened. Not quite human. Not quite dead.

He dropped to his knees beside one.

It was small. Its arm reached for him—charred and half-fused to its own body. A child.

Lily stopped. She knew.

The thing moved. Just barely. It dragged itself into Zayir's arms—and fell apart.

He didn't scream. He just knelt there, unmoving, cradling what was left. Eyes wide. Paralyzed.

When the air thinned enough for visibility, the others joined them.

"We should try to reach the shuttle landing site," Caris said, voice soft but clear. "If any equipment survived, we may be able to contact the ship."

But Zayir wouldn't move.

Lily crouched beside him. Her expression was unreadable—soft, but flinty beneath the surface.

She met his eyes. This time, the lust was gone. All that remained was the raw, stunned face she remembered from the day his mother had been arrested. A face that said, *help*.

"Zayir," she said gently. "You're one of the few people who can actually change lives. Directly. You affect millions."

She let that sit.

"You have a good heart in there. Let Vaishali guide you to be better. Govern well. Help people."

He looked away.

"It's not your fault your mother was awful," she added. "But don't become her."

He turned back to her.

"You just need to learn something most people never do," she said. "You can't have everything you want. If you chase that—if you *need* it—you'll always want more. And you'll always be unhappy. And that will consume you."

She leaned in just slightly.

"And then you won't be a good person who's made some mistakes. You'll be a bad person who's running away."

Zayir blinked. His voice cracked. "Running away from what?"

She stood.

"Take your pick. Everything. Nothing. You name it."

She extended a hand.

For a long moment, he just stared at it.

Then, slowly, he took it.

As they turned, Lily caught Malik's lips moving on a private channel to Caris. She didn't hear the words, but she could read them:

"This guy somehow manages to make the extinction of an entire race all about him. Wow."

No one said anything else.

They started toward the landing site.

One step at a time.

Chapter 9: The Valley of Dry Bones

THE STARS PULSED LIKE a wound above the chaos.

The Salamander twisted through the void, hull lit in flashes of stormlight, its flanks scorched and groaning as it spun beneath the shadow of the Warden of Tarshish. The massive vessel loomed above, black as a scar, vomiting lightning from the storm that birthed it.

On the bridge, Calan sat forward in his chair, every line of his body taut—not with fear, but with rhythm. The old reflexes had returned. He didn't bark commands; he threaded them, weaving a pattern through smoke and static as explosions hammered the shields.

Charlie had joined the bridge despite the captain's initial protests. They needed the help. His unique physiology let him operate at multiple stations at once. He moved like mercury across the deck, pseudopods forming and reforming to seal leaks, plug ruptured conduits. His senses, strange but deep, felt the desperation in every corner—and he leaned into it. This crew would hold the ship together through sheer will.

In engineering, the Raath-Ka moved in tandem—Ka-Lorrin rerouting power through the aft coil while Taran clung to the reactor chamber wall, the fur on his paws singing as he stabilized a failing conduit. Sparks flew around them like fireflies in a storm.

Beside them, Alrek shouted into the comms, his voice raw as he called out stabilization codes manually, guiding the team through brute-force resuscitation of the engines. His cobalt-blue skin was streaked with smoke, his eyes alive with fire. He would not let this ship die.

Up on the bridge, Glover was down. Dryst Amaris didn't know if he was dead—and couldn't afford to find out. He slid into the weapons station, blood dripping into one eye as he keyed in fire sequences with shaking hands. The deck jolted beneath him with another direct hit. He braced himself against the console, vision doubling, and muttered through clenched teeth, "We will not let this monster win."

In the medical bay, Dr. Thesari worked with surgical grace, her hands stained but steady. The doors hissed open—Xynn's tall frame silhouetted against the corridor light. A welcome sight amid the tide of wounded.

She'd seen the ship's status reports. Medical was short-handed. Those poor crew in shaft seven—gone in an instant when the Warden scored a direct hit. The hull breached. The lift lost to vacuum. No one survived.

Xynn stepped in without ceremony, sleeves rolled, her Saravethi field training taking over. She moved between patients with practiced precision—patching wounds, administering care, catching those who staggered in search of treatment or rest. Her voice was a constant, crisp current in the din. There was no time to grieve. No room for fear. Only motion.

Elsewhere, Tevya had lent her skills in both weapons and engineering, rerouting plasma from the backstop engine buffer into the auxiliary cannons, pushing them to over 150% capacity. She coaxed the ship like a stubborn child—stern, but protective.

On the bridge, Basco's hands trembled as he piloted through wreckage, breath caught between whispered prayers. His first real battle, unraveling like a nightmare across his eyes.

And through it all—

Ronin's voice broke through the comms in jagged bursts, slicing the air like a sabre. Laughing. Gloating. Singing, sometimes, as if the destruction unfolding were a symphony.

Lightning curled around the Warden like a crown. The Salamander was burning. Bleeding. But still breathing.

"This is just the overture," the voice rang through the halls of the ship, and their minds. "The real show has yet to begin."

• • • •

The shuttle landing site was a graveyard.

What remained of their craft lay half-buried in ash—a blackened crescent, its outer plating peeled back like scorched bark. Twisted struts jutted upward at wrong angles, one stabilizer melted into a glassy smear across the stone. The air hung heavy with the stink of ozone and fused metal.

No lights. No pulse. Just the soft tick of once-living circuitry cooling into silence.

Caris crouched by the remains of the comm array, her fingers moving over melted casing and warped relays. Her face stayed flat, but the tilt of her jaw said everything.

"It's gone," she confirmed. "Nothing left worth salvaging."

Malik kicked at a cracked panel. It crumbled beneath his boot.

"So that's it. No contact. No transport. Five hours of air left, and no home to call for help."

Lily stared at the wreckage, then turned upward.

The sky had darkened—a charcoal ceiling pressing down on the world. Fallout churned in swirls of gray and rust, a bruise-colored storm smeared across the heavens. But then: a rift. A narrow wound in the sky's skin.

And through it, color.

Not the warm gold she remembered.

Violet. Seething.

Streaked with jagged lightning—arc after arc of brilliant purple threading through the gas giant's fury. It pulsed like a living thing, clouds rippling in a hypnotic, deadly rhythm.

Leviathan.

Lily felt it before she spoke. A pressure behind her eyes. The silence before a scream. A sick twist in her stomach that hadn't gone away since the first time she'd seen it.

"It's in orbit," she whispered. "Leviathan's here."

Caris squinted upward beside her. "And if Leviathan's here..."

"Then the Warden of Tarshish probably is too," Malik finished grimly.

Datch checked his readout. "I'm picking up plasma fluctuations. High output. Could be a space battery."

"Which means the *Salamander's* already in the fight," Lily murmured. "They couldn't help us even if we could call them."

A long silence fell. Only the soft hiss of wind stirring ash.

Lily glanced down at her suit's gauge. **4:42.**

King Zayir's voice came over the helmet comm for the first time since the explosion—soft, trembling.

"Four hours and forty-two minutes of oxygen."

Then—movement.

A glint through the haze.

Caris lifted her arm, zooming in with her helmet display.

"There," she said. "Small craft. Just cleared the upper atmosphere. Heat signature and configuration are consistent with—"

"Ronin," Lily cut in. Her voice had gone sharp.

They watched the speck descend through the ash.

Toward the far ridge.

Toward the crystal fields.

Their enemy had arrived.

· · · ·

Zayir crouched low in the half-shelled ruin of a collapsed structure, its jagged walls half-swallowed by ash. Malik had found the spot—a good fallback shelter. Just enough cover, just enough metal to reflect a signal if the *Salamander* came looking.

"This is your best shot," Lily said, checking her blaster one last time before unclipping the smaller one from her belt. She handed it to him. "Stay here. The *Salamander* will be looking."

Zayir took the weapon slowly. "If they survive the battle."

Malik muttered, "And if His Majesty doesn't shoot his royal foot off. Watch the safety."

Lily ignored him. But Caris turned, eyes sharp. "He's breathing. Let's keep it that way. We have to stop the Storm Riders—whatever it is they're doing."

Malik grunted and stepped away.

Zayir finally looked at Lily. "Lily... I'm sorry."

"Later," she said. "If we make it through this, I'll accept any groveling you want to perform."

She paused, then added quietly, "If we don't... just try to be good, Zayir."

He didn't answer. Just gripped the blaster and nodded once.

They left him there, half-shadowed in ash, the faint hum of his suit's regulator the only sound as they vanished into the gray.

· · · ·

They moved in silence, the world reduced to wind and weight and the crunch of boots through brittle ash. The route they'd taken down from the landing site had already vanished, obscured by drifting fallout and flickers of heat still rising from the charred hills. Flames licked from fractured stone outcrops, fed by unseen vents beneath the surface. The air shimmered with heat distortion, making the ridgelines ripple like ghosts. The quickest path forward was blocked—first by fire, then by collapse.

So they took the long way.

Each time they thought the bend ahead might lead to an opening, it revealed only more ruin—another blackened outcrop, another dead ravine. The terrain coiled in on itself, a serpent of burned stone and buried history, winding ever lower. The farther they walked, the more the land felt wrong. Angled. Pulled. As if they were descending into something more than just a valley.

The sky stayed close above them, the air thick and flat. Every few steps, Lily found herself glancing back—toward the place they'd left Zayir behind, toward the ridge where the shuttle had once been whole. But there was no sign of it now. Just a smear of smoke and the long slope of the land folding away.

"How far down have we climbed?" Lily finally asked, her voice muted by the atmosphere filter. "Are we even going to be on the same level as the Storm Riders if we manage to catch up?"

Caris was already ahead, wedging herself between a crevice to get a better view. She adjusted her helmet display and nodded. "Look," she said, pointing. "I think that bank stretches around further."

They followed her gaze. The terrain opened slightly, revealing a low basin—gray and sunken, its surface cracked and rippled like cooling lava.

"Jesus," Malik said, staring down. "Was that a lake?"

Datch confirmed it with a nod. "Affirmative. Topographic data suggests it was the village's primary water source."

The silence returned as they picked their way down into the former lakebed. The ash here was softer, finer—every step kicked up small clouds that clung to their suits and visors. Dull, mineral-rich sediment painted the walls of the crater in reds and silvers, like ancient blood. Nothing moved. No birds. No insects. Just the slow hiss of filtered breath and the crunch of boots in dust.

They walked for a long time.

The weight of it all pressed closer now. Every direction looked the same. The only landmarks were the ones they'd already passed.

"Are we even going the right way?" Lily asked, voice low.

"I think so," Datch replied.

And for the moment, that had to be enough.

. . . .

They walked in silence across broken terrain, ducking low behind outcroppings of rock and slag. The ash dulled every sound—each step a whisper, swallowed by the world.

Lily checked her oxygen gauge again. 3:54.

"We're losing time," Malik said. "Still no sign of them."

"Keep moving," Caris replied.

They continued single file, climbing down another steep slope—

Then, quickly stopped in their tracks.

A low whine cut through the stillness. A thruster pack.

They turned just in time to see a figure break through the mist, ash swirling in his wake like torn silk.

Zayir streaked overhead on a thruster pack, descending with all the grace of a wounded albatross.

He landed hard, stumbling only once before he righted himself. His breathing came ragged over comms.

"Wasn't easy finding you," he said, winded.

Lily stared. "You should've stayed put."

Malik scoffed. "You probably burned through half your oxygen just getting here."

"Sixty-one minutes remaining, to be exact," Caris reported, checking his gauge.

Zayir let them react, then raised his voice over the channel. "Comms weren't reaching you. I was watching you through the scope. I could see the

Storm Riders moving in the opposite direction. I watched you move further and further away from them."

He flicked his wrist, projecting a flickering holomap. A curved path marked due east. "I made a route to intercept."

Lily gave him a genuine hug.

Datch nodded in approval. "Welcome to the party."

He pulled up a tactical overlay, light spilling from his wrist. "Now that we're five, we can run tactical formation Delta-17. We'll try to flank them."

Zayir looked to Lily. Said nothing. Just gave a small, steady nod.

She returned it. "They won't know what hit them."

Caris checked her com tag. "We're on a deadline now." She flipped her blast shield down and drew her blaster. "Let's get this done."

The next leg of the journey passed faster—more focused. They crept along the rim of a ravine until they reached the edge of a high outcropping.

There, through the haze, they saw them.

A loose circle of Storm Riders moved with purpose around a half-formed dig site, their black suits shining dully in the gloom. Heavy equipment surrounded a field of crystal—frames mounted with drills and cutting beams. Biting into the land like hungry animals.

The raiders worked like locusts.

It was now or never.

• • • •

They moved into position one by one, taking cover behind jagged boulders and low ridges that lined the crest overlooking the Storm Riders' operation.

Lily scanned the scene carefully, eyes narrowing behind her visor. "Ronin's not with them," she said over comms.

"I guess I shouldn't have expected him to be," she added after a beat.

Datch's voice came through sharp and low. "I have some questions to ask him."

Below, the Storm Riders worked like drones—efficient, tireless. They moved in synchronized lines, harvesting pale mineral shards from the crystal field and packing them into matte-black crates. Automated carts hummed along, ferrying the materials back toward the shuttle. It was methodical. Mechanical. Like watching a hive.

Lily knew the plan. One of them would step forward to draw attention—force the Riders to reveal themselves—while the rest stayed hidden, waiting until the last possible second before springing the trap. A burst of fire. Close the gap. End it quickly.

This was Caris' operation. But before she could call the move, Datch did something he almost never did—he pulled rank.

"I'll go," he said simply, already moving.

"Be careful," Lily whispered into her comm.

Datch didn't answer.

He walked into view without hesitation, shoulders squared, every step deliberate. No showmanship. No bravado. Just a man with a purpose.

The Storm Riders noticed immediately. Their movements faltered, then turned. Twelve—no, more. Clad in matte armor, faceless helmets glinting in the dull light. They spread out fast, surrounding the dig zone in a loose arc, weapons rising like teeth.

"There's way too many of them," Malik said.

"Stick with the plan," Caris snapped, voice taut.

The ambush had begun.

"Greetings," Datch said calmly over an open channel, raising his hands in what might pass for surrender. "We're surprised to see you. We thought everyone on this planet was dead."

The Storm Riders didn't lower their weapons. Black-clad figures turned toward each other with subtle glances—silent, wordless acknowledgments that, while maybe not the sharpest in the galaxy, they weren't that gullible.

One of them stepped forward. His armor was trimmed in pale silver, marked with insignia—clearly a leader. He lifted his blaster rifle and aimed it squarely at Datch.

"Who are you?" the man barked. "Don't take another step."

From her vantage point, Lily spotted movement—four Riders flanking Datch's position, two to either side, slowly circling to trap him.

"We go on my mark," she said over the private channel.

"Lily..." Caris warned. "Hold..."

Then all at once, every head turned.

Zayir.

He'd climbed down from the ridge and was now walking straight into the open. Fully exposed.

"Zayir, what the hell are you doing?" Lily hissed into her comm.

But he had already switched to the open channel.

"Gentlemen," Zayir called out, spreading his arms dramatically. "I see you've found my robot butler..."

Datch visibly bristled at the term "robot."

"Stop right there!" the Storm Rider leader barked, shifting his aim to Zayir. "What is going on here?"

Zayir kept walking, hands still raised. "Come now, I'm a diplomat. Surely we can talk. I'm confident we have mutual interests—"

The leader fired.

A bolt of violet energy tore through the air and struck Zayir in the chest, the force of it throwing him backward several meters. He hit the ground hard, smoke curling from his armor.

Datch dropped into a shoulder roll, diving behind a nearby generator just as—

Chaos erupted.

Caris fired first. A clean shot that clipped one Rider's shoulder and sent him spinning. Then Malik and Lily moved together, advancing fast, blasters hot.

Zayir, stunned but miraculously still alive, groaned as he rolled beneath a low hover cart. He pulled out the sidearm Lily had given him and started laying down cover fire—more noise than threat.

"I really wish you'd given me a bigger gun," he muttered.

The battle had begun.

The crystal field erupted in gunfire.

Bolts of purple and red streaked through the smoke-choked air, carving molten scars into stone and steel. The Storm Riders pressed forward in waves, disciplined and unrelenting, their rifles humming with deadly charge. Lily ducked behind a metal storage crate as a blast passed inches from her shoulder, turning the panel beside her into liquid slag.

Caris surged forward, picked off two Riders with surgical precision, then took a hard shot to the upper arm. Her cry broke through the comms as she crumpled behind cover, one hand clamped over the smoking wound. "I'm hit—suit breach," she gasped. Already her voice was slurring, head reeling from the radiation leaking into her bloodstream.

"Hold still," Malik shouted, but he barely finished before a fuel cell behind him exploded, sending a shockwave through the ravine. He dove, landing hard and twisting his ankle with a sickening pop.

Datch dragged Zayir by the collar, half-carrying, half-hauling him behind a shattered mining cart. The king was breathing, barely, but his armor was scorched and cracked. Datch shoved a fallen console upright to block fire, eyes scanning for an escape they didn't have.

Lily had been closest to the blast. The force slammed her backward into a pile of debris, and now her ears rang with a high, relentless whine. The world around her pulsed in and out of focus—just color and light and pain. But she forced herself upright, teeth clenched, and stumbled toward the others.

They regrouped at the base of a massive rock crusher, a hulking piece of mining machinery they'd managed to topple on its side. It groaned under repeated impacts as the Riders' blaster bolts slammed into it, the metal hissing and warping.

Behind them, nothing but smoke and open air. To their left, a sheer wall of rock. To their right, the black hull of the enemy shuttle. And dead ahead—dozens of Storm Riders, guns blazing.

Pinned. Trapped. Nowhere left to run.

And the fire never stopped.

"Well team," Malik said, "I guess now's the time to say it was nice knowing you."

No one argued.

The silence that followed sank its claws into Lily. This was it. She felt it—not just the fear, but the resignation. They weren't getting out.

And then something tugged at her leg.

She looked down.

At first, she thought it was a hallucination. A child—the little girl she'd seen earlier—stood in the ash. But it wasn't her. Not quite.

The red vines.

They had poked through the ground, threading through soot and slag, weaving themselves into the vague shape of the child. A facsimile. A memory.

"Are you seeing this?" Lily asked, but the blaster fire had stopped. Everything was still.

The girl made the same motion she had before—a slash across her throat—then crumbled, the vines slithering back into the dirt.

Lily spun around, heart pounding.

A wall was growing in front of them. An enormous, pulsing barrier of crimson vines, lashing up from the ground, hardening into a shield. The Storm Riders stared, weapons frozen mid-air.

Above them, the ash began to clear.

Sunlight broke through the clouds.

And the crystals—those strange, jagged remnants—began to glow.

Magenta light pulsed across the field as the vines multiplied, curling and growing, emboldened by the sun. All around, the ruined terrain shifted.

The Storm Riders panicked.

Some screamed. Others dropped their weapons. One shouted something about omens. Then they ran—racing toward their shuttle, scrambling aboard as the vines reached up, latching to the hull like fingers desperate to hold it back.

The shuttle roared and lifted, barely tearing free of the vines' grip. It vanished into the sky, trailing smoke and shredded red tendrils.

The world stilled again.

"What is this?" Malik said.

Caris stared up at the widening sunbeam, then around at the flowering red growth all around them. "It's life," she said. "It's *life*."

Lily followed her gaze.

The vines were still climbing, but now they were *shaping*. Morphing. Twisting upward into structures—first abstract, then familiar. Arches. Walls. Roofs. A vehicle chassis. Window frames. Streetlamps. Animals.

People.

It wasn't just reconstruction. It was *resurrection*.

"I'm reading clean air," Malik said, scanning with disbelief. "I mean *perfectly* clean."

"That's not the half of it," Lily murmured. "Look."

Before their eyes, the red vines transformed not just into the shape of things—but the things themselves. Matter rewriting itself. Roads returned. Doorframes solidified. Chimneys puffed pale smoke.

A town was being reborn around them.

"How is this possible?" Lily whispered.

"It isn't," Malik said, his voice oddly reverent. "It *shouldn't* be."

Within minutes, people filled the streets—talking, walking, laughing. As if the world-ending blast had been nothing more than a passing storm.

Caris blinked, then looked at her arm. The burns were gone. The suit's radiation warnings had vanished.

"My arm's healed."

"My ankle too," Malik added, stunned.

Lily turned.

Zayir stood beside her now, adjusting his collar and smiling.

"Fit as an Aldebrin fiddle," he said.

She took off her helmet. The air was crisp and cool, tinged with something sweet. The kind of morning air that came after rain. She let herself breathe it in.

"I think the life forms on this planet are colony-based," Malik said, reading the scanner. "They're all connected to that red vine. It *feeds* on radiation."

Caris frowned. "So what... they just... blow themselves up every few generations?"

"Seems that way," Malik replied. "As population grows and energy use rises, the vines weaken. Nuclear detonation restores the radiation levels—supercharges the vine."

Lily looked at the glowing crystals in the distance. "And if those crystals are a catalyst... no wonder Ronin wanted them."

"The fountain of youth," Zayir said softly. Then turned. "Mr. Datch, I owe you a debt of gratitude once again. I—"

He froze.

Lily scanned the crowd.

"Where's Datch?"

Caris was already tapping her scanner. "Caris to Datch. Please tell me you're still on the planet."

His voice came through, cool and unhurried. "I told you—I have questions for Ronin."

Then the line cut out.

Lily's stomach dropped. "He stowed away."

Zayir blinked. "And here I thought *I* was the troublemaker."

Lily didn't smile.

Caris turned toward the sky, trying the Salamander. "Come in, Salamander. Respond."

A garbled voice sputtered through. "...pffft... engaged in battle... zzzpt... transmit your coordinates...psssst..."

"Transmitting now," Lily said, boosting the gain on her comm tag.

Then she looked up.

Zayir was in the town square, laughing with newly reborn children as they tossed vine-made toys in the air. The whole village pulsed with energy, motion, and renewal.

And then—

Lily. Malik. Caris.

All turned at once, eyes widening.

"The shuttle," they said in unison.

· · · ·

They crested the rise—and there it was.

Their shuttle.

Fully restored. Not just repaired, but *pristine*. The hull gleamed beneath the sunlight, untouched by ash or fire, as if it had never known damage at all.

"It even looks cleaner," Caris muttered.

No one hesitated. They rushed aboard, boots thudding against the ramp. Malik slid into the pilot's seat, hands already flying across the controls. The startup hum was smooth, fluid—familiar.

He blinked at the diagnostics.

"My god," he said. "It's working perfectly."

The shuttle creaked, then lurched upward—its usual complaints voiced in low groans of metal and pressure. And then it rose, steady and strong, lifting through the haze like a column of hope.

Zayir whooped, clapping a hand to the bulkhead.

"This is *remarkable!*" he shouted, a broad, genuine smile lighting up his face for the first time.

Malik nodded, strapping in beside him.

"You know what, Your Majesty?" he said. "I'm inclined to agree with you."

But they weren't out of it yet.

As the shuttle rose into open sky, the scene above unfolded like a nightmare carved into sunlight: the *Warden of Tarshish* loomed enormous, casting its long shadow across the stars. The *Salamander* held position below it, shields flaring with every impact—valiant, but clearly straining.

"Care for some tandem maneuvers?" Caris said, her voice light, almost flirty.

Lily glanced at her—then at Malik, who looked far too eager considering the odds. "Umm, you two..." she said nervously. "I hope you've been practicing."

Malik just grinned as his fingers danced across the console. "Bearing twenty-two mark five. Keep close."

"Copy that," she said, already adjusting trajectory.

Together, they spiraled through the chaos—cutting low beneath a wave of plasma fire, then banking hard starboard to avoid the shockwave ripple from the *Warden's* heavy cannons. The shuttle jolted and groaned, but Caris held her line, skimming close enough to the *Salamander's* hull to trigger a docking override.

"Brace," Malik warned.

The shuttle slammed into the bay's magfield, slowed sharply, then glided into a hard but clean touchdown. The doors hissed open.

"Lily, is that you?" came Calan's voice over comms, tight with tension.

"We made it," Lily said, breathless as she unbuckled. "But Ronin's people got a lot of that crystal. Sir—it's powerful. Beyond what we thought."

"How powerful?" Calan asked.

Malik didn't pause as he unstrapped. "That's a long story."

"And Captain," Lily added, her tone shifting. "They have Datch."

And they sprinted around the horseshoe corridor, heading for the bridge.

• • • •

They burst onto the bridge like a wave breaking through a dam.

Xynn was the first to reach them, throwing her arms around Lily and kissing her without hesitation—briefly making the storm outside disappear.

Then the noise rose around them.

The *Salamander* shuddered under another direct hit. Sparks flew from an overhead console. The lights flickered.

"Shields at twenty-two percent!" Basco called out from his station.

"Hold position!" Calan barked, bracing against the railing. "Datch stowed away aboard that monster. Let's not make it in vain."

Tevya stood off to the side, hands clenched, eyes locked on the tactical display.

The bridge swarmed with motion. Alerts flashed. Systems rerouted. Another blast rocked them hard enough that everyone staggered.

"Suggestions," Calan snapped.

Silence.

Malik looked at Caris. Caris met his gaze, jaw tight. Lily felt Xynn's hand wrap around hers, grounding her.

Then—

"Captain!" Basco shouted. "Their weapons have powered down!"

A stunned beat.

Tevya stepped forward, barely a whisper. "Datch... well done, my love."

Calan snapped back to the moment. "Fire everything we've got left!"

The *Salamander* unleashed a desperate salvo—every torpedo tube, every pulse cannon, every ounce of fury it could muster. Energy streaked across space, slamming into the retreating hull of the *Warden of Tarshish*.

The great black vessel turned slowly, deliberately, back toward the churning eye of the storm. Its hull was scorched, but not broken. Even wounded, it looked invincible.

Then came the voice—smooth, unbothered.

"It seems I have worn out my welcome," Ronin said, his tone almost amused. "Farewell, Captain. I have better things to do anyway."

And with that, the *Warden* vanished into Leviathan's coils.

The storm began to roll away with it, retreating across the sky like a great beast withdrawing its claws.

"Good riddance," Malik muttered, exhaling hard.

But no one relaxed. Not yet. The storm was moving on—but the damage was done.

And somewhere inside that monstrous ship, Datch was alone.

Chapter 10: The Lakehouse

"THE ORDERS ARE CLEAR," Calan said. "We're to break orbit immediately and bring King Zayir to Starbase 12. No pursuit. No deviation. No exceptions."

No one spoke.

The soft lights of the briefing room flickered once overhead, a reminder that the ship was still healing. Outside, the stars wheeled by—distant and indifferent.

Lily leaned forward. Her voice, when it came, was quiet but firm. "Ronin's heading to Gherion Prime. We're sure of it."

She didn't look at the others. Just at him.

"We need to go after him."

Calan met her gaze. And then, with something like permission softening the line of his jaw, he said, "Yes. You do."

He straightened, and when he spoke again, there was weight behind it. A shifting of gravity.

"There's something else."

Caris looked up sharply. Malik leaned back in his chair, brow furrowed. Tevya's hand, resting against the edge of the table, curled in slightly—quiet tension gathering like thread on a spool.

"I've accepted a reassignment," Calan said. "I'm transferring to the *Vanguard* to be with Joren. I'll be a senior engineer. So, I'll be stepping down as captain when we reach Starbase 12."

The words landed like a bomb at first, but after only a moment, it was like a door finally creaking open.

Caris offered the first nod. "Congratulations, Griff."

"You've earned it," Malik added. "Probably three times over."

Tevya's lips pressed into something like a smile. "They're lucky to have you."

Calan gave the barest smile. It reached his eyes, barely.

Lily was the last to speak. "What changed your mind sir?"

Calan looked thoughtful. "There will always be another crisis," he said. "Another mystery to solve. But it's not worth putting your life on hold—at least, it isn't worth it to me anymore. I can forgive myself for missing a good mission. But I can't lose my family."

Lily didn't exactly know how to feel. But she knew this was a good thing. She thought maybe she was just distracted. Worried about Datch.

There was a brief silence, Lily wondered if she was the only one who felt like it was a little awkward.

Calan's voice returned to its steady register. "Dryst Amaris and I will take the Salamander and transport the king to Starbase 12. There I will officially transfer command to the Dryst who will serve as acting captain."

Then he turned toward Lily, Caris, and Tevya.

"But you three? You're going to take a little unsanctioned detour."

Caris met his eyes, her smile quick and sharp. "Tell me more..." She said a little too eager.

Lily gave Tevya's arm a little squeeze.

Calan continued, "Assemble your team discreetly. Make sure you bring people you trust. Amaris and I will vamp as long as we can to buy you time."

Then he looked directly at Lily. "And make sure you bring Xynn with you."

Lily blinked, caught off guard—but only for a moment. Of course. He was right. Probably more right than she wanted to admit.

As the others stood to leave, gathering into loose motion, Lily lingered a step behind.

"I think," she said quietly, "I should make a call."

• • • •

The call connected with a flicker, and suddenly the Scales and Feathers bloomed into view—dusty light slanting through the old stained-glass windows, casting fractured color across the worn wood floor.

Behind the bar, Trish looked up from a battered datapad and arched one eyebrow. She wore her usual utility vest over a faded synth-cotton shirt, sleeves rolled, collar frayed. A pot of something steamed behind her, and someone was tuning an old guitar in the background. The inn was alive, in its own gentle, lived-in way.

"Well, well," Trish said, one hand on her hip. "Lily Starling, darkening my holo screen so soon. You look like someone who's about to ask for something."

Lily offered a small, weary smile. "Trish. Good to see you."

Trish's tone softened. "I was glad to hear your friend pulled through."

"He's doing better," Lily said. "Thank you."

A pause followed—quiet, but not empty.

Lily glanced offscreen for a moment, then looked back. "How have things been on Earth since we left?"

Trish exhaled, chuckling dryly. "Well, not dull—I'll tell you that much. The Ludon and the Hedon haven't torn each other to pieces, so I'd call that a win. They're talking. Cautiously. Testing boundaries like two cats who just realized they live in the same house."

She walked around the bar and leaned against a column, arms crossed. "They've been cooperating, surprisingly. Trying to track any leftover cells from Leviathan's Hand. Nothing like a common enemy to bring people together. It's not sunshine and roses, but it's a start."

Lily nodded. "That's actually why I called."

Trish tilted her head, the warmth in her eyes giving way to something more guarded.

"Your intel before..." Lily began. "We never would've gotten this far without it. That data gave us just enough of a lead. I was wondering if you could—" she hesitated "—send me the rest of the storm cult packets. Anything you haven't shared yet on Leviathan... or Gherion Prime."

She paused again.

"To a private channel."

There was a beat. Trish didn't say anything right away.

She just looked at her.

And Lily could feel the silence, thickening with implication.

"One of our crew, a friend—Datch. He's been taken by the Storm Riders," Lily said finally, quietly. "He's like family to me. I'm going to get him back. I need every edge I can get."

Trish didn't break eye contact. But her arms tightened slightly.

"Lily..." she began, voice low and deliberate. "You're putting me in an awkward position."

"Trish—"

"No, listen to me." Trish shook her head. "I didn't leave the fleet on a red carpet, I realize that. I've been critical of fleet operations... but I also still believe in the principles of the Union, when those principles are upheld."

Lily shifted uncomfortably. She was not in the mood for a lecture.

Trish continued. "And to be quite frank, one of those principles is not leaking restricted intelligence for a rogue mission. No matter your intentions."

Lily blinked, her mouth opening slightly. "Trish, I'm not asking you to give up Union defenses or anything crazy. It's what, some ancient history..."

"Sorry, Lily," Trish said, almost sharply. "You won't get me to budge on this. Besides, this isn't my mission. I'm not saying I don't care. But I'm helping where I can—here, on Earth. You go help where you can—"

Lily's jaw tightened. "Don't think I'm taking this lightly."

"I don't. I think you're exhausted. Scared for your friend. Maybe a little desperate?" Trish replied, not unkindly. "I don't blame you. But I'm not the silver bullet here, Lily."

Lily stood there for a long second, hands flat on the console.

"Ronin is going to Gherion Prime," she said. "And if he gets what he's after—whatever that is—it won't just be one more attack. It'll be something worse. I don't even know what yet, but I can feel it."

She looked right into Trish's eyes through the transmission. "You know I'm right."

Trish didn't answer right away. Her eyes searched Lily's face for a flicker longer, then drifted downward, jaw tightening.

"Like I said," she said quietly. "Not my mission."

Lily inhaled slowly. Her throat felt tight.

"Understood," she said.

There was no bitterness in her voice. Just tired resignation.

"Goodbye, Trish."

The signal blinked out.

• • • •

Lily stepped into the hallway, still thinking about the call with Trish—that hadn't gone to plan, and now she felt like she'd stepped through the wrong door into unexpected territory. She briefly closed her eyes and exhaled.

Footsteps approached. Her eyes snapped open.

She turned and saw Basco, posture crisp, expression boyish—as always. He had that ever-present cadet energy.

She smiled teasingly. "You still haven't switched to the navy blue?"

He glanced down at his own Fleet HQ whites. This time, he didn't blush quite so much. "It's not at the top of my to-do list." Then, more purposefully: "I'm glad I found you. Just wanted to let you know the Storm Rider scout vessel is just about ready to go. Final checks are finishing now."

Lily smiled, dry but fond. "You're always doing that."

He blinked. "Doing what?"

"Tracking me down to tell me things instead of using the comms."

Basco flushed, his shoulders hunching just a little. "Guilty."

Lily examined him, feeling a little guilty about how much she enjoyed making him squirm.

He shifted his weight. "I guess... I still feel really fortunate to work with you. It's been a while since a human made the headlines like you did."

Lily stayed silent, her gaze inviting him to go on.

"When I was finishing up at the Academy," he continued, "you were already out there, winning the war. I followed all the whispers, the rumors... read between the lines of every report. You were like..." He trailed off, then laughed quietly. "Kind of a ghost. A legend. Sorry for the hero worship."

She let the moment breathe. The lights above flickered ever so slightly, reflecting off the polished floor.

"Trust me," she said at last, "I'm not a hero."

He met her eyes. "What are you even talking about?"

Then, after a second: "I mean, you're not perfect. But that's kind of the best part."

She looked at him, surprised.

"You're human. You mess up. You doubt yourself. You get things wrong." He rubbed the back of his neck. "But you keep trying. You don't give up. What could be more heroic than that?"

Lily's throat tightened in a way she didn't expect. She wasn't always great at knowing what to do with pure, guileless kindness.

He went on. "I see these ranking officers—like Calan. Don't get me wrong, their exploits are impressive. But they all act like heroes. Like they're perfect. Never doubting themselves. It's all a show. I try to be buttoned up, but I could never be like them. You've helped me see there are different ways to be a hero."

She gave a small nod. "Thanks, Basco."

He straightened. "Good luck on your mission. Go get Lieutenant Commander Datch back. The *Salamander* will be here when you return."

"Make sure you keep her in one piece," she said, the corner of her mouth lifting.

He smiled—wide, real. "I will."

He turned on his heel.

• • • •

The corridor lights dimmed as Lily approached Zayir's quarters, the hush of the ship settling into its quieter rhythms. She paused outside his door and pressed the buzzer.

A beat passed.

Then the door slid open with a sigh.

Zayir lay sprawled on the narrow bunk, one arm flung over his face. He didn't move.

Lily leaned against the doorway. "Bad time?"

He sighed and dropped his arm, blinking at her. His hair was a mess. A bowl of untouched food sat precariously on the edge of the bedside table. "Just hoping for a dreamless coma."

Lily stepped inside. "Sorry to disappoint."

He sat up slowly, legs swinging over the edge of the bed. He glanced around at the mess, then down at himself. "I'm a disgrace. I know."

She didn't answer that. Just crossed the room and moved the bowl to a safer spot.

"You're not a disgrace," she said at last. "Just being dramatic."

He gave a dry, humorless laugh. "I've replayed it a hundred times. I messed up, Lily. I was a fool—and worse, a coward."

"No argument from me," she said, with a faint snicker.

Zayir looked at her, posture tense with shame. "And I've probably ruined our friendship... So why are you here? Why are you still speaking to me? Don't you hate me for how I've acted?"

Lily crossed her arms, thoughtful. "Hating you would be easy. You know me—I'm the difficult type."

He blinked at that.

She went on. "Look. In the grand scheme of privileged, powerful men doing sleazy things—trust me, Zayir—you don't even come close to the top."

He let out a short, surprised laugh. "Is that supposed to make me feel better?"

"No," she said, stepping closer. "It's supposed to make you see the opportunity."

He frowned, but didn't interrupt.

"You have so much," Lily said. "Endless chances to do good. But here's the lesson: you can't have everything. That's the trap—thinking you deserve it all."

His mouth opened, then closed again.

"You don't," she added. "None of us do. And guess what? That's a good thing."

Zayir looked up at her like he was searching for something solid to hold on to.

She softened, crouching so they were eye level.

"If you can celebrate the joy of others," she said gently, "you'll always find something to be happy about. Even on your worst day. Even when the crown doesn't fit. That's the kind of man your wife believes you can be. That's the kind of king your people need."

He stared at her for a long moment. Then, quietly, "You always know how to make me feel worse and better at the same time."

"I take that as a compliment."

She leaned in and kissed him—softly, once, like punctuation.

Then stood.

"Take care of yourself, Zayir."

And with that, she turned and walked out—leaving him in the dim quiet of his quarters. Alone.

• • • •

The shuttle bay doors stood open, bathed in the pale light of the docking cradle. The Storm Rider scout vessel loomed ahead—sleek, shadowed, humming with unfamiliar energy. Its hull bore the faint scars of battle.

Lily arrived with her pack slung over one shoulder, Malik already beside her, adjusting the strap of a utility harness. Caris stood just behind, her calm expression at odds with the sharp precision of her posture.

Waiting near the base of the ramp were the others. Lily felt both touched and mildly uncomfortable that they'd come to see her off.

Alrek was the first to step forward. His expression was softer than usual, the corners of his mouth pulled tight with worry. "Come back in one piece," he said simply.

Lily pulled him into a hug—brief, but firm. "I'll do my best."

Charlie gave a brisk salute with one pseudopod. "Way to hog all the action," he said.

Lily smirked. "I'm sure you'll find a way to put yourself in grave danger soon enough. Thanks, Charlie."

The Raath-Ka stood side by side, their small and large frames a study in contrast. Both nodded solemnly.

Ka-Lorrin blinked. "You will succeed."

Taran rumbled, "Hurry back. Hurry back."

Lily smiled. "That's the plan."

Dryst Amaris stepped up to Malik, offering a hand. "I heard your name is up for Dryst next quarter at the Council," he said. "You'll need to return for the honor."

Malik raised an eyebrow, then nodded with quiet pride. "Yes, sir."

Calan approached with a touch of hesitation. He shook Caris's hand first, offering a steady "Good luck."

Then he turned to Lily. His expression was calm. A little tired. Maybe a little sad.

"I appreciate everything, Lily," he said. "Especially the patience. No hard feelings?"

She didn't answer with words—just leaned in and hugged him.

They stood that way for a beat.

"You take care of yourself, Captain," she whispered.

Behind her, the ramp to the scout vessel hissed open.

Xynn and Tevya stood waiting at the top, silhouetted by the red interior lights, ready to go.

Lily stepped back and took in everyone one last time.

"I love you all," she said. "Thank you."

And then she turned, following Caris and Malik up the ramp to join the others.

The doors sealed shut behind them.

She exhaled. "Ready or not, here we go."

. . . .

The Storm Rider vessel wasn't built for comfort. The corridors were narrow, the walls too close—everything cramped and buzzing with low-grade menace, like the ship itself was irritated by their presence.

Lily crouched near the engineering console, sleeves rolled up, her pack tossed aside. Grease smeared one forearm where she'd been elbow-deep in tangled power lines. Above her, Xynn was halfway inside an open panel, peering through a mess of wiring and half-familiar circuit trees.

"Okay," Lily called, "if I'm reading this right, that's the secondary jaco-grid—or something like it. There on your left, see it?"

"It's throttling power to the main engines," came Tevya's voice through the overhead comm. She was up on the bridge, managing the helm and watching proximity alerts.

"I'm reducing restrictors," Xynn said, fumbling with a narrow metal lever tucked beneath the exposed lattice.

The lever gave with a whine.

Lily tapped a few keys. The console hummed, then purred—cleaner, steadier. Engine efficiency climbed by twelve percent. The whole ship seemed to exhale.

"That's more like it," Tevya announced. "Holding course."

Nearby, on the other side of a low partition: Caris—calm but firm—and Malik, groaning something sarcastic. She was giving him another injection for the lingering symptoms from his mental trauma. Their shadows stretched toward Lily under the low strip lighting.

Then she noticed Xynn staring, transfixed.

"There's something back here," Xynn murmured. "Writing. Really old. These are some of the same symbols Charlie and I were translating from Bimara."

Lily moved closer. "Can you read it?"

"Look." Xynn shifted aside, pointing behind the casing. Carved into the alloy was a cluster of geometric glyphs. They were faint—like the memory of a language—but Xynn's sharp eye had caught them.

"It's a name," she whispered, tracing one carefully. "Veyrik."

Lily didn't know why, but the word sent a chill through her.

Xynn squinted, fingers moving across the shapes. "There's a pressure plate hidden here. Maybe a panel release."

"Wait—" Lily started.

Too late.

Click.

The deck shuddered.

Lily turned just in time to see Caris and Malik, just stepping into view, slide cleanly out of sight—swept sideways into a narrow seam in the wall that hadn't been there a second ago.

"Leena!" Caris's voice echoed.

She reached instinctively toward the wall—but the moment her fingers brushed the edge, a searing charge snapped through it.

She yelped, jerking back. "Electric shock. Some kind of security trap."

"Well that's just rude," Xynn muttered, gripping the edge of her chair.

The lights flickered. The floor continued to shift beneath them.

• • • •

The floor tipped without warning, sending a jolt through Lily's boots. She lost her grip on the console as a charge ripped up the metal, forcing her to let go. Xynn cried out beside her, thrown sideways as the floor gave way beneath them.

They crashed down hard—right on top of Caris and Malik in a tangle of limbs.

Above them, two panels groaned open in the ceiling, revealing gleaming metallic plates studded with sharp, electrified spikes. They began to descend—slowly, methodically, the hum of live current filling the room.

"Oh, and the oxygen is being removed," Malik muttered, eyes on his scanner as he pushed himself up under the weight of the others.

"Jesus," Lily snapped, brushing hair from her face, "either skewer us, electrocute us, or suffocate us. Pick one."

"Don't forget crush us," Xynn added, coughing.

They all turned toward the panel release—now sealed shut, sparking faintly. The lights dimmed again. Something deep in the ship growled.

Caris braced her back against the wall and tried to jam her hypo into the descending mechanism, but it barely slowed. The panel shuddered, and the spikes continued their path toward the floor.

Lily reached out. Xynn found her hand, their fingers clasping tightly in the dim.

Across from them, Malik and Caris locked eyes.

"Leena," Malik said softly, voice raw. It startled Lily—she had never heard him say her first name before.

Caris leaned in and kissed him, fiercely, like it might be the last.

Xynn gave a small, crooked smile. Lily squeezed her hand tighter. She saw Xynn close her eyes, bowing her head slightly. Lily instinctively did the same.

The sound of grinding metal grew louder—then stopped.

Dead silence.

Lily opened her eyes.

The panels had frozen, inches above their heads. The lights flickered once more, steadier now.

Tevya's voice came over the comms. "You're lucky I was monitoring. Sorry for the last-minute save—I was adjusting the flight path when I noticed you'd all vanished."

"Oh thank God, Tevya. We all owe you one," Lily said sincerely.

"You're welcome," Tevya replied, her synthetic voice betraying a hint of superiority.

• • • •

The conference room was quiet, lit by the soft amber glow of the overhead panels. The ship cruised on autopilot. Tevya had joined them after locking in their flight path.

Everyone looked a little rattled—bruised, dust-smeared, but alive.

Xynn stood at the console, arms folded. "I cross-referenced the name *Veyrik* with the Gherionite records we recovered. It appears in an old historical theory—supposedly one of the original organic beings who helped create the Gherionites."

Caris leaned forward. "As in... built them?"

Xynn nodded. "The name *Veyrik*, specifically, was from a story. More legend than history. The original artifacts and records haven't been seen in over a century."

"I know the story," Tevya said, stepping closer. "It's not a popular or widely accepted theory of our origin. But it goes like this: the androids on Gherion Prime weren't built as servants or equals. They were meant to be vessels—empty bodies for the original Gherionites to transfer their consciousness into. To live forever."

Lily and Caris turned to each other, the realization dawning. "Fountain of youth," they said in unison.

Tevya pursed her lips. "But something went wrong. The transfer process started driving the organic Gherionites mad. The androids—originally designed to help—took control of the bodies to keep society from collapsing."

"Doesn't seem unreasonable," Malik said.

"Eventually," Tevya continued, "they determined it was a lost cause. The androids put the people down. A mercy kill."

Malik raised his eyebrows. "Less reasonable."

Tevya gave a wry smile. "Like I said—not a very popular story."

"So Gherion Prime is the throughline," Xynn said, cracking her knuckles. "Do you think Ronin could be... a descendant of one of the slain?"

"According to the theory," Tevya said, "no one survived. But history is written by those who live to tell it."

Lily scratched her head. "Still a lot of puzzle pieces missing. No wonder Datch had so many questions."

"If I know my husband," Tevya said softly, "he's already getting answers."

Malik tilted his head. "How much longer till we reach Gherion Prime?"

Tevya checked the display. "Another hour and ten minutes."

Without another word, Malik stood and headed for the exit. Caris followed a beat later, brushing dust from her uniform as she went.

Xynn tilted her head toward Lily, eyes narrowing slightly. "I'm going to our bunk, and I'm closing my eyes for exactly fifty minutes. Want to come with?"

Lily nodded and followed her into the corridor.

As they passed the bunks, Lily slowed in front of the door she'd seen Caris and Malik enter. She was pretty sure she caught just a hint of some unmistakable sounds.

She grinned. "Will wonders never cease."

Then she picked up her pace, hurrying after Xynn.

An hour till showtime.

Chapter 11: Knitted in the Womb

THE SALVAGED STORM Rider vessel rattled as it cut through the upper atmosphere of Gherion Prime. Lightning cracked across the bow, crawling over the scarred hull like veins of living fire. Beneath them, the ochre haze of the planet bloomed—roiling and golden, streaked with rivers of molten glass and continent-sized scars.

Tevya stood at the front of the bridge, silent at first. Her fingers hovered above the console, not quite touching.

"He stowed away," she said quietly. "And now Ronin's carrying him home. Like a soul returning to the cradle."

No one responded. There was something too final in her voice—like the last line of a monologue.

Lily turned toward the viewport, watching the ochre clouds peel back in slow, deliberate waves. The planet looked empty. Abandoned. Not dead... expectant. As if something had been sleeping beneath the crust, gathering its breath.

Then the shuttle banked sharply—thrusters flaring as they dropped into a narrow canyon carved deep into the fractured crust. Jagged scoria walls rose around them, tall and sharp as knives.

They landed hard enough to rattle teeth.

Outside, the wind screamed.

· · · ·

Lily looked out the portal window into the firelit dusk. Basalt pillars surrounded the landing site on all sides, twisted by centuries of tectonic violence. Overhead, flashes of stormlight pulsed in a slow, silent rhythm—like a heartbeat buried too deep to reach.

Caris activated the holodisplay, projecting a map of the region in soft blue light.

"We're here," she said, pointing to a blinking mark. "This canyon puts us about three kilometers south of the citadel complex called Guhrotu. The scans show Datch's signal somewhere inside."

"Guhrotu?" Lily asked.

"A temple of sorts," Tevya answered, stepping forward. "Built on ruins left behind by the progenitors."

Malik leaned in, gesturing toward a glowing line that pulsed faintly on the map, connecting Guhrotu to a second point farther south. "We're also seeing some kind of energy buildup here. It's feeding directly into the citadel through a buried conduit."

"That site," Tevya added, "is Yavero. A collapsed shield volcano. It sits right above the mantle's edge." She paused. "Looks like they're using it as a power source."

Lily exhaled. "But what is he powering?"

Xynn rolled the tension out of her shoulders. "What if we blow it up?"

Caris looked at her. "Volunteering?"

Xynn held the moment, her expression half challenge, half anticipation.

Lily straightened. "We'll set charges. Xynn and I can hit the conduit at the base of Yavero. That should disrupt whatever he's powering."

"Oh," Xynn said, almost surprised. "You all agree... nice."

Caris gave a tight nod. "The rest of us will move toward Datch's position."

• • • •

The terrain around them looked like it had been melted, crushed, and carved in the same breath. Ochre-yellow rocks jutted up from the earth at chaotic angles, brittle and sharp-edged, as if the planet had never quite healed from whatever catastrophe had cracked its crust in the first place. The sky above was a strange, seafoam green—muted, swirling, electric at the edges. It looked like it should have been sweltering, baking them beneath the haze.

But the air was cool. Not cold, but oddly crisp, with an occasional breeze that whipped past hard enough to raise goosebumps. A chill, dry whisper across the skin.

Lily followed Xynn over the next ridge, eyes half on the path, half on the curve of Xynn's hips as she moved—muscle and grace working in perfect, infuriating harmony. She looked effortless, even in the rough terrain. Like she belonged to it.

Lily exhaled, forcing her focus forward. Her mind drifted to Tevya, to the trust she was placing in Caris and Malik. Trust that was earned—but still heavy to carry.

"We'll get him back," Caris had said, *before they split off—calm and certain, like it was fact.*

Lily had believed her.

She still did.

"Psst."

The sharp whisper snapped her back. Xynn raised a hand, palm flat, eyes narrowed. Lily dropped low, slipping behind a slab of jagged rock at the edge of an outcropping. They crouched in silence, hidden by stone and shadow.

About a hundred meters below, figures moved—at least six of them. Ronin's men. Storm Riders in full gear, armor dull and crackling faintly with residual energy. They stood around a cluster of supply crates and gear pylons, weapons slung or leaning close at hand. Most looked bored.

Then the air changed.

A low whine grew into a full-throated roar as a speeder bike tore into view from the east, kicking up trails of ash and dust. The rider was enormous—a Bimaran, easily over seven feet tall, with shoulders as wide as Lily was tall. Every muscle looked like it could split stone.

He skidded to a stop just outside the perimeter. One of the Storm Riders jogged over to meet him, exchanged a few nods, then jogged back toward the others.

"Shift change," he announced.

One of the guards frowned. "He didn't say anything about a shift change."

The first man scoffed. "What are you, new? Grage doesn't say words. Grage *shows up*. And if you question him, he'll grind your bones into paste."

"Three minutes," the first man said, glancing at the others. "On the landing pad."

He pointed toward a flat outcrop high on the far ridge, half shrouded in seafoam haze.

Xynn leaned close, her voice barely above the wind. "Perfect. Shift change. That's our chance to sneak by."

She nodded toward the massive figure still looming near the speeder. "We just have to dodge the walking landmass over there and we'll be fine."

Lily squinted down at him. "He looks like he could squish me like a bug."

"Bigger they are," Xynn whispered with a shrug. "And all that."

Lily didn't look convinced.

She pointed instead toward a squat structure at the base of the ridge—a smooth, metallic silo nestled into the rock like a buried needle. "Are we blowing *that* up?"

Xynn tapped her scanner, eyes flicking over the data. "If we set charges there, it'd make too big a boom. Might trigger an eruption."

She pointed a few yards east, just beyond the perimeter of stacked supply crates. "But over there—the conduit's close to the surface. We plant charges behind those crates, we might be able to sever it clean."

"Might?" Lily echoed.

But they didn't have time to argue. A low hum filled the air as a transport vessel coasted into view, wind from its thrusters kicking up loose grit. Below, the guards began their climb toward the landing pad—at least a dozen of them, armored and armed, boots heavy against the slope.

Grage, thankfully, was lumbering the other way, circling around the silo with the slow certainty of a boulder deciding to roll downhill.

Xynn crouched lower. "Now."

Then she was already moving—sliding down the ridge like a shadow with a pulse.

The heat hit like a wall.

The mouth of the volcano was over a hundred meters away—but even from there, the air shimmered, thick and punishing. Lily staggered a step as the wave rolled over her, searing and dry, like stepping into an oven mid-breath. Every instinct screamed to retreat, to shield her skin, her eyes. If they got any closer, it felt like it would strip them raw.

A few seconds ago, from their perch above, it had all looked so simple. They could see everything—the silo, the crates, the transport, the ridges curling in like the ribs of a vast machine. Now, down on the ground, Lily realized just how tall the stone outcroppings really were. The moment they'd descended, the landscape had swallowed them whole.

Walls of rock surrounded them on all sides—cracked and jagged, hot and rough like red sandpaper. It was like trying to navigate a maze that breathed. The view was gone, replaced by oppressive walls and disorienting heat.

Xynn checked her scanner, angling it toward a narrow split between boulders. "This way," she muttered, already moving.

Lily followed close behind, footsteps muffled against the cracked ground.

They emerged into a wider channel, just enough of a break to glimpse the activity ahead. In the distance, the transport was offloading fresh guards—twelve of them stepping into formation. The previous group handed over equipment, data slates, gruff exchanges of orders and notes.

"See?" Xynn said, a grin twitching at her lips. "Piece of cake."

That's when Lily felt it—the shift in air, the shadow.

Towering. Silent. The ground shook with a rattled breath—Grage was right there.

Lily's blaster was in her hand before she had time to think—but it was gone in the next second, swatted away with an almost lazy motion. So was she. The blow knocked her sideways, her body slamming into the rock with a crunch of bone and breath. The pain lit up her back like fire.

"You jinxed it again!" she groaned, trying to get her breath as Xynn grabbed her arm, hauling her up.

Grage pressed something on his chest plate. A soft *chirrk*, and a red glow spread across the panel—an alert.

From the landing pad, the new and old guards both turned. All two dozen began to run toward their position.

"Shift change, huh?" Lily muttered.

Xynn shrugged helplessly.

They bolted—ducking into the maze of rock, hoping the twisted, narrow passages might work to their advantage. Anything to put space between them and the literal mountain chasing them.

• • • •

They ran.

The maze twisted in on itself, every turn indistinguishable from the last—walls of red stone looming close, throwing back the echo of their breath and boots in scattered fragments. The heat was still everywhere, pressing in like a second skin.

Xynn skidded to a stop at a fork—four jagged passages branched away into darkness.

She held up a hand, listening. "They're coming from all sides."

Lily spun, heart pounding. "What if we go... up?" She gestured to the jagged embankment of rock beside them.

Xynn hesitated. "We'd be wide open—they'll pick us off."

Footsteps. Close now.

"Back the way we came," Lily said, already turning. "Gigantor can't fit in these tunnels. We double back, climb up, cross over."

They sprinted around the bend and scrambled up the narrow ledge, using cracks in the stone to pull themselves up. Just as they crested the ridge—boots. Close.

They dropped down hard—right behind a squad of four guards.

One turned. "Hey—!"

Xynn fired first, crisp and fast.

The other guards spun around, shouting, returning fire. Plasma bolts hissed past. Xynn shoved her blaster into Lily's hand without missing a beat and drew her energy blade.

The weapon came alive in a sweep of amber light.

She moved like lightning—cleaving through the guards in a blur of heat and motion. Lily dropped behind her, firing clean, covering their flank. One of the guards collapsed with a sharp, brittle sound.

Then—more footsteps. Dozens.

"More incoming," Xynn said.

"Of course there are," Lily muttered.

They ran again—through a narrow passage flanked by steaming vents, ducking low. Then suddenly, they were out in the open.

The silo loomed ahead.

They locked eyes for half a beat. Wordlessly, they began prepping the charges.

"If we get blown up or swallowed by lava," Lily said as she worked, "for the record—I love you, even though this was a terrible plan."

"In theory," Xynn replied, fingers flying, "it could've been a great plan."

Lily looked up, one brow raised.

Xynn smirked. "Okay. Maybe not great. And—I love you too."

Then, the ground rumbled beneath them.

Grage rounded the corner, a storm in motion.

"I'll slow him down," Xynn said, already moving. "Set these for a quick detonation—I'll meet you on the other side of that chute." She pointed to a red metal slide built into the far wall, half-obscured by debris. It led down into darkness—no telling how far or where it came out.

Lily nodded. It was a long shot. But maybe their only one.

Xynn turned and sprinted toward a heavy equipment crate—solid alloy, probably weighing as much as she did. With a roar, she hurled it like an Olympic hammer. It spun through the air and crashed square into Grage's chest.

He staggered two steps back. Then kept walking, brushing the crate aside with a flick of his arm like it was made of paper.

Xynn sighed. "This just isn't your day, Xynn," she muttered grimly.

Lily finished wiring the last charge just as more guards came pouring out of the tunnel mouth. She snapped up the blaster and fired into the crowd, forcing them to scatter. Then she turned and bolted for the chute.

Behind her, Grage advanced. Xynn backed up onto a raised metal platform jutting from the scaffolding. He swung; she ducked and spun. Another swing—miss. Sparks flew as the rings on his fist hit steel.

"Come on, Xynn…" Lily hissed under her breath, laying down another volley to keep the guards pinned. But there was no time. The first charge detonated with a sharp, concussive boom.

The shockwave caught both Grage and Xynn mid-motion—hurling them backward. Xynn hit the platform hard; Grage slammed into a control panel.

A sudden whine filled the air.

The platform was a lift. And it began to rise—fast.

Lily's eyes widened as Xynn clung for balance, the lift surging sixty feet into the air. Flames bloomed beneath them, licking at the scaffolding.

The guards scrambled to their feet—just in time for the rest of the charges to go off.

This time, a massive explosion ripped through the base of the silo. Fire. Shrapnel. Bodies. The whole ridge shook as the ground split and vomited smoke.

Lily dove into the chute headfirst as the fireball chased her. She tried to slow herself, gripping the metal walls, but they were slick with dust and debris. Her back slammed against a bend in the slide. Sparks flew. Rocks pelted her from above.

She looked up through the narrow opening—Xynn and Grage, still on the lift, silhouetted against the raging inferno. Grage lunged. Xynn twisted. Fire flared all around them.

Lily watched, horrified, as Grage grabbed Xynn by her ponytail, holding her close to his face like a tiger savoring the moment before the kill. She reached for the blaster, which had followed her partway down the chute—but her fingertip nudged it the wrong way, and it slid into the dark.

She wanted to close her eyes. But she didn't. She forced herself to watch.

Then—Xynn sliced through her ponytail with her blade. As she dropped, the look on Grage's face was priceless. She twisted midair and, with both feet, kicked him hard in the chest.

With a mighty shove, Grage toppled backward—down into the fire below.

Lily exhaled sharply, pulse racing, the metallic tang of fear still sharp in her mouth..

That's when the top of the shaft gave way.

And she dropped, out of sight—swallowed by the tunnel, the roar of the explosion echoing after her.

• • • •

She came to with a mouthful of dust.

For a moment, everything was noise—wind, blood, the distant rumble of fire—and then stillness. It took her a second to orient herself. She'd expected to be underground, buried or entombed or trapped in some smoking ruin.

But no... she was lying on a wide stone platform near the far edge of the volcano.

A cliff.

From where she and Xynn had approached earlier, she'd only glimpsed the drop-off. Now she was right on top of it.

Lily groaned, pushing herself up with aching arms. Her body screamed in protest, but nothing seemed broken. She brushed soot from her face, coughing, dazed—but just enough relief began to trickle in. Maybe, just maybe, that was the end of Grage.

Then she saw it. The silhouette.

Leaning casually against a matte-black hoverbike. Arms crossed. That same nauseating, shit-eating grin.

"No fucking way," Lily breathed.

"Language, Starlight," came the reply.

She turned, already furious. "You've got to be kidding me."

Rhyder Dane winked.

"You piece of—"

"Hey now," he said, holding up both hands in a mock surrender. "At least let me explain. You know how sexy you are when you're all worked up, Starlight."

"It's *Starling*," she snapped. "You *know* it's Starling."

He only smiled wider.

"What the hell are you doing here? Don't tell me you're a true believer now. Here to ride the storm to immortality?" she sneered.

His eyes twinkled with something between amusement and danger.

Rhyder tilted his head. "You want to hit me? I know I deserve it."

Lily's glare could have melted alloy. "If I wasn't in so much pain, I'd knock you off this cliff."

He smirked. "Noted."

A beat.

"Ready to listen now?"

Lily's expression didn't change. In fact, it sharpened.

She launched at him.

Rhyder moved faster than she expected. In one fluid motion, he drew a blaster and leveled it at her chest—not shaking, not cocky, just calm and matter-of-fact.

"Ready to listen," he said again, his tone flat this time. "Now?"

Lily stared down the barrel of the blaster.

How did we get here? she thought. This guy got me all worked up—this is what happens when you mix up *bad boy* with *bad guy*.

She raised her hands a little, voice steady despite the pulse pounding in her ears. "Okay. I'm listening."

Rhyder's expression didn't shift. He kept the blaster leveled, his other hand gesturing out to the chaos behind her—smoke, fire, the churning throat of the volcano.

"Look around you," he said. "You think this is about the storm?"

He gave a low chuckle. "Ronin? He's two hundred years old, Starlight. Did you know that?"

Lily's brain snagged on the name.

It was him.

It was Ronin the entire time.

"He was there before the storm even started," Rhyder said, almost like he could see her thoughts lining up. "He's not some prophet. He's a relic."

He stretched his arms out wide, a mockery of reverence. "I don't care what he's preaching. Let the cult chant whatever they want. I'm not in it for the dogma."

He dropped his arms, expression sharpening.

"I'm in it for the gift."

From his coat pocket, he pulled out a slender data rod, tossing it once, then again, like it was just another game. It glittered faintly in the light—Union-grade tech.

"He's going to give me eternal life," Rhyder said, catching the rod with a snap of his fingers. "Because as many times as I've cheated death? I just can't imagine a galaxy without *yours truly* in it."

He pointed the rod at her now, like it was a wand or a weapon—hard to say which.

"In fact," he added with a grin, "I'm just getting started."

"What are you going to do?" Lily asked, her voice shaking more than she wanted it to. "Are you going to shoot me, Rhyder?"

He hesitated—then lowered the blaster. Not all the way, just enough to make a point. He kept his distance, watching her.

Lily tried to ignore the stabbing pain in her ribs, the way her shoulder throbbed every time she breathed. Her vision blurred at the edges. She was running out of time.

"You going to make yourself a god?" she asked, panting. "What'll you do, Your Almighty-ness?"

Rhyder tilted his head like he was considering it seriously—and, to her disgust, looked vaguely aroused by the idea.

"First thing? Not take people's crap all the time," he said. "And maybe—just maybe—let the underdogs have a shot now and then."

Lily raised a brow, voice flat. "So you're a hero now?"

He spread his arms again like he was accepting a standing ovation. "I'll tear down the whole system. Let people choose how they want to live."

Then his expression turned serious. "Ronin needs energy from certain progenitor species. He still needs Human and Saravethi."

He took a step closer. "Think about it. You and Xynn could be part of the new order—forever."

"Pass," Lily said coldly.

He stepped again, slower this time. "You'll be immortal."

Another step.

"We'll be immortal."

He reached out, placing his hands lightly on her arms.

"Don't touch me," she snapped, jerking away.

"Don't be like that," Rhyder said, his tone maddeningly playful.

The volcano answered for her.

A thunderous crack split the air. The ground lurched beneath them as lava exploded to life below, a fresh shockwave tearing through the cliffside.

They were both hurled sideways, dust and debris raining down in a choking cloud.

Lily slammed into the ground—tried to tuck into a roll, teeth clenched against the pain. Her vision swam. But then—there. The blaster. Teetering near the edge.

With everything she had, she forced herself up and kicked it.

It skidded once—twice—then sailed over the cliff.

"Damn it!" Rhyder shouted, scrambling after it—but not fast enough.

He spun back, grabbed her boot, and yanked—dragging her down hard.

They tumbled into the dust, limbs tangling, struggling for leverage. Lily clawed at his chest, but the searing pain in her ribs dulled her strength. She gasped as he pinned her—one knee on her thigh, the other hand grasping for her throat.

And still, the volcano raged.

"Last time I was on top, it was so much more pleasant," Rhyder grunted, struggling to pin her.

Despite the pain, Lily twisted hard and broke free, spitting as she rolled clear.

"That makes one of us."

She forced herself upright, breath ragged. Focus.

She remembered Leena's voice in training.

Remove yourself from the moment. Let go.

Then Alrek's calm. Xynn's steadiness.

She centered herself, shut out the pain—and moved.

A clean roundhouse kick snapped across Rhyder's temple.

Unarmed, he staggered, dropped to one knee, trying to catch himself.

Then—another blast.

The cliff shuddered, a deafening crack splitting the earth. Lily barely kept her footing as a fresh chasm tore open between them.

Rhyder slipped—then landed hard on a jagged outcrop just below. A fluke. A miracle. He scrambled up, now a full level down from her, a yawning split of lava-lit rock between them.

He looked up, breathless. Contrite.

"Lily... you're right. I let it all go to my head. I'm sorry."

The rock beneath him crumbled.

Lily hesitated—just for a second—then yanked the strap from her field jacket and tossed it down.

He caught it. She pulled.

But the moment he reached solid ground, he spun—bolted for the hoverbike.

"Rhyder—!"

Too late. He pulled a compact blaster from the storage compartment and fired.

Lily dove behind a rock as the bolt scorched past.

She spotted him struggling with the speeder's ignition.

Not this time.

Lily charged. Full speed. No hesitation.

Rhyder looked up, eyes wide, blaster raised—

But he hesitated.

Just for a heartbeat.

Genuine conflict flickered across his face.

He's a worm, Lily thought. *Not a killer.*

She hit him like a wave, shoulder-first, full-body contact that knocked the wind from his lungs and sent him sprawling. He hit the ground hard, coughing, stunned.

She straddled the bike, swung it upright with a grunt, then extended a hand.

"Look, if you let me drive, I'll get you out of here so you don't die. I'm nice like that."

Rhyder scrambled onto the back, clutching the seat, and as they lifted off, he slid open a side panel.

A soft *ping* as he activated a control override.

"Thanks, Starlight," he said, voice syrupy and smug.

Lily's reflexes took over. In one breath, she latched her safety harness, spun the stabilizer, and rolled the bike midair.

Rhyder didn't stand a chance.

He flew off like a ragdoll—arms flailing, shouting something that got lost in the wind.

He landed with a crunch on the same jagged rock, now almost fully swallowed by the churning lava below.

Smoke coiled around him, thick and black and rising. It made him look like a devil rising from the pit.

She looked down at him—surrounded by smoke, broken rock beneath him. For half a second, her hand twitched on the controls.

Then she whispered, "Goodbye, Rhyder," and left the rest unsaid.

"Damn it, Lily, I'm sorry!" he called after her, hands clasped like a prayer. "Give me another chance!"

She didn't look back.

The smoke curled around him. And Lily flew on.

· · · ·

Lily circled wide, the speeder bike rattling beneath her as another shockwave split the sky. Smoke spiraled upward in greasy columns, and below—darting across the crumbling scaffold—was Xynn.

She was climbing from platform to platform, her clothes torn, face streaked with ash, but alive. The path behind her was gone. The ledge ahead? Already falling.

Lily dipped low, one hand on the controls, the other outstretched.

"Need a lift?" she called.

Xynn grinned—wild and beautiful and somehow still joking. "My hero," she said, and jumped.

Lily caught her wrist and hauled her up with a grunt. Xynn swung her leg over the seat and clung tight as the bike lurched upward. Below, the entire cliff face detonated in a fury of fire and sound—silos rupturing, magma bursting from fresh wounds in the earth.

They landed near their borrowed vessel to regroup.

As they stepped inside, the doors groaned closed behind them. The air smelled like scorched plastic and ozone, and the console lights flickered hesitantly to life. Lily leaned over the comms panel, tapping through the interface to initiate a secure signal.

They waited in suspicious silence for a beat.

Then Lily gave a faint grin. "Sorry about your hair."

Xynn took a deep breath. "Is it that bad?"

Lily tried not to make a face.

"It's bad, isn't it," Xynn muttered, reaching up and wincing as her fingers grazed the singed stubble. "Well... it'll grow back."

"Makes you look tough," Lily said.

With a sharp chirp, the screen blinked—and Caris's face appeared, flushed with adrenaline, her pale skin stark against whatever dark room or cave they were in.

"Whatever you just did," Caris said, "you made waves."

Malik leaned into the frame beside her. "Big ones. They're not happy down here."

Xynn gave a half-laugh. "And we broke their only Grage."

Caris raised an eyebrow, but let it go. "Oh—and someone would very much like to say hi."

The screen shifted—and there was Datch. He was holding Tevya's hand, a little battered, but unmistakably alive.

Lily's heart gave a joyful lurch.

"Datch," she breathed, her hand rising instinctively toward the screen. "You're okay."

"Indeed," he said, offering one of his small, earnest smiles. "The team found me like a Rigelian homing pigeon. However, I'm afraid Ronin knows I'm here. I suspect he let me stow away."

Xynn leaned in. "Why would he do that?"

"An excellent question," Datch replied. He glanced at Tevya, then back to Lily. "I believe I've uncovered some... interesting information about Ronin's past."

Lily crossed her arms. "Let me guess. He's two hundred years old."

Datch shook his head. "Try two thousand."

Lily pieced it together slowly. "Coinciding with the ancient Gherionites... but how is that even possible?"

Caris stepped back into frame. "Remember what my brother and the captain found on Earth? That... thing. The immortality experiments."

"Veyrik," Xynn said. "From the inscriptions."

Datch nodded. "Veyrik and Ronin are one and the same."

"As in," Malik added, "the Gherionite progenitors. But the experiments weren't just them. They involved ancient Humans, Saravethi, Bimarans, and Krythar. Eternal life. But just like the legends say... they went mad. Turned on each other."

Tevya's voice came next—quiet, but steady. "Their creations—the android inhabitants, my ancestors—they purged them. Killed them. Somehow, Ronin survived."

Xynn frowned. "So what's he trying to do? Finish what they started?"

Tevya leaned forward, eyes dark. "He's going to use the chorosh to control the inhabitants. Turn them into what they were originally meant to be—slaves."

"Restoration," Datch said quietly. "That's how he sees it. Resetting the galaxy to the way he believes the storm intended. He's been working toward this for centuries. Something about the storm's proximity... and gathering all the elements here. I don't know how much of it is science, and how much is ritual."

Malik nodded. "And that blast you triggered—whatever device is at the heart of this consciousness transfer—it's destabilizing. Fast."

"The seismic readings are worsening," Tevya added. "Whatever he's doing—it's unraveling."

Caris reappeared. "Ronin's in a rage. He's isolated himself. Killed his own guards."

"We're on our way," Lily said, already moving.

"You'll need all the help you can get," Xynn added.

They cut the comms and bolted from the shuttle, mounting the speeder.

Xynn caught Lily glancing at her scorched buzz cut and made a face.

Lily tried to hide her smirk. "It's growing on me."

And she dropped the throttle.

· · · ·

Lily and Xynn roared in on the speeder, dust spiraling around them as they skidded to a stop outside the ruined citadel. The others were already there, gathered in the shadow of the crumbling structure—once grand, now more like a monument to hubris, its fractured stone towers looming against the flickering sky.

Datch stepped forward, the wind catching his coat. "Ronin has a lab inside," he said, voice taut. "It's fortified. Not much left of the structure's beauty, but more than enough strength to keep people out."

"Shyra'thel is in there," Malik added, reading his scanner. His tone was grim.

Lily's stomach dropped. A pulse of something sharp and aching flickered in her chest. She hadn't let herself hope—had almost come to peace with never seeing her again.

Malik went on. "She's not alone. Several other life forms, all in a state of stasis."

"We have to get them out," Xynn said instantly, already scanning the broken entrance for a path inside.

Datch didn't flinch. "While I don't disagree, stopping Ronin has to be our top priority now. Even if it means—" he hesitated, then said it plainly, "casualties. He poses a threat to multiple inhabited systems. We still don't fully understand the extent of his power."

Tevya nodded once. "Plus I just really want to kill him."

The silence that followed was immediate—and weirdly loud.

Lily exhaled, lips twitching at the edge. "Okay," she said. "How do we take him out?"

Malik's face was tight with frustration. "He's blocking our scanners with some kind of ancient encryption."

Datch glanced over. "It's old Gherionite code—deep algorithms. We'll need some sort of..."

"Ancient Gherionite encryption key?" Lily interrupted, holding up her comm tag. Its holo-display flickered to life, revealing a spinning cipher. Underneath it, a short message scrolled across the screen:

Hope this helps. If anyone asks, you didn't get it from me.
—Trish.

Lily felt a flicker of warmth. Trish was standing by her principles—but she cared too much not to help.

"It's working," Datch confirmed, eyes flicking across the stream of new data. "I've got a route. It's narrow." He looked up. "I want the rest of you focused on getting the stasis hostages out. I'll handle Ronin."

"I'll be your backup," Xynn said, without hesitation.

"We will," Lily added, stepping up beside her. Her voice didn't waver. She wasn't ready for another goodbye—not today.

Datch paused, then nodded. "Very well. Thank you both."

—

They moved fast, weaving through the shattered ruins to a side wall cracked just enough to hint at passage. Datch keyed a sequence into a field emitter, attaching it to the stone. A low hum rose, vibrating in Lily's molars, and then—

Boom. The wall gave way in a blast of crumbling dust and fractured masonry.

They surged inside, weapons drawn.

The corridor was dim, the walls alive with strange tubing and the glow of ancient circuits pulsing like veins. A pair of guards in twisted storm rider armor rounded the corner—then dropped fast as Caris and Malik opened fire. No time for subtlety now.

"Clear," Caris said.

"Move," Datch called. "This way."

They reached a split in the path—two heavy doors at odd angles. One led deeper toward the energy signature. The other sealed off a chamber glowing with cryo-suspension pods.

"Go," Lily told the others. "We'll find Ronin."

Malik nodded. "We'll get them out. Cryo integrity's too fragile to wake them here. We have to transport the pods back to the shuttle."

Tevya was already unhooking cables with surgical efficiency. Caris stood over her, guarding the door.

Lily turned toward the far corridor.

She looked once at the cryo chamber as she passed—and caught sight of Shyra'thel through the frost-rimed glass. Pale. Unmoving. But her vitals blinked steady and strong.

Lily's throat went tight. She touched the glass—just once—then ran.

Xynn fell in beside her. Datch led the way.

The ground shook beneath them from seismic activity.

The deeper they went, the stranger their surroundings became.

Lily had seen tech. She'd seen temples and labs, sanctuaries and tombs. But this place was something else. The walls pulsed faintly, an eerie bioluminescence bleeding from between mechanical plates and bone-like ridges. Veins of copper and black tubing ran along the floor—breathing, almost. Like a tightrope strung between the living and the built.

They rounded a corner into what had once been a great hall and stopped cold.

Bodies.

Storm Riders, scattered like broken dolls. Their black armor cracked. Faces slack in death. Burn marks scorched the walls. Blood sprayed in long, furious arcs.

"He killed them," Datch said quietly, stepping over one of the fallen. "In a rage."

"Why?" Xynn asked, her voice barely above a whisper.

"Because they failed him," Lily said. "Because in the end, you can never please a monster."

They pressed on.

The circuitry on the walls grew denser, more organic—some of it still sparking, crawling with faint glimmers of code like phosphorescent insects.

And then they reached the chamber.

A massive space that narrowed upward like the inside of a spire. High above, at its apex, was a platform that looked almost like a throne—or a torture device. A jagged nest of rusted steel and ancient alloy, stitched together with coils of translucent wiring and petrified tendrils.

And there, with his back to them, was Ronin.

He was working at a console embedded into the structure itself, his fingers flying over interfaces they couldn't see, entering sequence after sequence into the ancient machine.

Datch raised his weapon.

Paused.

Scowled at his scanner.

"He's behind a forcefield," he muttered.

"Very perceptive," Ronin said, without turning around.

His voice echoed around the space—too calm. Too amused.

"It's fitting that the three of you are here," he went on, still facing the console. "You've been... persistent. Unexpectedly effective at slowing me down."

Then he turned.

And smiled.

"No matter," he said. "Gherion Prime was only the beginning. My path leads elsewhere now—to higher planes of existence, where I will no longer be bound by this... primitive shell."

"I thought you wanted to restore the ancient order," Lily said. "Rebuild things the way they were."

Ronin's face twisted, like a switch had been flipped—sending him into a tantrum.

He reached down and hurled a large metal console into the forcefield wall. It struck with a sound like thunder—arcs of lightning exploding outward, making Lily flinch.

"You!" he snarled. "You were meant to rule! You and the chosen four. You could've restored the line. Instead, you chose ruin."

He paced behind the shield, fists clenched. "So now? Now all I can do is accelerate the end. Reverse the energy flow. Push it into the planet's core."

Datch's voice cut in, sharp. "That will destroy the planet."

Ronin tilted his head, mockingly thoughtful. "I believe I already said I was moving on."

He turned again to the console, typing with renewed speed. "It's frustrating, really," he said, calmer now. "To be hindered by such..."

He paused, as if searching for the right word.

"...lesser beings."

With a final keystroke, a hidden passage yawned open in the wall behind him, revealing a sleek, obsidian vessel docked and pulsing with light.

Ronin smiled. "Enjoy whatever comes next. I plan on never finding out."

He stepped toward the open hatch.

Xynn reached for her weapon. "What's our next move?" she asked, glancing at Datch.

Lily was already pulling up the encryption code from Trish. "Can we use it to drop the shield?"

Datch studied the field, calculating. "It's too powerful. But..." His eyes narrowed. "I might be able to modify a comm tag to emit a tunneling signal. Just enough to let one of us through."

Lily looked from the barrier to him. "Won't we be fried?"

"You might be..." Datch said, matter-of-fact.

He worked fast, punching commands into his comm tag.

Then he handed Lily his scanner.

"Take this," he said firmly. "Please don't lose it."

She blinked. "Datch—"

He didn't let her finish.

He ran.

Straight through the field.

The forcefield screamed.

Like the sound of some sort of tortured beast. Datch's body seized the moment he crossed the barrier—electric arcs lashing across his limbs, peeling away synthetic skin in wet, sizzling sheets.

"Datch!" Lily shouted, stepping forward—but stopped short of the field's edge. All she could do was watch.

His uniform burned away. Exposed circuitry sparked from his back. Biomechanical fluid poured from the seams in his arms. But he didn't stop. Didn't falter.

He cleared the barrier and threw himself at Ronin.

They collided in a blur of metal and fury, crashing against the base of the machine. Ronin swung first, wild but fast. Datch absorbed it, countered hard—his arm snapping upward to drive the heel of his palm into Ronin's jaw.

But Ronin twisted with unnatural speed and kicked Datch away. Debris rained from above as the room shuddered again—huge slabs of alloy crashing between them.

Smoke and sparks filled the air.

Across the divide, Ronin straightened, half-limping now, his movements disjointed. He raised his weapon and fired.

Two shots struck Datch in the chest—one sparking off metal plating, the other punching through softer tissue near his shoulder. Datch fell to one knee.

Lily gasped, her fists clenched at her sides. "No—"

Ronin didn't wait. He turned and ran, ducking through the exposed corridor toward the waiting ship.

Datch pushed himself upright. For a moment, he hesitated—gaze fixed on Ronin, torn between vengeance and duty. Then he turned toward the console.

Outside, Ronin streaked across the hangar like a burst of flame. He launched in a flash, the vessel soaring toward orbit faster than Lily thought possible.

Datch limped toward the device. His movements were deliberate now, slowed by damage. One arm hung uselessly at his side, the joint sparking with every step.

"The controls are fried!" he shouted. "Only seconds left!"

"Is there anything we can do to stop it?" Lily called from the other side of the field.

Xynn's voice followed, sharp and trembling. "Oh no…"

Datch looked up.

"Sometimes," he said, gruff but clear, "the only options are bad options."

Without another word, he drove his fist into the exposed core—hard enough that his whole body followed. Lily saw the metal housing split in two.

And then—

Light.

Blinding. Total.

A wall of white radiance erupted in every direction—but the forcefield held. Just barely. It groaned and sizzled, fractures spiderwebbing through the barrier as it strained to contain the blast.

The sound was deafening.

Lily and Xynn hit the ground, eyes shut tight, hands over their ears as the room came apart around them.

Lily felt the shaking in her bones. Her teeth chattered. The entire citadel buckled, walls tearing apart as pressure vented through the cracks. For a moment, she thought—this was it.

Then—

Silence.

A deep, awful silence.

They stood.

The blinding light had vanished. The shaking had stopped.

And before them, within the radius where the device had been, was nothing.

No trace of the machine. No wreckage.

Just a wide, perfect circle of ash. Pale as snow. Smooth as glass.

The device, the lab, much of the citadel's interior—along with Datch himself—gone.

Lily stepped to the edge. The silence pressed in from all sides.

"Datch..." she whispered.

And then, with a final flicker of dying energy, the forcefield collapsed.

Ash drifted down through the air like snow—spiraling around them, weightless and strange.

It was almost... beautiful.

Chapter 12: Elegy for the Living

THE FLECKS SWAM AROUND shapes of color, drifting like oil in water.

Not just lights—though there were plenty of those, gliding across the dark like fireworks with no sound—but shapes. Familiar and strange. Patterns in motion. Sometimes they looked like home. Sometimes like entire worlds.

Once, someone had told her—she couldn't remember who, or when—that the way to Never-Neverland was hidden in those shapes. If you followed them just right, you could fly there. Lift up and out, past gravity and grief, past time, past everything.

She imagined it sometimes: a place beyond the physical. A dream-world where she could glide like the pteranodons of Korolith III, wings outstretched, catching the currents over oceans and fields, fire and ice. A place where centuries passed below like weather patterns—where time didn't move forward or back, but through. As if her heartbeat could carry her to everything she'd missed—and everything still waiting.

In her dreams, she was often flying.

But she was also often alone.

Even in the good ones. Even when the sun was shining and the trees were tall and strange music played in the background—she was still the only one there.

The light woke her.

Not loud or jarring—just a slow flood of warmth across her face as the tent flap stirred open.

"Hey," came a soft voice.

Xynn, kind and careful, just inside the entrance.

Lily blinked against the brightness, vision swimming as she pushed her tangled hair off her forehead. Her back ached from the cot. Her whole body ached, really. But it was a reminder—still here. Still fighting.

"Sorry to wake you," Xynn added, crouching beside the cot, her eyes gentle. "I'm glad you got a nap. I don't think you slept at all last night."

Lily didn't answer right away. She wasn't ready to sit up. Her limbs felt like stone—solid, reluctant. She stared up at the ceiling of the tent, trying to gather the pieces of herself. There were too many lately. Some sharp. Some soft. None that seemed to fit quite right.

They were staying on Tevya's property—what remained of it. The already-damaged house had been nearly destroyed during the seismic event, along with much of the neighborhood. So the crew had helped set up temporary shelters: tents, mobile generators, portable medics. The kind of makeshift village that appeared when people didn't want to leave a place behind, even if it had hurt them.

It had been a few days since Ronin's escape.

A few days since Datch had saved them.

Saved them all—

Lily pressed her eyes shut again. The flecks were still there.

Gherion Prime had, in many ways, reset itself. The network of the chorosh—the invisible web connecting every citizen—had been suspended by the council. Temporarily shut down to address "any compromise."

But underneath it all, a strange new tension had begun to rise. Androids eyeing androids. Whispered questions. Unease that clung like static.

They were learning, collectively, that the stories passed down were incomplete. That their ancestors—organic and synthetic—had not walked peacefully into one another's arms. That the purge had been real.

Some refused to believe it.

Others took it too far.

The whole planet felt like it was holding its breath.

"They're here," Xynn said softly. "The *Salamander*. I just got the call—they should be sending down the landing party for the memorial any minute now."

Lily finally turned her head.

Xynn stood silhouetted against the sunlit flap of the tent, her buzzed hair backlit like a horizon. The stubble had grown in just enough to look intentional now—elegant in its own way.

"Dryst Amaris is in command," Xynn added. "Calan didn't come."

Lily nodded slowly.

She knew Calan and Datch had their disagreements, but he was probably still getting settled in his new assignment.

She was looking forward to seeing everyone. But the service—that she was dreading.

Sober events where everyone pretended to feel the same thing had never been her idea of comfort. She had a hard time with grief on a good day—let alone in public.

But it wasn't about her.

This was for her friends. For Tevya.

. . . .

Lily stepped out into the fading light, alone.

The path up the ridge was narrower than she remembered—worn to smooth dust by emergency boots and supply crates, the kind of soft erosion that happened not over centuries, but days. Beneath her feet, the ground felt fragile, like the planet hadn't fully decided to stay whole.

She adjusted the collar of her shirt, fingers snagging on the fold. Nothing fit quite right today. The fabric clung too tightly in the wrong places, like it remembered Xynn's hands and wanted to be back on the floor.

Xynn had stayed behind, still fussing with what passed for formalwear. She'd laughed—bitterly, then almost shyly—about trying to find something that didn't make her look like "a soldier in a pageant," given the new buzzed hair. She hated ceremonies. Hated expectations. Lily couldn't blame her.

She hated them too, a little more than usual.

The Salamander crew dotted the clearing above like starlight breaking through cloud cover—shining and sharp in their Union-issue uniforms, every badge polished, every crease crisp. They didn't look *out of place*, exactly, but they didn't look like they belonged to the terrain either. The glint of metal trim caught the low sun, flashing like the chrome of a car parked in a garden. Gleaming. Perfect.

A beacon of hope, she supposed.

Or something too clean. Too manufactured. Like the glittering towers in the cities she used to haunt, before the world went to hell and back. She'd seen this shine before—on Earth, in places that pushed out the soul to make room for the showroom.

She shoved the thought down. Not now. Not today.

Then she saw Basco.

He stood near the edge of the crowd, feet planted too wide, uniform slightly askew, like it had been assembled mid-run. He caught sight of her and offered a grin so big it nearly split his face in two. His discomfort with the formality was visible from orbit, but it made him *more* himself, not less.

Lily nodded. Smiled back. That was enough.

She kept walking—closer now. And then she felt it.

The gravity of them.

Charlie's gelatinous pseudopods opened first—already mid-reach, halfway toward her like someone had removed the waiting part of a hug. Alrek followed a beat later, awkward but certain, his eyes wide and wet at the edges.

And without needing to think about it, she walked straight into their orbit.

Wrapped up. Held fast.

Held home.

Lily didn't know how long they stood there. Long enough for the wind to rise and fall again. Long enough for her heart to stop pounding quite so loudly in her chest.

When she finally pulled back, Alrek's eyes were glassy.

"I'm just glad you're okay," he said, his voice cracking around the edges like something old and breakable.

She opened her mouth to answer—but then Charlie let out a strange, almost musical *snrk* from his voice module, followed by a stuttered *blurp* and a warbling hum that echoed somewhere between a car alarm and a goose with a head cold.

"Sorry," Charlie said quickly. "I've been working on the crying patch. It's... it's still not ideal."

Lily blinked. "That was supposed to be—"

"Crying," he said. "I know. I hate it too."

Another hiccup of noise escaped him—some awful mix of a trumpet and a sigh.

"I always get emotional at funerals," he added miserably. "Even when I didn't really know the individual. But I *did* know Datch. I mean, not as well as you two, obviously. But I think of us as kindred spirits."

Lily reached out and rested a hand gently against the side of his squishy form, where she thought his shoulder might be. "It's okay, Charlie. If you had a heart, it would be a big heart."

Charlie burbled softly. "He really saved my gelatinous ass on our mission here."

A wet laugh slipped out of Lily before she could stop it. "He really did."

"But," she added, squeezing his side, "you weren't so bad yourself. I happen to remember you saving all of us."

She was pretty sure he beamed at that.

Alrek sniffed, wiping his face on his sleeve, a display of the bit of childhood left in him. "So... I just got approval..." he said, a little too fast, like he'd been holding it in. "From the Academy. I get to finish my training aboard the *Salamander*."

Lily looked down at her shoes. "That's great news," she managed.

Alrek hesitated. "Wait—" he tilted his head. "You *are* coming back on board, right?"

She looked up at him, eyes tired but kind. "We'll talk about it later. Okay?"

His smile was small but real, the kind that didn't need to be whole to be honest. "Okay," he whispered.

Then her gaze caught on something past his shoulder.

The Dryst's silhouette, backlit dramatically by the afternoon sun. He stood tall as always near the paved path leading toward the community hall—what was left of it. The volunteer crew had worked day and night to clean it up well enough to hold the service. The building still bore scorch marks and broken windows, but the roof had been patched, and the walls painted with soft streaks of color from the morning sun.

Lily swallowed the lump in her throat.

She squared her shoulders and managed her most professional walk.

"Captain Calan was sorry he couldn't be here," came the voice before Lily had fully reached him.

Amaris stood with his back to her, tall and still and unmistakable. The afternoon sun etched a faint aura around his shoulders, his lavender skin catching the light like polished sea glass.

"He's already on the transport headed to deep space," The Dryst continued. "The *Vanguard* needs its new engineer."

Lily paused a few steps behind him. "So it's official, then," she said. "Congratulations are in order, Captain."

Now he turned.

She'd almost forgotten how tall he was—nearly seven feet of easy grace, silver hair neatly tied back, uniform crisp. But it was still the uniform of a first officer.

"I declined the offer," he said simply.

Lily raised her eyebrows.

"While I do take seriously the opportunity to command," he began, smiling just a little, "I've always been better suited to the needs of the crew. I'll remain first officer, once they name someone to replace Calan."

Lily's grin came despite herself. "Well. Congratulations, then. For *not* being captain."

Amaris chuckled, his slim shoulders lifting slightly. "Best promotion I ever turned down."

The mirth faded gently from his face. "He left for what I'd call an inarguable reason. I must say, I'm quite proud of him."

Lily nodded. Then they both faced the hall again. The lump in her throat hadn't left—just softened its grip.

"Datch was a rare breed," Dryst said quietly.

She gave a broken smile. "He was my first friend when I came to the future. He always looked out for me."

The tears were back. Not sudden this time—just steady, like rain that had waited too long.

Damn, she thought. *I hate funerals.*

She stepped into his arms and let them come. Amaris held her gently, saying nothing, simply giving her space to fall apart without fanfare.

When they pulled apart, he tilted his head. "Who's officiating the service?"

"Tevya," she said. "It's Gherionite tradition. The closest loved one gives the service."

Dryst nodded, absorbing that. "They're a passionate people," he said. "Despite being synthetic."

Lily looked at the gathering crowd of friends, neighbors, colleagues. "They certainly are. If there's one thing we've learned through all of this, it's that."

· · · ·

The community hall was fuller than Lily expected.

Xynn sat beside her in the second row, silent and still—though her fingers had curled around Lily's early in the ceremony and hadn't let go since. She'd chosen a dress from Tevya's small collection of Earth clothing that had survived the fires. Asymmetrical, shimmering, much more classically feminine than her usual fare—but it contrasted beautifully with the blunt line of her new hair. Lily was grateful to be next to her. Grateful to be touching something alive.

The tears had stopped for now. What replaced them was something quieter, deeper—fascination, maybe. Wonder, even.

So much ritual, she thought. *On a planet of androids.*

Low chants echoed around the darkened room, more harmonic than musical, as if the voices were designed to vibrate through the floor itself. Light shimmered above the darkened platform at the front of the room—rainbow threads, dancing like airborne spirits. They coalesced into creatures that didn't exist: long-bodied, antlered things with wings like petals. When one flickered out, another took its place.

The whole thing felt impossibly ancient.

Then Tevya stood.

Lily's stomach clenched. She wasn't sure what Gherionites called this ritual, but she knew the meaning was the same. A eulogy. A farewell. And what do you say, really—what could you possibly say?

It hardly seemed fair for the spouse to be the one to do it. But Tevya's voice was clear as ever, even if the usual sweetness had thinned.

"Datch," she said, smiling faintly, "did not like any of this ritual. But he tolerated it for me. And I appreciate him knowing it would give me comfort."

She paused, gathering breath, gathering weight.

"I am a lucky individual. Our time was too brief together. I mourn my loss, and the loss of what we would have built. Of who... we might have become. Growing our family. Traveling together. Listening to him complain about new things."

There was soft laughter—just enough to remind everyone they could still feel joy.

"But Datch had one quality I'm sure we all admired," she went on. "On the one hand, enviable—for its virtuous nature. On the other, something many avoid. Because it so often ends... like this."

She didn't need to clarify.

"And that was selflessness."

Tevya's voice didn't break, but it softened.

"He always put the needs of others before his own. The needs of a single individual—even a stranger—above himself. And often," she added, a corner of her mouth quirking, "above mine."

Another ripple of laughter, gentler this time.

"I doubt I will ever see another specimen like Datch again," she said. "Which is a loss for the entire galaxy. Because we could use more like him. More who are willing to see beyond their own nose. Who find the good. Who are, frankly, obnoxiously tenacious."

She closed her eyes.

Silence followed.

Not for effect, not for ceremony. Just silence. Long enough that Lily felt her breathing shift. That the light-creatures above them flickered, faded, and did not return.

Then Tevya opened her eyes.

And she spoke, in words that felt both sacred and deeply personal.

"As now I have passed through this darkness,
The light has faded and met my being once again.
I invite you all to pass now—
Through the dark, and back into the light."

Around her, heads bowed. Lily did the same.

She closed her eyes.

Darkness.

• • • •

Someone had set out low urns of pale blue blossoms along the perimeter of the gathering space—a Gherionite tradition, Lily guessed, for remembrance maybe. It lent the air a kind of soft sanctity.

Then, the Raath-Ka arrived.

Ka-Lorrin approached Tevya with a solemn air, spine perfectly straight, hands neatly folded behind his back. "On behalf of the Raath-Ka, I wish to convey our formal respect for your grief," he said. "Datch was a valuable presence. We mourn his passing with you."

Tevya inclined her head, clearly touched.

Ka-Lorrin paused, then added with careful sincerity, "If you require a memory preservation, or would like a philosophical transcription of today's events for posterity, we remain at your disposal."

"That's... very kind," Tevya said gently.

Behind them, Taran was trying to fix a tray of appetizers he'd bumped, but it had become a game of dominoes wrapped in a Rube Goldberg machine of dishes.

With a massive clatter, a river of trays cascaded to the floor. A few guests turned to look. Tevya snickered.

Taran winced. "Oops... Big oops."

"Worry not, friend," Ka-Lorrin said tightly. "It was a valiant effort."

Tevya bit back a smile as she crouched to help. "It's alright," she said. "It was much too elaborate anyway."

Lily stood nearby, watching the whole thing with arms loosely crossed. A breath of laughter escaped her lips—not loud, but real.

Tevya patted the Raath-Ka and they made a quick exit—Taran muttering "Sorry, sorry," and Ka-Lorrin doing his best to assure him that most people hadn't noticed.

As the pair shuffled away, Lily caught Tevya's eye, and they shared a look.

"Dear god," Lily said under her breath, smiling faintly. "I needed that."

• • • •

The crowd had drifted toward the makeshift refreshment table, voices low, movements gentle. The air had shifted—not lighter, but looser somehow.

Grief had taken its shape, spoken its name, and left behind the kind of quiet that made room for conversation again.

Lily stood with Xynn, Tevya, and Dryst Amaris. The table was laid out with a patchwork of food—some local, some brought in from the *Salamander*. A string of lights someone had rigged up flickered overhead, as if they weren't entirely convinced of their purpose. Caris and Malik drifted over—closer to each other than they would've stood a few weeks ago.

"I got your official request for leave," Amaris said lightly. "I'll leave it to you to break the news to the others."

Lily nodded. "Thank you, sir."

With a gentle dip of his head, he excused himself and moved off toward a cluster of guests near the window.

"News?" Caris asked, picking up the thread.

Lily glanced at Xynn, who reached down and laced their fingers together. Her voice came quiet, but steady. "I already told Alrek. Well... the truth is—"

"The truth is," Xynn cut in smoothly, "we're getting married."

There was a beat.

Malik blinked. "Wait—really?"

Caris's eyes went wide. "You are?"

Tevya's smile spread, warm and genuine. "Congratulations."

"And you're sure you want to spend your honeymoon cleaning up debris on Gherion Prime?" she asked with a teasing grin.

Lily shrugged. "Apparently, Saravethi don't believe in honeymoons."

"Not quite true," Xynn said. "We still do the part where we have lots of sex."

Caris's drink went up her nose. Malik dropped his fork.

"Oh—sorry," Xynn added, with mock innocence. "I forget to temper myself around repressed species."

Lily gave a sideways smile, saving it with, "They believe in doing some kind of service together instead of just a vacation."

Malik tilted his head, considering. "That's actually kind of... neat."

"Sex and service," Caris said, raising a brow. "Sounds like a good time to me."

"How long will you be on leave?" Malik asked.

"We're keeping it open," Lily said. "Maybe a few weeks."

Tevya's voice was warm. "I'm so happy to host you here. We could certainly use the help." She gave Lily a grateful glance before slipping away to greet someone near the back of the hall.

Caris and Malik lingered just a moment longer, then wandered off toward the food—still talking, still standing closer than before.

Xynn leaned in.

"Do you think that'll buy us the time we need?"

Lily didn't answer. She just squeezed Xynn's hand, her eyes steady, her posture quiet and ready.

Whatever came next—they'd face it together.

• • • •

The night sky was different here.

Above the hills of Gherion Prime, ochre clouds coiled through the stratosphere like brushstrokes across canvas, lit from beneath by a red moon and the shimmer of distant stars. It reminded Lily of a painting—one she hadn't known she'd been missing until she saw it. Hard to believe there was ever a time she hadn't looked up at alien skies. Harder still to imagine she'd once thought of just one planet as home.

She sat near the mouth of their tent, the data tablet resting against her knee, Trish's message still glowing softly on the screen.

Trish's smile filled the frame. Her voice was warm. Congratulating Lily on the mission's success. Offering condolences for Datch. But it was the final line that had anchored itself in Lily's chest:

"You need to come back to Earth and see me soon, hon. I've found a record I think you'll want to see. Just a little family history... Take care."

Xynn approached and sat tailor fashion on the ground next to her. "There you are." She brushed a wild bit of Lily's hair out of her face. "You okay?"

Lily nodded, but Xynn didn't look convinced. "Seriously." She gestured to the tablet. "She might have something about your family..."

Before Lily could answer, footsteps crunched on the gravel path. Alrek approached, his duffel slung across one shoulder. He'd stayed a few days longer than planned, but was now headed to catch a transport and rendezvous with the *Salamander*. He stopped when he saw them, and Lily reached out—one hand for Xynn, one for Alrek.

"I have my family," she said. "It may sound cheesy, but even when we're separated by lightyears, I know you two are with me."

Xynn's expression softened. Then her eyes went distant. "That reminds me of a song. A Saravethi one. Very old. I think every caste knows it." She glanced at Alrek. "We used to sing it when we were scattered."

Alrek raised an eyebrow. "Many still do."

Xynn gave him a look. "I'm not much of a singer, but... how does it go?" She hummed a few scattered notes. "From the fields, to the hills..." she began, a little off key. "From the hunting lands of our mothers, to the ships of our fathers—"

"Boats," Alrek corrected gently.

Xynn narrowed her eyes, then smiled. "Right. Boats."

"Or fishing boats," Alrek added. "Depending on the version."

She tried again. "They climbed the mountains and soared through the sky..." She paused, then frowned. "Sky? Atmosphere?"

She looked helplessly at Alrek.

For a moment, he smirked.

Then he closed his eyes.

When he sang, his voice came clear and warm—a high, aching tenor that surprised them both.

"In the current of the clouds, driven up and away.
Like the sands on the shore, washed apart.
Though we be not found,
And the ruins still burn—
Yet our home is there, in the spaces between.
//
Be ye slave or king, yet we know not why.
When life is called away.
Those who murder and maim,
They have tried to end—
Yet our home is there, in the spaces between.
//

As we call, yes we call.
Though the caste may be set.
And whispers seem to fade into dust.
Yet through all that strife,
And for all we know—
Our home still lives, in the spaces between."

Lily didn't close her eyes—but the vision came to her nonetheless.

With every note, the galaxy unfolded in her mind. She saw it all. Earth. The *Salamander*. The Krythar lab where she was reborn. All of it.

She drifted through it—not lost, not afraid. Moving at will, forward and backward, fully in control.

Moments flickered past like constellations. People. Places. Heartbeats. All things, good and bad.

And somehow, through it all, this moment too was present. Like a harbor in the current.

Xynn beside her. Alrek before her. Alien skies overhead.

Nothing was more perfect than this moment now.

Because she was home.

Coda

TWO WEEKS LATER. BIMARA.

The air was thick—humid, heavy, clinging to Lily's skin like wet silk. She moved through the underbrush with slow, deliberate strides, machete in hand, hacking her way through the riot of green. Each step sent up the smell of moss and heat and something faintly metallic beneath it all. Insects buzzed in bursts. The canopy overhead filtered the sunlight into shafts of gold and shadow.

"Still nothing?" she muttered.

A voice crackled in her earpiece. Calm. Dry. "Define nothing."

"You know. Secret hatch. Glowing monolith. Moderately suspicious tree stump."

"Nothing yet."

She pushed through another curtain of vines and slapped away a low-hanging frond. Her boots squelched in the mud, and somewhere behind her, something howled—low and bone-deep.

"You're sure this is the right valley?"

"Coordinates match. Ground-penetrating scan shows a chamber beneath the slope ahead. Ten meters, give or take."

"You could've just said keep going."

"I could've."

She grunted and pressed on—then stopped.

Half-buried in the cliffside, beneath layers of soil and tangled roots, was a circular slab of stone. Its surface was etched with spiraling carvings worn almost smooth by time. Lily crouched and brushed away the dirt, her hand slowing as the glow beneath the markings flickered to life.

One word emerged.

VEYRIK

Her breath caught.

She tapped her comm. "Xynn? We found it."

Xynn's voice answered, clipped but steady. "Confirmed. I'm getting a faint energy reading. Still stable, but be careful."

"Copy that." She turned back to the stone. "Alright," she said to the other voice, "read me the code again."

A short pause. Then:

"Four-two-seven. Pi glyph. Double spiral. Root symbol."

She keyed in the sequence, eyes narrowed. A click sounded. Then a low, harmonic hum began to vibrate underfoot. Light seeped from the seams of the stone.

Lily stepped back. "That did it," she said, watching as the seal pulsed softly.

She smiled faintly at the stone. The air around her shimmered with heat. She began to make her way into the dark passage, brushing cobwebs aside and feeling dust fill her lungs.

"I can't wait until you have a body again."

"You and me both," Datch replied.

Epilogue

THE ALERT BEEPED, SHARP and insistent, breaking the quiet of the royal bath.

Queen Vaishali rose slowly from the steaming pool, droplets sliding in rivulets down her naked body. She didn't reach for a towel. Her attendants stepped back in silence as she crossed the stone floor, each footfall soft and certain. Steam curled around her like a veil. Water hissed where it met the heated tiles.

She reached the console and tapped in a command.

The feed blinked to life.

There she was.

Lily Starling.

Alive. In real time. On Bimara.

Vaishali smiled—slowly, knowingly.

"So," she murmured. "Full of surprises, aren't you."

• • • •

Love on Adius II
A Lily Starling Story

By Christian Hurst

• • • •

Between the Events of Voyage of the Salamander and Storm Riders.

Introduction

THE TERMINAL ON ZANADAR IV was alive with motion.

Travelers moved through the wide concourse in steady currents—pilots in worn flight jackets, Union officers in crisp uniforms, merchants guiding cargo drones that hummed softly along the polished floor. Above them all, the vast glass ceiling framed a piece of open sky, white clouds drifting lazily across the blue.

Lily Starling stepped into the flow of bodies, wide-eyed despite herself.

It had been six weeks since the end of the Krythar conflict. Since the Nullstorm Region—and the beginning of her new life.

Most of that time had been spent at the Zanadar Union recovery facility—medical evaluations, therapy sessions, and the sort of rest that never quite felt like rest when half the galaxy seemed to want a piece of your story. There had been debriefings too. Official ones. With lots of official-looking people who never bothered to introduce themselves.

Captain Calan had told her not to worry.

Her standing in the fleet was secure.

Still... Lily knew her situation was anything but ordinary.

Given the complicated history she carried—the impossible chain of events that had brought her here—she wouldn't have blamed the Union for keeping her at arm's length. Trusting her as an officer, of all things, would have seemed almost absurd only months ago.

But they had respected Calan's wishes.

And the name Lily Starling carried weight.

Even if it wasn't truly hers to begin with.

Somewhere along the way, the name had become something larger than the person wearing it. A symbol of sorts. A story people were telling.

It wasn't the most comfortable idea for Lily. But she had decided to wear it anyway—for better or worse—and accept the honor that came with it.

And the responsibility.

But she also knew, deep in a place that still ached, that she had another responsibility as well.

One to herself.

She moved through the terminal more easily now, the strange sights of the future no longer stopping her in her tracks. Not long ago she would have stared in open disbelief at alien travelers, hovering luggage carriers, or the quiet elegance of a Union starport.

Now it felt almost... normal.

This was her life.

Her home.

Starships. Alien worlds. A galaxy larger and stranger than anything she had ever imagined.

And somehow she had taken to it like a fish to water.

At the security gate she presented her identification. The officer scanned it, pausing for a brief moment before giving a small, respectful nod.

Lily returned the gesture and continued toward the departure corridor.

A simple line of text glowed above the gate.

Adius II – Boarding Soon

She slowed for a moment as she read it.

Adius II.

The largest of the Saravethi colony worlds. A thriving settlement built by refugees who had carved out a future for themselves on the edge of Union space.

It was also where Xynn had made her home after volunteering for the Saravethi Relief Effort.

Lily felt a quiet smile tug at her lips.

Lily's eyes drifted toward the great glass wall just as a sudden cloudburst swept across the terminal. Raindrops began racing down the pane, each one chasing the other toward the bottom. She watched them merge and divide again, carving tiny water highways as they went.

She barely knew Xynn, if she was being honest with herself. Not really. Their time together had been brief, complicated, and charged with more unspoken emotion than Lily quite knew how to handle.

She had tried, more than once, to push those feelings aside.

To pretend the connection between them was just another passing moment in a life that seemed determined to move faster than she could keep up.

But the switch never stayed off.

There was something there.

Something real.

And that realization brought her back to the responsibility she had been thinking about.

Not to the fleet.

Not to the legend of Lily Starling.

To herself.

Because the universe wasn't handing her a path.

Not really.

Choice was something people gave themselves—usually after painting themselves into a corner.

The boarding signal chimed softly through the terminal.

Passengers began filing through the gate.

Lily took a breath and stepped forward with them.

Her heart fluttered once, quick and uncertain.

She lingered a moment longer, watching the rain trace its wandering paths across the glass.

She was on her way to Adius II.

On her way to discover which path her own little droplet might follow.

Tea with Razh

I WAS NOT SUPPOSED to fall in love.

That was the unspoken rule of the thing—the quiet agreement between my brain and my body, between the part of me that could breathe when I was alone and the part that tightened every time she smiled. I was here for a break. A pause. A few weeks of sun-warmed cliffs and whatever passed for relaxation in a galaxy still unraveling.

But then there was Xynn.

She moved like gravity didn't apply to her. Like the wind asked her permission before it changed direction. And me? I stumbled around the colony pretending not to care, pretending I was just passing through, like always. That I'd leave without regret, without the music of her laugh etched into my skin.

That evening, we stayed out too late.

The markets had closed hours ago, the last transport shuttles quiet on their pads, lights dimmed to that soft amber glow designed to suggest safety. She tugged me by the wrist, wordless, leading me toward the cliffs overlooking the sea.

"You need to stop thinking so loud," she said, not unkindly.

I opened my mouth to answer—probably something sarcastic—but she pulled me down beside her before I could.

The night was warm. Our bodies pressed together. And my brain, ever the saboteur, reminded me: *This can't last.*

Fortunately, my thoughts were interrupted by the smell of her hair.

Her fingers traced mine, deliberate and slow, and for a few long minutes, I didn't ruin anything.

We must've floated back to the apartment, because the memory of falling asleep in her bed—naked in each other's arms—was more sensation than sequence. A blur. A feeling. A truth wrapped in warmth and skin.

I woke to the sound of her humming.

It wasn't a song exactly—more like a rhythm she carried in her core, wordless and bright, the kind of sound that wrapped around you like morning sun. I didn't open my eyes right away. The bed was warm. So was she. And whatever ridiculous hour it was, I already knew it was earlier than I wanted to be conscious.

But then came the tug at the edge of the blanket.

"Lily. Come on."

Her voice was soft, but insistent. There was joy tucked into it. A promise. That tone she got when she was about to drag me into something wild and good and entirely too energetic for someone who'd barely slept.

I opened one eye. She was already dressed, hair damp and curling from her rinse in the tiny washroom sink, her skin kissed by that early Adius II light—golden and heavy, like honey dripped on a blue flower. I'd never tell her this, but waking up to her might've been the only thing I believed in without question.

"I just got comfortable," I mumbled, voice still hoarse with sleep.

"You can get back to Lily-levels of comfortable later. Today, I'm showing you the cove," she said, bright-eyed. "I packed the napsacks while you were sawing logs." She paused for a grin as I wiped toothpaste from my face. "We'll hike straight through the cliff basin. You've never seen light like this, I promise."

I rinsed and spat into the sink. "You said that yesterday."

"And I was right, wasn't I?" she laughed, tightening the straps on her bag.

There was no winning once she got like this.

I rinsed my face and picked through the pile of clothes Xynn let me get away with. She didn't say anything aloud, but I could *feel* the judgment in her eyes—the quiet contrast between my half-wrinkled, over-curated mess and her precisely folded drawers.

My limbs ached in the best way—slow and heavy, the kind of soreness that came from long walks, too much laughing, and the way we'd moved through the night like we belonged to no one but each other.

"You know," I muttered, instinctively smelling my bra to determine its place in the wash cycle before strapping it on, "not every day has to start with a vertical scramble through thorn-covered terrain. One of these mornings, I'd like to wander around the local shops. Maybe sit in a café. Touch something that's been in a dishwasher."

Xynn grinned. "You'll forget all about that once you feel the water on your skin."

She offered me a hand, and I took it.

Of course I did.

The breakfast stall at the corner of the main square was exactly as I remembered it: a faded blue canopy strung between two crumbling stone walls, the air thick with the smell of steamed grain and boiled root. No signage, no menu. Just an old woman with deep blue skin, silver hair, and a ladle that looked like it had fused with her arm sometime in the last century.

"Two," Xynn said, handing over a few clipped tokens.

A moment later, we were each holding a biscuit the size of a fist—grayish-white, mildly damp, and stuffed with something that tasted like gym socks but blander. I took a bite, chewed once, and gave her a look.

"I'll never understand how your people survived the siege without any flavor in their food."

Xynn smirked, tearing her biscuit in half. "It's not about flavor. It's about balance."

"Oh right. Saravethi cuisine..." I ticked the rules off on my fingers. "Rule one: breakfast must be as bland as possible, preferably something that could also be used as a sponge."

Xynn nodded. "Correct."

"Rule two: lunch should strip the enamel off your teeth with salt."

"Only if it's good."

"And dinner? Enough spice to flay a boar-beetle. And never, *ever*, anything sweet, because sweetness is—"

"—only for sex," she finished, smirking again. "We don't waste sugar."

I rolled my eyes. "It explains so much."

We turned onto the walkway near her apartment, the sun already beginning to stretch across the white stone facades. The streets were just waking—shutters creaking open, early deliveries clattering in alleyways, the air still cool and clean.

And there he was.

The old man sat on the stool beneath the herbal shop downstairs, his milky eyes turned toward the street. I was never sure how much he could see. He wore the same tan shawl every day, its hem decorated with beads that clicked together faintly when he moved. A chipped porcelain pot rested beside him on the wooden crate he used as a table.

"Would you two care for tea?" he asked, as he always did, his voice thin but warm. "I have an extra cup today."

"No," Xynn said flatly, not slowing.

I hesitated, offering the man a small smile. "Sorry. Another time?"

He didn't seem bothered. Just nodded, slow and serene.

As we passed the corner, I glanced at her. "You know, I keep meaning to ask—why are you so sharp with him? He's just being polite."

Xynn didn't answer.

And I remembered—yesterday, I had said the exact same thing. And she had answered the same way she had today.

We turned down the trail that led out of town, the path rising gently as it curved toward the cliffs, the ocean's scent drifting in on the breeze. The day was clear, the light spilling golden across the valley below. Xynn reached back, lacing her fingers with mine, and for a moment, the silence felt deliberate.

I didn't press.

We still had a long walk ahead. And the cove, she'd said, would be worth it.

The hike wasn't nearly as bad as I'd expected.

There were still thorns, sure, and I might have grumbled once or twice about the incline, but Xynn knew how to find the paths less taken—and less steep. The trail curled like a ribbon through hills flecked with silvery moss, the breeze tugging at our sleeves as if guiding us forward. She kept looking back at me with that stupidly confident grin, the one that made my chest hurt in a good way.

And then the cove opened up below us.

It was quiet, hidden by the cliffs and unreachable by shuttle. A crescent of smooth stone and pale sand, the water so clear it was hard to tell where the ocean stopped and the sky began. We scrambled down the rocks, slipping our boots off the moment we hit the softest part of the shore.

I expected her to wade in. Maybe test the temperature. But no.

Without a word, she peeled her clothes off and tossed them onto a sun-warmed rock.

I blinked. "Seriously?"

She didn't answer. Just gave me a look over her shoulder—the kind that said everything it needed to—and then she dove.

Her body cut through the water like light.

I stood there for a beat too long, heart hammering, skin suddenly aware of itself. The sun was high, the beach empty, the sea unfolding in a shimmer of impossible blue. I kicked off the rest of my clothes and sprinted in after her, gasping as the coolness wrapped around me like silk.

We didn't talk. We splashed, dove, laughed too hard, floated on our backs with fingers grazing.

And for a moment—for one perfect, impossibly bright moment—I forgot everything else.

No past. No war. No expectations. Just the salt on my lips, the light on her face, and the ache in my chest that told me I was exactly where I was supposed to be.

I don't know if I've ever felt freer than I did, naked in that water.

That night, we slept under the stars.

She built a fire in a ring of stones, her hands moving with that quiet confidence I'd started to trust more than my own instincts. I laid out the blankets while the light faded into the horizon, that pale blue giving way to gold, then to violet.

I'm not usually one for roughing it. I don't like bugs. Or uneven ground. Or the fact that sand inevitably finds its way into your clothes no matter how hard you try to keep it out.

But that night didn't feel like the wild—not in a dangerous way.

It felt sacred. Still. Safer than anything I've ever known.

I remember lying beside her, the fire crackling low, the stars spread out like a thousand open doors. Her breathing slowed before mine. I stayed awake just long enough to trace the shape of her hand curled beside mine.

I wish that night could've lasted forever.

We got back just before midday, still damp from the ocean, windblown and sand-dusted, our boots half-full of gravel and blisters. My shoulders ached, my hair was a mess, and I was deeply aware of how my clothes had not been designed for post-skinny-dipping hikes. But I was happy. Worn out in the best possible way.

As we rounded the corner to Xynn's apartment, the old man was already there—perched on his usual crate under the shop awning, teacup balanced on one knee like it had grown roots there overnight.

"Would you care for tea today?" he asked, tilting his blind eyes toward us with the kind of serenity that made me feel immediately guilty for ever making noise near him.

"No," Xynn said, as flatly as ever.

I raised an eyebrow.

She sighed. "No, *thank you*, Razh."

He nodded, apparently satisfied.

I let her pull me up the stairs, but as the door shut behind us, I couldn't help myself.

"Okay, but seriously... why don't you just have tea with him? Or at least try not to sound so... confident."

She opened her mouth—and that's when we heard it.

Drums.

And not just one. A dozen at least. Followed by cheering. And rhythmic stomping.

I blinked. "Umm..."

Xynn's eyes lit up like she'd just remembered it was her birthday. "Oh! It's the Procession of Kar! I *totally* forgot it was this week."

"The what now?"

"Come on!" She grabbed my wrist, practically dragging me back out onto the walk in front of the café.

The path along the road was now *packed*—a sea of Saravethi shoulder to shoulder, buzzing with excitement and sweet-smelling oils.

And that's when I saw them.

A parade of entirely naked Saravethi men, marching—no, *dancing*—down the cobbled street. Tall, statuesque, gleaming with sun and oil, muscles flexing in slow, deliberate rhythm. Their bodies painted in swirling copper and blue sigils, glitter catching in the afternoon light like living constellations.

I blinked again, unsure if the dehydration was finally getting to me. "Okay... okay, so this is real?"

"Oh, very real," Xynn said cheerfully. "Tradition. The whole valley is celebrating." She happily accepted some strings of flowers and draped them around us like necklaces.

I opened my mouth to respond, but then two of the men—smiling wide, their oily blue muscles glistening in the sunlight—stepped from the procession and gently hoisted a bystander into the air like she weighed nothing. She squealed, delighted, and the crowd erupted in cheers as she was passed overhead like some kind of sparkly, grinning tribute.

"Oh no," I said flatly.

"Oh yes," Xynn whispered with glee, yanking me by the hand into the street.

Before I could protest, we were both lifted—pairs of golden arms hoisting us into the air, our feet leaving the ground as we were carried like goddesses in a wave of bronze and sunlight. Xynn was *howling* with laughter. I clutched the nearest shoulder like it might keep me from falling through the clouds three thousand feet up.

"Never a dull moment?" I shouted over the drumming.

"You're blushing so hard your face looks like *Tressia!*" she cackled.

"Stop laughing!"

But she didn't. In fact, she laughed harder. I'd never seen her like that—completely unguarded, her eyes creased, her whole body shaking with joy.

They set us down gently in the central square, and I staggered upright—half-laughing, half-horrified, fully pink.

All around us, vendors had set up stalls with garlands and sweet-smelling treats—little bottles of nectar, pastel jellies shaped like flowers, and an alarming number of soft, sticky candies that made my mouth water and my eyebrows raise.

I looked around warily. "Okay. Serious question. Is this an orgy?"

Xynn grinned. "Not quite. It's a fertility festival. Symbolic. Celebratory. I mean, no one's *doing it* in the square—" she gestured vaguely, "but there's definitely a lot of going home together, if you get my meaning."

Just then, a very attractive—and very naked—Saravethi man approached, with a very large crooked... smile, and balancing two nectar bottles between his hands. He offered them with a small bow.

I took one on reflex.

Xynn accepted hers, then turned to me with a smirk that should've been illegal.

"So," she said. "Should we bring one back to the room?"

I raised an eyebrow. "The nectar or the guy?"

She just smiled at me—that look that let me know she wasn't bluffing.

I went beet red. "Nooo," I groaned, punching her gently in the arm.

She doubled over laughing again, nearly dropping her bottle. "You're too easy."

"You're too *much*," I muttered.

But I was grinning too, despite myself.

That night, I couldn't sleep.

Xynn was out cold beside me, her breath slow and even, one arm flung over her head like she owned the bed and the stars and the sky itself. The window was cracked, letting in the sound of wind in the trees and the faint, far-off echo of festival drums that hadn't quite died out.

But my thoughts were loud. Too loud.

I stared at the ceiling, willing my mind to hush. It didn't listen.

You're leaving in three days.

This was never meant to last.

You'll ruin it if you stay.

You'll regret it if you go.

Round and round, a carousel of doubt, spinning under the quiet rhythm of her breathing.

She shifted in her sleep, and I caught a glimpse of her profile in the moonlight—lips parted, one brow twitching like she was fighting invisible enemies—on guard even in sleep. And for a second, I saw it all laid out: the shared mornings, the bad food, the arguments about hiking versus shops, the space between us shrinking until there was no more space left to run from.

It hit me, soft and sudden.

I want that.

I want her.

I don't want to leave.

The thought landed in my chest like a stone tossed into still water—and then, warmth spread outward from the center. Slow, deep, impossibly calm.

My toes wiggled under the cool sheet, my fingers curled against the mattress. I felt like laughing. I *did* laugh—just a little giggle, one I buried in the pillow so I wouldn't wake her.

I was staying.

Not because it was perfect. Not because I knew how it would turn out. But because I was done running. Done pretending I didn't care.

I smiled like a fool in the dark, eyes fluttering closed, the soft rhythm of the wind outside echoing in my bones.

And I did something rare for me, I fell asleep happy.

The morning sun filtered through the curtains in soft streaks, casting golden lines across the bedspread and the half-empty bag I was *definitely* not repacking anymore. I'd woken up still smiling, body loose and warm, heart humming like it had finally been tuned correctly.

Xynn was already up, humming as she stirred the hot water for breakfast. Her hair was a mess—sleep-tangled and perfect—and she wore the chain of flowers from yesterday. She hadn't taken it off since.

When she turned, she narrowed her eyes at me playfully. "You're in a good mood."

"I'm always in a good mood," I said, taking a seat at the table.

She raised an eyebrow. "Lily. You've never smiled while eating *dalcha*."

I glanced down at the biscuit—grayish, damp, aggressively flavorless. And I *was* smiling. Beaming, even. I took another bite.

She sat across from me, watching with a half-smirk and just enough suspicion to make me laugh.

I swallowed, tilted my head.

"I love you."

The words hung in the air like an electrical current. Not a whisper. Not a slip. Just truth, plain and clean.

Xynn froze.

Her eyes widened. "What?"

I blinked, breath caught in my chest. It was too late to take it back, even if I'd wanted to. My heart pounded against my ribs like it was trying to climb out and beg for mercy.

Then I managed a tiny breath—a hitch, really—and nodded.

She blinked, once, twice. A tear welled in one eye, catching the sunlight.

"I love you too, Lily," she said softly.

And then we kissed.

It wasn't long or dramatic or fireworks exploding in the sky. Just warm. Real. The kind of kiss that fits—like breathing in the morning air, the way it fills your whole body all the way down to your fingertips.

We dressed slowly, still brushing against each other like gravity had no effect on us. The morning stretched wide, the world briefly perfect.

Xynn tied her boots, glancing up with a smile. "You know what?"

"What?"

"I think I *do* fancy a trip to the book shop today."

I blinked, mock-shocked. "You mean not a six-hour climb through snakeweed and cliffs?"

She nudged my shoulder with hers. "Don't get used to it."

We stepped outside, hand in hand, into the sunlit street.

We hadn't gone ten steps before we saw him again.

Razh was in his usual spot beneath the awning, same shawl, same quiet smile. The chipped teapot steamed gently at his side.

"Would you care for tea this morning?" he asked, his voice a feather against the morning air.

And I don't know why—maybe it was the sunshine, maybe it was the way my heart was still glowing, or maybe I just finally wanted to be kind in return—but I smiled and said, "You know what, sir? I would love—"

Before I could finish the sentence, Xynn slapped a hand over my mouth like an assassin neutralizing a target mid-sentence.

I yelped, muffled and indignant.

"No thank you, Razh," she said smoothly, steering me away by the shoulders like I was a malfunctioning equipment cart.

I flailed, trying to talk through her fingers. She didn't let go until we rounded the corner.

I spun on her. "I can't believe you did that! What the hell was that?!"

"Are you going to make a scene," she said calmly, "or are we going to the bookshop?"

I didn't answer.

I walked behind her, several feet of dusty street between us, arms crossed so tightly I thought I might dislocate something. We didn't speak. The breeze stirred the edge of her tunic. My fists clenched and unclenched.

By the time we reached the bookshop, I wasn't mad—I was *boiling*. Furious in that quiet way where the world feels like it's holding its breath.

We sat at one of the little café tables out front, sunlight spilling across the weathered tabletop, a cluster of ceramic cups still drying on the tray beside us.

Xynn sighed, resting her forearms on the table. "Look," she said gently, "I should've explained earlier."

She paused, waiting for me to meet her eyes.

I didn't.

"Razh is a village elder. Priest caste," she continued. "His wife died a few weeks ago."

My head lifted—just slightly.

"In Saravethi tradition," she said, her voice soft but steady, "you don't say goodbye all at once. When someone you love dies, you ask a friend to join you for tea. It's symbolic. You drink the tea together, and that's when you let their spirit go. It's how we release grief—with company."

I stared at her. Her expression was calm. She didn't look sad, not exactly—just... reverent.

"If someone agrees," she said, "you have to let them go. If they say no... the spirit stays another day."

She took a breath.

"I know he's not ready to say goodbye. So he keeps asking me. Because he knows I'll say no."

Silence.

I opened my mouth to apologize—but I couldn't.

Tears were already streaming down my face. Not a single elegant tear. I was bawling, and I couldn't stop.

The kind of crying that comes from a place too deep to name. A grief that wasn't entirely mine—but hurt more than words could explain. For Razh. For his wife. For the impossible act of loving someone long enough to make goodbye unbearable.

Xynn slid her chair closer without a word and wrapped her arms around me.

I let her.

I didn't care that people were staring. I didn't care that my face was blotchy or that my shoulders were shaking or that I couldn't breathe right through the sobs.

I just cried.

And she held me.

There was something very beautiful about that moment.

But also something terrifying.

Some part of me grew up that day.

And I knew—I was different forever.

That night, I couldn't sleep.

Not like before—not smiling and giddy, toes wiggling under cool sheets. This time, I lay awake staring at the ceiling, the dark pressing in from all sides. My heart felt tight, like a fist I couldn't unclench.

Fear crept in—quiet, persistent.

Fear of staying. Fear of what I might become if I let myself have something this good. Fear of waking up in ten years and realizing I didn't know who I was without running. And worst of all... the image of Razh, curled in bed alone, after a lifetime spent beside someone he loved.

The ache of it hollowed me out.

I turned away from Xynn, pretending to sleep.

The rain started before dawn.

Of course it did.

By the time we were dressed and ready, the city streets were slick with silver. Umbrellas bloomed in the crowd like muted flowers.

We were headed to a concert we'd bought tickets for weeks ago—a local symphony, half traditional Saravethi strings, half experimental fusion from some planet I wasn't familiar with. I didn't really want to go.

But we had the tickets.

We didn't talk much that morning. The warmth between us hadn't gone cold, exactly—it just felt... fragile. Like a soap bubble you're afraid to breathe near.

We walked in silence, hand in hand, her fingers squeezing mine gently once or twice.

I didn't say it again.

My feelings hadn't changed. I loved her.

But the words stayed stuck somewhere between my chest and my throat. My brain and my body were at war again—and right now, it was a draw.

Razh wasn't on his usual crate.

We both looked around instinctively—then spotted him inside, seated at a table. Through the rain-fogged window, we saw him in the corner, surrounded by a fresh tea set. Three cups. Everything polished and laid out with care. Steam rose around his face like ribbons around a dancer.

Xynn stopped in her tracks.

I watched her whole expression shift—gentle disbelief giving way to something deeper.

"Razh," she whispered, voice cracking. "No..."

He looked up and smiled—a tender thing, like sunrise on an old memory.

"Won't you both please join me?" he said.

We just stood there, motionless, until he gestured again. Warmly. Kindly.

"It's time."

Something inside me wanted to bolt. To run, hard and fast, as far as I could.

This wasn't mine. I didn't belong here.

But Xynn held my hand.

And somehow, that anchored me.

We sat.

The three of us drank tea in silence at first, the warmth of the cup soothing my shaking fingers.

And then Razh began to speak.

About Yessif—his wife. About how they met at a spice stall on a moon he couldn't remember the name of, only the smells. About how she used to hide notes in his clothes when he had to travel offworld. About the night she proposed—in an emergency room, while they were both battling food poisoning.

He told us how they survived the Krythar occupations. How they stayed together. How, finally, they were free again.

He spoke of the final weeks. The long quiet. The way she always asked him to sing to her, even when his voice cracked. And how grateful he was that she got to have her garden before she died—*because it meant she could plant things again.*

He only wept a little.

But Xynn and I were wrecked.

And when the last of the tea was gone, Razh nodded to himself—like a door had finally closed.

"Thank you," he said simply, with an air of readiness in his voice.

The concert was the most beautiful thing I've ever heard.

Maybe it always would be. The music didn't just fill the room—it lifted us. Rewrote our bones. I cried again, the barrier gone at this point. Xynn held my hand the whole time, thumb tracing a slow rhythm over my knuckles, not asking for anything more.

That night, we made love.

Not the breathless kind. Not fast or fiery.

It was slow. Deep. Like we were carving something into the stars with our bodies, something neither of us could erase. I didn't think. I didn't doubt. I just loved her.

And afterward, as we lay tangled together in the hush of that small room, hearts still catching up, she asked:

"You're not going to stay, are you?"

I didn't answer right away.

My throat was thick. My breath felt shallow.

"No," I said softly. "I'm sorry, Xynn."

Silence.

And then—

"I love you, Xynn."

A beat. Her fingers brushed the side of my face.

"I love you too, Lily. Always."

We fell asleep like that, wrapped in each other, not knowing what tomorrow would bring.

But somehow, we both understood—

The stars had something in store for me out there.
Neither of us knew what it was.
But I would soon find out.

About the Author

Christian Hurst is a Creative Director and author of the *Lily Starling* series, a character-driven YA science fiction saga that blends epic adventure with emotional depth. With over 15 years of experience in advertising, marketing, and content creation, his work is shaped by a strong sense of story, pacing, and imagination.

His writing explores identity, connection, and the courage to forge your own path in a vast and unpredictable galaxy. Known for immersive worldbuilding, inclusive storytelling, and a balance of heart, humor, and high-stakes tension, Christian's work resonates with readers who are drawn to science fiction with both scale and soul.

He lives in Pennsylvania with his wife, son, and three dogs.

About the Series

The story doesn't end here.

Lily's journey continues in the Lily Starling series. What begins aboard the *Salamander* leads to ancient mysteries, impossible choices, and a threat that spans the galaxy.

Continue the adventure at **LilyStarlingBook.com**

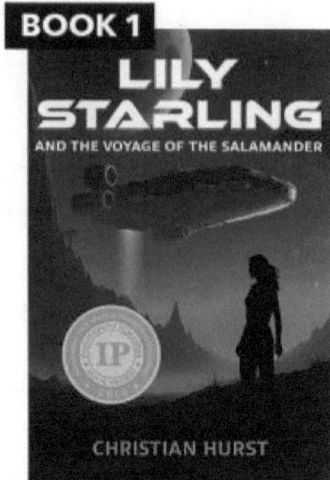

Leave a Review

If you enjoyed Voyage of the Salamander, please consider leaving a review on your favorite book site. Reader reviews help independent books reach new audiences and play a direct role in the future of series like this one.

www.ingramcontent.com/pod-product-compliance
Lightning Source LLC
Chambersburg PA
CBHW030230120726
47903CB00005B/1430